A Song of Joy

Books by Lauraine Snelling

UNDER NORTHERN SKIES

The Promise of Dawn
A Breath of Hope
A Season of Grace
A Song of Joy

SONG OF BLESSING

To Everything a Season
A Harvest of Hope
Streams of Mercy
From This Day Forward

An Untamed Heart

RED RIVER OF THE NORTH

An Untamed Land
A New Day Rising
A Land to Call Home
The Reapers' Song
Tender Mercies
Blessing in Disguise

RETURN TO RED RIVER

A Dream to Follow
Believing the Dream
More Than a Dream

DAUGHTERS OF BLESSING

A Promise for Ellie
Sophie's Dilemma
A Touch of Grace
Rebecca's Reward

HOME TO BLESSING

A Measure of Mercy
No Distance Too Far
A Heart for Home

WILD WEST WIND

Valley of Dreams
Whispers in the Wind
A Place to Belong

DAKOTAH TREASURES

Ruby • *Pearl*
Opal • *Amethyst*

SECRET REFUGE

Daughter of Twin Oaks
Sisters of the Confederacy
The Long Way Home
A Secret Refuge 3-in-1

Under Northern Skies

4

A Song of Joy

LAURAINE SNELLING

BethanyHouse
a division of Baker Publishing Group
Minneapolis, Minnesota

Published by Bethany House Publishers
11400 Hampshire Avenue South
Bloomington, Minnesota 55438
www.bethanyhouse.com

Bethany House Publishers is a division of
Baker Publishing Group, Grand Rapids, Michigan

Printed in the United States of America

Library of Congress Cataloging-in-Publication Data
Names: Snelling, Lauraine, author.
Title: A song of joy / Lauraine Snelling.
Description: Bloomington, Minnesota : Bethany House Publishers, [2019] | Series: Under Northern skies ; 4
Identifiers: LCCN 2019003835 | ISBN 9780764232923 (trade paper) | ISBN 9780764232930 (cloth) | ISBN 9780764232947 (large print) | ISBN 9781493418701 (e-book)
Classification: LCC PS3569.N39 S658 2019 | DDC 813/.54—dc23
LC record available at https://lccn.loc.gov/2019003835

Scripture quotations are from the King James Version of the Bible.

This is a work of fiction. Names, characters, incidents, and dialogues are products of the author's imagination and are not to be construed as real. Any resemblance to actual events or persons, living or dead, is entirely coincidental.

Cover design by Dan Thornberg, Design Source Creative Services

Author is represented by the Books & Such Literary Agency.

19 20 21 22 23 24 25 7 6 5 4 3 2 1

Prologue

Heinrik Schmitz stared at his three brothers around the table. "Our discussion today will go no further."

Jacob, in charge of the lumbering arm of the family business, asked, "Is someone going to record this meeting?"

"Yes, Jeffrey will." Heinrik nodded to his son, who leaned slightly forward and spoke.

"It might help if I had some idea of what is going on. I have another class in two hours. What could possibly be causing—?"

Heinrik barely raised his hand. "I am getting to that."

Jeffrey reached for paper and a pen, sending his father a slight frown at the same time.

The brothers were gathered around a small table in a private room off Heinrik's office. The door was locked. Usually they met in the boardroom with their elder sister, Gertrude Schoenleber, sitting at the head of the table. Lately Miss Carlson, her assistant, was always at her side.

"What is bothering you?" Jonathon, who was in charge of the railroad branch, scraped a match and lit his cigar. After an initial puff, he narrowed his eyes and studied his brother.

"I had a horrible nightmare two nights ago." Heinrik stared at each brother as his voice deepened. "I know this might be hard to believe, but I am convinced it was not a dream but a portent of things to come."

Jeffrey looked up from his notes. "Fa—"

Heinrik's hand came up again, just off the edge of the table. "Let me finish."

Everyone stared at him.

"In my dream, our elder sister died and left all her property to Nilda Carlson, including her seat on this board."

The scratching of the pen stopped, along with every other sound.

"I have made lists of ideas." He motioned to a notebook on the table in front of him. "And the only feasible thing—actually the easiest and most brilliant—is to neutralize Miss Carlson by having her married into the family."

He nodded to Jeffrey.

Chapter 1

June 1911

Life in America certainly wasn't like Nilda had dreamed. She closed her eyes for a moment, letting memories of home float through her. The house with the big kitchen, the farm, the *seter* where she had helped take the cows, goats, and sheep to summer pasture.

Making cheese. School, friends, the church. But mostly her family, the laughter in their house, all the parts of home.

Now, looking out the window again, she could see that farming here and farming in Norway were similar, but here it was so flat in comparison and so much larger. Cattle, horses, and farm animals dotted the pastures, while wheat and corn and other crops stretched for miles. This land used to be covered with gigantic pine trees, but loggers had cleared this land and moved north. Her onkel Einar's farm in Blackduck, Minnesota, grew white pine or red pine trees like the thousands of acres left to be logged. Like many other immigrants, he paid for the tickets for other family members to come help him clear the land so they could farm it. First, her brother Rune and his family immigrated, then she and their younger brother, Ivar. While helping on Rune's farm, she had hoped that one day she would meet a young man, and they would have a farm of their own.

Little did she know what God had in mind for her.

Indeed, who could have dreamed such a life as she was living now? A verse her mor had often quoted tickled her mind. "God would provide far beyond anything she could dream or imagine." True, she had scrambled the words a bit, but still, her life now fit that verse.

She stared out the window of the train as it rocked from side to side. Two fishermen in a boat on one of the sky-blue lakes caught her attention. How her nephews loved to fish. And hunt. The bounty of the trees extended to the land and the water too.

Not once since arriving in this country had she gone to bed hungry. Nor had any of the others. Porridge was no longer their staple food.

And look where simple, country-bred Nilda was riding now. Mrs. Schoenleber's private railroad car was as lavish as her home, with flocked wallpaper, a lovely little writing desk and other fine furniture, a separate sleeping compartment, *and* a small private room with porcelain fixtures in which to answer nature's call.

The towns, roads, and farms grew closer together as they drew nearer to St. Paul and the quarterly meeting of Schmitz Enterprises. Accompanying her employer, Mrs. Gertrude Schoenleber—mentor, employer, and friend, and a driving force in her town—to these meetings had become a part of Nilda's life.

"Are you concerned about the meeting?" Mrs. Schoenleber, slim and slight, smiled from the seat across from Nilda.

Nilda thought for a moment. "Not so much concerned as . . ." She paused, the movement of her seat setting the feather on her navy hat to nodding. She had lifted the veil to be more comfortable. If she had her way . . . But she didn't.

Mrs. Schoenleber waited. She was good at that. Even with her back straight, not touching the seat, she still looked comfortable and patient.

"I think I am a bit apprehensive, but then, these meetings often cause that." Not that she'd been to the Twin Cities more than three times. "I just want to do my best. I believe they want to intimidate me to the point of being ineffective."

"Of course they do. That is their way of doing business, especially with a woman, and a young woman at that. My brothers will do anything to succeed, and right now they are worried about the timber running out, where to get more, and how to compensate for its loss with other branches of the company. I often wonder how none of them inherited the kindness of our father. After all, he accomplished all he did without destroying other people."

"I wish I could have met him."

"He would have loved you."

Nilda stared at her. She felt her mouth drop. Never had Mrs. Schoenleber said anything like that to her. While she was generous with approbations, this . . . Nilda closed her eyes and swallowed. The *clickety-clack* of the train wheels nearly drowned out her words. "Thank you."

"Fifteen minutes until arrival in St. Paul," the conductor called as he passed by.

"Excuse me while I visit the necessary," Mrs. Schoenleber murmured as she stood.

Nilda nodded. "Can I get you anything?"

"No, thank you."

When the door closed, Nilda stood in front of the mirror on the inside of the door.

Never had she dreamed she would be wearing a dark navy traveling suit of heavy silk with a gored skirt that swished her ankles, a fitted jacket decorated in jet beads, and fitted long sleeves banded at the wrists with the same beads. A hat with veil and feather finished the ensemble. She tucked a light brown strand back into a chignon at the base of her head and smoothed her eyebrows. Satisfied, she picked up her navy leather gloves from her seat and slid her hands into them. Ready. She knew she looked every inch the formal traveler of 1911. Mrs. Jones, the dressmaker, made sure of that. But getting used to this fashionable look—in fact, this entire new life—took exquisite and dedicated training. Training that continued every day.

Speaking, reading, and writing in English; proper etiquette, dress, and manners; how to assist with correspondence; business principles, history, and politics; music; and overall confidence. Between Mrs. Schoenleber, her friend Miss Walstead, and those serving them, Nilda had time to visit her family near Benson's Corner only one weekend a month. While Nilda ached to see her mor, who had immigrated to America after her husband passed away, and the others more often, whole seasons seemed to fly by.

Mrs. Schoenleber returned to the small room. "I think we will have supper at the hotel tonight. I believe we need to go over our ideas one more time at least. Something is niggling at me."

Breathing a sigh of relief, Nilda set their bags up on the seat, including the leather briefcase that was a recent gift from Mrs. Schoenleber.

"St. Paul, next stop, St. Paul," the train conductor announced from the door to their compartment. "Is there anything I can get for you before we arrive?"

"Thank you for asking." Mrs. Schoenleber smiled at him. "You help make the trip more comfortable."

"You are welcome, ma'am." He touched the bill of his hat.

"And thank you for . . . for . . ." He swallowed and exited the room.

Nilda sent a questioning look at her employer across the narrow space between the two seats.

"His son is attending college."

"I see." Nilda raised her eyebrows. "A little bird told you and you decided to help?"

"Something like that. Treating employees well makes sure they want to continue to work for your company. My brothers and I have had a few discussions on matters of this sort. My father tried to instill this in all of our heads, but . . ."

"Women learn more easily than men?"

"Possibly." They shared a look of agreement. This was one of the principles the older woman had dwelled on often. "I think we women learn to care more about people. Perhaps we are born that way. My father lived by the principle 'do unto others as you would have them do to you.'" She glanced out the window. "He was a kind man. I'm not sure what happened to my brothers. I think success has gone to their heads."

Nilda's mind skipped back to her onkel Einar, who had died of his obsession with cutting down the big trees, all at the cost of the people around him. He was not missed much. *Like Dreng.*

She shuddered and forced her mind back to preparing to leave their compartment.

The conductor assisted them down the train steps. "I believe your driver is coming now."

"Thank you, and please congratulate your son for me on the hard work he is accomplishing. He hopes to go to medical school, right?"

"Yes, ma'am."

"Good. Doctors are much needed."

"The carriage is outside," their usual driver said in greeting.

"Good to have you back." He took their handbags and led the way, their shoes tapping against the black and white tiles in the cavernous station. The cacophony of arriving passengers surrounding them made conversation impossible.

Nilda knew the conductor's son was in his fourth year of college and dreamed of going to medical school after graduating. Since she now took care of the accounts, she knew of most of the contributions Mrs. Schoenleber sent out behind the scenes.

Good thing the driver had brought the carriage today, as when they reached the portico, the rain was coming down in sheets.

"It appears we will not be doing any shopping," Mrs. Schoenleber commented as they settled into their seats.

"We weren't planning on it, were we?"

"I had thought of a couple of things, but they are not worth the effort. It is not that long to supper anyway."

Nilda breathed a sigh of relief. Shopping had yet to become a pleasing pastime.

After greeting them, the clerk at the front desk handed Mrs. Schoenleber an envelope. "This came for you. And thank you for coming to stay with us again. Your rooms are ready." He motioned to a bellman who was waiting.

"This way, Mrs. Schoenleber," the bellman said. "Welcome back."

"Thank you. Could you please have a maid come to our rooms when she is able?"

"I believe one is already there."

"Thank you."

As soon as they entered their rooms, Mrs. Schoenleber removed her hat and handed it to the smiling maid.

"Very well, madam, would you like your bath drawn immediately or . . ."

"I think I will lie down for a few minutes. That train was

wearisome today. Nilda, bring your notebook into my room as soon as you've changed into something more comfortable. I have some ideas. Oh, I almost forgot." She picked up the envelope from a small table by the door and handed it to Nilda. "You read it."

Nilda did as asked. "We are invited to the symphony. Hmm, Jeffrey is included. Isn't he still in college?" He'd not attended most of their social events in St. Paul.

"Yes, but here in the Cities. That is unusual. I am sure Fritz would enjoy attending. It's a shame he can't."

Nilda felt herself smile inside. Fritz Larsson, nephew to Mrs. Schoenleber, taught Nilda's nephews at school in Benson's Corner, where he also played the organ at the Lutheran church. He and another young man, Petter Thorvaldson, whom she had met on the ship to Duluth, had become friends. They both attended the monthly socials held at Mrs. Schoenleber's home. Fritz loved music and taught piano lessons also, including a few to Nilda.

"Should I decline?" Nilda asked.

"No, tell Heinrik thank you. At least we brought appropriate clothing. There will most likely be a late supper afterward." The older woman sat down on her bed and swung her legs up. "Ah, this feels heavenly. Feel free to lie down a bit if you would like. We can talk later."

Nilda adjourned to her own room and divested herself of her outfit, allowed the maid to hold up a wrapper for her, and then sighed her way to lying down. *Heavenly* was indeed a good description.

At least she was no longer in awe of the boardroom and the men standing around talking the following morning. The four brothers each had at least one assistant, sometimes two, and the other department heads came, along with the male secretary, who also had an assistant. Cigar smoke already dulled the crown moldings decorating the high ceiling, making her think the meeting had begun well before the official starting time.

And what was this? The recording secretary set up a heavy black machine in front of himself. Nilda had seen pictures of such things. A typewriter, it was called. Mr. Jurgenson cranked a sheet of paper into it on a roller, adjusted it, and placed both hands over the bank of keys. *CLICK CLACK-CLACK-CLACK CLICK CLICK CLACK-CLACK-CLACK*. Good heavens, what noise!

Someone had just wheeled in a cart with coffee, hot water for tea, and all the accoutrements, including a lovely tray of pastries. As the servers filled the orders, Heinrik showed Mrs. Schoenleber and Nilda to their seats at the head of the table.

Mrs. Schoenleber smiled and nodded, greeting the others in attendance as they made their way to the table. Once everyone had assumed their places, with Heinrik on her left, she began. "Heinrik, will you please open our meeting with prayer? Remember, Father always used to do that, and today it seems most appropriate." She glanced around the table. "If I remember rightly, we used to take turns. I think we shall return to that practice."

Nilda looked at the woman beside her. This was something new, or at least she'd never known of it.

Heinrik shot his sister a questioning look but did as she requested. "God and Father of us all, we thank you for the great success you have given our companies, for wisdom now as we traverse the morass of today's business world. As our father always said, please show us the way to go and help us to remember who is indeed in charge in this country and world. Amen."

"Would that we believed and lived that all. Thank you." Mrs. Schoenleber smiled around the table, her white hair catching the light from overhead. "Are there any questions before we begin?"

The meeting continued as had all the other meetings with one new and jarring element: the constant *CLICK CLACK* of Mr. Jurgenson's typewriter.

Heinrik spent twenty minutes on his overall report. Jacob closed his report with "We still have a few years, but we are running out of timber in Minnesota. There are still pine forests in other states, such as western Montana and northern Idaho, but they are remote. Shipping costs money."

Jonathon nodded. "We ship more than just logs and lumber, but that is a significant part of our profit."

At the end of day, Mrs. Schoenleber stood. "The size of this corporation has grown far beyond the scope of anything we or our father ever envisioned. It would be easy to rest on our laurels, but we must not. Nor must we neglect the charity that was our father's primary aim. Everyone is dismissed."

Everyone gathered their papers and prepared to leave, general conversations raising a hubbub in the boardroom and down the halls. Mrs. Schoenleber turned to Nilda, started to say something, then turned back when someone asked her a question.

"Will you be joining us for supper at the club tonight?" Jacob asked.

"You mean they are allowing women entrance now?" Mrs. Schoenleber asked.

"Oh, yes, they are quite progressive. There is one dining room set apart for couples."

"Well, thank you for the offer, but I prefer a quiet supper after a long day like today. Will you be joining us at the symphony tomorrow night?"

He shook his head. "The symphony is just—just . . ."

"You mean you'd rather sleep in your bed at home?"

He nodded and leaned closer. "But don't go telling Heinrik.

He thinks everyone enjoys classical music like he does. Now, if there were dancing at the same time, we would be there."

The next evening, as the maids assisted them in dressing and styling their hair, Nilda asked, "Why do I have a feeling that there is something deeper going on here than attending the symphony? After all, they've never invited us before."

"They used to. When I was younger and enjoyed attending music and theater and such events. But I stopped going a few years ago." Mrs. Schoenleber stared into the mirror, nodding slowly. "I have a suspicion you might be right, but we will follow along, innocent as lambs, until we know what is behind it. Have you been to a symphony before?"

"No, but I love to listen to Fritz play both the piano and the organ. I'm looking forward to hearing and learning more."

"Another good experience for you. And I do enjoy it too." She stood and thanked the maid. "We will return late, so we will expect your help then."

"Of course, ma'am. Can I get you anything else?" A knock at the door called her away.

"They are here," Mrs. Schoenleber said.

A young man bowed in the hallway. "Your driver is downstairs waiting for you."

"Thank you."

The maid helped them into their wraps and saw them out the door.

Mrs. Schoenleber settled herself in the cab. "Hmm. I assumed Jeffrey would come for us."

Nilda shrugged. While Jeffrey seemed an intelligent and charming young man, she'd much rather have attended with Fritz.

The thought stopped her. Now, that was a surprise.

As they descended from the cab, it appeared to Nilda that

thousands of people were here for the concert, but it was probably only hundreds. Mrs. Schoenleber spoke to an usher, and he led them to their seats. Heinrik and Jeffrey were there already. They stood as Mrs. Schoenleber and Nilda sat down between them.

Nilda found herself next to Jeffrey. He said excitedly, "I'm glad you came. I bet this is your first symphony concert."

"It is, yes."

"They're playing Beethoven, you know."

She consulted the program the usher had given her. "So I see." Jeffrey pronounced it as Fritz had; you would think the name would be pronounced *Beeth Oven*.

She turned her attention to the huge concert hall. The seats were all of dark red velvet. And look at the intricate and interwoven designs on the domed ceiling! Everything from leaves and grapes to a few cherubs here and there protruded in three dimensions. That could not all have been carved; it must have been plaster. The orchestra members were taking their places on a large stage, scraping chairs around and playing odd bits of music. This was the new word Nilda had recently learned: cacophony.

The electric lights dimmed. Electric lights! Would Rune's farm ever have electric lights one day? Now that would be real progress!

When one of the violinists stepped up on a riser and turned his back to the audience, the orchestra hushed. From the rear, an instrument played a single wailing note. All the violinists played that note. The man on the riser looked around, nodded, and sat down.

An august gentleman in formal attire came out onto the stage. The audience applauded enthusiastically. Why? He hadn't done anything yet. He stepped up on the riser, bowed deeply, turned his back, and raised his arms. One hand held a small, thin stick. He brought his arms down sharply.

Da-da-da DUMMMMM!

Nilda jumped a tiny bit in surprise. But then the second *da-da-da-dum* and the music that followed swept her away. This was amazing. And loud. Brilliant. Indescribable! There were too many voices in the orchestra to keep track of them all. She could not begin to analyze how all this could blend together so perfectly, so she simply sat back and let herself be lost in the beautiful music. The piece ended, but no one clapped. She glanced at Mrs. Schoenleber, who sat serenely.

The orchestra began again with another theme. How long did she sit here? She had no idea. She knew only that she was surrounded by something absolutely new and absolutely wonderful.

The ending was thunderous. The audience clapped wildly, and voices all around her shouted strange new words: "Bravo!" and "Encore!"

Jeffrey sounded bored. How could he be bored after that? "Oh, I do hope they don't play the *William Tell Overture* again. That piece is becoming so dreary."

The man on the riser announced, "*William Tell Overture*, Rossini," and turned his back again. The music began quietly, reminding Nilda somehow of farm country, with birds singing. Then it pepped up.

"Here we go again," Jeffrey grumped.

Now it was a galloping piece with lots of triplets. Fritz had tried to teach her the proper way to play triplets, but she was not good at it, her fingers not fast enough. This orchestra was perfect with triplets! Oh, how she loved this! Finally she was allowed to clap as the audience again burst into applause.

Mrs. Schoenleber looked as pleased as Nilda felt. "It has been far too long since I enjoyed an evening of music this splendid. Nilda, we must come to these concerts more often."

"Oh, I would love to!"

Heinrik smiled broadly. "So, what did you think?"

Jeffrey sniffed. He didn't look nearly as pleased as Mrs. Schoenleber and Nilda. In fact, he looked tired. "All right, I suppose. But the brass seemed a bit behind the beat, and I heard the woodwinds go off-key in the third movement. Of course, I've never much liked the woodwinds anyway, oboes especially. Too whiny."

Nilda stared at him. "If you find this so wearying, why do you come?"

"It's the thing to do, of course. At our level of society, everyone goes to the symphony."

Nilda said nothing, but she thought plenty. If his social level had to do what they didn't feel like doing just because it was the thing to do, she didn't want to be part of it. Instead, she would come to the symphony for the same reason Fritz would: because it was the most wonderful music in the whole world.

Chapter 2

"Welcome home." Charles opened the carriage door, and Nilda stepped out into the front yard of the Schoenleber house. Behind her, Mrs. Schoenleber descended from the carriage.

Nilda drew a deep breath. "Ah, it is so good to be back. The city is exciting, but I much prefer less excitement and more natural beauty."

Mrs. Schoenleber grinned broadly. "Wonderful! That was a complex thought, and you articulated it well in English. Nilda, you have come very far indeed. And incidentally, I agree with you. This is a much better place to call home than is St. Paul."

Charles cleared his throat. "Ah, madam, you have a guest awaiting you in the parlor. The gentleman is a detective employed by the Pinkerton National Detective Agency."

Mrs. Schoenleber frowned at Nilda, but Nilda knew the frown was not because of her. "I do hope he was not sent by Schmitz Enterprises." She squared her shoulders. "Let us go see."

Detective agency? One of Nilda's assignments from Miss Walstead, who was tutoring her in English, was to read every article in the English-language newspaper. As much as she could remember, the Pinkerton National Detective Agency mainly worked for large companies, quelling labor strikes and arresting people who tried to start unions. Did this mean that Schmitz Enterprises was having labor trouble?

Mrs. Schoenleber marched to the house. "Charles, we will receive the gentleman in five minutes. We will freshen up first. It is a long journey under the best of circumstances."

"Yes, madam. I will tell him."

Nilda followed Mrs. Schoenleber upstairs and went to her room. She handed Gilda her hat and wool cape, took advantage of the facilities, and returned downstairs. She followed Mrs. Schoenleber into the parlor.

The Pinkerton detective was a tall, solidly built man. He was not fat by any means, but stocky. How old was he? Thirty? About so. He was sitting by the fireplace. He set his teacup aside and leapt to his feet as the women entered the room. "Mrs. Gertrude Schoenleber?"

"I am. This is my assistant, Nilda Carlson."

Nilda nodded to him. "How do you do, sir."

"Miss Carlson." He gave a slight bow.

"Do be seated." Mrs. Schoenleber sat down in her favorite chair near the fireplace, so Nilda took her usual straight-backed chair nearby.

"Thank you." He paused to show Mrs. Schoenleber an official-looking silver badge before he sat down. "My name is Crawford Galt, and I am employed by the Pinkerton agency. You may have heard of us."

"I have. Yours is a private law enforcement agency and is known as a union buster. Let us get right to it. Is this conversation regarding Schmitz Enterprises?"

"No, it is not. In fact, I would greatly prefer that Miss Carlson not be present. This is a private matter."

What should Nilda do?

Mrs. Schoenleber just sat for a moment. Then she said, "Very well, as you wish. Nilda, go tend to your duties in the alcove."

The alcove? And then Nilda realized what Mrs. Schoenleber was saying. She hopped up. "Yes, ma'am."

She left through the big doors, closing them behind her, and quickly turned the corner into the alcove beside the parlor. Here was the dumbwaiter, the vertical shaft used to transfer things from floor to floor. She opened the square, waist-high door. On the opposite side of it was a similar door, closed, that served the parlor. With this door open, she could hear everything that was said in the parlor! She leaned into the shaft, listening.

Mr. Galt was speaking. "I understand you were acquainted with a young man named Dreng Nygaard."

Nilda almost cried out. She clapped her hands over her mouth. She must not make a sound, or Mr. Galt would hear her and realize she was listening.

Mrs. Schoenleber said, "Yes. There are very few opportunities here in Blackduck for young people to become acquainted and socialize, so I conduct a social each month. Mr. Nygaard was a guest."

"The Pinkerton agency has been retained to look into the matter of his untimely death. I would like to ask you some questions."

Nilda's heart thumped. Everyone told her that she had not caused Dreng's death, but what if this detective found reason to accuse her? What if he decided that she actually was responsible?

"The local sheriff, Daniel Gruber—who is fully competent, I might add—undertook a careful investigation of Mr. Nygaard's death. I recommend you talk to him."

Mr. Galt replied, "I already have. I understand that Miss Carlson, the assistant who just left, also knew Mr. Nygaard."

"That is true. They emigrated from the same town in Norway and were acquainted."

"How well acquainted?"

Nilda thought that Mrs. Schoenleber's voice hardened. "I have no idea, nor have I ever inquired. Other than our gatherings, I never saw them in each other's company on a social basis, nor did Mr. Nygaard ever come calling on a social basis."

"Miss Carlson is an attractive young woman. I trust she is well chaperoned."

If Mrs. Schoenleber's voice was hard before, now it was stony. "She has proven herself to be a responsible adult in no need of chaperoning. Never have I—nor has anyone else—seen her engage in even the most innocent of flirtations. In the language of the local farmers, Mr. Galt, Miss Carlson tends to her own chickens."

Behind her, Charles was coming down the hall. Nilda stood erect and made shushing motions, her finger to her lips.

Charles paused and frowned. He must have caught on, because he turned away from her and opened the big doors. Nilda heard him ask, "Is there anything I may bring you?"

Mr. Galt asked, "You are the majordomo, is that correct?"

"That is correct, sir."

Mr. Galt said, "Mrs. Schoenleber, I wish to interview this man regarding the matter at hand."

"You may do so."

"Miss Carlson and the hostler as well."

"For the complete picture, you have my permission to interview the downstairs maid and the cook also, who are both privy to the situation. Miss Carlson, however . . ." She paused. "Either Charles or I will be present any time that you interview Miss Carlson."

"Oh?" Mr. Galt's voice sounded instantly suspicious.

"Miss Carlson had a very difficult time in the aftermath of the matter at hand; the circumstances of Mr. Nygaard's death caused nightmares and intense, intrusive memories. She needs emotional support."

"I see."

Mrs. Schoenleber suggested, "If you need nothing more from me, perhaps you ought to sit down with Charles here and complete that little chore on your list of conversations. I will leave the two of you alone."

After a moment, the big doors opened and she emerged. The doors closed. To follow her or continue listening? Nilda followed her. They went straight to the kitchen, and Mrs. Schoenleber plopped down at the kitchen table. Nilda sat beside her.

"Verna, tea." Mrs. Schoenleber was obviously furious. The anger poured out of her. She kept her voice tight, controlled. "You did listen, correct?"

"Yes, ma'am."

"What do you make of it?"

Nilda licked her lips. "I don't know, ma'am. The sheriff said the case was closed. Why would this Mr. Galt come?"

"You knew the Nygaards in Norway and told me about them, the missus in particular. I am thinking that perhaps Dreng's parents, most likely the mother, engaged the detective agency. After all, we are merely a small, backwater town in a rural area. Surely the local investigation was superficial at best. Incompetently done."

Nilda had to think a moment, translating the words Mrs. Schoenleber used. "It was not! Sheriff Gruber was very thorough. Oh, wait. I see what you are saying."

Cook set cups, saucers, tea dishes, and a pot of tea by Mrs. Schoenleber and then poured.

Mrs. Schoenleber sat quietly, studying nothing at all. Then

she said, "The facts are on record, and there is nothing to hide. We will remain candid with this Mr. Galt but volunteer nothing. Answer only the questions asked."

Cook brought a plate of maple-syrup rolls and set it between them, but Nilda was too upset to eat one.

They sat in silence. Charles returned and sent the cook to the parlor.

Mrs. Schoenleber waved a hand. "Join us."

"Thank you, madam." Charles brought a cup and sat down across from Nilda.

"Have you any insights?"

He grimaced. "I asked a few questions of my own. From his answers and the general tenor of his questioning, I'd suggest that our friend in there is certain that some horrific crime is being carefully covered up. Whoever hired him gave him incomplete information and an incorrect description of what occurred."

"In short, he is looking for trouble."

"I believe so. Was that your impression also?" Charles seemed angry too, but not so angry that he didn't take a maple-syrup roll. He poured himself tea.

"Yes. His whole approach suggests that Dreng's family in Norway sent the Pinkerton agency out here."

Nilda thought about this. What a terrible thing to come home to. A person trying to dig up dirt that wasn't there. "What if he . . ." She could not think of an English word for it. "What if he comes to a, uh, wrong decision? If he hears things and reads them wrongly. Is 'read' the right word?"

"It is. Very good." Mrs. Schoenleber almost smiled. She picked up a roll.

Charles almost smiled too. "Miss Carlson, your English is coming along very well. I suggest the phrasing you seek is 'come to the wrong conclusion' or 'misconstrue the evidence.' It could well happen. He is not investigating this with an open mind."

"An open mind?" Nilda thought she understood but she wasn't certain.

"From his approach and the questions he is asking, I perceive that he has already made up his mind; he is not very open to evidence that would prove false the case he invented."

"Or was invented for him." Mrs. Schoenleber nodded.

Nilda asked, "Isn't there anything we can do?"

"Unfortunately, no."

Nilda's heart sank into her shoes. Dreng's evil had made her life very unpleasant in Norway. She came to America, and Dreng made her life very unpleasant here. His attack on her and his death were making her life horribly unpleasant yet, plaguing her mind and heart. He had tried to kill her, and then, when she managed to injure him and escape, he had frozen to death in the snow. And now, here was this big-city detective adding to a woe she was trying so hard to put behind her.

One of her reading assignments had been a soliloquy from a play by William Shakespeare. "The evil that men do lives after them; the good is oft interred with their bones."

Dreng's evil was still alive.

Chapter 3

Rune's groan brought Signe out to stand beside him on the front porch. "What is it?" She leaned her cheek against his shoulder.

"I cannot see the trees at the west end of the field."

"Not even a blur?"

"Not anymore."

"And the pain?"

Rune hadn't answered her, but she didn't ask again. She could always tell. He'd first noticed the glaucoma some fifteen years ago. No surprise, since the disease had plagued his father and uncle too. It seemed to run in the Strand family.

"Call the boys, will you please? I'll go get the milk pails out. Got a lot to do today." When he stepped off the porch, Rufus leaped ahead of him, then sat down a few yards ahead, as if to wait. "I'm coming. You want to go open the barn door for me?" The cheery mutt danced beside him. "You can go make sure everyone is up in the barn." Rune waved an arm, and Rufus took off, fluffy tail waving like a flag.

Signe watched them go, her heart heavy. Signe caught her breath as she saw Rune stumble and catch himself before he hit the ground. She'd have one of the boys check to see if a rock had protruded and dig it out. Anything to help make life easier. Rune's shoulders were growing more rounded and his stride not so sure. Perhaps a cane could help him. The hat that shaded his eyes also protected the top of his head that had succumbed to baldness.

"He looks older than his years." Gerd, moving silently as always, stood at Signe's elbow.

"Ja, that he does."

"I'll get breakfast started."

"Takk, you always do so much."

Together they entered the house. Signe climbed the stairs, woke her three sons, and returned to her room to dress swiftly. Glancing out the east window, she could see the sun was already above the treetops. She'd chosen this bedroom because of that window, for the joy of seeing the sun bring light to the world again. She heard the boys going down the stairs, although bare feet did not make as much noise on the treads as boots. If they were going out into the woods today, they'd put boots on after breakfast. Leif was especially thrilled by swishing his bare feet through the wet grass on the way to the outhouse.

Back in the kitchen, she slipped an apron over her head and inhaled. The sun was up and coffee boiling, two portents of a fine day. She told Gerd, "I'll go get the buttermilk and cream from the well house. Anything else?"

"Milk too, and sausage patties. You better take a basket."

Signe smiled, snatching a basket off the hooks on the wall. The rooster crowing announced that Leif had opened the chicken house door. The rooster sounded so much closer when not locked in the coop, not that being inside stopped him from welcoming the sun.

"Good morning to you too," she called from the well house door. He flapped his wings and crowed again.

The dim interior felt almost chilly as she stepped down to the packed dirt floor. Water from the windmill flowed into the trough made of fieldstones, cooled the containers of food in it, and flowed on out the other end, this time to empty into a water tank for the cows. What they didn't drink watered a good crop of grass around it, along with pigweed and sow thistle that sprouted and grew with impunity.

The milk pans needed skimming and cream would need to be churned later in the day. She'd have one of the boys bring the churn and cream up to the back porch. Now that the cows were in full production, they were churning almost every other day.

With her supplies loaded in the basket, Signe shut the door behind her and returned to the house.

"Hungry." Kirstin met her at the door, rubbing her eyes. She lifted her arms and waited until Signe set her basket on the table. Once in her mother's arms, legs encircling her waist, Kirstin laid her cheek against her shoulder and popped her thumb in her mouth.

Signe squeezed her little girl, making her giggle. "Toast?" she asked. Kirstin nodded.

"You said the magic word." Gerd held a piece of bread over the open fire. "Jam?"

Another vigorous nod. Signe lifted the tray on the high chair that Rune had seen in a magazine and built during the winter, and let Kirstin slide down to stand on the seat. As soon as she sat down and her mor settled the tray in place, the little girl slapped her hand on the wood.

"What do you say?" Signe asked.

"Takk."

Both Signe and Gerd nodded, Signe smiling and Gerd close to it.

They set bowls of oatmeal around the table, and Gerd slid the plate of pancakes back in the warming oven after adding more. Milk-filled glasses sat at the boys' places, and coffee waited to be poured. Signe checked the syrup, the jar warming in a pan of hot water. Mrs. Benson had brought them a quart of maple syrup the last time she visited, made from their own trees. She had offered them seedlings, which they would transplant in the fall. It was too early in the season to transplant trees. The best time was fall before the ground froze. The thought of a maple grove of their own always brought a smile to Signe's face.

So many things had been started this past year. While Rune's ski business grew, so did their number of hogs, requiring a larger barn. Now that all the spring fieldwork was finished, beginning to build the barn went much faster with two teams and help from the Kielunds. They had already dug the trenches for the foundation for the hog barn and would start building it in the next day or so.

"Another sow is farrowing," Leif called as his feet hit the porch. "I need to be there."

Gerd drew out the platter of pancakes. "Oatmeal is there, and I'll roll these up with sugar so you can take them along."

At his mother's look, Leif washed his hands and slid into his chair. "Knute is staying with her until I get back." Between bites, he grinned at Kirstin banging her spoon on the tray and chanting "Ef, Ef" at the same time. While she was learning to talk remarkably early, "Ef" definitely meant Leif. "Go, Ef."

"Later, Baby." He shoveled a spoonful of oatmeal into his mouth.

"Where's your far?" Signe asked.

"Applying another coat of wax to that last pair of skis. He

said he'd be done in a few minutes. He wants to mail them today."

"I'll write down a list and get the butter packed."

Steps on the porch, and Gunlaug pulled open the screen door. "Sorry I am late. I wanted to finish the fringe on that rug so it can go to Mrs. Benson. Will anyone be going soon?"

"As soon as we can get everything ready." Signe handed her a cup of coffee. She could hear other voices outside.

Gerd handed Leif several rolled pancakes. "I put bacon in some. You go take care of your sow."

"Thank you." And out the door he charged.

"I think a whirlwind just went by," Rune said with a chuckle.

They took their places at the table. Knute blew into the room, plopped into his seat, and reached for the pancakes.

"Let's say grace." Rune bowed his head and waited for Knute to pay attention. "Thank you, Lord, for this morning, this food before us, and for each one here. Bless our work today. We thank you and praise your name. Amen."

Kirstin got the "men" part, sending chuckles around the table.

"She sure takes part, doesn't she?" Ivar, Gunlaug's youngest son, said.

While they ate, Rune delegated the work for the day.

"When can we go back in the woods?" Bjorn asked.

"When the barn is built. The lumber should be delivered today. You, Knute, and Ivar help them unload, I'll get the skis packed to ship, and one of the women will deliver them to Benson's Corner."

"Along with the rug I have ready," Gunlaug said.

"And the butter," Signe added. "Knute, please bring the full churn up to the porch before they come, and we need to skim the milk pans."

"Are you ready to start the cheese?" Rune asked.

"As soon as the new shelves are finished to hold the pans."

"That's right. I'll get on that as soon as the skis are ready to go. Knute can help me."

"Maybe one day soon we can go fishing?" Knute finished his milk. "Mor, can I have coffee now?"

Bjorn elbowed him. "Coffee is for adults, don't you know?" He drained his and raised his cup for a refill.

Knute shot him a dirty look. "Mo-o-r."

She rolled her eyes at Bjorn. "Enough."

When she started to rise to get the coffeepot, Knute jumped in. "I can get it."

"I'll have more coffee too, please," Rune said quietly. "I think I hear a wagon coming."

At that moment, Rufus leaped off the porch, started barking, and ran down the lane.

"Guess we'll all get out there and unload." Rune pushed back his chair. "Let's go, boys. Grab your gloves." He patted his wife's shoulder when he walked by.

Signe always loved his gentle reminders that he thought about her, and leaned her cheek against his hand. "Takk."

Gunlaug slid three pancakes onto Signe's plate once the men were outside. "I'll take Kirstin out to the garden with me. We'll make the trip to Benson's this afternoon." She scooped up the giggling Kirstin and went out the door.

Signe finished her breakfast alone, enjoying the peace. This was such a warm and comforting kitchen. Usually it bubbled with activity, but she loved this quiet too.

She knew where Gerd was; she could hear the churn thumping. As soon as she finished cleaning up the breakfast dishes, she walked out onto the porch.

"What are we having for dinner?" she asked.

"Canned chicken with the noodles we made yesterday," Gerd replied. "Good thing we still have canned corn and beans to add. The dried onions are all gone, but Gunlaug brought in green onions from the garden. The radishes are ready too. I'm thinking the watercress might be ready in the cow pond. And I think we can find enough dandelion greens for supper."

"Has Knute been setting snares? Some fried rabbit would be good. I could make biscuits."

Gerd nodded and stopped churning. "There, you hear that? Finally turned to butter. This batch took a while. We should have brought it in last night to warm up."

"Are you driving the cart this afternoon or is Gunlaug?"

Gerd shrugged. "Makes no difference to me." She poured the contents of the churn through the strainer and into a big pot. Once drained, the butter went into their biggest crockery bowl to be washed until the water ran clear. They kept the first drain of buttermilk for the house, and the rest went into a milk can to be fed to the pigs and chickens.

Drives to Benson's Corner had grown more frequent as the family created additional things to sell. Besides the butter and eggs they'd been selling for the last year or so, and sides of pork in the fall, this year they had added skis and rugs. Since the ewes had produced only two ewe lambs this year, they would butcher the wethers and add to their flock with the ewe lambs. Soon they would have a couple of bales of wool to sell too. Not to mention their main source of money, the giant pine trees they sold every spring. This year they had as many logs as they'd ever had, partly thanks to Oskar Kielund and his team. Since he had become a member of the family by marrying a cousin of Rune's, he was often at the farm to help out.

That afternoon, after dinner and the dishes were done, with the cart loaded and Gunlaug guiding Rosie at a trot down the driveway, Gerd and Signe sat out on the porch. Gerd swished the dandelion greens in a pan of water while Signe rinsed the watercress. She raised her chin to catch an errant breeze on her face and neck. "I love this time of year. Warm but not unbearably hot, plenty to do but almost within a window of time."

With all of them working, they were not only accomplishing a lot more but able to start and work on some dreams. Like the orchard and the maple grove. She and Gunlaug had loaded the cart with chicken manure and straw manure from the barn and had spread it in circles where each of the fruit and maple trees would be planted. By building up the soil in advance, their trees might grow far more sturdy, as well as quickly. Oskar had plowed more space for the garden and extended the fencing in case any animals got out.

Rune and the boys had blown out more stumps and turned another acre into oats for cattle feed. The cornfield had been expanded also. With their growing number of livestock, they needed more feed. The men had just closed off the pasture that would become the hayfield. With extra fertilizer from the added animals, they had more manure to spread for the future orchard.

As Rune often said, "*The wheel goes around, so now we pray for rain and sun in the right proportions.*"

Gerd stood and threw the wash water on the rosebushes on either side of the steps.

Signe announced, "I'm going out to pick more onions, perhaps pull a few weeds."

Gerd nodded and went inside. Thank God she had the strength to take part in not only the household chores, but working in the garden and attending church. Such a miraculous change from the woman who screamed complaints from her bed when Signe and Rune first arrived. Even now Signe shuddered when she thought about how Gerd used to be.

As she stepped off the porch, she heard the screen door open and shut. Gra, the cat, chirped a welcome and, she knew, twined around Gerd's legs. Gerd, who for so many years had not been permitted a cat in the house, would be bending over and stroking the silver-striped back.

Life was so different now without Onkel Einar. The only thing that would make it perfect was if Nilda were here. Perhaps tonight Signe would write her a letter. Strange how Blackduck seemed so far away when it really wasn't.

Chapter 4

Three nights. Three nights in a row.

Nilda stared into the mirror while Gilda finished her hair. Putting it up herself had seemed insurmountable. She looked ghastly. Purple shadows lurked under her eyes, which seemed to have lost their blue. Even her hair did not want to behave, which was why she had called for help.

That horrible dream about what really happened. Actually it was more like reliving things than a dream. Each time she woke up screaming, and her throat felt like raw beef.

Gilda laid her hands on Nilda's shoulders. She had been the one to answer the screams this time. Hopefully Mrs. Schoenleber had slept through the ruckus. That Nilda woke others made her feel even worse. "Miss, please take a nap today before the supper."

"I-I'm afraid to go to sleep." She stared down at her fingers knitted together in her lap. *Which is why I look so exhausted. As if I've been fighting off some horrible disease.* Actually, that was a good description of Dreng. He not only was a horrible sickness, he'd been sick in his head. She was not the only young woman back home in Norway who had fought off his advances or was afraid to and, in at least one case, paid a horrible price. After all, Dreng's mother thought her son could do no wrong, so it had to be the young women's fault.

Nilda had left the Nygaards' employment before she could be fired.

When Dreng showed up in Blackduck, he charmed all the women he met, no matter their age. Even Mrs. Schoenleber—well, almost. But while Nilda had tried to do her Christian duty and forgive him when he pleaded that he was a changed man, something inside warned her. To this day, she was not sure what that had been. But it no longer mattered. Even dead, he made her life miserable.

She'd never told anyone all of the story. When he attended the socials, he was the epitome of a fine young man, impeccable manners, funny. The other women in attendance competed for his attention. Nilda had wanted to warn them.

A headache pounded behind her eyes. Even though she rubbed her temples with her fingertips, it persisted.

"Let me bring you a cup of tea and one of the powders the doctor prescribed for Cook. She says it helps her a lot."

"Thank you, but no. I'll go downstairs. Perhaps breakfast will help me feel better. If it doesn't, then I'll try one." Nilda pushed herself to her feet. "Thank you. As always, you did a fine job." Now, if only food and coffee were the answer.

When she walked into the empty dining room, she started to turn back to the morning room, but the thought of facing Mrs. Schoenleber without first having coffee encouraged her to sit down at the table set with one place setting. Of course, by this late hour, what did she expect? After all, her employer always rose early, contrary to most wealthy women, who liked to lie abed and have breakfast brought to them on a tray.

"Good morning, Miss Nilda." Charles set a steaming cup of

coffee in front of her. How could he always sound so cheerful? "What can I get you for breakfast today? Cook took a pan of cinnamon rolls out of the oven just a few minutes ago. While she plans to serve them for midmorning coffee, I'm sure I could abscond with one for you." Cook's cinnamon rolls put any others to shame. He frowned and added, "But then, you don't look like you feel so good. Might just toast be a good starter?"

Nilda added cream to her coffee before taking a welcome sip. "A cinnamon roll sounds wonderful." At least she hoped it did.

Gently tipping her head from side to side, she stared out the tall window, its sheer drapes pulled back to let the sun in, and held her cup with both hands. Perhaps if she took her coffee and roll outside . . .

Without further thought, coffee in hand, she strode into the kitchen, nearly slamming into Charles with the swinging door.

"Sorry, I just decided eating at the table outside might help."

"Good idea. I'll wipe it off." He grabbed the rag Cook tossed him and, plate in one hand, rag in the other, marched outside. "Give me just a moment." After wiping down both the small round table and a matching iron chair, he set down her roll. "I could have brought your coffee out for you."

"You could have, but you didn't realize what I was going to do. Neither did I." She sat when he pulled out the chair and raised her face to the sun. "This is wonderful. Perhaps we need to do this more often."

"Eggs, biscuits? What is your pleasure? The baked eggs were perfect."

"Eggs scrambled, bacon, and a piece of toast. Oh, and please make it only one egg."

"Shredded potatoes? Jam?"

"No, thank you."

She was just unwinding the last bit of cinnamon roll when

Mrs. Schoenleber stepped through the French doors and onto the verandah of gray slate warming in the sun. Pots of nasturtiums that had been started in the greenhouse lined the windows with splashes of bright yellow and orange. "Do you mind if I join you?" she asked, her smile spreading both comfort and concern.

"Not in the least." Nilda pushed back her plate.

"I thought I smelled cinnamon rolls. That is another excuse to join you." When seated, she leaned forward, resting a hand on Nilda's arm. "Bad night again?"

"Did I wake you? I'm so sorry."

"As if you could control your dreams—or rather, in this case, nightmares."

"I'm becoming afraid to fall asleep."

Charles stopped at their table with a tray and set a cup and saucer in front of Mrs. Schoenleber. After he filled her cup, he refilled Nilda's. "Your breakfast will be out in a bit." With a flourish, he lifted a domed lid covering more cinnamon rolls, now drizzled with frosting. "Cook was saving these for later, but I suggested that later has already arrived."

"You figured right." Taking a bite even before setting the roll on her plate, Mrs. Schoenleber closed her eyes. "The better to taste it," she said. She wiped her lips with a napkin and studied Nilda. "I have a suggestion, if I may."

Please not another trip to the Cities. Nilda swallowed. "Of course."

"I've been thinking. Perhaps a trip home would break the cycle." She raised a hand to stop Nilda before she got out more than the "but." "I know we have a lot to do, but you and your health are far more important to me than the proposals. Beyond that, you have everything in order for the social, and since it is ten days away, I suggest four days at home. That will make up for the days you missed."

"Your breakfast, Miss Nilda." Charles set the domed plate in front of her and lifted the lid. "Now, can I get you anything else?"

Nilda shot him a smile as she shook her head. Home. The kindness of the offer made her eyes burn. To see her mor and all the rest of the family. "When?"

"Tomorrow. I will call Mrs. Benson and have her run a message out to the farm. Unless you would rather surprise them."

"Yes, I would. Surprising them sounds wonderful. Thank you." She clasped her employer's hand. "Thank you."

"Now we will pray that this is the perfect cure. Charles will have the horse and buggy ready by seven thirty so you arrive before dinnertime."

Home. I get to go home. Was she really this homesick, or were the nightmares affecting her more than she realized?

That night her clock read 3 AM when she turned on the light, still shaking from the horror. Every time she closed her eyes, she could hear him, see him, smell him. Each night the dream seemed more real, or maybe she was just more susceptible.

A tap at the door caught her attention. "Y-yes?"

Gilda pushed open the door. "I brought you tea and toast. My ma always said tea helped her relax." She set the tray on the seat of the chair. "Here, let me help you get settled. My goodness, you are shaking something fierce." She took the shawl that Nilda kept looped over the frame at the foot of the bed and tucked it around Nilda's shoulders. "There now. Ma always said add sugar, and I brought milk in case you might like to try that. I was real quiet, so I didn't wake Cook. You know how she don't like anyone fussing in her kitchen." Stirring the cup one more time to melt the sugar, she handed it to Nilda.

"I'm sorry I woke you."

"I know you don't mean to." Sitting on the edge of the bed,

Gilda turned to face Nilda, who dutifully sipped the tea. The warmth going down her throat did feel good.

"Thank you. I think having another person near helps the most, like the dream is afraid to come out in the light and company." Her eyes felt branded by hot coals.

"How about a warm cloth for your face, or would cold be better?"

"Warm, I think."

Returning after a moment, Gilda took the cup and saucer and handed Nilda the warm cloth. Burying her face in it, Nilda heaved a sigh. Such horror to endure months after Dreng had gone to the darkness where he belonged. How could he hate her so? Why would he? She'd done nothing to hurt him—well, not physically, but she had hurt his pride. His mor had spoiled him something fierce, but the justice meted out by her brothers and some friends should have made him think twice. He'd thought, all right—all about how to get even, all aimed at her.

She drained the cup and set the saucer on the stand by her bed. A kerosene lamp took up a good part of the surface, kept there just in case the gaslights failed. "Thank you again." She looked toward her valise near the chifforobe, already packed but for her hairbrush and comb set, a gift from Mrs. Schoenleber last Christmas.

"That is all you are taking?" Gilda asked.

"I have clothes at the farm, and if I need more, I can borrow from Signe."

"If you're sure, then?"

"You go back to bed now, and thank you again." Nilda snuggled down under the sheet and light summer blanket. Was there any chance she could fall asleep again and not dream?

Nilda set her valise outside her bedroom door and made her way down to the kitchen as soon as she heard Cook up and about. While the sun still lurked below the horizon, the eastern sky wore a cloak of lemon. The diamonds that hid in the dew of the grass had yet to sparkle and glitter. Even the birds sounded sleepy. The rooster out in the pen behind the stables crowed once, as if he had just awakened himself. The next attempt revealed his full range. Nilda didn't usually hear him because she slept later now at Mrs. Schoenleber's . . . at least she used to, before the nightmares. Perhaps being back on the farm would help her sleep well again.

The five miles of road seemed to fly past as the horse trotted to Benson's Corner. Nilda waved to Mrs. Benson, who was helping a customer load her supplies in the back of a wagon.

"Wonderful to see you, Nilda," Mrs. Benson called.

Nilda could hardly hear her over the noise of the buggy, but she waved and nodded.

"So we really are going to just show up and surprise them?" George looked over his shoulder, pulling the horse back to a slow jog now.

"Yes, just in case something happened and I had to change plans."

She watched the familiar farms pass by until they finally turned left onto the lane to the Carlson farm. Rufus came charging down the two lines of dirt with a strip of green between, barking a warning. But as soon as he heard Nilda's voice, he switched to happy, welcoming yips.

"Good boy." She looked ahead to the old house, the one she'd lived in from the time she and Ivar arrived. Right now, only Gunlaug and her youngest son slept there. Rune's family and Tante Gerd lived at the new house that glowed between the barn and the woods. The distance between house and virgin timber had widened; they had taken out so many trees.

No one came to the porch in spite of the dog barking. But just as George helped Nilda down from the buggy, Gunlaug pushed open the screen door.

"Oh, goodness, look who's here. I was at the loom and didn't realize why Rufus was barking. Oh, my."

Nilda met her mor at the bottom of the porch steps, burying herself in her mor's arms. Their tears of joy left them both sniffing.

"What a surprise. Did anyone know you were coming?" Gunlaug asked.

"No, I just learned myself yesterday."

"Where would you like this?" George asked, his smile wide as he hefted the valise.

"Up on the porch. Thank you." Nilda kept her arm around Gunlaug's waist.

"Can you stay for dinner or at least coffee?" Gunlaug asked George.

"Thank you, but no. I need to get back to town, and Cook sent a sandwich and coffee along with me." He looked at Nilda. "I will be here as early as I can on Monday morning."

"Yes, I know," Nilda assured him, "but you realize Norwegians make sure all guests have coffee and cookies at least. You wouldn't want to offend them."

"Of course not. See you on Monday. Good day, Mrs. Carlson." He tipped his hat and returned to the buggy.

"Takk, er, thank you." Gunlaug waved, and together they watched him turn the horse and buggy back toward the road. Arm in arm, they climbed the steps and entered the quiet house.

"Don't you all eat over here any longer?" Nilda asked.

"Usually, but today Signe and Gerd decided to fix dinner at the other house. We are planning to eat outside to celebrate Rune's birthday. I baked the cake here so he wouldn't know this was coming." She pointed to a round layer cake iced in white boiled frosting.

"A surprise?"

"Ja, and will he ever be surprised. Leave your bag here, and we'll walk on over. We can take turns carrying the cake."

Leif ran out from the barn to accompany them. "Tante Nilda, you're here!" He threw his arms around her waist. "I was beginning to think you were never coming back." He grinned up at her. "When are you coming home to stay? After dinner I'll show you all my baby pigs. One of the hens hatched another batch." His words tumbled over each other as he threw a little jump into his stride every now and then.

"Let's see. I think my home is now in Blackduck, at least as far as I can tell, but I will come to visit, and perhaps this summer you can ride Rosie into town to visit me."

His eyes rounded. "You think so? Really?"

"Why not?" Mrs. Schoenleber had encouraged her to invite her family to visit. "Perhaps you and Grandma could come together on the train."

He grinned at Gunlaug. "Soon, Grandma, let's go soon. Well, as soon as I can leave my pigs. All the sows are done farrowing now."

Signe brought a tablecloth out to throw over the table set on the porch. When she turned, she dropped the cloth and tore down the steps. "Nilda, you came home. Oh, my. What a shock, what a wonderful shock." She threw her arms around Nilda, the two of them hugging hard. She drew back. "Are you all right? Is something wrong? Are you home to stay?"

"Yes, no, and no. But I don't go back until Monday."

Signe laughed. "I can't believe this. You can be Rune's birthday present. Couldn't have planned anything better if I'd tried."

"They should be up pretty soon." Gunlaug looked out over

the fields to where the men were blowing up stumps. An explosion sent a stump, dirt, and rocks into the air. The debris almost settled before the second stump blew, followed by three more.

When all was quiet once more, Signe said, "They just blew their morning's work to smithereens."

Nilda burst out laughing. "That's for sure. What a show. Let's hurry and get inside before they see me. Seeing Rune's face when he comes through that door will be something."

Kirstin looked up from her place on the floor where she had blocks scattered around her.

"My land, look who's here." Tante Gerd skirted Kirstin to hug Nilda. "Welcome home."

"Thank you." Nilda blinked and felt the tears trying to attack her. This was her family, and she did not see them often enough. What would it be like to leave Mrs. Schoenleber and move back to the farm?

"You feeling all right?" Gerd studied her. "You been sick?"

"No, not sick." Well, perhaps sick at heart. Should she tell them all or . . . ? Not now. This was Rune's birthday, and while he didn't care a lot about birthdays, today they would have a party.

Gerd tipped her head to the side. "The prodigal has come home?" She nodded. "Today we have much to celebrate."

Nilda swapped questioning looks with Signe. As best friends for so many years, often they could read each other's minds. Signe nodded and smiled. Yes, there were great changes, all to be talked about later.

"Ma?" Kirstin tugged on Signe's apron and held up her arms, all the while eyeing the visitor. When Signe swung her daughter up to her hip, she kissed her cheek. "You remember Tante Nilda. She's not been gone that long."

Kirstin's thumb and forefinger found their way to her mouth as she leaned her cheek against her mother's shoulder.

"You're right, little one, this must seem like a long time to you, but I haven't forgotten you." Nilda reached over and tickled the bottom of a little bare foot. Kirstin jerked her foot back, then let it slide forward again. The next tickle brought out a smile and the third a giggle. The thumb left her mouth, and she waved at Nilda. They giggled together. "Oh, baby girl, I've missed you. There are no babies where I live."

"You could come back home, then," Leif suggested.

Kirstin reached for him. "Ef, Ef."

"She can't say my name yet."

"Well, she's pretty young to be talking much at all," Nilda said.

"She knows lots of words."

"Leif teaches her," Signe said. "She goes with him all over, mostly in the wagon."

Kirstin looked toward the door. "Go? Go, Ef?"

"See?"

Boots hit the steps. The women stared at each other, then started to laugh.

"Where's the dinner?" Rune asked as he stepped in the doorway. "Oh, my word." He crossed the space and swept Nilda into his arms. "You finally decided to come home. I was beginning to think you'd given up on us."

Nilda hugged him close. "Never. Happy birthday." She leaned back. "You know, you could come calling when you come to Blackduck."

"I know, but we are always in such a hurry. And besides, I don't remember when we last went there."

"We pick up most of what we need at the train station, or the Bensons order for us." Ivar looked her up and down. "I guess life there agrees with you."

"I guess it does." She studied him back. "Between you and Bjorn, are you trying to out-muscle each other?"

She hugged her younger brother, then Bjorn, who ducked his chin, trying to ignore the red creeping up his neck. Knute pointed at him and snickered.

"I think you might bring Bjorn with you when you come for the next social, brother. You received an invitation, right?" Nilda asked.

Ivar nodded. "I thought perhaps I would miss this one. There is so much to do here."

"There will always be so much to do." Rune slapped his shoulder. "And if Bjorn would like to go . . ."

Bjorn shook his head. "I don't think so."

"Why not? A chance to meet some lovely young women and have a good time." Nilda looked to Ivar, who subtly motioned to his clothes. "Ah, I see. Well, we can take care of that."

Nilda looked down at a tugging on her skirt. Kirstin stood with her arms raised. "So now you remember who I am?" She swept the little girl into her arms and twirled her around as she used to do. Kirstin went from hesitant to giggles to chortles to shrieks in three turns.

While they'd been talking, the other women had moved the platter of fried chicken, bowl of potatoes, greens with bacon, and fresh rolls to the table outside. They all trooped out to sit at the table there.

"Just think, soon those trees we have planted will shade this house, like they are beginning to the other." Signe motioned to the birch and cottonwood trees planted at either corner. She had insisted they plant them the previous fall after she and Knute went searching for saplings. Both had new growth, thanks to all the wash water thrown on them, just like the rosebush that Fritz had given them at English class one evening when Nilda and Signe attended. Well, Fritz had delivered them, but Mrs. Schoenleber was the one who had given them. Why did she think of Fritz first?

After grace, Nilda watched and listened to her family. They were speaking English with sprinkles of Norwegian when an unusual word was needed.

"How long are you here?" Rune asked while they were passing food.

"George will pick me up Monday morning. But I am serious about Bjorn coming with Ivar. I have a feeling he is concerned about his clothes, so I will make sure that is taken care of. I think Ivar probably needs a new shirt too. He's broadened out in the shoulders so."

"They work hard, those two." Rune tackled his food.

"You all work hard."

"That's what it takes to survive out here. And we want to do more than survive."

"Spoken like a true Norwegian." Gerd bobbed her head.

"God has given us so much, how can we do less than our best?" Signe said.

"Yes, I feel the same."

Rune studied Nilda. "What is going on that we have this surprise visit? I have a feeling it being my birthday was purely accidental."

To tell him or not? "I need to talk with Mor."

"Can I help?"

She stared down at her plate. "I think I need her wisdom. She's lived a lot more years than you or I."

"If I can help you, you know I will."

Blinking back tears, she laid her hand over his. "I know that. With everything in me, I know that."

He turned his hand over and clasped hers. "I finally believe that you—that we all—are right where God would have us to be. I didn't at first, but sanding skis leaves a lot of time to think. If I believe He loves us, I must believe that He knows best and that He alone is the one who can make things happen."

"Both the good and the bad?" Nilda asked.

"I don't think He makes the bad happen, but He allows it. One day when I was working in the shop, Reverend Skarstead dropped in to visit. He and I had quite a discussion. Would you believe he picked up a sanding block and went to work right along with me? Like he did on the buildings, especially this house." He motioned to the building around them. "Somehow I think Jesus did the same. You can iron out a lot of problems when your hands are busy with something else." He nodded gently as he talked.

"Thank you. You gave me lots to think about." She turned at Leif's nudge to pass him her empty plate. She really had no idea what she had eaten, but it had to have been good.

"The birthday cake," Leif whispered to her.

I wish I had brought him a present, she thought as a silence fell.

Gunlaug pushed open the screen door with her foot and stepped out carrying the cake on a platter. "Happy birthday, Rune, and we pray you have many more."

The others echoed her wishes as she set the cake in front of him.

"Frosting, even." He smiled up at her. "Your famous boiled frosting?"

"Ja, my arm is sore from beating it fluffy. You get the first piece."

"You mean I have to share this?"

The boys groaned as if on cue. Gunlaug shook her head, her smile belying the stern look she tried to wear. "You want me to cut it, I suppose?"

"Might be a good idea. I never excelled at cutting cakes."

"That's because you never cut them." Nilda flashed him an arch look with her lips rolled together. Ah, the delights of home.

But how would she broach the topic of her nightmares with her mor? Surely she should be over it by now. After all, it happened months ago.

Chapter 5

The Blackduck life has spoiled you.

Nilda shifted to get comfortable on the rope bed, with its straw-stuffed "mattress" supported by ropes. This used to feel good at night. But then, she was always so tired that a blanket on the floor was sufficient. She stared up at the beams that held up the roof, not able to see them, but like so many things in life, knowing they were there. Her mor was already snoring softly in the bed beside her.

Fear had her by the throat. She didn't want to wake up screaming. *Lord, help me. My mind says it is only a dream, but the memories only get worse.* The gentle rhythm of her mother's breathing finally accomplished what her mind could not.

Sometime before the sky began to lighten, it attacked again. His fingers clenched around her throat. *No breath, fight back, buck him off, the ski pole.*

A voice, someone shaking her. Not Dreng, her mor's voice. She was not lying in a snowbank, she was in her bed at home.

"Nilda, wake up, it's a dream. Wake up."

"Ja, a dream." She puffed the words out. The dream, always the dream. She started to sit up, then flopped back.

"You were screaming and thrashing around. A miracle you did not throw yourself out of bed."

"I'm home, safe."

"Dreng is dead and buried. He cannot hurt you or anyone else anymore."

"I know, but the dream . . . how do I make it stop?"

"I wish I knew." Gunlaug sat up. "We know this is not of God."

Nilda did the same and leaned into her mother, who wrapped her arm around her. "Takk."

"Velbekomme."

"I always get so cold."

"Ja, it happened in the winter. If he weren't dead already, I'd want to kill him."

Nilda nodded. "I think you are not the only one."

"But instead I remind myself to pray for you, although I have thought of sending his mor a rather forceful but honest letter. She . . . well, we won't go into that."

Peace crept in through the open window and settled around them.

"I have to keep reminding myself that it wasn't my fault. That I didn't kill him." Nilda stared at her hands. Folded together as if praying but clenched so hard that she knew the knuckles were white. *Relax, let go,* she ordered. *This is crazy.* Her mor's hand covered both of hers. Always in motion, Gunlaug's touch, so full of love as to seem to glow. She rubbed gently, that gesture of love flowing from her hands directly to her daughter's heart, and that released the tears.

"I pray our God will use your tears to wash away the horror of that day and all the days before. We are not meant to suffer from fears and things that happened in the past. As you said, his death was not your fault, so I pray that God will bring about healing from that time and free you to grow in the grace He is pouring out upon you." Gunlaug gathered her daughter into her arms. "Ah, my Nilda, my strong and beautiful daughter. Lord, let it be no more." They breathed together, in the silence and peace of the night.

Nilda felt sleep flow in through her mor's arms and peaceful murmurings, washing away all thoughts and responses.

She woke slowly, breathing gently, listening to the song of the meadowlark that floated in on the breeze through the open window. She knew she was home on the farm, but where was everyone? It was too quiet. Had they all gone away and left her here alone? Not that being alone was a problem. Right now she must have needed that.

You should get up and get going. Not waste your precious time at home lying in bed.

Oh hush, she ordered that scolding voice that always seemed so happy to be after her.

Last night—had she dreamed her mor's arms around her? No, surely not. The amazing thing was that she'd not heard nor felt her mor get up and begin her day. Where were all the others?

Curiosity got the better of her. Stretching brought on yawning, and yawning brought on the urge to settle back into wherever she had been floating on a sea of peace. The meadowlark sang again, this time joined by an answering song from a distance away.

Nilda swung her feet over the side of the bed and stood. First order of the day? The privy. How spoiled she had become with the indoor plumbing of the Schoenleber house in Blackduck. Not bothering with shoes, she snagged her wrap from the foot of the bed and hustled down the stairs and out the door.

She could hear several voices now, the chickens clucking, the dog barking. Happy sounds. Most of the dew was already gone from the grass along the path. On the way back, she checked the sun. As she suspected, the morning was half gone. How could it have been so quiet? How could she have slept so long?

"Tante Nilda, you finally got up!" Leif waved at her from the barn.

She strolled toward him. "Where's everybody?" How tender her feet had become. She never went barefoot in town. She realized she missed this. It was as if she lived two lives, her farm life and her town life.

"At the other house or out in the woods. I just came to check on the sow. Mor said that if one of us woke you, we would know the wrath of Mor." He giggled as he spoke.

As if he were afraid of his mor. The thought made her laugh. Today anything would make her laugh.

"We're going on a picnic for dinner, down in the woods." He and Rufus joined her at the well house. "You want me to pump water over your feet?"

"What a grand idea, though they're not real dirty."

Leif raised and pressed down on the handle, and in a couple of pumps, water gushed over her feet, soaking the nightdress she'd neglected to gather out of the way. "Change places?" he asked. They did, and he rolled his summer-toughened feet from side to side. "Feels good, huh?"

"It sure does."

"Your feet are all white."

"I know. I wear shoes or slippers all the time."

"You need to come home more often." He smiled at her, no longer the little boy who used to look up at her with a grin.

"Leif, you are getting so tall."

"I know. My pants are all too short."

"I could sew ruffles on the bottom for you."

He rolled his eyes. "You better hurry so we can go picnicking."

"Yes, sir." Nilda patted his shoulder. "Thanks for the foot bath."

She gathered her wet gown up so she wouldn't trip over it and strode back to the house. A picnic in the woods. What a grand idea.

"Sorry I slept so late," she announced when she and Leif arrived at the other house, the *new house* as they now called the home Rune had built for his family, the one the entire community had helped build. In the last year, so much had happened on the Carlson farm that it was hard to believe they hadn't been there for years.

"Let's get our things in the wagon and go enjoy the coolness of the shade. It's been too long since I've been out there," Gunlaug said.

Signe handed one basket to Leif. "Did you throw feed sacks in to sit on?"

"And the horse blankets."

"What else do we need?"

"We could take Tante's rocking chair." Leif chuckled as he escaped with the loaded basket.

Tante Gerd tried not to laugh but gave up when Signe rolled her eyes. "That boy."

"You know, that is not a bad idea," Signe said with a nod.

"I do not need the rocking chair. How old do you think I am, anyway?" Gerd planted both fists on her hips and shot him one of *those* looks when he came back inside.

Leif shrugged and backed up a bit. He scooped up the two jugs, one of coffee and one of tea with chokecherry syrup in it, a recent innovation by Signe. Kirstin took off right behind him. Now that she could walk well, she usually ran.

"Are we all loaded?" Leif asked a bit later from the wagon seat of the cart with Tante Gerd beside him and Gunlaug sitting in the wagon bed. "Far, Mor, anything else?"

"I sure as heaven hope not, or we'll have to bring the larger wagon," Rune said.

Rosie tossed her head and stamped her front foot, clearly as impatient with all the waiting as Leif.

Nilda and Signe followed the wagon, Kirstin swinging between them, giggling and chattering as if taking part in the conversation.

"It feels so good to be here. Especially this time. It's not like I've not been here since Dreng attacked me, but . . . but . . . this time is different." *How is it different?* that other voice in her head chimed in. The two often had arguments.

The little girl's chortle brought her back from wherever she had been. She looked down at the child when she whimpered.

"'Bout time you asked for a ride." Signe stopped and swung Kirstin up into her arms. "You, my little one, are getting so grown up, walking along with us like this." She kissed the rounded cheek with a loud *smack*, bringing forth another giggle. Kirstin patted her mor's cheeks with both pudgy hands.

"Let me carry her." Nilda stopped and held out her arms. Kirstin studied her hands, then her face, and then leaned over to be hoisted into Nilda's arms.

Nilda hugged the little girl even closer on her hip. "She is not so hard to believe as Bjorn is. How could he become a man so quickly?"

"He's not even seventeen yet. Maybe if he'd not taken on a man's job so soon and instead had gone to school, he could have remained a boy a bit longer."

Since they'd been strolling rather than striding, Rosie and the wagon were already to where the most recent trees had been felled. Just that morning, Bjorn, Knute, and Ivar had brought it down and started on the limbing.

"Over here." Leif waved to them from where the team and now Rosie were all tied. "We're going over to the creek."

"We're coming."

Nilda and Signe swapped smiles. As if they did not know the way. Leave it to Leif to make sure.

Nilda suggested, "If we take our time, they will have it all set up, and we can just sit down and enjoy ourselves."

"Nilda Carlson, whatever has gotten into you?" Signe tried to look shocked, but a chuckle escaped instead. "I know, it's living in town with staff to take care of you. Be careful you don't get spoiled."

"You might be right. I'll be careful." She thought of the bed she'd slept in. She already was spoiled.

"Mo. Mo." Kirstin had her own names for her family.

Signe reached for her. "Come on, baby. You must be thirsty by now. I know we are."

The creek gurgled over rocks and slid under ferns and moss as it meandered toward the river, not seeming to be in as much of a hurry as in other seasons. The broad, shallow hole they had finally dug out upstream for swimming was a deep wading pool right now. Even so, the boys shucked their boots and splashed in, clothes and all. While it wasn't deep enough or big enough for real diving and swimming, the clear, singing water did a grand job of cooling off anyone who jumped in.

While the boys whooped and splashed in the water, the others set out the food and drinks on a massive stump they had leveled for a table. When they had logged off the big trees and created this clearing, they had left the smaller ones, and pine and maple had already grown tall enough to create shade.

"Surely this is paradise," Nilda said as she stared up at the blue sky and puffy clouds floating above the virgin forest on the other side of the creek.

"Food's ready," Signe shouted to be heard over the boy noise.

Gerd sat on an old log they had rolled over on another visit, shaded by the young pine. "All those years we lived here and I never . . ." She heaved a sigh. "I guess that makes me even more grateful now."

Signe handed her a plate. "Enough here to share." She smiled at her daughter, who was sitting still for a change, next to Gerd.

"Let's have grace." Even Rune's voice sounded more peaceful.

But would peace, even lots of peace, quiet the nightmares?

Chapter 6

Hurry up, we're going to be late," Rune called from the wagon.

"Here, you take Kirstin." Signe glanced around the room. She knew she was forgetting something. Gerd was already out on the wagon seat. Today the whole family would be at church together.

Shutting the door behind her, she paused at the top of the steps. Such a glorious morning. Gunlaug, Nilda, and Ivar were waiting at the other house. She let Rune help her up into the wagon bed. He'd built a bench for the women to sit on right behind the wagon seat. Bjorn was driving, so Knute and Leif jumped in after her.

At the other house, Ivar helped Gunlaug and Nilda up into the wagon. As soon as they were seated, Bjorn clucked the team into a trot.

"Looking mighty prosperous," Nilda whispered in Signe's ear as they watched the houses and farm buildings go by.

Rufus always stopped at the corner of the fence and sat down.

"You think he waits there the whole time we're gone?" Leif

asked from his seat at his mother's feet. Kirstin sat beside him, banging her rattle on the wagon bed, then on up Leif's leg.

"Ef, Ef, Ef." She played with his name.

"Who's this?" he asked, touching Signe's skirt.

"Mo." She waved her rattle and beamed at her mother.

"And this?" He touched Gunlaug this time.

Kirstin studied her and nodded. "Momo." She rolled her lips on the m's.

"And her?" He pointed up to Gerd.

"Momo." Her smile widened. "Momo, Momo." She giggled and pointed her finger at him. "You Momo."

Nilda and Signe swapped astonished grins. Kirstin was teasing her brother. "Kinda young for that, isn't she?" Nilda said under her breath.

Leif shook his head so hard that his cap almost came loose. "I'm not Momo." He pointed to his chest. He poked her chest with one finger. "You Momo."

She stared at him, then frowned and shook her head. "You Ef."

"So who are you?"

She looked puzzled.

"You Kirstin."

"B-Bebe." She studied him, then pointed her finger. "Ef. Ef."

He tickled her 'til she squirmed. "You used to be Baby, but now you are Kirstin."

"Bebe."

"Kirstin, Kirstin, Kirstin." He sang her name, making her smile again.

"She likes singing, doesn't she?" Nilda said.

"She should. Gerd sang to her so often." Signe felt a surge of joy. "I have a little girl, when for so long I figured I needed to be content with my three boys. God has been so good to us, far more than I ever dreamed."

Leif held on to Kirstin as she stood and reached for her mother. Gunlaug lifted her instead. Kirstin stood on her lap and reached for Gerd. "No, you stay here."

Kirstin stuck her thumb and forefinger in her mouth and studied her grandmother. "Momo."

"Ja, that I am." She kept her hands firmly locked around the little one's waist. "Don't you go taking a header off my lap now."

Kirstin pointed at Gerd. "Momo."

Signe watched her little daughter with delight. And gratitude for all the help she'd had.

Bjorn turned the trotting team onto the road toward Blackduck, then turned left past the school. He guided the team into the churchyard and joined the other wagons and buggies at the hitching rail that stretched the length of the church. More rails lined the street. The Lutheran church was painted white with a steeple that included a bell tower. Someone would ring the bell in a few minutes, calling the people of Benson's Corner to worship. Signe loved the song of the bell.

Nilda set Kirstin down, and she dove into Rune's arms. He propped her on his hip and held out a hand to Gunlaug.

Signe headed up the church steps for the open door, greeting people as she went. She smiled. It felt so good to be here, among good friends and close to God.

As always, Mrs. Benson greeted her warmly at the door. "I see that Nilda is home for a visit."

"A surprise. And for Rune's birthday too. She has to go back tomorrow morning, but we have had such a good visit."

"She still likes working for Mrs. Schoenleber?"

"Oh, yes. But I know she gets homesick at times. Such a different life."

"I have heard good things about her. Mr. Larsson says Nilda has quite a head for business and that his aunt sings her praises."

"Really?"

"Mrs. Schoenleber is one of the people behind much of the change in Blackduck. She wants to make sure Blackduck doesn't go into a decline when the lumber runs out and the lumber barons move on. Already some have left."

"Rune has mentioned that, which is why he is working hard to make sure we have other ways to make a living."

"Like the skis and the hogs?"

"And the rugs that Gunlaug weaves, although they won't bring in much."

"If she can get some woven ahead, I will carry them at the store. Even one as a sample. I think there is a furniture store in Blackduck that might be interested too."

"Thank you. We need to get more wool carded and spun. There must be a better way to do some of these things to make it go faster."

They went inside and sat in their normal pew as Reverend Skarstead took his place in the pulpit and cleared his throat.

"Let us pray."

Signe bowed her head and breathed softly.

After the prayer, the reverend continued. "Dearly beloved, let us return to the gospel record for today: Mark chapter eight, beginning at verse twenty-two." He read it again. "One of Jesus' miracles. I have wondered why certain stories were included and others weren't. Scripture says there were many other signs and wonders that Jesus did in those few short years of His life on earth. We know they are told to show us what He did, to increase our faith."

Signe listened intently. Rune needed healing in his eyes. The glaucoma was making it harder for him to see. If only God would reach down and touch his eyes. Even just stop the progression. Could that be why this story was preached on today?

To help them know what God had in mind? But did He ever do miracles like that anymore?

Signe forced her attention back to the sermon. *Lord, teach me, show me how to help Rune. He is such a good man and is trying so hard to provide for us all by looking ahead.*

Another hymn, the benediction—a favorite part of the service in her mind—and then the organ burst into the postlude. Fritz Larsson let out all the stops so that the music rolled across the land. If only she could hear such music more often than church on Sundays. Nilda said he was teaching her the piano. Someday, perhaps, he would teach Signe how to play the organ.

Silly, you dream up the craziest things. She walked beside her family as they left the church. Surely the Kielunds would come to the farm for dinner. The roast was in the oven, and she had stoked the fire well.

Selma Kielund stopped beside them with only her little boy in tow. The other two Kielund children were off playing with Leif and the boys. "So good to see you today."

"Can you and Oskar join us for dinner?" Signe asked. "I thought it would be good to have all the family together, since Nilda is home."

"I thank you, let me ask Oskar." While she was trying to learn English, she was having a hard time with it. She nodded to a circle of men talking by the buggies and then walked over to speak to her husband. She was smiling when she returned, so her yes was no surprise.

Reverend Skarstead joined them and warmly greeted Rune and Signe. He patted Kirstin, who stared at him as if trying to figure out where she had seen him before.

Rune smiled. "This one fell asleep during the sermon. Please don't take that personally."

Reverend Skarstead laughed. "I promise not to." He greeted

the children and finally Gerd and Gunlaug. "English class will be starting up again soon." He waited, then nodded when Gunlaug did.

Signe said, "I will make sure Selma comes too."

They glanced over to see Nilda talking with Fritz Larsson, the organist and schoolteacher. He'd been her first teacher for English too. The reverend raised his eyebrows and grinned at Gunlaug, then leaned closer. "He certainly looks forward to those socials and visits to his aunt's house. He never used to go so often."

"Really?" Gunlaug nodded. "Nilda is encouraging Bjorn to attend with Ivar and Mr. Larsson."

On the way home, Gunlaug leaned over and spoke in Nilda's ear, though Signe was sitting close enough to hear. "He's a good man, Mr. Larsson. Did you say he is teaching you to play the piano?"

"When he comes to town. Mrs. Potts also gives me music lessons."

"Do you think Bjorn will be terribly uncomfortable at the party?"

"He might be, but he might really enjoy himself too. I'm sure Ivar will give him good instructions. He usually goes walking around Blackduck until Mr. Larsson is ready to return home. Bjorn knows Petter, who will be there too, now that logging season is over."

Gunlaug nodded thoughtfully. "He needs more time with people his own age. Since he didn't attend school here, he's not met many people outside the family. Not like he would have in Norway."

Signe thought about what they were saying. Bjorn had been thrown into manhood so young. He'd adopted Onkel Einar's drive to bring down the most trees possible. He would be seventeen soon, and he both looked and acted more like a man than a boy. She turned her head and looked up at him, driving the team, talking with Gerd and his far. Was it only two years since they came to Minnesota? For some reason it felt like more.

Selma, her husband, Oskar, and their children drove far enough behind them not to be eating their dust. Kirstin leaned against Nilda's chest, thumb and forefinger in her mouth. Knute and Leif sat with their feet hanging over the lowered tailgate. When they turned into the lane, Signe began parceling out the tasks ahead.

"Nilda, will you fetch the baked chickens from the well house? Bjorn, you take the wagon down to the new house and bring up some chairs."

"How about if I make the biscuits?" Gunlaug volunteered. "Since we baked those pies yesterday, we have dessert. How about bringing up some cream for whipping, Nilda?"

Good thing they still had some canned goods down in the cellar. They'd need to can more this year.

Leif loaded Kirstin in the wagon and, taking his three cousins, headed for the barn to show off all his babies. Piglets, calves, chicks, and kittens. Signe watched them go. Leave it to Leif. She smiled to herself.

I know pride goeth before a fall, but Lord, these sons of ours are good boys. Thank you. And each is so different. Bjorn would as soon hunt as sleep. Knute would rather fish than anything, like his onkel Johann in Norway, but he's provided us a lot of meat with his rabbit snares. Leif has taken over the care of the baby animals, and watches over his little sister. I wish the other two liked school and reading as much as he does.

Listening to the laughing and talking in the other room made her even more content. *Thank you, Lord. We are blessed indeed.*

Chapter 7

So how was your visit?" Mrs. Schoenleber smiled from her desk chair.

Nilda heaved a sigh of delight as she unpinned her hat and let the maid, Stella, take it. "We had a marvelous time with only one bit of well, blood."

"What happened?"

"Kirstin tried to get out of the wagon by herself down at the barn, fell, and banged her forehead on something. Lots of tears and blood, but not severe. That child sure has a set of lungs."

"Are you ready for a cup of tea?"

"Coffee sounds better."

"I'm sure Cook has something left of the coffee cake she made for breakfast, although it is not that long until dinner." Mrs. Schoenleber pulled the cord to the kitchen. "Now, tell me more."

Nilda crossed to stand in front of the window. "Let's see. I invited Bjorn to come with Ivar and Mr. Larsso—" When she stumbled over the name, Mrs. Schoenleber rolled her eyes.

"For goodness' sake, I do believe you can call him Fritz now, at least around here." She gave the order to the maid and nodded for Nilda to continue. "Surely there is more news than that."

"Selma and her family joined the others for Sunday dinner. I do believe she is in the family way, but nothing was said about it. Mor told me. I'm afraid Rune's eyesight is growing worse."

Mrs. Schoenleber studied the desk in front of her, obviously pondering something. Nilda had learned to wait patiently when this occurred. Looking out the window, she sucked in a deep breath of pure delight at the buds on the rosebushes. A red one already had a full blossom. The daisies were entering their glory. A purple martin flew in the birdhouse with a piece of red yarn in its beak. Cook had hung a mesh bag filled with bits of yarn from the branches of the clump of birch trees in the corner. Bluebirds and house sparrows splashed in the bird bath, while another inspected one of the birdhouses on a pole by itself, like bluebirds demanded.

"There must be some way we can help Rune's ski-making business grow. I think there is an organization in Red Wing. Skiing has been growing in popularity. I wonder if they have a newsletter or a magazine. If we could get an article in it . . ." Mrs. Schoenleber wrote herself a note on the pad of paper she kept handy for just that purpose. "An advertisement in the *Minneapolis Tribune* might be a good idea." She wrote herself another note.

Nilda knew who would be doing the research on these new ideas. "I need to go to the mercantile to buy shirts for both Ivar and Bjorn for the social. They've both gotten broader in the shoulders and more muscular."

"I take it Bjorn wasn't too enthusiastic about coming." Mrs. Schoenleber smiled at Stella when she entered the room. "Please put the tray on the table in front of the window. Thank you."

When she finished pouring coffee for herself and tea for Mrs. Schoenleber, Nilda eyed the crumbly-topped breakfast cake. "Leave it to Cook to come up with something new." She moved two pieces to separate plates, placed a fork on each plate, and handed one to the woman who had become friend along with employer. Nilda took a bite, then set her plate down. "I would like to invite Mor to visit, and I thought she could bring Leif along. I know Rune would take her to the train."

"Of course. I'm glad you want to do that. I would love to see that little Kirstin again. This house needs the laughter of children."

"You really want them to come?"

"Of course. Why do you doubt it?"

"I-I—everything is so perfect here, and children . . . well, children can be messy."

"Ah, I see. Don't worry about that." Mrs. Schoenleber nodded and stared at nothing. "I—we, meaning Arvid, my husband, and I—always dreamed of having children to fill this house, but then God took them all away in that tornado. It's something I will never understand but have learned to accept. After that, I decided my oldest nephew, Fritz Larsson, would inherit the personal part of our estate. We had sent him to school in the hope that he would step into Arvid's shoes or perhaps become an attorney, but when he wanted to become a musician and a teacher, we agreed. Not everyone is designed to run a business. So, surprising as it may seem to many, I had a head for business, and when Arvid died, I stepped into his shoes. Much to the consternation of my brothers, as you know. But he also held investments apart from the family businesses, and perhaps someday Fritz will pick up the responsibilities there. In the meantime, I am training you to help me carry out the things that need to be done."

"Did Fritz know what you wanted of him?"

"Yes and no." She held up her cup. "Coffee this time, please."

Nilda filled both their cups. Never had her employer's plans and dreams been laid out quite like this. She paused, sipped, and studied her cup.

"You have a question?" Mrs. Schoenleber asked.

Nilda nodded, the slow motion of someone deep in thought. She sucked in a breath, and on releasing it, looked at Mrs. Schoenleber. "But why me?"

"When I first met you, that night you stayed here, I felt God saying, 'Pay attention to her.' I had no idea why, but I learned long ago that when I sense things like that, I must try to follow them. Arvid used to say that I had a special gift in sensing things. It took us some time to believe it, but so it is." She leaned over and patted Nilda's hand. "And I have not regretted my decision for a moment. When we follow where God leads, we receive all sorts of surprises. Any more questions?"

"Not at the moment, but I am feeling a bit overwhelmed."

"Don't be. God knows where all this is leading, so let's just hang on for the ride."

Mrs. Schoenleber's hostler, George, entered the room. "The mail is here." He handed it to Nilda. "Something for you too. I'm going to be washing the carriage if you need anything."

"We'll have more to go out later."

Nilda sorted the mail—business for her to deal with later, personal to those it was addressed to. She handed two letters to Mrs. Schoenleber, kept two for herself, and tucked the remainder in beside her in the chair.

They both slit open their letters and unfolded the sheets of paper inside. The letterhead on Nilda's piqued her interest. She must have made a noise, for Mrs. Schoenleber looked up.

"A problem?"

"I have no idea." Nilda skimmed the note, then went back and read it again. "Listen to this."

"'Dear Miss Carlson,

"'I've been thinking about our evening at the symphony and how much I enjoyed myself. I'm hoping you did too; you seemed to. I asked you at the end of the evening if you would be willing to correspond with me, and since you did not say no, I am writing this in the hope of getting to know you better.'"

"Well, well, well. Now this is a bit of a surprise." Mrs. Schoenleber tapped the edge of one of her letters on her chin. "Continue, please. I mean, if you would like to. After all, this is a private letter."

Nilda made a face and continued reading aloud.

"'Perhaps I should tell you about myself, since we've not had much time to become acquainted, in the hope you will return the same. I am in my final year of college with a major in business and economics. Lest you think I am studying this under duress, let me reassure you that it is not easy, but it is fascinating. I play on the tennis team, usually in the spring, but now that we have an indoor tennis court at the college, I play year-round. The competitions are held in the spring and summer, since not all schools have access to indoor courts.

"'Besides my studies and tennis, I enjoy dancing and parlor recreations. It has been brought to my attention that my Aunt Gertrude has socials in her home on a regular basis. Far be it from me to request an invitation, but I do believe the train goes both ways, so if there is to be such a party over the holidays when I am out of school . . .

"'I do hope you will write back to me and tell me about

your life in both Norway, which I visited on my European tour, and here in Minnesota.

"'Sincerely,
"'Jeffrey Schmitz.'"

Nilda laid the page in her lap. "What do you make of this?" She wanted to ask if Mrs. Schoenleber thought this was a ploy of some kind but thought better of it.

"I think I want to leave that for later. Let's just see what happens."

"You think I should extend an invitation? And how do I know when college breaks are?"

"Ask him that when you write back. Once we know for certain, we can plan our schedule."

"To include him?"

Nodding, Mrs. Schoenleber replied, "Yes, I think so."

"He might not be under duress, but I am," Nilda muttered under her breath.

"And when he invites you to an event in the Cities, I expect you to attend."

"Why would he do that?" Nilda stuffed the letter back in the envelope, wishing she had not read it aloud and instead just tossed it into the trash.

The other letter was a note of acceptance to the upcoming social, bringing the total to ten so far. Petter Thorvaldson, the friend she and Ivar had made on the ship to Duluth, had written and asked if Miss Carlson was planning to be there, which made Nilda laugh. After he'd told her he would like to court her, he had taken it well when she told him she valued him as a friend but that was as far as the relationship would go. Having him present would make it easier for Bjorn. After all, he was turning into a fine-looking young man, which would surely cause a stir.

"I have ordered the most up-to-date typewriter for you to use," Mrs. Schoenleber announced. "Have you ever typed on one?"

Nilda shook her head. "No, but it would make some things go faster, if what I saw at the board meeting was any indication. Mr. Jurgenson's fingers flew over those keys. Do you know someone who can teach me?"

"I'll ask Jane when she comes this afternoon. Surely they are using them at the bank." Mrs. Schoenleber stood up and left the room to consult with Cook about the meals for the next week.

Nilda smiled to herself as she leafed through the remainder of the mail. She liked Miss Walstead, who had been one of Mrs. Schoenleber's dearest friends ever since she and Arvid moved to Blackduck. Miss Walstead always explained things clearly.

Charles appeared in the door. "A Mr. Crawford Galt to see Miss Carlson."

Nilda's heart began to pound. She wanted to shout to Mrs. Schoenleber to come back. *No*. She was a grown woman who could handle complex business affairs. Surely she could talk to Mr. Galt. "See him in, please."

The detective entered the room, and a sort of dark cloud descended. An ominous feeling—the word *ominous* being another new word in Nilda's growing vocabulary.

"Miss Carlson."

"Mr. Galt. Please have a seat."

"Thank you." He sat down firmly, acting as if he were in control. "How well do you know Miss Olivia Amundson?"

"Very casually. An acquaintance."

"Hilda Rainer? Dolores Gruber? Maxine Murphy?"

"They are young women who attend Mrs. Schoenleber's socials. I know them only in that capacity."

"Then who are your friends?"

Nilda thought a moment. She didn't have any of her age, at least not in Blackduck. "Miss Walstead, of course. She instructs me in English and American history. Petter Thorvaldson is a good friend. And Mr. Larsson."

"No female friends your age? You know, intimate friends, confidantes."

"No. Not in Blackduck. My sister-in-law—"

"I find that quite odd, don't you?" He sounded almost accusing.

"No, not really, Mr. Galt. I am busy almost all day, handling correspondence, researching and planning as Mrs. Schoenleber requests, studying to perfect my English. I am taking music lessons and practice each day. My hours are eaten up by all this."

"Of course." He didn't sound like he believed her.

Was that fear or anger rising up inside her? "May I ask where this is going, Mr. Galt?"

His voice took on a knife-edge sharpness, and he had a smug look on his face. "Miss Carlson, a normal young woman your age has friends. Girlfriends who share secrets and titter and gossip. If the young woman does not, she is almost always of an unsavory character."

"I'm sorry. *Unsavory*?" The *savory* that Nilda knew referred to food.

"There are women who are pursued by men, and there are women who prey upon men. That is unsavory."

Nilda gasped.

"Miss Carlson, I believe you are one such woman. There is no way you would have met Mr. Nygaard by chance the day he was killed. There must have been an assignation, a—"

"Mr. Galt, he was stalking me! For days!"

"Or you were stalking him. I have talked to all the young women I mentioned and more besides. They all agree that he was a perfect gentleman and very desirable. That he never made untoward advances to them. I questioned them carefully on that. I believe that Sheriff Gruber's investigation was either flawed, tainted, or deliberately inaccurate. Miss Carlson, I am confident that you are directly responsible for Dreng Nygaard's death."

"The guests should arrive about five o'clock, so we will serve supper at six," Mrs. Schoenleber said to Cook when she served dinner on Friday.

"I thought as much. And the hors d'oeuvres for the party are all prepared, along with the cake that Mr. Fritz likes so much."

"He will be pleased. Nilda, the shirts for your young men are all pressed and hanging in the bedrooms. I know how much Ivar appreciated using the bathtub. I'm thinking Bjorn might too."

"He will try one, I am sure. Speaking of which, do you mind if I go up and get ready early so I can be here to greet them?"

"Of course not. You go right ahead."

"Is Miss Walstead coming?"

"Yes, for supper. I know she is looking forward to listening to Fritz play the piano. I suppose I should go up and change also."

As Nilda tripped up the stairs, she thought back to other evenings and the pleasure of listening to the piano. Surely she would have a lesson in the morning. Surely it wasn't climbing the stairs that made her heart dance just a tiny bit. Surely it was the memory of the music. Surely. The music floated through her mind as she sank into the froth-covered tub.

But then her joy came to an abrupt halt. Mr. Galt. Dreng's evil had transferred directly to Mr. Galt. Would Dreng Nygaard destroy her happiness forever? She tried to shake the troubling thoughts from her mind as she climbed out of the tub and dried off. She needed to focus on the social tonight.

She finished dressing and went back downstairs just in time.

"Aunt Gertrude, we're here," Fritz called as he, Ivar, and Bjorn entered the house.

"I'll show you in," Charles told him, but Fritz laughed.

"In the sun-room? I'll tell her you tried to be proper."

"I will take your bags up."

"Fine. Come on."

Nilda and Mrs. Schoenleber both rolled their eyes.

Fritz led the other two young men into the room and heaved a sigh. "It feels so good to be here."

"Then you should come more often." Mrs. Schoenleber's smile belied the slight tinge of sternness in her voice.

Fritz smiled at Nilda before kissing his aunt's cheek. "I brought your brother and nephew." He gestured to the two men standing in the middle of the room. "We would have been here sooner if we had another riding horse, but we had to drive the buggy."

Ivar nodded to Mrs. Schoenleber. "Good to see you again, ma'am." He gestured around the room. "Your house is so welcoming. Thank you for inviting us."

"Keep in mind, the invitation always stands, even if you are in Blackduck for supplies. Nilda and I would both appreciate family visits."

"Thank you. You remember Bjorn?" Ivar said.

"I do, but I remember a boy. Where did this young man come from?" She extended her hand to Bjorn. "I hear you have developed a love for the trees and lumbering. Also that you are a fine marksman."

Nilda watched a red tinge climb up Bjorn's neck. It was definitely time to help him become more social.

"Thank you," he said. "I do like to hunt. Knute is good too, especially with snares."

"He's provided meat for the family more than once," Nilda offered.

"A deer?"

"Yes, ma'am. Several of them. Ducks and geese also." He nearly bent his hat out of shape, he squeezed it so hard.

Nilda explained, "The feather mattresses on some of the beds at the farm are thanks to the ducks and geese. I know Tante Gerd, for one, is very grateful. We use both wool and down. As we harvest more wool, we'll do the rest." *Including mine,* Nilda thought.

Mrs. Schoenleber looked amused. "I've heard that people pluck the down off domestic geese, like shearing wool."

Bjorn shrugged. "I wouldn't know about that, but this year we will be shearing our flock of sheep." He looked at Nilda. "I was hoping you could come and show me how."

"Your mor is an excellent sheepshearer, you know."

"I know, but this way you might come home more often." His grin peeked out.

Mrs. Schoenleber chuckled. "Ah, I see. Very good, young man. We will have to make sure that happens."

"You could come too." Bjorn stumbled over his English. "I mean, you are invited to come. If you want to, I mean . . ."

Mrs. Schoenleber smiled and nodded. "We will keep that in mind. You must let us know when you will be shearing."

"It will be soon. Mor said we should have done it early."

"Do we have time to get cleaned up before supper?" Fritz asked.

"Yes, if you hurry a bit. Charles has the tubs running now."

"Your shirts are hanging in your room," Nilda added. "If you like, Charles will clean your boots."

Bjorn looked down at his feet. "Oh." He beat the other two men out the door.

"I've never heard him talk so much," Mrs. Schoenleber said.

"Of course, I was only out there one time. I would like to get to know that young man better."

Nilda nodded. "He caught me by surprise, that's for sure. I've always thought he was just a quiet sort, but to quote my mor, 'Will wonders never cease.' I hope he has a good time so he will come back."

"I think Fritz and Ivar will help with that. Do you have games chosen?"

"We'll do charades again. Everyone has such fun with it." *Dreng helped make it fun.* The thought knocked her against the seat back. Horrible, lying Dreng. Which, of course, also brought to mind that terrible Crawford Galt, the detective.

She sucked in a deep breath and, on releasing it, caught another passing thought. Warmth chased the cold away from her toes to her face, where a smile broke out. She could feel her smile both inside and out. She'd not had a nightmare since the night with her mor. Her mother's healing hands. Her love that had filled the bedroom and poured into Nilda's heart.

"What is it?" Mrs. Schoenleber's voice came gently, pushing aside her thoughts.

"I've not had a nightmare since the night I woke my mother with my screaming and she prayed for me—and held me like when I was a little girl."

"Thank you, God. I so hoped and prayed that would happen. What wonderful news!"

They heard Charles answering the front door, greeting Miss Walstead.

"Thank you. All ready for the festivities tonight?" she asked him.

"Oh, I'm sure we are. The young men from Benson's Corner have arrived and are upstairs. Madam and Miss are in their favorite room."

"You needn't show me in. I know the way."

"I know. It is good to see you. Did you have a good trip?'

"I did indeed, but home always feels best." She strode into the sun-room, removing her hat as she came. "Good to see you. Your flowers are lovely. But then, George is as good a gardener as a driver. You are so blessed."

"Indeed I am. And your sister is back on her feet?"

"Yes, and it's a good thing. She is getting a bit crotchety in her advancing years. Reminds me that I need to be careful. But then, she was always more like our father. I take after my mother."

"Well, we missed you. Welcome home."

"So what is the news?"

"I ordered a typewriter for Nilda. Do you know anyone who could teach her the best way to use it?"

"I know there is a specific way to hold your hands and strike the keys, for both speed and accuracy. I will look into this. What made you decide to take the plunge? I seem to recall suggesting this a few years ago."

"Yes, yes, I remember. But I did not want to learn. I still don't, but I believe Nilda will excel at it."

"And it will make her more efficient." Miss Walstead leaned over and patted Nilda's knee. "How are you coming with your reading list?"

"Not as well as you would like." Nilda was hoping she would not bring that up.

Miss Walstead looked over the top of her spectacles. "And the reason?"

"We had a trip to the home office that lasted longer than usual."

"The surprise was Jeffrey," Mrs. Schoenleber chimed in. "Heinrik had tickets to the symphony, and Jeffrey accompanied Nilda and me."

Miss Walstead's eyebrows rose. "Really? Now, that is a surprise. I wonder . . ."

Mrs. Schoenleber nodded, her lips tight. "Me too, but we shall see."

"Supper is nearly ready," Charles announced from the doorway. "I'll go tell the young men." He looked over his shoulder at the sound of male voices. "Here they are."

Nilda smiled and nodded at Ivar and Bjorn. "Don't you look ready for a party?"

"Thank you." Bjorn looked down at the front of his white shirt and stroked the fabric.

"I ordered it a bit large, but I figured you still have growing to do." She glanced at his feet and saw Charles had indeed been at work there. Their boots shone.

"Supper is served."

Fritz held out his arm for his aunt, and Ivar smiled at Miss Walstead, leaving Bjorn to imitate them and do the same for Nilda.

She patted his arm and whispered, "Just copy what Fritz does, and you'll be fine."

He leaned closer. "This is all *so* not like home."

"I know. Takes a lot of getting used to. If you like, I'll even teach you to dance when Fritz plays the piano."

"Ah . . ." His eyes widened. "I don't dance."

"Yet." She patted his arm. *Nephew, you have a lot of things ahead of you, and I want to make sure you experience them.*

Chapter 8

"I hope you don't mind my bringing my younger sister along. This is Cora." The young woman, nattily attired in a fur cape and lovely trimmed hat, stood smiling in the doorway.

Nilda ushered them inside. "Not in the least. The more the merrier. Come along, and I will introduce you around."

As usual there were two clusters, not mixing in the slightest—the young men on one side of the room, and the young women together on the other. Did they not realize what these socials were all about?

Nilda took the two guests to the women's circle. "Remember June? This is her sister, Cora. Please introduce yourselves."

As the others smiled and said their names, greeting June and Cora, one of the women pulled Nilda aside. "I thought Mr. Thorvaldson was planning on coming tonight."

"He sent a message that he is. Something must have held him up." The knocker sounded on the front door. "Perhaps that is him. I mean, he." Strange, she thought on her way to the door. He usually came early for supper. She opened the door and stared. "What happened to you?"

Petter lifted one crutch. "Some lumber fell today, and when I leaped out of the way, I fell over something else, and here I am."

"Is your leg broken?"

"Doctor said a greenstick fracture. That means the bones are still in alignment, but I have to stay off it for a while."

She grinned. "But you came anyway."

"I said I would."

"I'm glad. Come in, come in. At least this is not a dance tonight."

He stumped beside her on his crutches to join the others. Questions came from both groups.

Nilda returned to the door because someone was knocking. She opened it and gasped.

Fancy city hat in hand, Crawford Galt stood on the porch. "I understand one of your socials is taking place."

"That is correct."

"I wish to speak with the young men here."

"I, uh . . ." What to do? He would spoil the whole happy atmosphere. And he'd as much as called her a murderer. On the other hand . . . "Which young men, please?"

"Any who were acquainted with Dreng Nygaard. I would assume that is all of them."

A thought flashed through her head. She could not convince him of Dreng's true nature, but possibly Petter . . . "Petter Thorvaldson and Dreng Nygaard went to the logging camps together last winter. Mr. Thorvaldson is here tonight. He might be able to answer your questions."

"Excellent. May I speak with him?"

"Certainly. He is having a difficult time due to an injury. I will introduce you."

Petter had given an abbreviated report to the group on how he'd broken his leg and, at the urging of two of the ladies, had sat down in a wingback chair with a footstool to rest his leg on. He shook hands with the guys and smiled at all the girls.

Nilda stepped in front of him. "Petter Thorvaldson, this is Mr. Crawford Galt." She knew that to be proper, you must present the younger person to the older, more respected one. She did the introduction backwards on purpose; she respected the younger man much more. "Mr. Galt, I trust you will be brief."

She turned and clapped her hands. "Let's all congregate out in the sun-room to set up teams for charades, our first game." She led the way out of the room, leaving the Pinkerton man with Petter.

Amid a certain amount of confusion, at least part of it caused by the intrusion of Mr. Galt, the party poured into the sun-room, and two teams divided themselves out.

"Please count off by twos," Nilda instructed, "since we don't have an even number to set guys and gals against each other."

But everyone's interest seemed centered on whatever was going on in the other room. Nilda heard some of the whispers.

"He came to my home and asked me about Dreng Nygaard."

"Me too."

"Petter and Dreng knew each other. I bet that's it."

What a disaster Mr. Galt was!

Finally, Charles showed Mr. Galt to the door, and they returned to the parlor and to Petter with his poor leg still propped up. Nilda was so tempted to ask him what was said, but she did not.

Somehow Petter and Ivar ended up on a team of all girls, which made Nilda smile and helped distract her from the detective's appearance at the social. Bjorn was on the same team as she and Fritz. That too was good; he'd get some coaching as they went.

"Team captains?" she asked.

Petter raised his hand. "They said I have to earn my keep tonight." Titters danced around the groups.

Nilda stared at Fritz until he grudgingly raised his hand. "Good." She picked up an envelope from the table. "Our two chaperones compiled these so that I could play too." She held the envelopes out, and each of the leaders took one. "Our topic this evening is famous people. Fritz, will you please start?"

He pantomimed chopping something with an ax, and someone guessed George Washington. He shook his head and raised his hands above his head. Words bandied back and forth until someone shouted, "Abraham Lincoln!" Cheers from that team and groans from the other.

The teams each had four chances, and since Petter's team did not guess their last round in the required time, Fritz's team cheered.

Nilda smiled. "I had no idea we had so many actors in this group. Let's break for drinks and refreshments, and then we have a new game called twenty questions."

The only question in her mind was what Mr. Galt had wanted. She thought she knew, and she dreaded it. Feared it.

Charles and Stella opened the great dining room doors. Everyone but Petter strolled into the room where Cook had set out trays of delicate sandwiches and a huge punch bowl.

"Did you enjoy that?" Nilda asked Bjorn as they approached the table.

"I really liked winning."

She laughed. "That's good of you. Help yourself, there's plenty of food." She watched him turn to June's younger sister, who was holding a plateful of food, and stop beside her. Nilda smiled at June. "Looks like your sister and my nephew are getting to know each other."

June nodded. "Good. It's a shame he chose not to go to

school when they moved here. He'd have more opportunities to make friends."

"True. But apparently he never did like school."

"I didn't either, but my mother was adamant. Pa was more concerned about my brothers going to school than us girls. You know: 'You'll get this expensive, fancy education, and then you'll just get married and have children. Waste of money.'" June wagged her head. "Nilda? Can I tell you a secret?"

"Of course."

June leaned in closer. "Well, since you and Petter have been friends for quite some time, I . . ." She blushed. The rest came out in a rush. "He asked if he may escort me to the next social, and I said yes."

"That is wonderful."

"And you don't mind or anything? I mean . . ."

"Mercy, June. You have my every joy and blessing. Petter and I are friends; he feels more like my brother than anything else." Nilda laid her hand on the other woman's arm. "You two make a lovely couple, and he is a charming and hardworking young man. I hope your parents realize his value, if anything comes of this friendship."

"Thank you."

Nilda glanced down at the table, where a plateful of food looked lonely. Picking it up, she took it into the other room and gave it to Petter. "Here, you might want this."

He grinned. "Thank you. I was about to get up and join you all, but my body got lazy."

She laughed. "And here I was just telling someone how industrious you are." She returned to the dining room as Petter tackled his food.

Fritz turned from the table. "That was kind of you."

"Taking the plate in there?"

"No. The way you treated her." He nodded toward June, and his smile warmed his eyes. "You look lovely tonight."

"I—ah—thank you." She tried to look away from his eyes—and failed.

"You haven't eaten anything yet." He set a tiny open-faced sandwich on a napkin and handed it to her. "Try this one. Cook, as always, has done an exemplary job."

What was happening? She blinked and forced herself to look down, raise her hand, and take a bite. *Now chew.* Nodding and smiling, she ate the rest. "You are so right."

"Of course I am. The teacher is always right, didn't you know?"

"Oh really. I didn't know that." She made herself take a step backward. And bumped into the table. "I-I better get the party back on track."

He looked around the room. "Everyone seems to be having a good time, no one hiding in the corners." He ate another finger sandwich. "You've done a wonderful job."

"Th-thank you." *Nilda Carlson, don't be a ninny. You know you despise ninnies.* What had happened to those calm sensibilities Mrs. Schoenleber said she possessed?

Nilda cleared her throat and addressed the group. "Shall we return to another game? A new one this time. Twenty questions." *Ninny indeed! You already said that.*

As the participants assembled, Nilda said, "Let us keep the same teams, since that worked so well. The team with the fewest questions needed to guess the word will be the winners. One person on each team will keep account of how many questions were needed, up to twenty. And the leader can only answer yes or no. Say, for example, the word is *Paris*. The only hints the leader can give are whether the word is a person, place, or thing. Since Paris is a place, what questions might be asked? Remember, the speaker can only answer yes or no. Any questions?"

"Is this place in the United States or in Europe?" a young woman ventured.

"That's two questions," someone else pointed out.

"Oh, right. So I would ask if it is in the United States?"

"Correct."

The noise level rose appreciably as the two teams leaped into the game.

"Seventeen questions," reported Petter for his team after the first round.

"Didn't get the answer," announced the other team after theirs.

"That gives you a total of twenty, then."

The game continued until all ten words had been guessed.

"We are tied up, even. Look at that." Nilda pointed to the score sheet. "Call it a draw?"

"No, one more word."

What to do? "I'll go ask Miss Walstead for one. Be right back." Nilda slipped into the sun-room where the two women were playing dominos. "I need one more word for twenty questions. To break a tie."

Jane picked up a pen, wrote the same word on two pieces of paper, folded them, and handed them to Nilda. "Sounds like a great time in there."

"It is."

The last round began.

"Eleven," called Fritz.

"No, not already!" someone from Petter's team protested.

"And the answer is . . . St. Petersburg, Russia."

"I was just going to say that," groaned Ivar.

Fritz stood and made his way to the piano. As soon as he played a few chords and a lovely arpeggio, the others joined him.

Miss Walstead beckoned to Nilda from the doorway. "Everyone seems to be having a good time," she whispered in Nilda's ear.

"They are indeed." Nilda stood at the back of the room, sipping from a cup of punch. The others were gathered around the piano, where Fritz was segueing from one popular song to another so everyone could sing along.

"Get up, Petter," commanded Ivar. "We'll move your chair closer."

Fritz took requests, playing most of the songs from memory, with everyone singing and harmonizing, then moved from the songs into several hymns, closing with "Blest Be the Tie That Binds." When they finished singing that song, they returned to the dining room for cake.

"Lemon cake, my favorite." Fritz nodded as he picked up his plate. "I'm guessing Cook had a hand in this."

Later, Nilda stood at the front door, responding to compliments and promising there would be another gathering next month. "We're considering outdoors with a croquet match. What do you think? Any other suggestions?"

"You ever played badminton?" someone asked.

"No, never heard of it."

"You have a net, rackets like tennis rackets, and a feathered shuttlecock that you bat over the net. It looks easier than it is."

"I'll look into it. Good night. Thanks for coming." When the last guests had left, Nilda closed the door and leaned against it. How could entertaining be so tiring? Did Mr. Galt have anything to do with her weariness?

She joined the others in the sun-room. Fritz, Ivar, and Bjorn were all eating more cake while the two older women laughed at them. Nilda paused in the doorway. What a delight to see.

"You can always have the rest for breakfast," Mrs. Schoenleber said to her nephew.

"Why leave any for breakfast?"

"Why indeed?" Mrs. Schoenleber snickered.

"I think everyone had more fun tonight than at any of the others, or rather, all of the others combined," Miss Walstead said, nodding. "I think even this house had a fine time tonight. It needs music and laughter too."

"That's rather poetic."

"Good. We all need more music and laughter in our lives." She studied Fritz. "Would you mind playing some Chopin for me?"

"Not at all. If Nilda will turn pages for me."

"As if you need sheet music. I've heard you play for hours from the music stored in your head." Mrs. Schoenleber caught Bjorn in a yawn. "You are welcome to go to bed anytime you feel like it. I'm sure your morning started far earlier than ours did."

"Come on, Bjorn," Ivar said. "We can hear the music from upstairs just fine."

Nilda smiled at her brother. "Thank you. Good night to you both."

"There go two fine young men," Miss Walstead said softly. She reached over and patted Nilda's hand. "You can be proud of them. Tell their mothers too, will you, please?"

Sitting next to Fritz in the dimness of the parlor, Nilda felt like she was floating, with the music carrying her higher and higher. "I thought you wanted me to turn the pages."

"Aunt Gertrude is right. But I enjoy playing even more when you are sitting here with me. I thought I needed a good excuse."

"Hmm, I think that was a rather flirtatious comment."

"Really? I never would have guessed."

When he played the last notes and closed the lid on the keyboard, she hated to disturb the peace in the room.

"Lessons at nine in the morning?" he asked.

"Fine. Then a game of croquet?"

"Do you know how?" he asked.

"No, but knocking a wooden ball through those hoops surely can't be too difficult."

"We shall see." He smiled wickedly.

The feeling of peace stayed with her as she allowed Gilda to help her undress and get into her nightgown. She even allowed the maid to brush out the upswept hairstyle and finish the requisite one hundred strokes. Scenes from the evening slipped through her mind as Nilda drifted into sleep in a safe and hazy way.

The next morning, she entered the dining room to find all the others at breakfast already.

"Sleepyhead, lie abed, waste away the day," Ivar teased her.

"What can I get for you, Miss Nilda?" Charles asked with a smile for her and a stern glance at her brother.

"I'll have whatever Cook is serving this morning." She sniffed. "Cinnamon rolls? What, has she been baking all night?"

"These are my favorite." Fritz used the side of his fork to pick up every bit of sweet goo from his plate.

"You can always have more, you know." Mrs. Schoenleber tried to look stern. And failed. "What time must you leave for Benson's Corner?"

"Do you need to be home for anything in particular?" Fritz looked to Ivar.

"Rune said we need not hurry. I would like to show Bjorn the rest of the town that is not on the road to the lumberyard or the mercantile, if that is all right with you?"

Mrs. Schoenleber laid aside her napkin. "You do whatever you like. Nilda has a piano lesson, and Jane and I will be going over our lesson plans for Nilda and enjoying coffee or tea out on the verandah. It seems I heard a certain young woman challenge a certain young man to a croquet match this afternoon as well." She smiled at Nilda with arched eyebrows.

"You mean I have the day off?" Nilda realized the heat coming up her neck had nothing to do with the summer day.

Charles set a plate before her and another platter of cinnamon rolls on the table. "Can I get you anything else?"

"No, thank you."

"If we may be excused?" Ivar looked to their hostess.

"Of course."

"I'd like more coffee, please." Fritz eyed the rolls.

"Coming right up." Fritz finished eating and went into the parlor.

When Nilda was finished eating, she slid her napkin back in the ring and stood. "Thank you, Charles. Please tell Cook the same."

Piano music floated into the room, enticing her to listen. And enjoy.

Mrs. Schoenleber raised a hand. "Don't try to compare yourself to what you hear. Remember, he has been playing since he was three or four. Even then, we could tell that he was gifted, as he would hear a song, then go try to play it. We decided lessons were in order to encourage him. His father was not pleased, thinking that music was not a profitable occupation, so we made sure he had the lessons and could practice at our house." Mrs. Schoenleber closed her eyes, the better to enjoy the music.

Nilda smiled at Miss Walstead. "Will you be staying tonight too?"

"I believe so. I need to go home and feed Matilda sometime."

"I would gladly do that for you."

"Why, thank you, my dear. Are you up for a few hands of whist tonight?"

"Anytime." Now that she finally understood the game, she enjoyed the challenge.

When she went to stand by the piano, Fritz smiled at her, finished his song, and rested his hands on the keys.

"Ready?" His fingers moved as if of their own volition.

"As ready as I'll ever be." She sat on the bench beside him.

"Have you been practicing?"

She licked her lips. "Most days."

He scooted over to give her more room. "Play for me."

She warmed up on the scales as he had taught her, then moved into chords and finally "Goodnight, Irene," the song he had started her on. The scales and chords came easily now. She played the song from memory.

"Good, good." He pointed to a section of the music. "Play that section again, concentrating on each key, then pick up speed."

She did as he asked, finally focused on the notes and keys, forgetting about the man beside her.

"Good, go on to the next."

By the end of the hour, her shoulders felt glued to her earlobes, and her fingers ignored her wishes once in a while.

"Relax. This should be pleasure, not pain," Fritz said.

She dropped her head forward and groaned.

"You were relaxed on the scales and chords. Can you feel the difference?"

"Of course. But knowing and doing are two different things."

"Yes, they are, but repetition is the foundation." He touched the back of her hand. "You have pianist's hands, long fingers. I have seen these hands make knitting needles fly. You will have the same dexterity on the keyboard if you remember to relax." Even his voice wore a smile. "Now, let's do the second piece again, and this time remember to breathe."

Nilda blew out a breath and did as he said. Every time she felt her shoulders tighten, she sucked in a breath and, releasing it, felt them drop. "That was better."

"It was. Good. Now the third piece. Breathe."

She played the music as he asked. And when she struck the final note, she dropped her hands to her lap.

"Well done."

"Thank you."

He flipped the pages to the next piece. "Ready for three more?"

"Yes." *Why am I doing this? Because I was silly enough to want to. Did I really want to learn to play the piano, or did I want the time with him?* She could feel her stomach thud in surprise. Where had that idea come from? *But why would I have spent all the hours practicing, if that were the case?*

She heard Ivar and Bjorn come in the front door, laughing about something.

Fritz closed the keyboard cover. "Let's go play croquet."

She smiled and nodded. "Yes, let's."

Mrs. Schoenleber and Miss Walstead waved from the round table on the verandah. "Cook is sending out lemonade, and George has the croquet court all set up."

Miss Walstead waved a paper. "I'll read the instructions while Fritz demonstrates."

Nilda sank down on one of the wrought-iron chairs. *I sure hope this goes better than the piano lesson.*

Chapter 9

"How are you coming on your research for a way to assist Blackduck?" Mrs. Schoenleber sat down beside Nilda's desk in the library.

Nilda looked up from her papers, which were spread across the surface, filling it. "I've spoken with three of the local ministers, Dr. Andrews and his nurses, the midwife, and the owners of the mercantile and the pharmacy. They all seem to agree that housing for the immigrants is a primary problem. Reverend Holtschmidt took me out to see the tar-paper shacks. They aren't so bad now but will be when winter comes and the husbands go out to the logging camps. The loggers have to leave their families here with no support until they get paid at the end of the season."

Mrs. Schoenleber nodded. "This is a problem."

"I suggest that of all the proposals we've considered, this one would reap the best rewards, both in terms of benefitting the community and providing a return to investors. As Heinrik himself said, the universe revolves around money."

Mrs. Schoenleber laughed out loud. "I did not expect to see

this day so soon: that you would directly quote my brother. It is indeed all about the money."

"These men want to work and provide for their families. They are certainly not indigents." Nilda glanced down at her papers. "I went by the lumberyard and got estimates on the cost to build a small house and a larger building to divide in two. And one into four, an apartment house. Once we get one finished, we could begin another."

"Would the immigrants purchase their place or rent it?"

"I suggest they would rent. They do not have the money to buy one. The rent money could then go toward building the next."

"I see." Mrs. Schoenleber looked thoughtful. "How will the investors recoup their money?"

Recoup was not a word Nilda had heard, but she could easily guess its meaning. She was learning a lot of words that way. "From the rent paid when the building is completed. There would not be an immediate return. The best solution would be to look at the original amount as benevolent community service."

"Ah, but when you look at the other proposals, aren't most of them long-term investments that will not have a quick return? And for several, the risk is extremely high. I consider this enterprise a low-risk prospect."

"But they will have the greatest return—possibly." Nilda stared down at her totals. "What I am learning is that the real problem is the size of this. While it looks like a lot of money to me, it might be easier to get investment money for a new hotel or a chain of hotels or a new manufacturing plant. I've looked through the business's other investments. Your family company is like a centipede with a hundred legs."

"So true, and not all their investments have paid off. They

are good at selling off at the right time—pure luck. Sometimes they've just cut their losses and pulled out."

Nilda watched her mull this over.

"How many houses are needed?"

Their discussion continued until Charles announced that dinner was ready to be served. And picked up again once they were seated and being served.

"What about land on which to build?" Mrs. Schoenleber asked.

"Ideally someone who has land would donate a few acres." Nilda spooned up her soup.

"In reality?"

"You have a piece of property northwest of town by the lake."

"Arvid bought that fifty acres in the hopes of eventually building another house out there on the water. Someday it might be worth something, but right now it is too far away to be useful for our purposes."

"Perhaps someone else has a piece closer to town."

"You present your formal proposal at the next board meeting, but I would not hold out much hope. My brothers don't see a great deal of value in Blackduck, especially now that northern Minnesota is running out of pine trees. Some companies are already moving on."

Nilda smiled. "That leaves more for those left, then."

They ate in silence for a few minutes. Then Mrs. Schoenleber commented, "I see that Rune is aware of the end of logging and planning ahead to find other means of income. The land that grows those big trees is not good farmland without a lot of soil improvement."

"I know that is a big concern of his. He works manure and leaves, pine needles, sawdust, anything that will decompose, back into the land. Signe read that hog and chicken manure are best. In any case, it's much, much work."

"Ah, Nilda, the future. I am not so sure that I am ready for it."

The next day, when the telephone on the wall by the kitchen rang two shorts and a long, Nilda answered it to learn there was a parcel for them at the railroad station. She passed the message on to George and returned to answering letters for Mrs. Schoenleber.

"Must be the typewriter," her employer said. "I wonder if Jane has found us some help yet."

"Do you want me to telephone her?"

"No, she dislikes it worse than I do. Were you planning on taking a walk today?"

"Yes."

"Good, we'll send her a note."

"No lessons today?"

"She had something else to do. I know, I'll send George over on his way back from the station."

As soon as they finished their meal, Nilda wrote the note to Miss Walstead and dispatched George on the errands. The cool breeze coming in the window felt good, so she took her new leather-bound writing case outside on the terrace, in the shade. First on her list was a reply to Jeffrey Schmitz.

Dear Mr. Schmitz,

Thank you for your note of last week. I also enjoyed the symphony. I had never heard such glorious music.

As to your request to know more about me, I was born and raised on a farm near a town in the Valders region of Norway. It could hardly be called a town, its only buildings being the local school, a church, and the general store. In the late spring when the snow had melted on the higher valleys, the young women and the children took the cows, goats, and sheep up to the seter, where there was grazing for the cattle. We took care of the animals, sheared the sheep, and made cheese from the goats' and cows' milk. I have many good memories of those months.

I have three brothers, one of whom came to America before I did, then sent me and our younger brother tickets to come to help an uncle and aunt near Blackduck. Rune and his family are all west of Benson's Corner on the farm still. After my father passed away, my mother immigrated with a cousin and her little boy.

Mrs. Schoenleber employed me to be her assistant and has been training me ever since. As soon as we decide on a date for the next social, I will send you an invitation as you requested.

Sincerely,
Miss Nilda Carlson

She addressed the envelope and set it with the others in the basket for George to take to the post office. One proper thing done. Why Jeffrey would bother to answer was beyond her.

She wanted to spend another hour on the proposal, but since she would have to go inside to do that, she watched a butterfly flit from daisy to daisy and up to the roses. The purple martin chorus sang in full force, and it looked like the males were standing guard and bringing food to their nesting mates. Inhaling the sweet scent of roses, she closed her eyes in delight. This yard was certainly a piece of heaven. And such colors! The blue of the sky made the green in the trees glisten in the sunlight, the leaves dancing with the breeze while the piled puff of clouds changed shape before the sculpting winds.

She opened a leather-bound Dickens novel, one of the books Miss Walstead had assigned for her reading. Cold winter nights would be far better for this than a summer afternoon.

What were they doing out at the farm about now? Her mor was most likely at the loom. Signe might be weeding the garden. The men might be out in the woods or perhaps starting to build the long barn for the hogs. Next winter the sheep would spend the nights in there too. If Nilda were there, she could be weeding or carding wool or working at the spinning wheel.

"Why the sigh?" Mrs. Schoenleber asked from the doorway.

"Just thinking of all they are doing out at the farm. If Kirstin isn't down for a nap, Leif might have her with him in the wagon down at the barn or out in the garden. Wherever she is, she will need to be washed down before she goes in the house."

"I would be so pleased to have your mother come visit and bring Kirstin and Leif. Do you think it could ever happen?" She sat down in the opposite chair. "I don't come out here often enough. Thank you."

"Now, before canning season begins, would be a good time. Do you want to send her an invitation?"

"Yes, and I ordered tea and lemonade."

Nilda turned the pages of her calendar. "We also need to set the date for the picnic social." She tapped her pencil on the pages. "I suggest we schedule the social on the last Friday of the month and invite Mor for Wednesday two weeks from now, and she could return home on Friday. I'm sure she and Leif would come, but . . ." Nilda shook her head. "Kirstin is not much into leaving home yet."

"Hmm. Perhaps you are right. Will Gunlaug be offended if I order things for them? I have so much here, and I would like to share it with them."

"I will see what I can do."

"Remember, I did not grow up with all of this wealth. We were not poor by any means, but . . . but I do understand pride."

Her smile had a tinge of craftiness. "I guess I could purchase skis for relatives or half of the schoolchildren of Blackduck."

Nilda shook her head. The woman she so respected might just do such a thing.

"Or hams and bacon or . . . I'm going to do some thinking on this. You know, instead of housing, perhaps we should feed people. Buy from local farmers and such." Mrs. Schoenleber thanked Stella and chose a glass of lemonade. "These Norwegian immigrants are a proud folk; they would rather work for something than get a handout."

Nilda choked on her lemonade. She coughed, and Mrs. Schoenleber thumped her on the back. When she could breathe again, she nodded. "Sorry."

"Was it really that shocking?"

"No, no, of course not." She could not look at the woman across the table without laughing or at least shaking her head. "Probably the surprise was you saying that. I mean, I know about pride, but I've also come to believe the saying 'pride goeth before a fall.'" Nilda was assigned Bible chapters at each English lesson. If this kept up, she would read the whole Bible cover to cover. In English.

"Perhaps I can give them presents. I'll have to think about it. After all, you dealt with all your new clothing and schooling."

"Only because you were my employer and I was being paid to learn a new way of life. And no, before you ask, I am not one bit sorry. I always want to make you proud of me, because I know how important appearances are to you. It has to be that way for the position you are in."

"I'm glad to hear that."

Was that slight sarcasm she heard? "However, if you find me out weeding in the garden . . ."

"You realize George would be horrified."

"I'll tell him it is good for my soul." Nilda stared down at her leather-bound writing case under the book she'd been reading. "Do you think it at all a possibility that your brothers would consider investing in my proposal?"

"No. I could call for a vote, but four to one is not much of a help."

"Then I'll complete the proposal and move on to my next possibility. We can invite the key benefactors of Blackduck to a dinner meeting here. Several of them already know what I have been exploring, but if there is anyone else who should be included, may I please have their names?"

"Good. I can think of two, Thor Haglund and Mrs. Isabella Schwartz. She, like me, was widowed at a young age but has spent much of her life traveling around the world. I believe she just returned from somewhere. She usually attends the ladies' functions when she is in town." She reached over and patted the back of Nilda's hand. "I'm sorry to not be more positive about the board."

"Well, it's good to be realistic, I suppose. I'm surprised a couple of those other proposals made it past your brothers."

"If they read them at all."

Nilda wrote the invitation to Gunlaug and Leif to visit in a couple of weeks as she had suggested. They could telephone their acceptance from Benson's Corner, and the train tickets would be waiting for them there. Following that, she wrote six invitations to dinner next Wednesday, which would include a discussion about assistance for the residents of Blackduck. The next social would be the last Friday in July, but she went ahead and wrote the invitations and set them aside to mail later.

"Your shipment is in the kitchen," George announced. "Do you want me to uncrate it?"

Nilda pushed back her chair. "I'm coming. Mrs. Schoenleber

is upstairs taking a nap. I think we can unpack it and set it up here on the desk. I do hope there are good instructions."

Once the typewriter was sitting on the kitchen table and Nilda and George were trying to follow the written instructions and drawings, Mrs. Schoenleber followed the noise to the kitchen.

"See," Nilda pointed to a drawing on a page in the booklet. "They look to spool this way."

"Yes, miss, but I already did that and nothing happened." George crossed his arms over his chest. "Let's start from the beginning again. You read them aloud while I follow them."

Cook jumped back when she noticed Mrs. Schoenleber. "Sorry, I didn't see you."

"Would you please go ahead and fix whatever you had planned for tea?" their employer said.

"Just having a bit of trouble." George looked over at her. "You ever really looked at one of these contraptions?"

"Not the insides, no. We could always call Elmer at the bank. I know he uses one."

"Wait, I think we have it." Nilda touched one piece. George turned it with pliers, and the spools snapped into place.

"Good job, miss. I'll carry it in to the desk."

Nilda smiled in triumph. "I'll bring the book. I think we have all we need here. There are instructions on how to use it, including which fingers for which keystrokes. Something like playing a piano, it seems to me."

Wrapped in more brown paper and tied with string, they found a ream of paper, another spool of inked ribbon, and a strange pink eraser.

George set the machine on the desk and stepped back. Nilda sat down, picked up a single sheet of paper and, following the diagrams, turned the knob on the side of the carriage to roll the paper into place.

"Type a word, or your name." Mrs. Schoenleber sounded as excited as the rest of them.

Nilda set her fingers on the middle line of keys but switched to using just her index fingers to make something happen more easily. She typed her name, then *George*, then *Cook*. "Oh, I forgot to hit the capital letters at the beginning." She started again, pressing the shift key for capital letters. *I did it. I really typed words on this machine.* "I guess I will do all the lessons next." She looked up at Mrs. Schoenleber, who was standing on her right side. "Do you want to try it?"

"Not today, but I will at some point. Jane will be so surprised when she comes tomorrow. I didn't tell her when it might arrive." She nodded slowly. "I think this will be a turning point in the way we do business. Heinrik has been after me for the last several years, and we have now succumbed. Welcome to the twentieth century."

George pointed to a picture in the book. "According to this, that desk is too high for Nilda to use easily. We need to get her a low table like this one."

"I wonder if we can order one."

"Or I could build one. If you don't mind, I'll go over to the bank and see what they are using."

"You might ask where they bought them."

"Yes, ma'am."

Charles carried in the tea tray and set it on the table between the two wingback chairs. "Unless you would rather have this outside?"

"Not today, thank you. Come, Nilda, let's leave the new toy alone for now."

After tea, where they further discussed the needs of Blackduck, Nilda returned to working on the keystrokes at the typewriter. When the telephone rang, she went to answer it, flexing her aching fingers. Lifting down the earpiece, she reminded herself she did not need to shout into the mouthpiece.

"Hello, this is Miss Carlson speaking. How may I help you?"

"Good afternoon, Nilda, this is Fritz Larsson. Is my aunt there?" The sound of his voice made her smile.

"She is, but you know how she dislikes talking on the telephone. May I give her a message?"

"Yes, tell her I am coming into town tomorrow for a meeting at ten, and then I would like to come for dinner. Well, actually, I'd like to return home the day after."

"I'm sure that will be fine. We have no engagements on the calendar."

"Good, then I will see you around dinnertime."

"Fritz, have you ever typed on a typewriter?"

"I have, why?"

"We have one now, and I am trying to learn how to use it."

"Perhaps we can do two lessons tomorrow afternoon, then. Typewriter and piano."

"Piano sounds much more appealing, but thank you. I'll tell Cook that you are coming." She hooked the earpiece back on the prong and returned to the room that was becoming more study than sun-room. "Fritz asked if he could come here after his meeting and leave the next morning."

"And you said of course." Mrs. Schoenleber nodded. "That means we can have a foursome for cards, since Jane will be here too."

"True, and he knows how to use a typewriter."

"Now, why didn't I think of that? Of course he does. He worked for an attorney while he was going to college. Arvid hoped that would encourage him to become an attorney, but Fritz would have none of it."

When Nilda returned to her machine, her fingers seemed to be more cooperative, and she found herself humming. All because Fritz was coming?

Chapter 10

A letter for you from Nilda." Leif bounded up the porch steps.

"You and Rufus went out to the mailbox?" Gunlaug looked up from her loom. "If I had known you were going, you could have taken one down for me." She took the envelope and slit it open with a small knife she kept by the loom.

"So, is she coming home again soon?"

"Let me read it to find out." She scanned the single page. "Well, my word, she is inviting you and me to come in on the train and stay there for a couple of nights."

"Us?" He thumbed his chest.

"Yes. We are to telephone from Benson's, and the tickets will be there waiting for us."

"A train ride. I need to ask Mor." He started to dash out, then stopped at the door. "Do you want to go?"

"I most certainly do. I'm sure we have butter and eggs, oh, and some soft cheese to deliver. You want to drive?"

"I think we have more cream to churn. I'll ask Mor. She and Tante Gerd are out in the garden." He charged out the door and leaped over the steps. She could hear him through the open window.

Gunlaug slammed the bar down to tighten the weave and picked up the rhythm of throwing the shuttle, slamming the bar and pressing down on the footpad to change the color of the stripes. This one was so close to being done that perhaps she could finish it in the next day or so. What they really needed was to get the spinning wheel busy. Gerd was about out of yarn for knitting. They had plenty of fleece, and it was time to shear again.

Signe entered the house with Leif dancing beside her. "It's getting warm out there." She used her apron to mop her forehead. "The breeze through here feels good." Returning to the kitchen, she pumped herself a glass of water. "You want some too?"

"Yes, please." Gunlaug smiled at Leif. "Where's Kirstin?"

"Sound asleep in the wagon parked in the shade."

Signe handed Gunlaug a glass and sat down in the rocking chair, sipping while the chair rocked gently. She took the letter Gunlaug handed her and read it, nodding. "Do you want to go?"

"I do, and it will be a good experience for Leif."

"Kirstin will be lost without him."

"I know, but we'll be gone only two nights. I'm hoping to get this rug done before we leave and the loom restrung. Nilda seems pretty busy helping Mrs. Schoenleber. And all that studying she is doing."

"I'll ask Rune if he has any skis to ship or deliver. That last order was from someone in Blackduck."

"If it keeps going the way it is, he will have to hire help. Especially through haying season."

"So, we are going?" Leif shifted from one foot to the other. When Signe nodded, he tore for the door, careful not to yell until he was away from the house.

The two women exchanged smiles. "Leif and I will go make the telephone call tomorrow and deliver whatever is ready to go," Gunlaug said. "He mentioned there is cream in the churn."

"It is on the back porch, so he must have brought it up. We have the pot of chicken and dumplings left, so supper will be easy. We'll fry the two rabbits Knute brought in for dinner tomorrow. Good thing we have rice and beans, since there aren't any potatoes. But the peas are ready for a first picking."

"Did you dig under any potato plants?"

Signe nodded. "Not large enough yet. Another week might do it." She cocked her head. "I hear Kirstin."

"I'll go get her."

"Leif will bring her in." Signe rocked peacefully, the songs of the rocker and the loom playing counterpart. The sparrow family who had built a nest on the back porch were having an argument. Gul, the tabby cat who was big-bellied again, came and rubbed against Gunlaug's legs.

"Ef, Ef, Ef." Kirstin thumped her brother on the head as he carried her into the house.

"And who is that?" He pointed at Signe.

"Mo." She reached with both hands for her mother.

"No, sorry. And who is that?" He pointed to Gunlaug.

"Momo." She clapped her hands to her chest. "Es."

"You say *kuh*." He made the *k* sound.

"Es." She reached for Gunlaug's arms. "Momo."

"Yes, let's go change your britches. You stinky." Gunlaug wrinkled her nose. "*Ishta*."

Kirstin wrinkled her nose in mimicry.

"How are we going to get you to do your business in the potty?" Gunlaug asked.

"Catch her quicker. She's done so a couple of times." Signe called from the loom room. "How about a cup of coffee?"

A thunking sound caused Gunlaug to look up and find Leif at the churn. When he was finished, her next job would be to wash the butter. Surely it was about time he learned to wash butter. She snuggle-hugged the squirming little girl who was chanting "Ef-Ef-Ef" and ran to the screen door as soon as her grandmother set her on the floor.

She banged at the screen, continuing to chant. When she leaned against the door, it opened a foot or so. Gunlaug and Signe stood watching her. She pushed again harder, but by the time she got to the opening, the spring on the door caused it to slam closed right on her hand. Kirstin howled, jerked her hand loose, and turned to her mor, tears streaming down her face.

Signe scooped her up and motioned to Gunlaug to pump some cold water to run over the little one's hand. Kirstin tried to jerk her hand out of her mother's grasp and upped the noise level. "Shh. You're not hurt that bad."

When the water stopped, Kirstin opened and shut her fingers. She studied her hand, looked at Signe, and leaned toward the water again. "I know, you will do anything to play in the water, but it's all gone now."

Kirstin frowned and looked to her grandmother. "Momo." She waved at the pump.

"Sorry," Gunlaug said. "Let's go talk with Leif."

"Ef-Ef-Ef."

Gunlaug set the little girl down on the porch. "She lost a fight with the screen door," she told Leif.

He grinned when Kirstin held up her hand. "I see. Why don't you go talk to Rufus?" She headed for the dog lying in the shade by the wall, and Gunlaug returned to the kitchen.

"She has to try everything." Signe set the stove lids back in place and pulled the coffeepot forward. "There are a few cookies in the tin. Maybe that is what I need to do next." While the coffee heated, she brought out the ingredients for oatmeal cookies and set them on the counter.

"The butter is rising," Leif sang from the porch.

"Keep it going a bit longer, and make sure the butter is clumping." Gunlaug reached into one of the lower shelves and brought out the huge crockery bowl they used for washing butter and then set the strainer on top. Leif pulled the top with the attached paddles out of the churn and set it in the sink while Gunlaug hefted the churn and poured the butter and buttermilk into the bowl. She emptied the buttermilk into a crock and pumped water over the butter still in the bowl.

"Go tell Gerd the coffee is ready," Signe said. "She needs a rest. She's been out in that sun a long time."

As Leif darted out the door, it caught Kirstin and knocked her on her butt. She howled and pushed herself to her feet as her mother scooped her up.

"You're not hurt. You're just mad." She tapped a finger on the baby's bottom lip, which stuck out like a shelf. Then she hugged her and set her back down. "Come get in your chair. We'll have a cookie."

Kirstin jabbered back at her and caught the chair leg, raising her arms to be picked up and put in the chair. Once the tray was in place, she slapped her hands on the flat surface. All was well until Signe brought a dishcloth over and wiped her hands and face.

"Hold still and it will go faster." Kirstin jabbered back at her, clearly not pleased, her scrunched face a testimony to her feelings.

"I was about to come do this myself," Gerd said, washing her hands under the running water. She wiped them on a towel and sat down at the table. "What happened to you, little one? Your screams about scared the birds away." When they told her what had happened, Gerd turned and patted Kirstin's hand. "Poor baby. You just have to learn things the hard way, don't you?"

Gunlaug took a cookie off the plate and handed it to the little one, who tried to shove it in her mouth and instead broke it into pieces. She watched it crumble, then grabbed up a piece with each hand and shoved them in her mouth. Which set her to coughing.

Gerd held a glass of milk for her. "Drink this." She shook her head. "You can make messes faster than any baby I've ever seen."

Kirstin smacked her palms on the cookie pieces, turning them to small bits, which she studiously picked up between thumb and forefinger, only half of them making it to her mouth.

Supper that night in the new house was a quiet affair. The boys in the woods had managed to down a third tree, since the days had grown so much longer. Rune was rubbing his head and eyes more than usual. So when Leif announced that he and Gunlaug were taking a trip to the store, mostly what he heard back were groans.

"The reason we are going tomorrow is that Leif and I have been invited to visit Nilda and Mrs. Schoenleber," Gunlaug said. "We will leave on the train the Wednesday after next and return on Friday."

"So he gets to go play, and we have to keep working." Knute sent Leif a dirty look.

"I do believe you would rather go fishing," Rune said, "and I am sure that can be arranged. You choose when you would like to go."

Knute thought a minute, then looked to Ivar and Bjorn. "How about we bring down five more trees, get them limbed and dragged to the stack, then take a day and go fishing?"

"Fresh fish sounds wonderful," Signe said.

"The perch should be biting good by now," Bjorn said

thoughtfully, "along with the bass and bluegill. Maybe we could catch enough to smoke some."

Ivar and Bjorn nodded at each other. "Five trees? Three days. That will be Saturday. And maybe, if they are really biting, we could go again after church on Sunday."

Knute grinned, and Gunlaug relaxed. The last thing they needed was for the boys to be jealous of one another.

A rolling boom of thunder woke Rune and Signe long before dawn. He lay beside her in bed as they listened to it move closer. Signe slid her hand into his.

"Should we go down on the porch and watch the storm?" she whispered.

Together they slipped out of bed and padded down the stairs. A cool breeze blew through the house, so they quickly shut all the windows. They were sitting on the porch, watching the storm move closer, when the rain hit like a bucket being dumped. Lightning lit the yard and the buildings, then snuffed out as if it were a candle. The thunder seemed to crash right over their heads.

Signe couldn't help but flinch. "If this were daytime, we'd be out dancing in the rain, washing our hair, loving every cool moment."

"You could do so now."

"No, I'd rather go back to bed for the rest of the night than have wet hair, even if it is clean."

Rune smiled. "I can hear the garden and the fields sighing. This came at just the right time."

"Ja, that it did."

Without the sun to wake her, Signe slept longer than usual. When she got up, Rune was not in bed, but she could hear voices from the kitchen. She slid her arms into her wrapper and made her way downstairs.

Gerd was mixing batter for pancakes, the coffee was hot, and the day was gray and dripping. Bacon sizzled in the frying pan. "Good morning."

"You should have woken me up," she said to Rune.

"Why? You deserve some extra sleep. I think I'd better call the boys, though, or they'll sleep all morning."

Gerd poured Signe a cup of coffee. "To sustain you until breakfast is ready."

"Thank you."

"Far said no logging today because of the rain. Now we won't get all our trees down." Knute sat down on the stairs to shove his feet into his boots.

"Most people would be happy to have a day off," Signe pointed out.

"Most people don't want to go fishing. And Far said being out on the lake in the rain could be asking for a lightning strike."

"It will all work out."

Knute sounded bored. "That's what you always say."

Bjorn pushed by him. "Come on, let's get the chores done. I'm hungry."

"You're always hungry."

Bjorn shrugged as he followed the others out the kitchen door. "At least the garden is happy," he called over his shoulder.

The men returned to the house laughing at the water running down their hair and faces, their clothes drenched.

"The chickens just stood in the doorway, then turned back in their house. Even the rooster didn't come out." Leif took the towel his mor handed him and scrubbed his head before passing it to Knute, who was shaking his head like a wet dog.

He grinned around the towel. "I opened the door for the sheep, and they just stood there and watched it rain."

"The cows came into the barn shaking their heads and with

water running down their sides and dripping on the floor. It ran down my neck when I put my head into their flanks to milk." Bjorn spattered those around him with a head shake.

"And I got swatted with drippy wet tails."

"The horses were standing under the shed roof," Ivar threw in. "They went back out to graze when we let the cows out."

Leif shivered. "The pigs' pens are knee-deep in water, and they were running through it, tossing mud and muck. After breakfast we should probably go dig a trench to drain them."

Rune watched his boys, smiling at their antics. "So today we work in the shop. Too dangerous out in the woods."

"Figured you'd say that." Bjorn took his chair at the table. "I can't believe I slept through a storm like that. Not if the thunder and lightning was as bad as you said."

"You had the pillow over your head." Leif poked him with his elbow.

"What's your excuse?"

"No excuse. Just slept sound. I wonder how long I would sleep if no one woke me up."

"Let's have grace before the pancakes get cold." Rune bowed his head and waited. "Thank you, Lord, for this rain we so needed. Thank you for the food Gerd has prepared. And thank you for good health, work to do, and such a fine place to live. In Jesus' name we pray. Amen."

Kirstin slapped her hands on the high chair tray. "Eat."

The boys burst out laughing.

After digging the drainage trench, the men and boys gathered in the shop. Rune assigned their chores, with three of them on ski sanding. Ivar helped Rune with planning out another pair of skis and setting them to soak to turn the tips up. Rune had built a long water trough to soak the wood in, then carved clamps as forms to mold the tips as the wood dried. Once dried, the sanding would begin, starting with rougher and working into finer with a many layered finish, before waxing and more waxing.

When the bell clanged for dinner, they stepped out into drizzle.

"Unless it stops, we won't be going to Benson's today," Gunlaug announced.

"Wet as it is, even if it stops, I'd say wait until tomorrow. You don't want to slide off into the ditch." Rune helped himself to the fried rabbit and looked at Knute. "Thanks for snaring dinner for us. It's been a while."

"Something has robbed them lately. Coyote or fox, I s'pose." Knute speared himself a piece of meat too. "Maybe with the wet, I can identify any tracks. I'll check them right after we finish eating."

"Remember when that old cougar took our pigs?" Leif said. "Could be another of those. Or a bear!"

"Much more likely to be a coyote. You could try a blind, possibly," Rune suggested.

"What if I put the snares at the base of a tree and waited up in the branches?"

"Since we are in the dark of the moon, I'd say wait until the moon is near to full so you can see better."

Signe and Gunlaug both rolled their eyes and shook their heads.

Gerd added, "When we first moved here, there was a lot more wildlife than now. We even heard and saw wolves one winter. They would sure have a feast if they got in the sheep pen."

"Or the chicken house," Leif added.

"We didn't even have chickens then. A neighbor gave me a broody hen with eggs, and I built her a nest in one of the stalls in the barn. Einar got the chicken house built by the time they needed more room. That old hen raised six chicks the first time, and then when she got broody again, I got more fertile eggs. That lady gave me a rooster too, so I'd have my own eggs. She sure was good to me, but then she died in childbirth, and her husband sold his land and moved back to Norway."

Rune watched Gerd talking. To think this was the same woman who was near to dying when he and Signe came here. It was hard to believe that was only two years ago. So many changes, so much progress. Who ever would have dreamed all this?

Chapter 11

What to do, what to do, what to do?

Nilda gathered all her proposal papers together and tapped them into an even stack. She'd awakened that morning sure that taking the proposal to the meeting in Minneapolis was not the best route to follow. Yes, housing was needed, but what was the best way to accomplish that? She opened the file drawer she had claimed for her own and set the papers on the edge, wedged against the others with a wooden block so she could find them more easily. She would need them for the dinner meeting with the leaders in Blackduck the week after Gunlaug would visit.

She had already sent out the invitations. Hopefully she would have other ideas for the agenda. With her desk cleared off, she went to stand in front of the window. Fritz would be here any minute, otherwise she would have gone for a walk. A walk down by the river always helped her come up with new ideas, or at least different ones.

So did deadheading the roses. Or the daisies.

"I'll be out in the garden," she called as she passed the sunroom. Walking through the kitchen, she said, "Sure smells good in here." Inhaling the fragrances melding in the air, she kept going.

"Don't go far," Cook called. "Dinner is nearly ready. As soon as Mr. Fritz gets here, we can serve."

"Okay."

Nilda dug the hand clippers out of the apron pocket she'd hung on a hook by the back door and paused on the back steps to enjoy the colors spread before her. Reaching up onto a shelf, she fetched the flat-bottomed basket. Surely she could find enough flowers to change the bouquet on the entry table.

She snipped spent blossoms as she clipped the sunrise roses with the long stems, a couple of the white ones tinged with yellow, and daisies for filler, laying them all flat in the basket she carried over her arm. The peonies were budding but none were open yet, so she searched out the largest open rose blossom and, after inhaling the spicy fragrance, added it to her sweet-smelling collection. Interesting how different roses had different fragrances.

She was just turning back to the house when Fritz called to her from the French doors to the verandah and strode out to meet her.

"Let me carry that for you." He took her basket.

"Good day to you too." She smiled back. "Just think, you could have been out here helping me deadhead."

"I'm surprised George allows you to touch his precious roses."

"I made a bargain with him. I won't pull the weeds—not that there are ever any to pull out here—if I can cut flowers for the house and accidentally manage to snip off a few spent blooms. This time I forgot to bring the basket for the compost heap, so he will probably get disgruntled to find the spent blossoms on the ground."

"You want me to go back and pick them up? I'd hate to be on George's bad side." He smiled down at her. "You look lovely today. I mean, you do every day, but . . ." He rolled his eyes. "Sorry, I mean . . ."

Nilda shook her head with a teasing smile. Her eyebrows arched as she watched him stumbling. Should she bail him out or let him dig himself a deeper hole? Why was it more fun to tease him than her brother Ivar? Taking pity on him, she asked, "How did your meeting go?"

"I've been asked to accompany a choir for a concert coming up and play several organ pieces besides." He paused. "For pay."

"How wonderful." She slipped her clippers back in their pocket by the door and started the water in the deep sink in the laundry room. "Have you played for them before?"

He nodded. "A couple of years ago."

She laid the roses flat to submerge them and set the daisies in water up to their blossoms. Taking the biggest rose, she snipped off the stem, filled a clear round bowl with water, and sank the rose with its petals pointing toward the bottom. She finished it off by laying a matching plate over the mouth.

"Dinner is ready to serve," Charles said as she made her way to the dining room.

"Perfect timing." With her hand on the plate, she flipped the bowl over and set it on the table. The rose floated, submerged in the water. "There." She stepped back. The rose glowed against the white tablecloth, the water making the colors even more brilliant. "Miss Walstead taught me this when she gave me instructions on flower arranging. I've never had this array of flowers to choose from before. At home, we'd go pick wildflowers and put them in a jar. They never lasted very long."

"So lovely." Mrs. Schoenleber paused in the arched doorway.

"Hello, Fritz, I see you found her." She tipped her head for his kiss on her cheek. "I do wish you would come more often. You don't need an excuse, you know."

He pulled out her chair and seated her, then did the same for Nilda. "I know, but this summer I am redoing the history program for the eighth grade, and I have four new music students twice a week for the summer. Along with my English classes for immigrants. This year I have a couple from Germany and one Swedish family as well as Norwegian." He smiled at Nilda. "I'm glad to see your mother and Signe back again. They have really progressed over the winter."

"Thanks to the boys," Nilda said. "I wish Bjorn and Rune would attend too, but they are learning from the others. Knute and Leif can be hard taskmasters. Leif is making sure Kirstin learns to talk in English."

"It is interesting to me how quickly small children—well, children in general—pick up a foreign language." He smiled up at Charles, who was taking the soup bowls away. "Tell Cook she has outdone herself, as usual."

Charles leaned closer. "You might notice she cooks all your favorite foods when you are here."

Nilda watched the interaction. For someone so quiet, Fritz could be charming when he wanted to be. "How many languages do you speak?" she asked him.

"Three fluently—English, Norwegian, and German—and I'm working on French. I can understand and read more than I can speak. It'd be good to find someone around Benson's Corner who speaks French for practice in conversation."

"Jane speaks French," Mrs. Schoenleber said. "She spent a summer in France when she was young and became quite fluent. And she has a good accent."

"And you speak some," Fritz pointed out.

"I know, but my accent is abysmal. I would make a real Frenchman shudder."

"German is so similar to Norwegian that it is fairly easy to learn." Nilda smiled at Charles when he set her plate before her. "This looks and smells delicious."

"Wait until you see what she made for dessert."

"Dried apple pie?" Fritz smiled at his aunt, who shook her head.

"You are incorrigible. I think she was saving the last of the apples for your pie. We'll have coffee out on the verandah after."

Nilda smiled at the banter between them. Someday, perhaps, she would learn more of the family stories, but for the moment she was content to observe. Maybe she should ask Fritz if he had any ideas for assisting Blackduck.

After both piano and typewriter lessons in the afternoon, Nilda was not looking forward to playing whist, but she made sure she smiled and acted pleased. If asked what she wanted to do, she'd have said listen to Fritz play the piano, but perhaps that would happen anyway. At least it better.

"What if all four of us play a game of croquet while it is still light out? We can play whist after dark." Fritz looked from Miss Walstead to his aunt. They were just finishing supper, and dusk had not yet begun to creep in. Fritz looked from Miss Walstead to his aunt.

Nilda nodded. "I'd vote for that."

Mrs. Schoenleber smiled. "Only if you promise to be gentle with these old ladies."

Fritz snorted. "You mean no whacking the ball off the lawn?"

"I'm glad you understand me." Mrs. Schoenleber folded her napkin and slid it back in the ring. "We'll have beverages later, Charles. Tell Cook thank you for another delicious meal. Fritz, you have to come more often."

Charles and Fritz pulled the chairs out for the ladies, and they adjourned to the backyard, where the croquet game was all set up.

"Confident, weren't you?" Mrs. Schoenleber said.

Fritz grinned. "If not tonight, I figured Nilda and I could get in a game before I have to leave tomorrow."

"You'll stay for dinner?"

"It's either that or kidnap Cook." He waved his hand. "I know you've offered to find me a woman to cook and clean house, but no, thank you."

"Stubborn," she muttered under her breath.

Mrs. Schoenleber won the game with a perfect shot that knocked Fritz's ball out of the court and then rolled her ball in to touch the finish post.

Fritz stood, open-mouthed. "But you said . . ."

"You agreed not to knock ours out of the court. I did not agree, for you didn't ask me."

Fritz sputtered, Nilda almost choked trying not to laugh, and Jane nearly doubled over laughing. Mrs. Schoenleber gave Fritz a sideways look, her eyes twinkling.

"Let's go have something to drink, and I do not want to play whist either. What are you trying to do, destroy my manly pride?" Fritz huffed.

"Now, now, let's not pout." Mrs. Schoenleber dropped her croquet mallet back in the holding frame and patted his shoulder.

"I'll agree to one game of whist, and then I think Nilda wants me to play the piano. She mentioned that earlier this afternoon."

Miss Walstead won the card game, which was not unusual, and they adjourned to the parlor, where Charles served his special drink. Glass in hand, Fritz moved to the piano. He sat down on the bench and lifted the keyboard cover.

"Any special requests?" His fingers moved up and down the

keyboard, filling the room with music that bathed the senses in peace. When no one responded, he moved into a passage from Debussy's "La Mer," followed by that composer's "Clair de Lune." Thanks to her piano lessons, Nilda was beginning to recognize the works of the major composers. Well, a few of them. Debussy seemed to be Fritz's favorite.

Nilda rested her head against the back of her chair and let herself float. What bliss! When she opened her eyes, she saw Fritz watching her, a smile playing hide and seek with the music. *Dreamy* was the only word she could think of. He finished with "It Is Well with My Soul," and after the last note lingered, he sat with his eyes closed and let the peace of the moment remain.

"Amen," Mrs. Schoenleber whispered. "And thank you for blessing us with your amazing gift." She stood. "Good night, my dears." One by one, they all drifted up the stairs.

Fritz walked Nilda to her bedroom door. "Thank you."

"I am the one to be thanking you." Hand on the doorknob, she smiled over her shoulder. "Music flows out of your fingers and sings to my soul. Good night."

"'Night."

Inside her room, she crossed to the window and pulled back the sheers. Gilda had learned not to close the drapes, and the window was already open a foot or so. The breeze wafted in the fragrances from the garden. First peace for her soul and now incense. "Lord God, how can I ever thank you for such soul-bathing gifts as these?"

When she woke in the morning, all she could think of was a walk. Down by the river. With Fritz. As the pieces fell into place, she smiled to herself. They could be back by the time breakfast was served.

She dressed quickly, pulled her hair back with a tie, and descended the stairs as if she were floating. Six thirty, and voices drew her to the dining room. Fritz and Charles were talking as Charles poured the coffee and set a plate with a roll in front of Fritz. She paused in the doorway.

"Good morning, Miss Nilda, what can I bring you?"

"Nothing right now, thank you. I just wanted to tell someone I am going for a walk."

"Do you mind if I come along?" Fritz already had frosting on his mouth.

"Not at all, but you might want to finish your coffee. I guess you could catch up."

He swallowed, made a face, and set the coffee back in the saucer. "Hot!"

"Yes, sir, that's the way you like it." Charles kept his face straight, but his eyes twinkled. "I am sure Cook will keep your roll for you."

"No, she won't. I can walk and eat." He pushed his chair back, grabbed the rest of his roll, and followed Nilda out the door.

"You want to take one with you?" Charles called after her.

"No, thanks. I'll eat my share later."

When they cleared the shadows of the house, she lifted her face to the sun already arching into the sky, as if in a hurry to complete his work for the day. They picked up the path heading east. Once they passed the place where Dreng had attacked her, she exhaled the tension that always tried to trip her but no longer succeeded.

"Your smile is back."

"That is no longer a terrifying place, but I still have to make myself keep walking. Once I get past it, I am good again. The farther I get beyond it, the more I enjoy my walk."

"But you make yourself do this."

She nodded. "I cannot let him influence how I feel. That is

over and done with, and I have to go on. If I never heard his name again, it would be fine with me."

"Is he buried here in Blackduck?"

She shook her head and picked up the pace. "I have no idea where he is buried, and I have no way to find out."

That is a lie, Nilda Carlson. You could ask that Detective Galt, and he would know. But if you never see Mr. Galt again, it will be too soon.

She stopped when they reached the river that now flowed gently on its way to the Mississippi. "In the spring, when the ice breaks up and the logs are floated down, this is a whole different scene. It's hard to believe it is the same river as now."

"I know. I used to come down here and dream of being a log roller. They looked to have such an adventurous life."

"What kept you from doing that?"

"I saw a man fall off the logs one day, and they found his body way downriver. I've never forgotten that. Logging might sound like a wild adventure, but Aunt Gertrude didn't have to talk hard to dissuade me. The thought of smashing my fingers and not being able to play the piano and organ was more than enough to put me off the idea."

Nilda realized she was puffing, so she slowed her steps just enough to catch her breath. *Ask him. Ask him.* The words kept time with her feet. "You like Blackduck, don't you?"

"Of course. I love it here. The proximity to Blackduck is what made me accept the teaching position in Benson's Corner. I came to live here after Uncle Arvid and the children were killed in the tornado. Aunt Gertrude was withdrawing into her grief, and my mother—her sister-in-law—was afraid she would die of a broken heart."

Another piece in the puzzle that was Gertrude Schoenleber. "She has assigned me the task of determining what she, er, we can do to make life better for the people who live here. Or at least of coming up with good ideas. Then we will need to find others who want to help. I've talked with Reverend Holtschmidt and Father McElroy and several others, and they said housing and support for immigrant families while the men are at the lumberjack camps in the winter. The women and children have little to live on until the men are paid at the end of the season. So that is one idea, and I've researched the costs to build houses and developed a proposal that I was going to present to Schmitz Enterprises at the next board meeting. But I have come to understand that they don't much care about Blackduck."

"They don't much care about anything that doesn't have a high profit return."

"Or at least the possibility of one. So we have scheduled a dinner, and the leaders of Blackduck are invited, both those with wealth and those who care but need help." She paused and studied the man beside her. "Would you like to come to the dinner and share some ideas and suggestions?"

"I'd be glad to come, but I'm not sure I can help."

"Do you have any dreams for this town?"

"Right now, the timber industry is pouring money through here and has created a booming town. But what will happen when the trees are all harvested and the timber industry moves out? We know that is going to happen. It has in other places in the northeastern states."

"Have you heard any estimates of a timeline?"

"No, but then, I am not following the industry. You need to talk with Jacob Schmitz. He handles the logging arm of Schmitz Enterprises. Talk with those who own the other logging companies too."

"I know." Nilda felt increasingly hopeless.

"It seems to me that the best way to assist would be in services that will benefit the community in years to come. My dream would be of a music program starting with the elementary school and on up through the high school, including a theater with a stage and plenty of seating—big enough for concerts and even bringing in performers."

"Will you write all that down and send it to me before the meeting?" She stopped on the edge of the back lawn where she saw George cleaning out the greenhouse. The house basked in the sunshine. "Let's go have breakfast. Thank you."

"For what?" He held the screen door open for her.

"Your ideas and for going with me."

"Anytime, Nilda, anytime."

Chapter 12

Dear Miss Carlson,

Thank you for responding to my letter. I feared you might not, and then I didn't know what I would do.

Nilda stopped reading and shook her head. Whatever made Jeffrey Schmitz write something like that?

I need to fulfill my obligations in the office starting after the Fourth of July, so I will telephone my aunt and ask when might be a good time. I do hope that you might be willing to show me around. When the heat and humidity smother us here, we adjourn to the lake north of town, but not as far north as you are. That is usually in August. Perhaps you and my aunt could join us there.

Here I am, forging ahead on my own, rather than waiting for invitations. Pardon my forthrightness, but I really would like to see you again soon.

Sincerely,
Mr. Jeffrey Schmitz.

Nilda laid the letter in her lap. "Hmm." On one hand, this was beginning to sound interesting, and on the other, she had no desire to travel to the city before the next board meeting, and that wouldn't be until September.

Mrs. Schoenleber wagged her head when Nilda told her of Jeffrey's letter. "Of course I will invite him to visit. The last time he was here, Jeffrey moped and moaned the whole time. And if I remember right, they were glad to return to the city life. Perhaps this time around we could encourage him to look at our town with vision instead of derision."

"I hadn't thought of that." Nilda nodded. "Good idea. He might bring a good word back to the board when they convene, and I could still present our proposal." She read through the missive again. "If he is to visit here in July, it will have to be near the end of the month now, and he doesn't have to stay long, does he?"

"No, and we will fill those two days with so many activities that he will run back to the Cities with his tail between his legs." Mrs. Schoenleber did not look pleased. Nilda noted the contrast between her warm delight in Fritz and her rather sour attitude toward Jeffrey.

Miss Walstead looked over her glasses, her eyes wide in astonishment.

Mrs. Schoenleber huffed. "Oh, I know that is a bad metaphor, but . . . oh, all right. Riding the train back to the Cities, grateful he did not promise to return."

"I think inviting him for a social would be enlightening. Do they play croquet and badminton on the estates, or is it all tennis?" Nilda emphasized *estates*. "I know they don't have Cook to prepare the repast, or music like Fritz plays."

Mrs. Schoenleber looked thoughtful. "I seem to remember that Jeffrey played the piano when he was younger, but he really didn't want to practice. He always gravitated to sports and physical activities. I don't know how he will manage to work in an office."

Nilda stared down at the letter. "I think I'll ask Fritz to knock his ball out of the yard, let alone the court." She heard the chuckles from the other two but glared at the letter instead.

"I will have Charles telephone him tomorrow." Mrs. Schoenleber shook her head. "No, this is something I should do. I will invite him to arrive on the thirtieth and leave on August second. How does that sound?"

Nilda's sigh could have been heard in the kitchen. "All right."

"Isn't it better than your going down there?"

"Yes! The board meetings are bad enough. Although I did enjoy the symphony. I'm grateful I got to do that."

Mrs. Schoenleber warned, "If he insists on your going down there for something, I will chaperone. And no, we will be too busy to visit them at their lake house in August. Besides, Heinrik only joins them there on weekends."

Interesting that she never mentions her sister-in-law. Nilda tapped the folded letter on her skirt. She'd wait to answer until after the telephone call. Since Mrs. Schoenleber disliked the box on the wall so intensely—more than she had ever hated anyone or anything, she said—for her to agree to do this was a real sacrifice on her part.

That taken care of, Nilda put her mind on the next task, the dinner for the town leaders tomorrow. She had all the paperwork together and condensed to a short presentation. Fritz was returning in time for the meeting, and so far everyone had accepted the invitation. Cook and Mrs. Schoenleber had the menu planned and the supplies all purchased, so Cook would be up early, and breakfast might be a bit sparse. Not that Nilda felt much like eating anyway, since every time she thought about the coming dinner, her stomach clenched.

She did not sleep well that night. After breakfast, Nilda absently tucked a strand of hair into the figure-eight chignon at the back of her head that the maid had fashioned for her. *I wish I could go home to the farm, at least for today.* Life there was far simpler than life here. Harder work for certain, but no one cared how she looked or walked or talked, be it English or Norwegian. She'd come to this country dreaming of becoming a farmer's wife—not that she knew any farmers looking for a wife at the moment, but that had been the dream.

A knock at her bedroom door made her turn from the peaceful view of the rose garden. "Yes?"

Gilda stuck her head in the door. "Mrs. Schoenleber said to tell you the guests will be arriving in the next ten minutes or so."

"All right, I'm coming." Nilda paused. "Do I look all right?"

"Oh, miss, you look perfect. You need not worry about this meeting. You will do just fine, a real credit to Madam. So never fear."

Nilda glanced in the mirror one more time. The summer-sky blue of her watered-silk dress not only matched her eyes but made her dream of her homeland fjords, the land she'd so gleefully left behind to begin her new life in America.

She returned Gilda's smile, even though she felt it wobble a tiny bit. Her presentation papers were already in the dining room so that the meeting could be conducted after the meal. As Mrs. Schoenleber had said, meeting in her home instead of in someone's office gave them a slight edge.

Nilda inhaled and blew out a breath, as she had been taught, to help her relax. Her back straight and head high, she followed the maid down the walnut staircase, putting to use all the training in social graces Miss Walstead had spent hours drilling into her. Like her mor so often said, one should dream and plan but always know that God had the final say on what would truly happen. *Lord, if this is what you have planned for me, give me the right words to say and help them see the possibilities.*

"You look lovely, my dear," Mrs. Schoenleber said, a smile accompanying her nod. She rose from her chair in the morning room, setting her navy silk rustling. "You know who these people are, and they are of the same mind as we are. All for the good of the people of Blackduck. Just remember, for several of them, the dollar sign is most important. It is our job to convince them that this will not only profit the people but them as well. A big order I know, but you—*we*—are up to it."

They both turned at the chime of the front door and Charles' footsteps as he answered it.

Mrs. Schoenleber puffed out a breath, one eyebrow lifting as she smiled again at her protégé. She leaned closer. "Remember, these are the same men who played croquet on our back lawn last summer when we hosted the picnic."

"Ja—yes, I know, but I remember something else. Several of them like to win at all costs."

Together, they swept into the parlor, where Charles showed two men inside and then turned to answer another chime at the front door.

"Good day, welcome, so good of you to come." Mrs. Schoenleber extended her hand to shake theirs. "I hope your day is going well."

Mr. Mathew Amundson, president of the First National Bank, took her hand with a slight bow. "I know you have something up your sleeve again, and I am looking forward to our coming discussion." His eyes twinkled. The two of them had been friends for more years than they liked to count.

"You know me well, Mathew. Together we have accomplished a great deal for our town. Today is one more opportunity."

Mrs. Schoenleber greeted the others as they arrived by twos

and threes until twelve people were gathered, including one other woman, Mrs. Schwartz, who always managed to be on the other side of any issue Mrs. Schoenleber took up.

Fritz joined them in the parlor. "Sorry I'm almost late."

Nilda nodded. "I'm just glad you're here."

Charles appeared in the arched doorway to the dining room. "Dinner is served."

"Thank you, Charles." Mrs. Schoenleber turned to the guests. "If you will. Miss Carlson put nameplates at the settings."

"So we cannot gang up on you?" Henry Mueller, head of the local Lumbermen's Association, said with a grin.

"Henry, you found me out."

Chuckles danced through the group as they found their places. They greeted each other, all relaxed, fully expecting a fine meal and a good, possibly memorable discussion.

Nilda took her place to the right of Mrs. Schoenleber, watching as they all discovered where to sit and stood behind their chairs. "Reverend Holtschmidt, will you please say the blessing?"

"I'd be delighted." He waited for the rustlings to settle. "Father in heaven, we gather here to learn how we can best serve you in our positions of leadership in this town. Thank you for the many ways you have blessed us and for each one gathered here. Give us your wisdom and foresight to do and be our best. Thank you for this meal and the hands that prepared it. All to your glory and honor, amen."

"Thank you, please be seated."

While Mathew Amundson seated Mrs. Schoenleber, Henry Mueller pulled out Nilda's chair. "Thank you." She smiled at Henry over her shoulder. She had planned to seat him beside her because he reminded her of one of her uncles at home in Norway. Besides, he had given them the idea in the first place.

Henry leaned closer to Nilda to whisper, "I see your cook has been at it again. My wife and I envy you all with such a cook to feed you. I'd hire her in a minute if only she were looking for a different job."

"Why, what happened to your cook?" Nilda spread her napkin in her lap.

"She had to go take care of her sister, so my wife says we have to find a good cook very soon. Do you know of anyone?"

"I will ask Cook if she knows anyone."

He nodded. "That is a very good idea. Thank you." He smiled up at the butler, who set a bowl of soup in front of him. "What kind of soup is this? I was busy talking."

"Cream of mushroom with a touch of lemon, sir."

"And Mrs. Solvang's secret ingredient? I know she always adds something."

"Now, surely you don't expect me to give away her family secrets."

Nilda could hear the smile in Charles' voice. He always enjoyed hearing their cook be praised, and he would be sure to tell her.

While conversations blossomed around the table, as far as Nilda could hear, they stayed away from discussing the business of the coming meeting. When Mrs. Schwartz directly asked Mrs. Schoenleber a question about it, she smiled and deftly changed the subject. The man next to Mrs. Schwartz turned and asked her a question, earning Nilda's gratitude. With every social event, she managed to learn something new. In this case, how to manage conversations with contrary guests. Nilda glanced up to catch Mrs. Schoenleber's slight nod. How she kept track of everything going on was beyond Nilda's comprehension. It was all she could do to answer any questions pointed to her and to keep Henry entertained. Good thing he was such a pleasant man.

While Charles and the maid cleared the table and set the chocolate mousse pie before them, Mrs. Schoenleber stood, waiting for their attention. "In order to keep our meeting from going all afternoon, we will begin while you enjoy your coffee and dessert."

"Hoping to encourage agreement by sweetening us up?" Mr. Durfield, head of the school system, said, his smile encouraging similar responses from others.

"Now, that is not a bad idea, thank you." Mrs. Schoenleber's response brought a sprinkle of chuckles. Everyone was indeed in a good mood. "I know all of you have met my assistant, Miss Nilda Carlson, and today she will be our presenter. In fact, she has already asked many of you for suggestions on how we can provide opportunities for the residents of Blackduck. I hope you have been thinking on this and brought your ideas to add to the stewpot."

She nodded to Nilda, who stood and smiled at those around the table.

Lord, please help. "Thank you for coming today. As Mrs. Schoenleber said, I have been talking with many of you already. She assigned me the task of discerning what the needs of the people who live in Blackduck are and how we can help."

"The Bible says God helps those who help themselves," Mrs. Schwartz said.

Reverend Holtschmidt grimaced. "Actually, that is not in the Bible." Nilda caught the look that passed between him and Mrs. Schoenleber.

"But the Bible does say for those who have to share with those who have not." Nilda almost bit her lip. How had that slipped out? Several undercover chuckles let her breathe again. "The general consensus has been that housing is needed, especially for the families of the men who come to the logging camps for the winter. I know they are encouraged to leave their families behind, but that might not be feasible for many of them. So I asked Mr. Mueller to give us a five-minute overview of an estimate for building something besides tar-paper shacks."

He stood, thanked her, and gave cost estimates and income projections, passing out papers with diagrams and costs. "We propose that we form a charitable foundation and, with the money donated, have at least ten homes ready for occupancy by logging season. If we were assured of more funding, we could erect more."

"I am opening the floor for discussion," Mrs. Schoenleber said. "To begin with, we are seeking someone who will donate land close enough to town."

"Money, money, money. All you ever want is money for this and money for that. I should have known better than to come today." Mrs. Schwartz scowled.

"You know you came because you are proud to be part of the community of Blackduck." Mr. Amundson leaned forward to make her look at him. "And, Isabella, you like your name on the plaques. That does not come for free."

Mrs. Schwartz glared at Nilda and sputtered into her napkin but said nothing more.

Nilda breathed a sigh of relief. "Any more questions for Mr. Mueller?" She paused. "Any further questions on any topic?"

Thor Haglund, whom she had just recently met, signaled her. "Yes, thank you. I been in this town since I was a young man, and I believe what my far always said. 'Start your own business and save your money.' Investing in land was what he advocated. So we worked and did that, then sold the trees and bought more land." He looked around the room. "Folks were kind to us immigrants, and I believe we need to pass that kindness on. Now, it seems to me that we were all invited here for two reasons. We have money, and we care about our town and community. I have a piece of land a mile southeast of town, and I can donate ten acres without losing any sleep over it. The pine trees are long gone, but brush and deciduous trees are sprouting up, just like the Lord God ordained them to do. If I do that, we still have to come up with money for the supplies. I know some strong young men who would be grateful for the work and might just do so as a down payment on one of those houses. I know that Miss Carlson was proposing rentals so the investors could recoup their money, but what is needed here won't make any of you go hungry. And you got to admit, we have a lot to be thankful for."

He sat down to a moment of silence. Henry Mueller started clapping, and one by one, the others chimed in.

"Thank you, Mr. Haglund." Nilda looked around the group. "Anything to add to that?"

"Charles, would you please bring a basket to pass around?" Mrs. Schoenleber nodded as she looked around the group. "There are twelve of us here. You can put a note in the basket of what you are willing to contribute today, and I know Mr. Amundson will see that a fund is set up at the bank, to be drawn on as needed."

He nodded. "And if you desire, you are always encouraged to invest more later. I suggest we put Reverend Holtschmidt at the head of this, with Miss Carlson assisting. Those of you who are willing will be the board that he reports to. Thor, if you can get us the plot of land and bring together a corps of men who are willing to start clearing brush immediately, that will be good. Henry, you provide the plans and deliver the lumber. Thor, they need an overseer, and I suggest you would be a good one. I know you are not afraid to get your hands dirty."

Should Nilda intervene and regain control? She decided not. Things were flowing well, however rapidly.

Mr. Amundson turned to the lady beside him. "Mrs. Schwartz, since you have that good solid barn that you are not using, that would be a good place for these men who might not have a home here to bed down. I also know that your cook loves to feed a crowd, so perhaps you could provide supper every night."

Mrs. Schwartz's mouth fell open. She looked aghast. "But . . . but . . . I never . . ."

He stared right at her. "I know that is what Fredrich would want you to do with a portion of the money he so richly left for you. He and I often talked about building a town we could be proud of and continuing the tradition of caring for others."

The glare she sent him could have curled what little hair he had left, but she finally jerked a nod. "There will be no spirits imbibed on my property."

"You have every right to demand that, and Thor will make that clear to those who stay there."

Thor raised one eyebrow and stared right at her.

"Any questions?" Mr. Amundson nodded. "Back to you, Miss Carlson."

"Thank you, sir. Since I—we had no idea this meeting would turn into a whirlwind like this, I asked several others if they had suggestions for us to consider today. Mr. Larsson, please begin."

"As a musician and schoolteacher, I, of course, am most interested in the best education for our children. That includes education and training in the arts. I believe that Blackduck would benefit from the addition of an arts center, for lack of a better word. A theater or auditorium, studio space, and classrooms. This would be open to the community to use and to bring traveling performers to this town. Ideally the theater would include an organ and piano along with other musical instruments. Students and the public could put on plays, bring in speakers and teachers. This would open a window of opportunity beyond what we can envision. I have here cost estimates that were produced for another town that had similar facilities." He handed his pages to Reverend Holtschmidt on his other side. "Thank you." He sat down and smiled at Nilda with a slight shrug.

Nilda announced, "We have another proposal from Dr. Andrews."

The doctor pushed his glasses up on his nose. "This town and the surrounding counties need at least a clinic, but preferably a hospital. I can't keep up with all those needing health care. The three beds I have are all that is available, as you know. The more people we have here, the more there are to get sick or injured. We've talked about this before, but talk is all we've done. If we ever have an epidemic here, people will die for lack of health care. If we had a hospital, we could attract a dentist and maybe even a visiting nurse and at least one other doctor. Now, you know I am getting up in years, and I don't move as fast as I used to. We need to draw in young folks to help, and having a hospital would help that happen. It would be good if the donors and investors are from this group but not this group alone. The whole community would benefit, so I say the whole community needs to invest." He nodded as he sat down. "Thank you."

Mrs. Schoenleber stood. "I don't know about you all, but I feel like I've been run over by a logging train." Several others nodded. "I think we are all clear on our assignments on the housing project that has gone beyond a mere proposal. If anyone has anything else to question or add, now is your chance." The pause stretched, but no one spoke. "I have asked Fritz to take notes on our meeting, and we shall get them to you all in the next couple of days. Again, thank you for coming and for your participation. Father McElroy, will you pronounce the benediction, please?"

He'd just lowered his hands after the *amen* when Isabella Schwartz stood and gathered her purse. "Well, I never. Mathew, you and I will talk." She thumped her stick on the floor and sailed out of the room.

"Don't worry, she will do what I asked." Mr. Amundson scrubbed the palm of his hand over his burnished head. He smiled at Mrs. Schoenleber. "It always helps to know someone's secrets."

She smiled back wickedly. "I notice that you did not ask—you told her, in no uncertain terms. Every mother knows the value of using bribery and guilt to advantage, but you have honed it to a fine art."

He bowed. "Why, thank you, my dear Gertrude."

Charles stopped in the doorway. "We are serving afternoon beverages out on the verandah."

The remainder of the guests made their way outside. Nilda breathed in the fresh air. At least that meeting was over. She heard the opening strains of Debussy. Fritz had moved to the piano. She could feel her shoulders relax.

"I look forward to working with you, Miss Carlson." Reverend Holtschmidt handed her a glass of lemonade.

"Thank you—I think." She leaned closer. "Is this typical for meetings like this, or did we just see miracles happen?"

"I always opt for miracles. Makes good sense." He patted her arm. "I think we just needed someone to get the ball rolling. After all, in the scheme of things, ten small houses is not a big undertaking."

"It seems so to me. You will have to guide me if I am to assist you."

"Oh, I will, never fear. Excuse me, I want to catch Mr. Durfield before he leaves."

Nilda watched her project's new benefactors mingle on the verandah. What had she gotten herself into?

Chapter 13

Two more hours, and they would be here. *Mor is coming! Mor is coming!*

Nilda felt like running to the station so she would be the first person they saw. She was already planning to go with George to meet them, but the running might take away her jitters.

"You could try sitting down." Mrs. Schoenleber's smile took any sting out of her words.

"I can't. It's like I have ants crawling over me."

"While that is a good description, the picture is rather warped." Mrs. Schoenleber patted her chest and looked around and in her chair. "I must have left my glasses upstairs. Could you please fetch them for me?"

"Of course."

As soon as she was out of sight of her friend and mentor, Nilda took the stairs at a run, two at a time. At the top she bent over to catch her breath and walked to her employer's bedroom and sitting room. First she checked by the bed, then, shaking her head, went over to the sitting room, running her hand around the chair cushion. They weren't in the bathroom either. Finger to her chin, Nilda searched the room again. No glasses. The stand that held them during the night was empty, as was the shallow dish by the sink. Since Mrs. Schoenleber used them only to read, she inspected the dining room before returning to the sun-room.

"I've searched everywhere. Here, let me look in your chair." Nilda found the glasses under the chair, hidden by the upholstery ruffle, and handed them to their owner.

"Strange how they could get there. However, I'm grateful you found them." Mrs. Schoenleber set them back on her nose. "There, that's better. I wish Fritz were here to play like he did yesterday."

So do I. Nilda crossed to stand at the window, looking out over the verandah. The potted ferns guarding the wall were beginning to block the view if one were sitting down. Her fingers itched to go trim them back, but she hated to offend George, since he was rather possessive of his garden and plants. She'd already picked and arranged the roses and daisies for the house.

She drifted over and sat on the piano bench. Practicing would take her mind off the anticipated arrival. Starting with the scales she now knew by heart, she segued into "In the Shade of the Old Apple Tree." She loved the tune of that one. But her relaxed manner tightened up as soon as she started on the pieces Fritz had assigned to her this week. As he instructed, after playing them so she would know how they sounded, she played the hard parts one note at a time, making sure she was using the proper fingers, then gradually picking up speed as she smoothed them out. Focusing, she moved on to the next page. Sharps and flats could cause all kinds of havoc.

"Miss Nilda, we'll be leaving for the station in about five minutes," George announced.

"Oh. Oh my goodness."

She shut the cover over the keys and headed for the powder

room just down the hall. Checking her image in the mirror, she made a face and dried her hands. *Mor is almost here. Oh, I have so much to show her.*

"You think they will want to go shopping?" she asked as she stepped back into the sun-room.

"I assumed that would be on your list," Mrs. Schoenleber replied. "Dinner will be ready by the time they are settled."

Nilda flew out the front door, and only at George's arched eyebrows did she not jump into the buggy without assistance. More than once she had received a rebuke via George's eyebrows.

"I am so excited." She settled into the seat facing forward.

"I can tell."

"It shows?"

"It most definitely shows, miss."

She knew he added the *miss* to make his point.

"Where is your parasol?" he asked.

Nilda tried to touch the broad brim of her straw hat with her own eyebrows. "In the hall closet. We won't be out long."

"Unless the train is late." The team trotted smartly down the street, kicking up a bit of a breeze. "We are early, Miss Nilda. You will not see the train yet."

Nilda made herself sit back against the seat. Decorum might be ladylike, but right now all she cared about was seeing her mor here in Blackduck for a real visit, albeit a short one. But short was better than nothing. What would Leif think of the house and the way she was living? What might he enjoy doing? There were no animals here for him to take care of. Would he be lost? Was Knute jealous, or did he even want to come to town? It seemed all he wanted was to be fishing or out in the big trees with Ivar and Bjorn. Now, Bjorn, he did enjoy the social, even though he was the youngest there. And while he had never played croquet before, he caught on quickly.

The whistle announced the coming train. George climbed down and, with a smile of approval, held out his hand to assist her.

"Thank you, George. You have been most circumspect."

"As in proper?"

She recognized the laughter lurking in his eyes. "Disgustingly so."

"You never know who might be watching."

Nilda had come to realize that she should care about appearances because of Mrs. Schoenleber's position in the town, but she still struggled with it. At least out on the farm, the cows and chickens and dog and cats did not care if she were proper or not, as long as she fed them on time. There were pluses on both sides of the equation.

The train steamed and screeched, wheels locking to stop the heavy engine. The engineer returned Nilda's wave, and as soon as the conductor set the steel bench by a door, she headed toward it. The door slid open, and Leif stood at the head of the steps, already waving at her.

"We're here. We're really here." He didn't bother with the conductor's assisting hand, instead leaping over the step and flying into Nilda's arms. She squeezed him tight, all the while watching Gunlaug carefully descend the three steps and take the conductor's hand for the final one.

"Uff da. Er, thank you."

"You are welcome. I think there is someone having a hard time waiting for you." He reached into the train and picked up her carpetbag. "Enjoy your stay."

Nilda threw decorum over her shoulder and let herself be enveloped in her mother's hug. "It feels like months since I saw you, not just weeks. I am so glad you are here."

"We came so fast, we could hardly see the country." Gunlaug resettled Nilda's hat on her head. "Leif was so excited he couldn't sit still."

"Do you have more baggage?" Nilda locked her arm through her mor's.

"Yes, those two boxes they are just unloading. Oh, and two pairs of skis I am to deliver." She watched the cargo being carried off the train. "Ah, there they are."

Nilda caught George's eye and pointed down the platform. "Goodness, did you come to stay?" she asked.

"No, but Rune made a gift for you. Now, keep in mind that if you'd rather not have it here, his feelings won't be hurt. We can use it at home."

A gift? Nilda put the thought aside for later. "If he had known you were bringing so much, George would have brought a larger carriage."

They walked over to where the horse and buggy waited.

Leif was already helping George load the baggage. "He said we need to keep the skis with us."

"George, I'd like you to meet my mother, Gunlaug Carlson, and my nephew Leif."

"Very pleased to meet you, madam." George turned to Leif. "If you would ride up with me, we could put that last box inside."

"Yes, sir, Mr. George. I'd be glad to." Leif scrambled up to the driver's seat. "What is your horse's name? I drive Rosie at home. Knute and I ride her to school too."

Nilda caught George's eye when he turned to make sure all was ready. "Thank you." She slid her hand into her mother's. "I am so very glad you are here. I have a feeling George will have a shadow for the time." She pointed out the landmarks as they trotted home.

"My, but this is a busy place," Gunlaug said.

"If there is anything you would like to see while you are here, just tell me."

"I have a list for the mercantile. Things the Bensons aren't carrying, although she will order anything we want. She said to greet you and ask when you are coming to the farm again, that perhaps you can stop for a visit."

"That's nice of her. That's the Schoenleber house up there on the left."

Gunlaug started to stand as soon as the buggy stopped, but Nilda laid a restraining hand on her arm. When George had the step lowered and held out his hand, Nilda nodded.

Leif swung down and stood looking at the house, his head tipped back as he surveyed the roof line. The look he gave Nilda made her smile. He would have plenty of questions; she could nearly see his curiosity bubbling over.

When Gunlaug reached for her carpetbag, George got it before she could. "Let me get that, madam. You and Miss Nilda go on in. I'm sure dinner is ready and waiting. You go with them too, Master Leif. Your things will be up in your rooms for later."

Leif shrugged and shot Nilda another questioning look. She would have to explain how things were different here. Leif was used to helping, often without being asked. He saw what needed to be done and went ahead and did it, a rare gift in a child his age. For that matter, in people in general.

"George is right, dinner should be ready. Are you hungry, Leif?"

"Tante Nilda, you know I am always hungry." Halfway to the door, he whispered to her, "How come Mr. George wouldn't let me help?"

"Because that is his job, along with the gardening and taking care of the grounds. And whatever else he sees that needs doing outside. You will meet Charles in a minute. He is the butler who takes care of things inside. He will serve the meals, along with the maid, Stella. Mrs. Schoenleber hires them. Oh, and Mrs. Solvang too, but she likes to be called Cook."

Leif was still pondering this when the door opened and Charles welcomed them in. Nilda introduced them, and Charles nodded with a smile. "I've been looking forward to meeting you, Master Leif. Your aunt, your uncle, and your teacher all speak very highly of you."

"Yes, sir. Thank you, sir." But his eyes screamed questions.

"If you would like to wash up in the powder room downstairs, madam, dinner will be served right away."

"Thank you." Gunlaug only hesitated a fraction of a second, but Nilda could see the effort it took to speak English.

"Come, Mother, I will show you the way."

When they were seated and grace had been said, Charles announced the soup as he set shallow bowls in front of them.

"Just do what I do," Nilda whispered in Leif's ear. He was seated on her right side. He nodded and did exactly that.

"Leif, I hear that you like to read." Mrs. Schoenleber smiled at him.

"Yes, ma'am. I do."

"I have a rather well-stocked library. Nilda will show you, and you are welcome to read anything you want. You could take some books home with you, if you'd like."

"Really?" He thought a moment. "Do you have books by Mark Twain? Like *Tom Sawyer*?"

"I do. He is a remarkable author. What books of his have you read?"

"Mr. Larsson read *The Adventures of Tom Sawyer* to us last year. If we get our work done, he reads to us every day. But I would like to read it myself, all the way through, without waiting for reading time."

"Then you shall do that. You might look at *The Adventures of Huckleberry Finn* too, and my favorite of all of his books is *A Connecticut Yankee in King Arthur's Court*. Have you read *Robinson Crusoe* by Daniel Defoe or *Treasure Island* by Robert Louis Stevenson?"

Leif shook his head. "But I will."

"Do you have a library at your school?"

"No, ma'am. The teachers each have some reading books in their rooms, but that's all."

"Hmm, we will have to see about that."

Charles removed the bowls. He said softly to Leif, "Never fear, you won't go hungry."

"Thank you." He leaned closer and whispered to Nilda, "How did he know I wanted more?"

"Oh, I think he knows about growing boys."

She watched his eyes grow wide as Charles set a plate of pork chops with applesauce, potatoes and gravy, and green beans mixed with baby onions in front of him. Charles then set a roll on each bread plate.

Nilda picked up the butter knife and sliced off a pat of butter to put on the bread plate, then passed the butter to Leif. Again he copied her exactly and looked across the table at Gunlaug. How to get it to her? He pushed back his chair and started to get up.

Charles came to his side and took the butter plate. "Let me do that for you. You just enjoy your dinner." He bent over and picked up Leif's napkin to tuck back in his lap.

"Thank you."

Nilda cared about Charles, but the way he was treating Leif made her want to hug him.

Mrs. Schoenleber suggested, "When we've finished dinner, Nilda, why don't you take Leif on a tour of the house, ending in the library, while Gunlaug and I visit in the sun-room?"

Gunlaug smiled. "I have some things in the boxes that I will show you when you get back."

Nilda smiled at her mor. "Of course."

When the meal was finished, Nilda led Leif up the stairs. "First of all, I will show you your room. You and your grandma will share a bath." She showed him the room and watched his face.

At the window he turned around. "All this for me?" He used the stool to climb up on the bed and flopped back on it, his arms straight out. Nilda knew exactly how he felt. She showed him how to use the facilities, including the hot and cold water faucets.

"No pump."

"I know. Pretty amazing. Now, my room is right there across the hall." She opened the door to show him. "Tomorrow we are going shopping to buy you and Knute boots and clothes for school. I can see your pants and sleeves are getting short."

"I'm growing, but I will have Knute's clothes, or what's left of them."

"Mrs. Schoenleber would like to do this for you. And you always need new boots."

Down in the kitchen, she introduced him to Cook. "You sure made a good dinner," he said. "Thank you."

"Did you get filled up?"

He nodded. "But I can always eat more." He looked around. "You have fancy stoves and lots of cupboards."

"A big pantry too." She bent over and pulled a pan of cookies out of the oven. "I hope you like ginger cookies. I found a cookie cutter just for you." She pointed at the gingerbread men on the cookie sheet. "Do you think I should frost them or leave them as is?"

He watched as she slid them onto dish towels on the table. "I think some of each. That looks like buttons on them. Are they raisins?"

"Yes. Help yourself, but be careful, they're hot. I thought if you like these, perhaps I could send some home with you."

"That would be good. Knute would love it." He picked up a cookie and blew on it.

"I warned you."

"I know, but I can't wait." He took a bite and sucked in air around it. "We're going to the library next."

Cook grinned. "You might want to take a couple with you, just in case you get lost or something."

Nilda laughed. "Come along, Leif. I'll show you the stables and the garden later, or you can just wander around and come ask me any questions."

"Okay."

When they reached the library, he stopped in the doorway. Bookshelves reached clear to the ten-foot ceiling with a ladder one could push along on a track to reach the high shelves. Many of the books were leather-bound, and all were arranged according to topic and alphabetically by author.

Leif stood in the middle of the room and turned slowly. "All these belong to her?"

"Yes. You can read the topics in that strip of printing on the shelves."

Gazing raptly at the walls, he bumped into the desk. "Is this your desk?"

"Yes, I work in here."

"And with all these books, anytime you like."

"I used to work out in the sun-room, but with this new gadget, I've moved in here. It's quite loud, you see." She laid a hand on the machine. "This is a typewriter. I am still learning to use it. I'll show you later, if you like."

She watched him walk slowly in front of the shelves, reading the topics. He reached out and touched them, as if to make sure they were real. "Look! Mark Twain. And Robert Louis Stevenson, *Treasure Island*! She really means I can read these?"

"Yes, you can."

"Oh, Nilda!" Like an archaeologist choosing a precious artifact, he carefully pulled a leather-bound book from the shelf. With legs crossed, he sank to the floor and opened it. "'Squire Trelawney, Dr. Livesey, and the rest of these gentlemen having asked me to write down the whole particulars about Treasure Island, from the beginning to the end, keeping nothing back but the bearings of the island, and that only because there is still treasure not yet lifted, I take up my pen. . . .'"

Smiling outrageously, Nilda left him there and went to find the ladies. They were settled in the lovely wicker chairs in the sun-room. "He's lost in *Treasure Island*," she reported. "Didn't get as far as Twain."

Mrs. Schoenleber smiled. "Your mother says he loves books as much as he loves animals. I would like to have seen his face."

"Rapture."

"Good. We will fix up a box for him to take home."

Nilda's heart quailed. "But what if—if something happens to one of the books?"

Mrs. Schoenleber shrugged. "It is just a book that can be replaced. The dreams and mind of that child cannot be replaced. I have a feeling God has great things in store for him, and I look forward to helping any way I can." She turned to Nilda. "First of all, we need to see about setting up a library for that school. No school should be without plenty of books for their students to read, not even small ones, or especially not small ones out in the country." She nodded slowly and seemed to be staring at nothing.

Nilda knew an idea was brewing. She also knew better than to ask anything at this point. When Mrs. Schoenleber had given it sufficient thought, then she would learn of it.

"Mor, would you like to walk in the garden?" she asked.

"Yes, definitely, and I have a surprise for you." Gunlaug looked to Mrs. Schoenleber, who was obviously thinking.

"Come along," Nilda said, "she'll catch up when she's ready." Together they paused in the doorway. "I love all of this." Nilda's sweeping gesture encompassed the beauty around them. "And look, a greenhouse."

They strolled across the verandah.

"The kitchen and herb gardens are out here behind the greenhouse. Whenever the flowers in the house start to fade, I come out here and cut more. Miss Walstead, my teacher whom you will meet tomorrow, taught me about flower arranging, and I take absolute delight in doing so."

Gunlaug bent to sniff several of the roses. "I hope ours bloom this summer."

"We'll ask George if he thinks they will. Perhaps he has a few more cuttings you could take home."

"At this rate, we'll need Rune to bring the wagon to carry all the boxes home."

"Would that be such a bad thing?"

"Wait. Look. Are these plant stakes?" Gunlaug pointed to the peavine stakes. The top several inches of each one was carved into a clever little animal or plant. She ran her fingers across a stake, shaped like a rabbit with its ears and feet tucked in.

"George carves them. No one asked him to. He does it for pleasure. He says that he and Charles were sitting in the garden one day, and Charles said everything was extraordinarily beautiful except the support stakes, so George got this idea."

"It is . . ." Gunlaug paused to find the word and ended up using Norwegian. ". . . gratifying to me that you work in such a pleasant, cooperative household. Everyone here seems to enjoy their work."

"That is very true." Nilda had not thought of it like that. Leave it to her mor to find another shining bright spot in her life.

Gunlaug cupped another blossom in her hands. "Such beauty. And look at you. It seems you have adapted quite well."

Nilda pointed out another rosebush, this one with white roses brush-tipped in shades of red. "Isn't that a beauty?" They wandered back to the kitchen garden plot behind the greenhouse.

"Not a weed in sight. How does he do this?"

"I think he has elves who work in the night, or he never sleeps. Cook is allowed out here to pick what she wants for the kitchen, but he likes to harvest too. He likes things done just so. We've had peas, and it looks like we're about to have more."

Nilda looked around to make sure George was nowhere in sight and picked two pea pods. Together, they split them open and popped the peas in their mouths.

"This is the best way to eat peas." Nilda looked around to find someplace to hide the pods, then tucked them in her waistband. "Thanks to the greenhouse, we had fresh lettuce during the winter and vine-ripened tomatoes." While she didn't say it, the thought that wealth could buy comfort had become very real to her.

"A far distance from life in Norway, and I'm not just talking miles."

"Tante Nilda, where are you?" Leif called.

"Out in the garden. We're coming back."

"Cook says tea is ready, and wait 'til you eat a gingerbread man."

Arm in arm, Nilda and her mother strolled back to the verandah. Mrs. Schoenleber was sitting at the glass-topped iron table, still in the shade. When the sun sank farther west, it would reach the flagstone verandah. A breeze came off the river and wafted around the women when they sat down.

"Mor, what was your surprise?" Nilda asked.

Gunlaug looked heavenward. “How could I forget that? I received another letter from Ingeborg. She added up the miles. She thinks that Blackduck and Blessing are only about three hundred and fifty miles apart, but the railroads do not go there directly. We would have to go south by rail, then west, then north. But it can surely be done.”

Nilda turned to her employer. “Mother and Ingeborg are cousins and were best friends when they were growing up. Until there was a fight over some land when one of their uncles died, and the families were never allowed to speak to each other again. Then Ingeborg married and moved to North Dakota to homestead. They never communicated again.”

“How terribly sad. Whatever is wrong with people who can carry a grudge like that?” Mrs. Schoenleber passed the cookie plate to Gunlaug. “Cook found that cookie cutter somewhere and always hoped she’d have a young visitor to bake for.”

Nilda grinned at Leif, who was eating the legs off his gingerbread man. “We Carlsons were finally able to visit back and forth, but Ingeborg had moved to America by then.”

“And you’ve never heard from her? Or about her?” Mrs. Schoenleber asked.

“They would send letters, asking for relatives to come and work for them on their farm, but no one in our family wanted to go until Ivar, who kept saying that as soon as he was grown enough, he really wanted to go to Blessing.

“We’ve not talked about it since we came here. Now I don’t know.” Nilda looked at her mother. “What about you, do you want to go there?”

“I don’t know. It is a long and difficult journey to make, but I have made worse ones. Coming to America, for one. I’ll answer this letter and see what happens.”

Chapter 14

Blowing stumps again today?" Signe refilled Rune's coffee mug.

He nodded. "If we can get a couple more acres cleared, the cows can pasture there. We're going to run out of hay if we don't do something. Knute, take the sheep to graze along the road tomorrow."

Knute made a face. "Can't that wait for Leif to get back?"

Kirstin looked up from picking food off her tray. "Ef, Ef, Ef." She banged her spoon, looking for Leif.

"Now see what you started." Signe took a cloth to wash the child's hands and face, hoping to distract her. It didn't work. Once she set the little girl down, Kirstin headed for the screen door, still chanting.

Knute beat his mother to lock the screen door, since he was the last one in for breakfast. "Sorry, Baby, you can't go outside by yourself."

Kirstin banged her palms on the screen door, but when nothing happened, she turned to stare at the others, a frown taking over her forehead. Gerd handed her a toy, but she threw that on the floor. She was working up to a roar when Bjorn scooped her up, set her on his shoulders, and jogged her outside and down the steps.

Knute hung his head. "Sorry, I . . ."

"Let's get going. You and Ivar go harness up the team. I'll count out the sticks of dynamite. All the tools are still in the wagon, right?"

"Yes, sir."

Signe heard Knute muttering as he left. She shook her head.

"What's the matter with him?" Rune asked, pushing back his chair.

"I think he had no idea how much Leif does around here when the rest of you are out in the big trees. Besides having Kirstin with him so much of the time. He misses working out in the trees." She smiled up at him. Today one eye was more red than the other. "Remind me to wash your eyes in milk tonight." That always brought him some relief.

He nodded. "Takk."

"Please be careful out there."

He paused and looked over his shoulder. "We are always careful."

"I know, but . . ."

He waited, but she just shook her head. Why was she more worried today? She knew that her husband was extremely cautious around the dynamite. After all, they'd been clearing land for the last two weeks. After today, he'd have the boys clean up the pieces so they could plow and disk the cleared acres to plant grass and alfalfa seed. This year the cows could graze on it later in the summer; next year they would cut it for hay.

She'd heard the discussions many evenings. Between making skis in the shop, felling the big trees, and taking care of farming chores, all of the boys and Rune were working from dawn 'til dark and in the shop by lantern light.

"All will be well," Gerd said firmly. "You cannot worry about them. It does no good. We do our part and pray God protects them in theirs. You are the one who told me that more than once."

"Mor, here she is back," Knute called as he mounted the steps. He slid Kirstin into her mother's arms. "Far said to fill the water jugs for the wagon."

"Tell Knute thank you." Signe waved Kirstin's hand for her. "Thank you." She swung her daughter around and carried the giggling little girl back in the house. "You play with the kettles for a while." She opened the cupboard door and set Kirstin in front of it. "I guess I didn't realize either how much you-know-who entertains her."

"That and having Gunlaug here. Think how often Kirstin plays with her while Gunlaug works at her loom." Gerd handed the filled jugs to Knute and waved him off.

"Having them both gone has left a real hole." Signe sighed.

When Rufus tore off down the lane, barking, they heard the jangle of a harnessed team. "Who could that be?" Gerd walked out on the porch. "Oskar and Selma are here. He must have come to help with the clearing."

"Oh good, Eric and the others will play with Kirstin."

Selma stepped into the house. "I hope you don't mind our dropping in like this. Oskar felt he was supposed to be over here helping, and Eric got all excited to come, and since I am always thrilled to come, here we are."

Kirstin paused only a second before she ran to Selma and jabbered at her.

Eric looked up at his mor. "Kirstin wants to go outside. Can we?"

Kirstin put on her most imploring face.

The women looked at each other, shaking their heads. Signe

laughed. "I guess she does make sense, at least to someone. Maybe we should keep Eric here to interpret, and we won't have as many frowning faces."

Gerd nodded. "What sounds like jabber to us obviously has meaning."

"Where's Leif?" Eric asked.

Kirstin stopped her chatter. "Ef?" She ran to the door and banged on the screen.

Gerd told him, "He and Gunlaug went to visit Nilda in Blackduck. He'll be back tomorrow."

"Can't be too soon," Signe muttered.

Selma smiled. "Why don't I take the little ones down to the barn to play with the kittens? Unless there is something you'd like me to do here."

"That's a great idea."

The explosion in the distance outside was so loud that it rattled the windows. A minute later, another, followed by three more in succession.

"Well, we know they've been successful." Signe glanced at the clock. "An hour 'til dinner."

"Boom," said Kirstin.

"Big booms," Eric said with a nod. "Five booms."

Gerd smiled. "Very good, Eric. You've been learning to count."

"He can count to twenty and is getting close to figuring out the sequence to one hundred. He can print his name, and we keep singing the alphabet." Selma smiled at her son. "All in English. He knew some of that already in Norwegian. And Olaf and Katie are learning too. Oskar made them a chalkboard, and they play on that." She herded the three children ahead of her and out the door, then helped Kirstin down the porch steps.

Signe watched her cousin. Such a difference now from that

frightened young widow who came with Gunlaug. She and Oskar had been married nearly eight or nine months now. Sometimes meddling paid off. Why, Selma had blossomed; she was downright pretty.

Signe went to stir the ham and beans baking in the oven, which were giving the kitchen the fragrance of home.

Gerd inhaled deeply and smiled. "I'll make an extra pan of cornbread. There's plenty of beans." She paused. "That Selma, she's a whole different woman from that ghost who came with Gunlaug. And I would lay money that she's pregnant, though barely showing."

"Do you think so? Oskar looks happier now than I've ever seen him."

And Signe? She, too, was as happy now as she had ever been in her life. So much family, so much plenty, so much laughter. Her heart was singing.

"Welcome, Oskar, what brings you out here?" Rune leaned on his shovel handle.

"A little bird told me you could use some help." Oskar pulled his leather gloves out of his back pocket. "How many you got wired?"

"Three. The boys are digging out the next two. I just took a water break."

"You got a mattocks out there?"

"Ja, one."

Oskar reached into the bed of his wagon and pulled out another.

From the far stump came Bjorn's voice. "Far, we need a pry bar."

Rune looked in the wagon and shook his head. "Back at the shop."

"I have one." Oskar reached into his wagon again. "Anything else?"

Rune shook his head. "More hands than I'm used to. Thanks, I appreciate this." The two men walked out to where the boys were digging.

"We got a big rock here." Ivar pointed to a chunk of stone. "Way under the stump."

"Well, we sure don't want that flying through the air." Oskar rammed the pry bar into the ground at an angle until it hit stone. "That is a big one." He picked up his mattocks. "Come on, Knute, let's dig a bigger hole." They faced each other and swung the wider blades down in the hole, then pulled the dirt out along the side of the rock.

Rune drove the pry bar down farther, but it still hit the rock. "Might take dynamite to blow that out of there. You boys got the other side dug out for the sticks? The size this tree was, I felt bad bringing it down. One of the granddaddies."

Oskar nodded. "Had one like that over at my place. My pa wanted to leave it, but he really needed the money. Near to broke his heart when that giant hit the ground. He left the stump as a memorial. It's still there. We buried him and Ma both out there. Fenced the whole thing in for a burial site. Planted another pine tree there. It's thirty or forty feet tall now. We take picnics out there sometimes."

While he talked, he kept slamming the mattocks into the ground. Knute was slowing down. He gave up and handed his mattocks to Bjorn.

"We're going to have to climb down in that hole pretty soon." Rune handed the pry bar to Ivar, who jumped in the hole and stabbed the pry bar in at the same angle.

"Got it. But it's too big to pry out. What if we blow the stump, and maybe it will loosen the boulder?"

Oskar and Rune both nodded. They inserted three sticks of dynamite around the other side of the stump. "And we'll get far away."

Oskar took the boys to the next stump while Ivar and Rune planted the explosives and ran the fuse back toward the wagons. By the time noon was drawing near, they had five stumps ready to blow.

"What if we set off the others and after they go, do this one. It just seems safer to me." Rune looked out across their field and nodded. "Ja, that is what we will do."

"Bjorn, how about moving my team over there?" Oskar pointed a ways away. "And then I'll stay with them while you go back to the barn." He had learned of the lightning strike that damaged Bjorn's hearing and that since then, Bjorn never stayed near the blasting zone.

"Knute, you do the same," Rune said. "Before we set anything off, Oskar, would you please do another inspection? Ivar and I already did, but I don't trust this a bit."

When both horses and humans were back with the wagons, Rune handed Ivar the matches. "Don't take any chances." Sometimes the fuses went out or went faster than normal.

One by one, starting at the farthest, the sound hit them after the stump, along with rocks and dirt and pinecones, lifted in the air. Some of the lighter pieces came as far as the wagons and rained down on them. Knute pulled off his hat and slapped it against his thigh before setting it back on his head.

Rune and Oskar looked at each other, and both nodded. "Set off the big one, Ivar. I left longer fuses on that one."

They watched as Ivar struck the matches and waited to make sure the fuses were burning before he trotted back to the other side of the wagons. He turned and watched with the others. The first two blasts were simultaneous; the debris was falling when the next stick blew and then the final one under the rock. The stump lifted and fell to one side while the great stone rose six feet in the air, shattering as it blew.

"Well, at least we won't have to try to move that monster. Those pieces are big enough." Ivar brushed dirt and bits of wood off his shoulders. "You want to clear this afternoon or blow some more?"

"Why don't you blow more, since you have these extra hands to help you?" Oskar held out his hands. "Good thing you had the sheep penned up, or they would have hightailed it as far as they could get."

"I don't think the cows even looked up." Knute climbed up on the wagon seat. "Let's go eat."

They unharnessed the teams and let them loose in the pasture, where they immediately headed for the water trough.

Bjorn walked to the house with them. "That was something to see, even from the barn."

Rune shook his head. "Even the thought of using the dynamite gives me nightmares. Something can go wrong so easily."

Oskar nodded. "I know a man up north who lost his eye when some little piece of wood struck him. That's why I always say cover your head."

"I watched that big one," Rune confessed. "We could have added another stick, but this worked. Maybe we'll just bury the pieces of rock down in that hole. It should be deep enough for them not to work their way to the surface."

As they described the blasting over dinner, Signe shook her head. "It rattled the windows here. If there are flat pieces, perhaps we could use them to make a path to the outhouse."

"We'll look. That's a good idea."

"You should have seen that rock lift and break apart," Knute said.

Signe stared at Knute. "I thought you always kept your heads down."

"I did for the others, but that one was different. It was so big." Knute gave her his most pleading look.

She looked to Bjorn. "And you?"

"I was at the barn like you said I had to be. Good thing, because the explosion made the sheep panic, and they all piled together in one corner. I waded in and made them move. Some were too scared to even move, so I picked them up and set them back. How come sheep are so stupid?"

"When Jesus called us sheep, He wasn't paying people a compliment, was He?" Knute looked to his far, shaking his head.

Rune smiled. "You're right, son, but sheep are good followers. When their master calls them, they recognize His voice and follow. That's what Jesus wants us to do. A shepherd has a big responsibility to keep the sheep safe and alive."

"Leif is a good shepherd. They follow him."

"Ja, they know his voice."

Bjorn shrugged. "I sure hope none of them die. He'll blame me, but I tried."

"Good thing they were in the barn," Oskar said again. "They might still be running, right through fences, if they'd been out in the pasture."

Kirstin banged her spoon on her tray.

"That's enough." Signe caught her hand and held it.

Kirstin glared at her. "Ef, Ef."

"Sorry. He's not here right now."

Eric climbed down from his chair and went to stand by the high chair. He made a face at Kirstin. She stared at him. He made another. A smile started on her face. He stuck out his tongue, and she giggled and reached for his hair. When he backed away, he made another face.

The others watched the two children play.

"Thank you, Eric." Signe patted his shoulder. "You get back in your chair and finish your dinner."

Oskar smiled at his son. When he had married Selma, he got Eric as part of the package, and now he referred to both boys as his sons. Olaf, five, and Katie, three, had come into the marriage with him. Now, Selma and Oskar were making sure all three children felt like part of the new family. Eric was learning English a lot faster than his mor was. She and Gunlaug attended the English classes Mr. Larsson taught at the church one evening a week during the longer days.

When they finished dinner, including chocolate cream pie for dessert, the men and boys filled jugs with water and returned to the field. Rune stopped by the sheep pen with Knute. The sheep were milling around bleating their complaints about being locked in the pen.

"They look fine," Rune said, nodding. "Bjorn did just the right thing."

"I was scared to come look."

"Knute, you have a good head on your shoulders. Just keep using it and learning all you can."

"You mean school?"

"Well, that too, but there are many things you learn by doing them and by being curious and seeking answers to your questions. Like you did with Mr. Edmonds and the hunting and trapping. He enjoyed talking with you because you kept asking more questions." Rune let them out of the sheep pen and headed out to the field as he talked.

"Thank you. I hope we can go fishing again soon."

"We will on Saturday. Leif and Gunlaug will be back on Friday."

"Ivar and Bjorn both went to stay at Nilda's. Do you think I'll get invited sometime too?"

"Do you want to go?"

"I'd rather go fishing, I think, but I've never been there."

"I'm sure that will happen. Nilda asked me if you would want to come, and I said to ask you. You're almost a young man. You can say no if you want."

"No, thank you, huh?" Knute's eyes laughed up at him.

Rune realized the distance between their heights was not so much anymore. He tousled his son's hair, knocking off his hat in the process. "Smarty."

Knute grinned. "Let's go blow some more stumps."

Chapter 15

"Where's Leif?" Mrs. Schoenleber asked as morning tea was served.

"Somewhere holed up reading." Nilda looked at her mother. "I never dreamed he would spend so much of his time here reading."

"He was out helping George wash the carriage and polish the brass earlier today. I told him he could take the books home, but he hesitates." Mrs. Schoenleber looked over her glasses.

"I think he is afraid something might happen to them."

"I see. Well, I will have to do something about that." She paused, then looked at Nilda. "Did you talk with Fritz about starting a library in their school?"

"No, not yet. I thought to wait until he comes this weekend. Is there a library at the grade school here?"

Mrs. Schoenleber smiled mischievously. "Now, would he let a day go by without establishing one in this school? The town also has a library of sorts. A group you may wish to join, Nilda, the Young Ladies of Blackduck, have set up a modest library and reading room. It is still in its infancy, but they hope to make it a true public library."

The Young Ladies of Blackduck. Nilda had heard of them but had not known they were setting up a library.

"Our walk this morning was full of beauty." Gunlaug mixed some Norwegian words in with her English but was doing her best to speak mostly English.

"It is a beautiful area," Mrs. Schoenleber agreed. "Gunlaug, is there something special you would like to see or do here in Blackduck?"

"No, not really." She looked at Nilda. "I brought a list for shopping at the mercantile."

"Ah. Of course! When visiting a large town, shopping is always high on the list." Mrs. Schoenleber seemed to be enjoying Mor. "Why don't you and Nilda do that after dinner? Leif can go along or stay here, it is up to him. When George drives you to do your shopping, if you like, he and Nilda can take you on an extended tour of the town."

Charles entered and stood by the door. "Mr. Crawford Galt, madam. He wishes to speak with Miss Nilda's mother."

Nilda's heart thumped. That man again!

Gunlaug looked confused. "Who is Mr. Galt?"

"A private detective, Mor. He did not say who sent him, but we're pretty sure it was Dreng Nygaard's mother. She hired him to investigate Dreng's death. He has been asking questions all over town."

Mrs. Schoenleber looked grim. "His death was thoroughly investigated and the case closed. Then this detective came. Do you wish to speak with him?"

"Can it do any good?" Gunlaug looked from face to face.

Mrs. Schoenleber shook her head. "I truly do not know."

Gunlaug stood up. "Yes. I will speak with him." She followed Charles out to the parlor.

Nilda hurried to the alcove and opened the door of the dumbwaiter, listening.

Charles announced Mrs. Gunlaug Carlson and told her that

this was Crawford Galt. She thanked him. Nilda heard the door close as he left.

Mr. Galt's voice said, "Good morning, Mrs. Carlson. I am delighted to find you here. Several people I spoke with yesterday told me you are visiting. I hope your time here has been pleasant."

Mor replied, "Seeing my daughter is the most important reason. Now I will know what she is talking about when she comes home to visit. Please excuse my English. It is not very good yet."

"Your English is fine, madam. I understand you have not been here as long as has your daughter."

Mor explained to him about Far not wanting to travel, about missing Nilda and Rune and their sons, about Ivar coming as well.

Then Mr. Galt asked, "In Norway, were you acquainted with Dreng Nygaard?"

"I did not know him, really, but I certainly heard all about him. In a small town, everyone knows everything."

"But, madam, that is only hearsay."

"I am sorry. I do not know that word, *hearsay*."

Neither did Nilda exactly. She kept listening.

"Rumor. Gossip. Facts that everyone knows, but they are not really facts at all, and are often wrong."

"Dreng Nygaard made unwanted advances toward my daughter, Mr. Galt. I believe the gossip, as you call it. I believe her."

"But can you be certain they were truly unwanted? After all, that is only what she told you."

Mor sounded almost angry. "My daughter does not lie, Mr. Galt. Besides, who would want that horrible fellow?"

"A handsome young man from a background of wealth is very attractive to a young woman. Mrs. Carlson, I am going to pose a scenario here."

"I'm sorry, I do not—"

"Sorry. I will rephrase. Let me draw a picture of what possibly could have happened. Mr. Nygaard and Miss Carlson are both new to this country, and they happen to find themselves in the same town. They both go out to enjoy the new snow. They happen to cross paths. Mr. Nygaard approaches Miss Carlson, who is an old friend, with innocent intentions. However, she believes the ugly false rumors about him. She attacks him in self-defense, if you will, before he has a chance to attack her, or so she thinks, and then runs home."

"No. That was not it at all. He was lying in wait and—"

"You do not know that. You were told that by a person who intended to deceive you, to cover her own actions."

"That's not—" Mor sounded so frustrated and angry.

"Everyone who attended the dinner parties that Mrs. Schoenleber puts on for the youth in this town agreed that Mr. Nygaard was a perfect gentleman. Not the rogue you claim."

Nilda was sorely tempted to rush into the room and set this Mr. Galt straight. Would he believe her? Apparently not. She felt—how did she feel? Threatened! Accused of something she did not do. And she could see no way to bring the truth to light. Could this Mr. Galt get her arrested?

They talked awhile longer, but Nilda's brain was churning. Back in Norway, Dreng had sent her a note that said, *I will get you for this.* What if he got his revenge even from the grave? A perfect gentleman? Hardly.

Mr. Galt took his leave. Charles handed him his coat and hat as Mor came out of the parlor and continued to the study. As soon as Mr. Galt was out the door, Nilda ran to the study.

"Well?" was all Mrs. Schoenleber said, but it spoke volumes.

Gunlaug sat down, looking worried and shaken. "He does not believe me." She sighed. "And he does not believe Nilda."

"I fear he had his mind made up before he even left New York. I don't think we can do much at this point besides wait and see. Now, let us change the subject to something more pleasant than that unlikable man."

"Like the loom. What a lovely gift, Mor. Thank you!" Nilda beamed.

Gunlaug nodded. "It was good of George to put it together. Are you sure you want to keep it?"

Mrs. Schoenleber nodded. "If Nilda would like it here, that is all that matters. It isn't as if we are short of room." The women shared a smile. "There is a sewing machine in the sewing room too, but we have been so busy, I don't think you've seen that. George put the loom together there."

"I would like to warp the loom before I leave."

"Of course. I see that I am about to learn something new, namely, how weaving works. I have never seen a loom in use. This is a fine opportunity to learn."

Charles appeared. "Madam, Cook announces dinner. I shall go tell Master Leif."

Mrs. Schoenleber stood up. "Thank you. Shall we?" And she led them to the dining hall.

Nilda had no appetite and could hardly eat. Mr. Galt's obvious desire to lay the blame on her made her stomach turn. But she must not let Dreng ruin any more than he had already. She smiled at Leif. "I know this isn't what you want to do, but I want you to come along shopping." She shook her head at his pout. "Sorry, but this is important if you want winter clothes for school."

"Knute isn't here."

"I know. We will have to buy his at Benson's. But this way we can make sure yours fit well."

He heaved a sigh. "May I take my book along?"

Nilda chuckled. "If you must."

Dinner ended, Mrs. Schoenleber went to her study, and Nilda took Gunlaug out to the waiting victoria carriage.

George smiled and tipped his hat. "Madam. Allow me." He gave Gunlaug a steady hand up onto the carriage seat. He too seemed quite fond of Nilda's mor.

Leif asked, "Mr. George, is it all right if I read in the buggy while they finish shopping?"

George laughed. "Or I could bring you back here, or you could walk back. Pay attention to the way we go. This is the shortest and best way back."

When they reached the mercantile, Leif smiled at George. "I can find my way back."

"You'll miss out on a buggy tour of the town. Not that it is terribly large, but still."

Leif looked at Nilda. "Will I be sad to miss the tour?"

"You can sit out here and read."

"All right. Thank you, Mr. George. I won't bother you." He left his book on the seat.

Nilda caught George's look. He kept telling Leif that he ought to be addressed as plain George, but Leif insisted on prefacing the name with *mister*. Nilda half shrugged and led her family into the store.

Leif looked around. "This is lots bigger than Benson's."

"Yes, it is. They serve a lot more people."

"Miss Carlson, how can I help you today?" The proprietress came around the counter to them. She remembered Nilda, but Nilda could not remember her name.

"This is my mother from Norway, Gunlaug Carlson. She lives out on the farm and has brought a list for you today."

"Welcome, Mrs. Carlson. Do you want to give me your list to fill, or did you want to find things yourself?"

Mor pondered this a moment. "Both."

"How about we pick out the items that need choices, and then you fill the rest while George takes us on a tour?" Nilda suggested.

The proprietress smiled. "That will be just fine."

"We'll start with boots and a winter coat for my nephew here, Leif."

"Very good. This way." She led them to the shoe section.

Gunlaug said, "We want him to try on boots. And we have a traced foot here for a pair for his brother."

The proprietress nodded. "I'll take care of that."

"You mean I get a pair of new boots? I always have Knute's when he outgrows them."

Gunlaug smiled. "That you do. But I saw his boots. And Bjorn's too. You need new ones."

Leif sat on the floor and tried on two pairs before he made his choice. "These. I really like these. And I want them a little large so I have room to grow. I don't want to have to give them away too soon." He put the others back on the shelf and hugged his brand-new boots to his chest. "These are great. Thank you, Tante Nilda."

"Now let's get your coat." The brown wool one they chose was still too long in the sleeves, but it had an extra layer for inner lining, so it was plenty heavy.

"Mor would say this is just right." Leif looked at the sleeves. "I won't need it for months yet."

Gunlaug nodded, smiling. "You make wise choices, Leif."

Nilda led them to the dry goods. "Now let's look at some shirts and pants."

"That too? Tante Nilda, are you sure?"

"Yes, I am sure. Mrs. Schoenleber wants to do this for you boys."

Leif shook his head. "This is an awful lot."

"You let her worry about that, all right?"

Two shirts and two pairs of pants later, Leif joined George in the buggy. As Nilda was going back inside, she heard Leif say, "You have to wait a whole lot, don't you?"

And George replied, "Yes, but I don't mind. That's when I plan out things I have to do, like in the garden and the greenhouse. Sometimes I do the shopping for the house too. Cook gives me a list. And sometimes they call the list in and I just go pick it up. There are advantages to living in town."

There certainly were. And yet Nilda really missed the farm life, even though it meant hard work from dawn until dark.

When Nilda and Gunlaug exited the store with several bundles, Nilda noticed Mr. Galt across the street. He was leaning against a light pole, watching them. Simply watching. Whatever did he think he was finding out? Would he never go away? He made Nilda's stomach turn.

Leif had laid aside his book and plunged deeply into conversation with George. The topic, apparently, was telephones.

"I can see that a telephone is a big help," Leif said.

"That it is."

"They have one at Benson's Corner and at Reverend Skarstead's house."

George's voice held amusement. "I am sure there will be telephones out on the farms someday too, as the telephone company plants more posts and strings more wires along the country roads. It might help your pa with orders for his skis."

"You think?"

"Things are changing fast. In town we are supplied with both electricity and telephones, and I am sure they will eventually be available in all of Beltrami County. In fact, the *American* says they're already contemplating rural electrification in Beltrami County. We're growing fast."

As Nilda and Gunlaug reached the carriage, George put away his whittling knife and the garden stake he was working on. He stowed their purchases in the rumble at the back and gave Gunlaug a hand in. "Is there more?"

"Mrs. Renborggen is filling the rest of the list for us to pick up later."

"Good, good." He helped Nilda up into the buggy. "Now for the tour. Would you like to ride up front with me, Leif?"

"Thank you!" Her nephew placed his bookmark, closed the book, and tucked it tightly into a corner before climbing up on the driver's seat.

They drove through the parts of Blackduck that Nilda knew well and parts she had never seen before. This tour, in places, was as new to her as it was to Mor.

As they rumbled along a dirt path beside a brook, George said, "They plan to turn this area into a city park, much like that Central Park in New York City. However, we do not have their Mr. Olmsted to design it for us, so we must do that ourselves."

An hour later they arrived back at the house.

"I'll go back and pick up your purchases," George announced as he helped them down. "Do you need anything else?"

"Not that I know of," Nilda answered. "Thank you. We'll probably have to bundle things up to make it easier to load on the train."

"I thought as much. I have some cardboard boxes out in the carriage house."

"Afternoon tea will be served out on the verandah," Charles said as they filed in the door. "May I take those things up to your rooms?"

"I think George is going to box up the items that go home with my mother."

"I see. We'll take care of all that, then."

"Uff da," Gunlaug muttered under her breath. "Too much. Too much."

"As I tell you, life is different here." Nilda unpinned her hat and motioned for her mother to do the same. The maid took the hats upstairs. "It has taken me some time to get used to this kind of service."

They joined Mrs. Schoenleber and Miss Walstead out on the verandah. "Mor, I'd like you to meet Miss Jane Walstead, my teacher and . . ."

"Drill sergeant." Jane extended her hand. "I am so pleased to meet you. Working with Nilda has been one of the pleasures of my life. You reared a fine young woman, Mrs. Carlson. You can be very proud of her. She works very hard and learns so quickly."

Nilda kept herself from staring with her mouth open.

"We both feel that way, Gunlaug. Thank you for entrusting her to us." Mrs. Schoenleber looked around. "Did you lose Leif?"

"No, I think he is helping George." Nilda rolled her eyes. "When he hears the magic word, he'll come running."

"And that is?"

"Cookies." She nodded to the plate of gingerbread men, sugar-topped ginger cookies, and several other kinds. "I think Cook would like to keep him."

"Wouldn't we all? We have hot tea, iced tea, lemonade, and coffee, if you prefer."

Once they were all served, Mrs. Schoenleber turned to Gunlaug. "I have boxed up some books for Leif, and when he is finished with them, he can give them to Fritz to go on his bookshelf in the classroom until we can set up a school library. Nilda and I hope to have enough books gathered before school starts for both the school here in Blackduck and the one at Benson's Corner."

Gunlaug looked to her daughter, who nodded.

"That's one of my endeavors," Nilda said.

That night she joined her mother in her room, sitting cross-legged on the bed while Gunlaug sat in the chair. "I hope you have enjoyed your time here."

"How could I not? But I would have loved to join Cook in that big, wonderful kitchen."

"Maybe next time you can do that too."

"I, ah . . ."

"You don't want to come back?"

Gunlaug leaned forward and dropped her voice. "I feel guilty for letting other people wait on me like this. I like washing dishes and cooking and working in the garden."

Nilda chuckled. "Oh, Mor, I know you do, but look at this as a time to try new things. You had more time to knit, and you warped the loom for me. And you could have spent time up in the sewing room if you were staying longer."

"And if I knew how to use that machine. Gerd does all the machine sewing at home."

Nilda smiled. Yes, the farm was home now, and she was glad Gunlaug felt that way too.

"Is Mrs. Benson able to sell all the rugs you've made?"

"So far."

Nilda smiled. "Good. When you have more in stock, we could talk with several shop owners here who might like to carry them. The same with Rune's skis, since so far he is able to handle all the orders. He said he plans to make some ahead. After all, he can shorten a rough ski easily."

Gunlaug nodded. "He has a pair of shorter and narrower skis for children finished. Leif has been using them. The boys get to school faster on skis in the winter than on Rosie."

"Next time I am home, I hope to sit down and talk with

Rune about the business. The man here in Blackduck whom you brought the skis for is interested in talking with him next time he comes to town. With Ivar and Bjorn there, surely Rune could spend a night or two here. When he does, I will make sure he can meet with some of the competitive skiers. They have all their skis brought from Norway, but now perhaps they will buy from him."

"Life sure can change, can't it?" Gunlaug sat back and shook her head. "So much change."

Telling her mor and Leif good-bye at the railroad station the next day was harder than Nilda thought it would be. After all, they really weren't that far away, it just seemed like it.

She hugged her mor again. "Thank you for coming. And for bringing Leif. I'm sure Kirstin has really been missing him."

"They probably all have been missing him."

They turned to see Leif bidding George farewell and walking toward them with his book under his arm.

"I hoped to finish this before I left but . . ."

"Don't worry. Like Mrs. Schoenleber said, just give it to Mr. Larsson. Or Bjorn and Ivar will be coming for the social next Saturday afternoon. They can bring it back, if you'd like."

As the northbound train steamed and screeched to a halt, she hugged her mor again. "I'll see you in a few weeks."

"Don't make it too long." Gunlaug heaved a sigh. "And here I thought when I moved to America that I would have at least three of my family all in one place. You just never know what God has in store."

"Has Johann shown any interest in moving to America?"

"Not so far."

"Like you always say, we shall see." She passed her mor to the conductor. "Now you know how easy it is to come here. Perhaps you and Knute can come after haying."

"By then we'll be canning."

"Then he might have to come by himself." She stepped back. "Good-bye."

She waved until she could no longer see Leif's face at the window, then turned to walk back to the buggy.

Now to get back to work. After all, she needed to contact smaller schools to see about libraries or lending books. And she had an appointment to meet with Thor Haglund about Blackduck's future. Back to her real world.

Chapter 16

Gunlaug sure felt welcome. She was greeted as warmly as if she'd just arrived from Norway.

"I'm so glad to have you back home." Signe released the hug that had wrapped around her mother-in-law.

Gunlaug nodded. "While we had a wonderful time there, I too am glad to be home." She shook her head. "They wouldn't let me do anything there. I couldn't help in the kitchen or out in the garden, and I didn't learn about the sewing room until just before we left for the train station." She looked down at the tugging on her apron. "You missed me too, didn't you, little one?"

Kirstin answered her, but the only clear word was a new one: *g'ma*.

"Is she saying what I think she is saying?" Gunlaug asked.

Signe smiled. "She calls Gerd that too. G'ma Gerd is out in the garden."

Kirstin ran to the door. "Go." She banged on the screen. "Ef, Ef, Ef."

"He's down at the barn already, checking on his animals." Gunlaug glanced out the kitchen window. "Ah. Here he comes."

As soon as Kirstin saw Leif, she shrieked and, rattling the

whole door, yelled his name at the top of her lungs. Leif pushed in through the screen door. His face said that all his animals were happy.

Signe asked, "Can you take Kirstin with you, Leif? As you can see, she missed you."

"Sure." Grinning, Leif scooped up his little sister and trotted her to the sink, where he pumped a glass of water and downed it, which wasn't easy with Kirstin slapping on his chest and at the glass and doing a fine imitation of a wiggly worm. "You want to go to the barn?" he asked her.

"Go, go, Ef." She turned and, looking at her mother, waved good-bye.

Signe shook her head. "Thank you."

Leif asked, "You need anything from the well house?"

"Please bring up the churn and, if you would, empty the milk cans so we can skim the pans, please." The excess milk went to feed the pigs and chickens, along with the whey from churning butter. Now that the calves were off milk, the other animals got more.

"I'll set more cheese too." Gunlaug walked out the door with Leif and his babbling little sister.

When he set the toddler in the wagon, she banged on the slatted sides and told him something.

"Not now, we have to haul milk," he replied.

"What did she say?"

"She wants to go to the barn and see the pigs."

They had all learned that Leif could understand more of what Kirstin wanted than anyone else could.

"From what your mor told me, Kirstin will be so much happier now that you are home."

Leif frowned. "It wasn't like I was gone a long time."

"No, but when you're that small, it probably seems like forever."

"I still can't believe Mrs. Schoenleber sent a box of books home with me. She wants me to give the ones I've read to Mr. Larsson. So many books, all in one room in one house. I liked just reading all the titles. She said there are libraries with room after room of shelves of books."

Together, they loaded the churn in the wagon, and he pulled it to the back porch. Gunlaug tagged along, partly to help but mostly just to watch this little grandson. Although he wasn't very old yet, he was not a little boy. Gunlaug had learned that in the last few days. He was a mature young man, despite his young age and small stature. After taking the full milk cans down to the barrels for the pigs, he lifted Kirstin out of the wagon.

"See how big they are growing, K? Time to move them into a pen of their own." He now had two pens of growing hogs, one with the older litters, the other for younger pigs, where these would go. He set her on the ground so he and Gunlaug could empty the milk cans. She waddled to the rail fence and squatted down, hanging on to the rail. The little pigs came over to investigate. She touched their round noses, giggling and chattering to them.

Leif scooped her up and set her back in the empty wagon. "I'm going to have to build these frames higher, since you insist on standing up in here. All you need is to take another header over the side."

"Leif, can you come help me pick peas?" Gerd called from the garden.

"Be right there. Come on, K, garden next." Once there, he lifted her out of the wagon and set her in the corner they had fenced for her to play in. A stack of feed sacks cushioned part of it. With a pea pod in each hand, she sat down on the pile.

With Gunlaug, Gerd, and Leif all going down the row, they rapidly filled the oblong, flat-bottomed baskets.

"We have a good crop," Gunlaug observed. Good? It was amazing. She thought briefly of trying to grow peas in the worn-out soil of Norway, nowhere near as productive as this land.

"That we do. Plenty of jars to fill." Gerd nodded toward Kirstin's corner.

"Sound asleep." Leif grinned. "I think this afternoon I'm going to teach her how to go down the porch steps."

"We need a gate so she can be out on the porch," Gerd said. "And you need to split wood, since we'll be running the canner before supper. Knute can stay and help after dinner."

Leif nodded. "That'll make him happy."

Gerd sniggered. "He learned how much you do while you were gone and he had to do it."

"No wonder he was happy to see me."

Signe joined them. "You've done a lot."

Gunlaug waved a hand. "We haven't even started on that row."

Signe smiled. "Let's finish this row and start shelling. The men will be up for dinner in about half an hour."

Bliss. That was what this was. Gunlaug helped pick the bountiful crop. She helped shell the bountiful crop. She helped serve the bountiful dinner to family who laughed and chatted. She was doing! Working! Serving! So much better than having servants. And the bounty . . . oh my!

When they finished eating, Bjorn nudged Knute. "Come on, we'll all split wood for an hour. I bet I can split a bigger pile than you can."

"You're on." Knute elbowed him back. "Leif, you get to stack and keep score."

"Ivar and I will go work in the shop." Rune stretched his arms over his head. "When you're done, Bjorn, you and Knute can take the teams and disk up the land we cleared. Then, after we seed it, we'll all pray for rain."

"We're behind on the number of felled trees we planned on." Ivar drained his coffee cup.

"I know, but gaining more acreage is probably more important in the long run."

Gunlaug listened to her family plan out their goals for the week, her heart brimming with contentment.

Dear Miss Carlson,

Thank you for answering my letter. Life sounds more idyllic there in Blackduck than here in the Cities. I'm sorry my father was rather abrupt in declining to assist in your noble cause of helping those less fortunate in your little town. I understand Blackduck is booming due to the lumber industry, of which our company has a part, but still, in comparison to the Twin Cities . . .

I have been playing tennis as many hours each day as I can, since once I start in the office, evenings will be my only available time, and Mother insists on planning social events at which she would like me to appear. She is not happy with the idea of my being gone for a few days or even a week. I understand your next social is coming up soon. I plan to take the train up on Friday, but I have another event here on the next Wednesday, so will need to leave again on Tuesday. I had hoped to stay there a bit longer, and perhaps I could assist you with planning the program for the loggers' families.

Please, I know my aunt refuses to use the telephone, but I hope you are willing to be part of the progressive ways of communication we have at our disposal. So please telephone me if my plan is not acceptable.

I am looking forward to hearing from you, but more so to seeing you again.

Sincerely,
Jeffrey Schmitz, Esq.

Nilda dropped the paper in her lap. "Esquire. The epitome of pompous." She gave Mrs. Schoenleber her most plaintive look. "Do we have to accept his inviting himself to the social and to stay here for four nights?"

"And two of those nights, Fritz will be here." Mrs. Schoenleber shook her head. "I'm sorry, Nilda, but to keep peace in the family, I think we must accept this." Shaking her head again, she wore a puzzled look.

"What is it?"

"I'm surprised at his sudden interest. Not that you are not a lovely young woman, but when I think of the women he usually shows interest in . . ."

"I am not a society belle, and I never will be." She looked at her employer. "You won't ask that of me, will you?"

"Rest assured that I will not. Those are the very reasons I never moved to Minneapolis after my husband died. I'd had my fill of it growing up, but I was fortunate enough to have a mother who also had no interest in being a society queen. Two of my brothers married into the social set deliberately. One, Jonathon, has never married. I learned that he had loved deeply, but after his beloved passed away before their wedding, he has not shown an interest in marrying. He would rather travel, and that is why he holds the position he does. He is on the train, sometimes on ships, more than he is in Minneapolis. He lives in a hotel, not bothering with a house like the others." She stared at nothing, obviously in her thinking mode. Then she said, "I think I won't warn Fritz, for if I mention Jeffrey is coming, he will most likely choose to remain in Benson's Corner."

"I take it they do not get along?"

"Oh, they are polite, but there is no love lost between the two." She shook her head. "Here I am, dragging up the dirty family laundry. Pardon me, please. We will get through this, and life will be peaceful again."

"Monday we have a meeting with Mr. Thor Haglund. He requested it earlier this week, and while I've mentioned it, I neglected to write it on your calendar." She stared down at her hands. "I'm sorry."

"I see. Hmm." She reached over and patted Nilda's hand. "Don't worry, all will be well. I wonder what he wants."

Saturday morning, Charles brought an envelope to Nilda. "This just arrived for you, Miss Nilda."

"Who was that at the door?"

"The Amundsons' hostler, Mr. Hanson. Mrs. Amundson is rather old-fashioned, you know."

Nilda slit open the envelope and removed a folded card with an elaborate monogram embossed on the front. She read it aloud.

> "'Dear Miss Carlson,
>
> "'I am writing this to invite you and Gertrude to join us for tea at two PM on Tuesday, at my home. A niece of mine is coming to visit, and I am hoping you will help her and Olivia meet more of the younger people in Blackduck society. If this time is not convenient, please feel free to offer an alternate time.
>
> "'Thank you,
>
> "'Mrs. Mathew Amundson'"

Mrs. Schoenleber grunted. "Are we committed to anything that day?"

Nilda checked her calendar. "No. Do you want me to write an acceptance?"

"Please, and George can take it over. I do hope she moves this outside. Her house always seems stuffy."

"We can plead another appointment and leave after a certain period of time."

"I know, but perhaps this niece or the daughter could become a friend for you. At least she can attend the social and meet others, as Bernice suggests."

Nilda studied the calendar. This on Tuesday and Jeffrey on Friday. Uff da, as her mother always said. "I suppose I must telephone Mister Schmitz."

"That would be a good idea. Just get it over with. You are referring to Esquire?"

The two chuckled together at the little joke. Humor always made difficult things easier to tolerate.

Nilda sniffed. "He is probably out on the tennis court."

"Then he can return the call, and you can postpone the chore. But I suggest you pen that note to Bernice first."

"Yes, right now."

She wrote the note, gave it to George, and returned to get the telephone number of the Schmitz house, since she already had all the numbers for the company, not that she used them much. She turned the telephone crank, gave the number to the operator, and waited for a connection.

"Schmitz residence. Who may I say is calling?"

"Miss Nilda Carlson for Mr. Jeffrey Schmitz, please."

"I am sorry, Mr. Jeffrey is not available. Could I please take a message?"

"Yes, tell him that I called and the arrangements he suggested will be just fine."

"Would you like him to return your call?"

"If he must. Thank you."

She set the earpiece back on the hook without a qualm. *That was almost rude,* her inner voice grumbled at her. *No, it* was *rude, and right now I don't much care.* Sometimes her inner arguments surprised even her.

She stuck her head back in the sun-room. "I'm going out to cut flowers before the day heats up even more."

Dusk was creeping over the land when the telephone chimed their number. She rolled her eyes at Mrs. Schoenleber and went to answer it. "Schoenleber residence."

"Could I speak with Miss Carlson, please?"

She was so tempted to say she was not there that she had to bite her lip. "Speaking."

"Oh, you don't sound like you."

She ignored the comment. "Yes, Mr. Schmitz?" She waited.

"Oh. Ah, I'm looking forward to the trip. Is there anything you would like me to bring?"

"Like what?" The words slipped out before she could stop them. Did he think they had no stores here? She sucked in a breath. "Not that I can think of. George will be at the train to meet you. Your aunt and I are looking forward to your visit." Good grief, she was bordering on rude again. Whatever was the matter with her?

"Is your social more formal or casual?"

"Very relaxed. We'll be playing croquet and badminton, Cook will provide a repast, and we usually close with a sing-along with Mr. Larsson on the piano. Sunday morning we attend church." *My, you are getting downright loquacious.* "Oh. I see I am needed. Thank you for calling."

"No, I—ah—thank you for calling. Good-bye."

She dusted her hands together after replacing the earpiece. If only she could deal with him as abruptly in person.

Mrs. Schoenleber smirked. "You should be honored he is paying attention to you."

"That might be what he thinks." She sank into a chair. "I don't even like me right now. I was rude. Abrupt."

"Nilda, look at me. You were businesslike, and that is acceptable. I have a feeling, though, that the more you put him off, the more determined he will be to pursue you."

"Perhaps we can encourage him to spend time with Mrs. Amundson's niece. She is from a wealthy background too. Isn't she a socialite?"

"Yes, from someplace back east. I think her father or mother insisted she spend time here with her aunt."

"The plot thickens. Can we stir things up a bit?"

"Why, Nilda Carlson, you astound me." Mrs. Schoenleber pretended to be fluttering a fan.

Monday rolled around even faster because Nilda spent most of the days in between researching purchasing books for the school libraries and writing letters for the Assist Blackduck Project, as she had taken to calling it. They now had the land, and her list of donors was growing, albeit slowly. She stared out the window. Perhaps she could talk Jeffrey into contributing sufficiently for the materials for one house if she agreed to name it after him. The Jeffrey Schmitz House. *Put names on all the houses.* She jotted down a note to remind herself.

"Dinner is served, miss."

"Thank you, Charles, I'll be right there." She stopped to wash her hands on the way and paused when she entered the dining room. "Why, Mr. Haglund, I . . ."

"I asked Gertrude if I could join you for dinner, as my cook is not feeling well and I told her to take a few days off to get better." He rose as he spoke and came around the table to seat her. "Please don't be offended."

"I am certainly not offended, sir. I'm just sorry I didn't think of it when you asked for a meeting with us. Thank you." She smiled up at him. "I'm glad you are here." She knew she was not just being polite. While she'd heard that Mr. Haglund was basically a recluse, she wondered what his story was. Everyone in this town seemed to have some mysterious story.

The conversation was relaxed and pleasant as they finished their meal and adjourned to the verandah for coffee and dessert.

"Ah, so much better than what my housekeeper would put on the table." Mr. Haglund inhaled and breathed out gently. "Whenever I come here, I feel the worries sloughing off and peace taking their place. So let's talk about why I requested this meeting." He leaned forward, elbows on his knees and hands relaxed. "I've been thinking about what you are trying to do to help make Blackduck a better place to live. I believe that since the growth of Blackduck is due to logging, those of us who have benefited from the industry need to step up and pay something back. Folks helped me when I was new, and now I have the wherewithal to help others."

Nilda smiled. "I too am an immigrant, of course, a very recent one, who would not be here were it not for relatives who needed help."

"You set my mind to thinking about these things. And for that I will always be grateful." His smile made her feel warm all over. "My ten-acre parcel is just off Morris Avenue on the edge of town. I assume the houses should be rented, as we have said, with the residents being encouraged to purchase the home and settle here. Some loggers will move on to where there are still trees to cut, but I hope some will want to live here. They are industrious people. We need industrious people. And we need to have places for people to work. I have some ideas for that too."

"You're full of ideas today, Thor. What a pleasure to hear you." Mrs. Schoenleber poured him another cup of coffee.

He leaned against the back of his wrought-iron chair. "How about we drive out and see exactly what we're talking about? I am having the deed drawn up, but at this point, who is in charge?" He looked to Nilda. "You and Reverend Holtschmidt, is that correct?"

Nilda smiled. "Yes, although until right now, there was nothing to be in charge of. We have a list of people who have agreed to donate a certain amount, and thanks to you, we can spend the money on housing instead of land. Mrs. Schoenleber and I talked about hiring lumberjacks in the off-season and letting their labor count toward their house, so many dollars per day."

Mr. Haglund nodded, smiling. "I was thinking that as well. So they need to be recruited and organized, with someone overseeing the clearing of the land, measuring the plots, and running the construction crews. Would you mind if I took on part of that load? I haven't forgotten how to work and how to make others work."

Nilda and Mrs. Schoenleber stared at each other, then at him. "Are you serious?"

"You doubt me?" He looked ten years younger. "Gertrude, let's you and I meet with Ellis Carnes tomorrow. I will write up some ideas tonight and bring them along. But right now, you get George to harness up that team, and we'll go visit the site of future houses." He smiled at Nilda. "I never have been a patient man. When I get an idea, I want to get to work on it."

"I can see that." Nilda stood up and took the arm he held out to her. "Thank you, kind sir."

"I don't know about the *kind* part, but right now I think you've given me a new lease on life. And for that, I am grateful." He patted the hand tucked around his arm.

Nilda swallowed and sniffed. *But I didn't really do anything. He came to us with the ideas. All I've wanted is to help some of those less fortunate. And to make Blackduck an even better place to live.*

He helped Mrs. Schoenleber and then Nilda into the victoria before climbing in himself. "Thank you, George. Just go north on Main Street, and I'll tell you where to go. Should we stop by the bank and kidnap Mathew Amundson? He will have some good suggestions, I'm sure."

"If you wish. Good thing George brought the larger carriage."

They waited outside the bank while Mr. Haglund went striding in, and in a few minutes, came striding out with Mr. Amundson in tow.

"Did you send this crazy man in to fetch me?" the banker asked Mrs. Schoenleber as he settled into the seat across from her.

She raised her hands. "I'm innocent. This was all his idea."

"Well, if I am to be a part of this, I'd like at least to have a general idea of what is going on."

Mrs. Schoenleber nodded toward Nilda, so she explained. "You know that since the dinner meeting at our house, I've been collecting pledges from people that will be due when we are ready to start building. Mr. Haglund came to dinner today, and we are going to examine the piece of land that he will donate."

"It's unencumbered, right? You own the title free and clear?"

"Now, why would I try to give something away that I didn't own?" Mr. Haglund adopted a pained expression.

Nilda bit back a giggle by clearing her throat.

The carriage rolled through town and out a rutted backstreet.

Nilda explained, "According to the plan, we will have half-acre lots so that the people could have a garden, maybe a small barn or shed for chickens and a cow. So they can feed their families."

"That is some good thinking." Mr. Haglund nodded. "Very

good. We'll need space for streets, of course, possibly a community well." He leaned forward. "Right up there on the left; stop here, George."

They sat in the carriage and stared at the woodland beside them. Maple trees, a few young pines, birch, and tall beech, with lots of brush covering the ground. Birds must have been nesting all over. *Listen to their music!*

"It would be nice if we could leave those deciduous trees and build around them, the maples especially," Mr. Haglund mused.

Mr. Amundson was nodding. "Have you had it surveyed?"

"An old survey, but I'll have them plat it out into lots. We'll need to clear roads. That'll cut into the lot sizes."

Mr. Amundson sat back. "You know, we're going to have to cajole the town council into improving this road. It would be nice if they would grade the streets, but we may have to do that ourselves. It will add to the cost."

"Perhaps we could put the houses closer together, maybe in pairs," Nilda suggested. "It would be a better use of the land."

"Miss Carlson has a good thought. Leave enough land for gardens, maybe a barn, but build them close together." Mrs. Schoenleber scowled. "You said a community well. Has anyone dowsed this parcel yet?"

"Not yet," Mr. Haglund replied. "And where the well is situated will affect the whole plat."

"Who's going to build these houses?" Mr. Amundson asked.

"A crew of temporarily out-of-work loggers and me."

"You! But you're an old man."

Mr. Haglund's eyes turned steely. "Be careful how you talk. You might have to eat your words."

"Sorry, that slipped out, but . . ." Mr. Amundson wisely shut up.

Nilda suppressed a snicker. She noticed that Mrs. Schoenleber appeared amused too.

Mr. Haglund bobbed his head. "We will be in your office tomorrow morning to sign the paperwork, so we'd best get on it."

"I can't have it all ready by then. It's closing time as is. My secretary has already left."

"Very well. Day after tomorrow. But I want to get going on this. Winter will be here before we know it." Mr. Haglund sat back in his seat with a happy smile on his face.

They dropped Mr. Amundson off at the bank, and George set the team to a smart trot back home.

"I think I'll go talk to Mueller at the lumberyard," Mr. Haglund said. "You said he had plans that could be used."

"But first the land will have to be cleared." Mrs. Schoenleber echoed Nilda's thoughts.

"I know. I'll have the surveyor stake out both the lots and the houses. That way we can clear it down to the dirt where the houses will be. I'll talk to him about foundations too." He stepped out and helped the ladies down. "Thank you for a most exciting day." He turned to George. "Drop me off at the lumberyard, and I'll call my driver to come pick me up."

"I can wait for you, if you like, and take you home."

"It might be quite a while, but thank you."

George frowned. "Mr. Haglund, I don't want to butt in, but are you certain? I mean, you'll be taking on quite a lot, and . . ."

Mr. Haglund clapped him on the upper arm. "Thank you for being concerned, but I feel like I'm starting a whole new life. This might be the best thing to have happened to me in ages." He climbed back up in the victoria. "Let's get over there before Mueller closes the gates."

Nilda watched them leave from the front entry. Mr. Haglund felt he'd received a new life. She felt like she'd been caught up by a cyclone and was still spinning.

Chapter 17

They signed the paperwork the moment it was ready. There was Nilda's signature under Reverend Holtschmidt's, as if she, a simple immigrant farm girl, were in the same social circle as these august men, community leaders. And yet, in a way, she was. She thought about Jeffrey's single-minded attention to social status. She liked *this* status, earned by hard work, much more.

"The surveyors will be out there tomorrow, and Mueller and I are arguing over the house designs, so I will bring copies of the two we like best over for you to make the final decision." Mr. Haglund looked right at Nilda.

"Ah, the reverend is truly in charge of this project."

"But you are making remarkably accurate estimations," Mrs. Schoenleber said. "We will all be making these decisions, or rather all of us and Mathew at the bank, but you should be the spokesperson, since this whole thing is really your idea."

But I'm too young and inexperienced for such a role.

You have wise counselors in these three, so do not be afraid. The voices in her head often did nothing more than cause confusion.

"But I have no money to work with here," Nilda protested. "You are the people with the money."

"And we are trusting you to use it wisely." Mr. Haglund smiled at her, his face livelier than she had ever seen. Not that she'd seen him that often, but that day of the first meeting, he'd seemed like more of a recluse or someone who felt used up and no longer useful.

When Nilda and Mrs. Schoenleber returned home, Cook sent out tea, and they took it in the library, where Nilda's desk was split in half—one side for the housing project and the other for books for school libraries. The typewriter sat on the low stand George had built for it, so all Nilda had to do was turn her chair and she could begin typing—something at which she was gaining proficiency, just like she was at the piano. She practiced faithfully on both every day.

Nilda said, "I have spoken with the head of Blackduck School and have asked that he and Fritz compile a list of books he thinks should be available."

Mrs. Schoenleber sipped from her teacup, holding the saucer in her other hand. "I've been thinking. Since you are the one who uses the telephone the most, ours should be in here for you. I believe there are telephones on every desk at the head office in Minneapolis—new ones that don't require winding a crank like the one in the hall. Please look into that, and we will put one here in your office as soon as possible. I do fear, however, that if my brothers learn of this, my limited accessibility will be a thing of the past. Letters will no longer suffice."

Nilda dunked her cookie in her tea. They were better dunked in coffee, but she never mentioned that. It would be just one more thing for Cook to see to. "You remember we are committed to join Mrs. Amundson for tea this afternoon."

"Would that I could forget. On another subject, can you

believe the change in Thor Haglund? He figures he is having the time of his life, and I tend to agree. Why, he rolled right over Mathew's objections this morning. And since between the two of us we might own a good portion of the bank's assets, Mathew felt a mite out-voted." Mrs. Schoenleber tipped her head back, still nodding. "I think this might be very good for Mathew, not being in control for a change."

"The mail is here," George announced from the doorway. Mrs. Schoenleber motioned him in.

As Nilda leafed through the little clutch of letters, Mrs. Schoenleber asked George, "I am thinking of taking Bernice a bouquet this afternoon. What flowers do you not mind parting with?"

"We still have some roses. The peonies are showing color, but I think it's too early to cut them. Most of the annuals aren't blooming yet, so all we have right now are daisies."

"Let's do what roses we have and use daisies as fillers. Put them in a bucket, and then Nilda can arrange them in a vase just before we leave."

"That won't leave much for the house here, madam."

"What we have should suffice until the peonies are ready."

"As you say."

Nilda knew that any time George became formal, it meant he was not pleased with the situation. She laughed inside, which was difficult to keep off her face. She made herself read the page in her lap so he would not recognize the mirth in her eyes. He was a very perceptive man.

"I could have cut them," she reminded Mrs. Schoenleber.

"I know, but we are busy here, and we should have had them cut early this morning. They won't last as long now."

"Why are you taking her flowers, anyway?"

Mrs. Schoenleber pondered a long moment. "Because I don't like her very much."

Nilda blinked and made a questioning face. "Does she know you don't much care for her? I'm sorry, but I am now thoroughly confused."

Mrs. Schoenleber sat up straighter, if that were possible, and huffed a sigh. "Let's just say it makes me feel better."

Nilda started to say something but rolled her eyes instead. She pulled her calendar book out from under some papers. "All right, we have the tea this afternoon and Mr. Haglund is coming for supper. I plan to work in here all Wednesday and Thursday, then Mr. Schmitz arrives on Friday, and the social is in the afternoon and evening of Saturday. Fritz said he would beg out of playing the organ on Sunday or leave at the crack of dawn—well, not quite, but in time to get ready for church on Sunday."

So instead of enjoyable time with Fritz and Ivar and Bjorn, I will be entertaining His Highness. She'd not referred to him that way with his aunt, and she clamped her teeth shut. While she'd not said anything, she might have been thinking loudly. And as Miss Walstead often said, *"Sarcasm does not become you."*

"Thank you in advance for Jeffrey's visit," Mrs. Schoenleber said. "As you already know, he can be charming, so perhaps you will find yourself having a good time. And perhaps on Monday we can show him what is happening on the housing issue. By the way, perhaps you might steer the niece today in the direction of the Young Ladies of Blackduck group, or the YLB, I think they're calling themselves. Miss Lucinda might find some friends there."

After dinner, they both went up to their rooms to lie down for a bit and then get dressed to go visiting. They met downstairs at the appointed time, Nilda arranged the flowers in the vase with very little water, and after George helped them into the buggy, Charles set the vase of flowers on Nilda's lap.

"Don't worry. Unless we hit a deep pothole, I will be fine." Nilda tipped her head down to sniff the roses. "So lovely. Thank you, George, for cutting them." She looked up at George, who was now on the driver's seat. "And thank you for growing them and maintaining a yard that makes others jealous."

He grinned over his shoulder. "Thank you, miss."

Mrs. Schoenleber smirked. "Bernice tried to entice George away from my employ a couple of years ago. She has a hard time finding and keeping good help."

"And George has been with you how many years?"

"Since we moved into this house, I believe. Let's see . . . George, when did you come to work for us?"

"Must be fifteen years now. I know, it was summer of '95. They'd finished building the house, carriage house, and stables that spring, and the family had just moved in."

"We'd lived there a little over a year when the accident happened. I was recovering from some malady, or I would have been with them." Mrs. Schoenleber stared down at her lace-gloved hands. "For a long time, I wished I had been."

Nilda reached over and covered her employer's hands. "Would you rather not go to this tea? I can go alone and make your apologies."

Mrs. Schoenleber forced a smile to her lips and patted Nilda's hand. "No, I will attend. I promised myself and Jane that I would no longer dwell on the past, on what might have been. God has given me many years now, and then you and your family, to make a difference in people's lives. I believe I am where He wants me, and He has impressed upon me that with wealth comes not only possibilities but responsibilities to use the money wisely and for His glory. And you will help me do that."

"Would you like me to go around the block again?" George asked.

"Thank you, George, but no. And, by the way, I did realize what you were doing."

"As you say, madam." He touched the brim of his hat.

"Help me down first, and then I will hold the flowers." Mrs. Schoenleber made sure she had her reticule over her arm and stepped regally down to the graveled drive. "Two hours, unless I call to make it earlier."

"Yes, madam, I will be here. Do you have any errands to run in the meantime?"

"Ask Cook. Oh, and there is mail to send out."

George handed Mrs. Schoenleber the flowers and helped Nilda down. "Just be your sweet self, and they will be smitten."

"Thank you. How did you know?"

He shrugged. "Good guess."

She shook her head and took the flowers back. "Onward." Pasting a smile on her face, she joined Mrs. Schoenleber and walked to the door, where a maid ushered them in. Stuffy air met them at the door.

"Madam is in the parlor."

"Looks like outside is not an option," Nilda whispered as the maid walked ahead to announce them.

"More's the pity. Good thing we brought our fans."

"Gertrude, so good to see you. And Miss Carlson." Mrs. Amundson held out her hand to greet them without rising, which made Nilda wonder if she was ill. She motioned to the young women sitting on the sofa. "You know my daughter, Olivia."

Nilda handed her the flowers. "It's good to see you again. I'm happy to know you are joining us on Saturday."

"I wouldn't miss it." Olivia had the worn look of a daughter who was at her mother's beck and call.

Mrs. Amundson continued the introductions. "And my niece,

Lucinda, who is visiting us for part of the summer before she joins her family in France."

Nilda nodded. "Glad to meet you, Lucinda. I hope you aren't too bored with a stay in our little town."

"Oh, I am pleased to be here and not in the heat and humidity of the Cities. Aunt Bernice is most gracious. The last time I was here, Olivia and I managed to get into a few scrapes, but they let me return."

Curiosity dug in, like a gopher burrowing a hole. Now that, Nilda would like to hear about. "Well, welcome to Blackduck. I have some ideas of things you can do while you're here."

They sat down at Mrs. Amundson's request. Nilda followed Mrs. Schoenleber's actions and opened the fan dangling from a ribbon on her wrist. Why weren't the windows open, at least? Surely there was a cross breeze to help alleviate the humidity. She glanced up. There was a ceiling fan, but where was the switch? How did one tactfully ask if they may turn on the fan? She could feel a drop of sweat trickling down her spine.

"How long have you been in this country?" Lucinda asked.

"Just over a year. How time flies."

"Did you speak English while you lived in . . . Norway, wasn't it?" Lucinda looked to her aunt, who nodded.

"No. My older brother kept writing and telling us to learn English, so we found a man who emigrated but then returned to Norway. Now, of course, I wish I had worked harder at it, but thanks to the accelerated teaching I have had with Miss Walstead after beginning with Mr. Larsson in Benson's Corner, I am adequate now."

Lucinda replied, "I started learning French when my mother would take us back there to visit her family."

"You are fortunate. I've heard that children learn much faster than adults. I'm convinced now that being put in a position where one is not allowed to use their mother tongue but only the new language is the fastest way to learn." She smiled at Mrs. Schoenleber.

"That is what I made her do in order to work for me," Mrs. Schoenleber explained.

Lucinda nodded.

"I would say you are more than adequate," Olivia chimed in. "At the socials, I had no idea you had not been here for years and years." She turned to Lucinda. "We will attend the next one on Saturday. You will meet many new friends there."

"I hear there is a handsome young man attending too," Lucinda said, her eyes twinkling.

"Actually, several." Nilda leaned forward a bit, the better to let what air there was cool her. "They have to pass a handsome test in order to be invited." Now, where had that come from?

Both Olivia and Lucinda giggled and then broke into laughter. The proverbial ice melted, and Nilda felt herself relax. Perhaps this tea wouldn't be such a bad thing after all.

The tea was served in the dining room, and after fixing her plate and cup, she asked, "Wouldn't it be cooler outside on your verandah?"

"Well, I suppose it might," Olivia replied. She pushed open the door, and sure enough, there was shade on their table and chairs. "Mother doesn't like the bugs." But the three girls seated themselves and enjoyed the repast, all the while getting to know each other better.

"Have you heard about the group that recently formed called the YLB?" Nilda asked.

Olivia nodded slowly. "I think so. Young Ladies of Blackduck, right?"

"Yes, they formed to start a true library here in Blackduck. They began with a lending library that sends out a box of books to different towns that request them. I think that is what gave them the idea. I thought it might be a good place to make some friends and help the community at the same time."

"Are you going to take part, Nilda?"

"I don't know. I'm working on getting libraries, or at least shelves of books, in the local schools."

"Is this related to that Andrew Carnegie who builds libraries in different towns? I've been to one in Minneapolis. Anyone can go there and check out books." Lucinda helped herself to another triangular open-faced sandwich. "These are really good."

"There is one in Bemidji, right near the lake." Olivia added, "I think I will talk with the woman in charge. There was an article in the newspaper about the YLB. Thank you, Nilda."

Nilda nodded. "How long will you be staying here, Lucinda?"

"At least three weeks."

"But we might be able to keep her longer." Olivia crumbled a cookie on her plate. "Do you know if Petter will be there? He was seeing June until her family moved away earlier this month."

"Oh, I thought that was becoming serious." Nilda turned to Lucinda. "I met Petter on the ship from New York to Duluth when my brother Ivar and I came to America. We became good friends. He works at the lumberyard and came out to our farm to help us build a new house. He and a whole lot of people from around Benson's Corner."

"People still really do that? I read in a history book about barn raisings."

Nilda nodded. "That's how we got to know our neighbors."

"You mean people you didn't even know came to help?"

"We were surprised too."

Mrs. Schoenleber came to the door. "Nilda, George is here."

"Thank you." Nilda stood. "I need to go, but I will see you both on Saturday? Dress casually, as we'll be playing croquet and badminton outside. And if you find out anything about the YLB, tell us all at the social."

Olivia nodded and stood. "This has been delightful. Thank you for coming."

They said their good-byes, and Nilda and Mrs. Schoenleber adjourned to the buggy. Once they were settled, Mrs. Schoenleber smiled at Nilda. "It sounded to me like you young ladies hit it off well."

"We did, to my surprise. Olivia seemed a whole different woman than she is at the socials. I wonder why. How did you get on with Mrs. Amundson?"

"I would have much preferred being out with you girls."

"That bad?"

"Yes."

"I'm sorry."

"That's all right. We did our social obligation, and I learned that Olivia is her youngest child. There were four children, but one died in infancy and one simply left home. Her eldest, a son who is married and lives in Chicago, has three children, but she never sees him, hardly hears from him, and so all her focus is on finding a good husband for Olivia. Preferably a wealthy husband, as you can guess."

"Well, I think Olivia wants to do something besides be with her mother. She asked about Petter and said that the young woman he was interested in has moved away. I think Olivia would like to take her place."

"I see. And Lucinda?"

"She goes to the library in Minneapolis. Something makes me think her mother might be on the library board or some such. What do you know about the Carnegie libraries?"

"I know Blackduck is too small for one. There is one in Bemidji, but I have never been there."

"This makes me believe we are really on the right track. I don't know if the YLB plan to carry books for children in their library too. If they do, perhaps we could donate some boxes there as well."

"Perhaps we could."

"I've been thinking." Nilda looked up to see a smile on Mrs. Schoenleber's face. "What?"

"I've been thinking too. Jane and I are so proud of you. God sent me a great gift when you spent the night in my house on your way to your relatives' farm." She paused. "Now, what were you thinking?"

"Back to the immigrant question, learning to speak English is vitally important. What if Jane were to teach English to the immigrants here in Blackduck? I would be glad to help her."

"I like that. Go ahead and ask her."

"Something else."

"Yes?"

"That Detective Galt. Is there any way we can make sure he does not return? He makes me feel dirty. Dreng was bad enough, and now this."

"Sometimes, Nilda, we bear burdens that cannot be lifted."

Chapter 18

No, I won't pick one."

Nilda tried to look stern but knew she'd failed when Mr. Haglund laughed and shook his head again. "You have to choose."

They had finished supper in Mrs. Schoenleber's main dining room, the table was cleared, and now the schematics for several different house plans were spread out and weighted at the corners so that the table looked like it was covered with a new kind of cloth.

Nilda had studied the plans and asked plenty of questions, to which Thor often said, "These are general ideas. Things can still be changed."

"Do they all have to be alike?" she asked. "Why can't we do some of each?"

"Why not?"

"I wish we could put indoor plumbing in them. I've gotten spoiled living here. Going back to having an outhouse would be hard, especially in the winter." She studied the drawings, trying to picture families living there. Each house consisted of a large room that included the kitchen, then two bedrooms off of it. A cooking range would provide the heat. Two windows in the front wall, one in each bedroom, one in the kitchen. "They will be wired for electricity?"

"Yes, and will have free power until the lumber season is finished and the men get paid. That will be Beltrami Lights and Telephone's contribution."

"Then the big difference is that some will have an open loft. Actually, they could all have that, so older children could sleep up there."

"True."

"Some have a larger front porch and some a larger back porch, but both could be the same size too."

"I have eight men who could be ready to start clearing the house sites tomorrow, but the surveyors are not finished yet."

"And you think it will take how long to get ready to start on the first one?"

"Probably a week to get two plots cleared and supplies delivered. I'm sure once the word gets out, I will have more volunteers than I know what to do with. I'm thinking we can raise two at a time; that would be four men on each house."

"And if you had more men who wanted to work? Or volunteers who just want to help?"

"I figured we would clear four house sites, start building two. Others could then clear more sites, so they are always two ahead of the building crew. The surveyors will leave stakes for markers, and we can string line from one to the other. I'll get those houses built, but you'll need to find the money to pay for the materials. I will put pressure on those I know well, but we will not build more than the first four houses until they are paid for. Mathew and I agreed on that."

Nilda nodded. "I understand, and I am impressed. What kind of agreement are you setting up with the men working with you?"

"Mathew and I talked about that. One plan is to keep track

of the hours they work, decide on a wage, then put that total against either the rent of the house or the purchase of it. After we finish the first couple of houses, we'll know the exact costs."

"I see. So who will be the bookkeeper?"

"I don't have the answer to that yet. But at the end of the day, we can write down how many hours each man worked."

"Basically, these men will be working for the future, but they have to eat and have a place to sleep each night." Nilda looked at him.

Mrs. Schoenleber broke her long silence. "I will take care of providing one meal, and Isabella Schwartz will provide a meal. And her barn, as we discussed. Has she said anything since that meeting?"

Mr. Haglund smiled at her. "Very little, other than complaining to Mathew, but she can be convinced. Perhaps a box lunch at noon would not deplete her accounts too much."

Nilda almost giggled.

Mr. Haglund did indeed seem ten years younger. He almost bounced with enthusiasm. "We'll be working dawn to dark with the goal of moving some of the families with children in before school starts. As soon as the first two houses are roofed, the men could sleep on the floors there."

Nilda nodded. "And move to the next houses as needed."

She fell asleep that night with numbers running through her head and wondering how she could get the folks of Blackduck to agree to support the program.

She woke up knowing that the first thing she needed was the total cost of materials for each house, down to the nails and the screws. The big question was how this was benefiting Blackduck, other than as an altruistic gesture. Right now, canning string beans sounded a lot easier than what she was trying to do.

That thought made her want to go back to the farm. The

work was hard there, but the reward of having food through the winter was sufficient. As families moved into these houses, how were they going to pay for food? The men would be fed in the logging camps, but the women and children needed to eat here, have wood for their fires, and warm clothing.

She brought her questions up at the breakfast table.

Mrs. Schoenleber nodded. "As to food, I can talk with Homer and tell him to run a tab for each family, and if any renege on their bill, I will pay it. That takes the financial pressure off him."

Nilda frowned. "Who is Homer? Have I met him?"

"Homer Blanding owns the largest grocery store in town, the one that's open all year. I don't believe you've met him yet, but you will."

Yet another important local personage. Did Mrs. Schoenleber know every single businessman in Blackduck? It was beginning to look that way.

Nilda mused, "There are plenty of downed trees to be cut up where they have been cleared, but how to get firewood to their houses? That wood will still be wet this winter."

"Wet?" Mrs. Schoenleber frowned.

"Still green with a lot of moisture. Wet wood does not give off as much heat as dry, seasoned wood."

Mrs. Schoenleber stared at Nilda, a slight smile playing about her mouth. "Most young women your age would not come up with these things. I think we are all learning how brilliant you really are."

"That's not brilliant. We had to make do with so little all our lives in Norway that we learned to stretch every penny until it screamed, and then stretch it more. Here on Uncle's farm, we had real meat and food all winter, not just porridge—and if the winter in Norway was brutal, some porridges were weaker than others. I know what it is like to go to bed hungry and wake up still hungrier. Mor and Far did their very best, working at anything they could set their hands to in the hopes of bringing in a few *kroner*." She paused and sucked in a breath. "And I *never* want to do that again! Now I have an opportunity to help keep it from happening to people who come here for work. A roof over their heads, food for their bellies, and clothing warm enough to get through a Minnesota winter."

Mrs. Schoenleber was studying her. "I am beginning to see a side of you, and of all of your family, that I had not realized. Fascinating."

"The first year my family was here, Knute put snares out for rabbits. They ate a lot of rabbit, Signe said. Bjorn shot a couple deer and some ducks and geese. He loves to hunt. Knute would go fishing, another way to help feed the family. On a farm, you have milk from the cow and eggs from the chickens, but then you need feed for them too. The boys, even Leif, work hard, and they do it willingly, because they know what it's like to lack food."

"I know too. I grew up on a farm until my father started making money by cutting railroad ties. The railroads were moving west. New lines were starting and old lines consolidating. It was a booming market for railroad ties. He knew not only how to make money but how to use that money to make more. He built a company earning millions and passed that on to my brothers and me. We have helped it grow beyond his wildest imagination. But he also knew the importance of investing part of that money into people who need some assistance. He so believed the Lord's command to love your neighbor as yourself. That is what I grew up on."

"That's beautiful." Nilda had known some of this about her employer's life, but this made it so much clearer.

Mrs. Schoenleber continued, "And I plan to carry on the tradition he established of assisting others. My brothers have lost sight of that larger goal, so perhaps having Jeffrey here will bring home that lesson again." She called in George. "I plan to make some social calls today, so could you please have the buggy ready by ten?"

"Of course. Anything else?"

"You will be meeting my nephew Jeffrey at the train station at four. He will be our guest for several days."

George looked at Nilda. "Will you be going with me, Miss Nilda?"

She shook her head and smiled. "No one met us at the train in St. Paul, and there is no chance of him getting lost at this station." She thought of the monstrous train station in the city, with all the rail lines coming in and all the huge doorways leading out. She was grateful she'd been with Mrs. Schoenleber, who had plenty of experience with train stations—especially that station.

After Mrs. Schoenleber left, the house was quiet but for Nilda tapping the typewriter keys. In her practice every morning, she pushed for speed. During the day she worked for accuracy. When she could finally pull a perfect sheet of paper out of the machine, she felt like celebrating. She signed each letter and set aside the ones needing Mrs. Schoenleber's signature also. After typing the addresses on the envelopes, she applied the stamps and set them in a basket, ready for George to mail.

Charles rapped on the library door and stuck his head in. "Are you about ready for tea, Miss Nilda?"

"I'd rather have coffee, if that's all right. And thank you. You read my mind."

"Actually, Cook is the mind reader around here. I will be right back."

She began a letter to Clara Baldwin, who organized the practice of sending boxes of books to places that requested them and had become head of the State Public Library Commission.

After another tap on the door, Charles carried in a tray with not only a cup for coffee but a pot covered in a padded tea cozy. Along with a plate of cookies.

Nilda smiled and put her work aside. “Tell Cook thank you for me, please.”

Charles poured her a cup of coffee and left the room. Nilda settled back in her chair, elbows on the arms, and held her cup with both hands, the better to sip it. She had typed up all the notes about their housing venture so she wouldn’t forget anything. Now to bring it before the general public. Perhaps an article in the newspaper along with an advertisement, possibly a whole page. But was it time for that, or should they send a letter to every organization in Blackduck? But how to get such a list? Who might have one? She would ask the editor of the weekly newspaper, the Blackduck *American*. And was it time to include other towns, especially Bemidji, in her search for donations? She dunked a ginger cookie in her coffee.

Mrs. Schoenleber was planning to talk to the pastors of the local churches regarding feeding the men building the houses. Might they be wise to host dinners or suppers at this house to get other people involved? *Lord, help me, I have no idea what I am doing. And thank you for Thor Haglund and Mrs. Schoenleber, who care about helping those less fortunate.*

She dunked another cookie and refreshed her cup. The verse she had read about Queen Esther rolled through her mind. *“For such a time as this.” Lord, did you put me here for such a time as this, to help others who come from Norway and other countries so they can feed their families and make a new home here?* She resolved to go back and read Esther’s story again. God had trained Esther. Had He set Mrs. Schoenleber to train Nilda Carlson? Was this something she wanted to talk over with Miss Walstead and Mrs. Schoenleber? She knew God used ordinary people. The whole Bible was full of them. He even used donkeys and other creatures to get His points across.

She drained her coffee cup, set the tray off to the side, and got back to typing and making lists and searching for answers.

Mrs. Schoenleber returned in time for dinner, albeit a bit later than usual. She unpinned her hat and, after using the powder room, joined Nilda in the dining room.

"Need I bring my notebook?" Nilda asked.

"No, let's just eat and talk." She smiled up at Charles as he pulled out her chair.

"Please ask Cook to come in here for a moment."

Charles seated Nilda and then returned to the kitchen, returning shortly with Mrs. Solvang in tow.

"Verna, I apologize for returning late. I know how you like to serve dinner right at noon when you have it ready, so please accept my apology."

Cook rolled her eyes. "Well, thank you, but I had an idea today might go like this, so nothing was ruined by waiting awhile."

Mrs. Schoenleber shook her head. "I would be so lost without you. Thank you."

"You are welcome." Cook smiled back. "You have no idea how grateful I am to work here. Who could dream my life would be like this? You too, Miss Nilda. I am so pleased you have become part of this family." She sniffed and puffed a breath. "Now, can I get you anything else?"

"Only a reminder. Jeffrey will be here for supper and is staying until after breakfast on Tuesday. He'll return home on the morning train."

"I wonder if sauerbraten is still his favorite. I made it for him anyway, so we shall see." Cook returned to the kitchen, humming.

Mrs. Schoenleber nodded. "Anytime Verna is humming, you know all is right in this world. Let's have grace."

After dinner they adjourned to Nilda's office, where Mrs. Schoenleber gave her a list of what she had accomplished. She had commissioned the cook at Grandview Hotel to deliver sandwiches, coffee, and a dessert to the men at noon every day for a month with the possibility of continuing if all worked out well. The Catholic church would serve breakfast at daylight. The Presbyterian church would serve a big kettle of soup or stew, with bread, for two weeks, to be continued if it worked well. "I will shoulder the cost of food and try to coerce Isabella into sharing it. She's rather tight with her money," Mrs. Schoenleber confided.

Nilda felt good. "So the workmen are fed and housed. That is the biggest thing."

"Miles—that is, Mr. Goddard is special-ordering enough hardware to furnish four houses. And that is as far as I got. Next I will be asking for financial contributions. I suggest we target a group for each house. They will know they are donating for house one and so on. But first we need to know the exact amount needed. A thought that just came in—what if that same organization or someone else were to assist that house's family through the winter?"

Nilda nodded. "You are amazing. So much in one morning's calls. I think personal contact might make this work better."

From the doorway, Charles announced, "Miss Walstead is here."

"Oh good. Come into the war room, Jane."

They explained what had happened so far and watched her nod and make notes.

"I believe people like to help more when they know exactly what is needed and how long the need is going to last," Miss Walstead finally said. "I think the house-raising story that Nilda told us is a good case in point. The people who could give more time kept on until the house was finished, even after the family had moved in. I have read many stories of house and barn raisings as people have moved west. Communities pull together to help those in need if they know what the need is. Why should our community be any different?"

Charles tapped on the door with another announcement. "George is going to the station to pick up Mr. Jeffrey."

"Thank you, Charles."

"Oh my." Nilda looked down at her gingham dress. "Do I need to change?"

"How much do you want to impress him?" Mrs. Schoenleber asked.

"Why do I need to impress him?"

"There's your answer right there. You look very nice, but not the fashionable young woman he might be used to." Miss Walstead smiled.

"I believe you are the reason he is coming here," Mrs. Schoenleber repeated.

Nilda frowned. "I didn't invite him."

"No, he invited himself. I think his father wants to know what is really going on up here, so he is sending Jeffrey."

Miss Walstead shook her head. "My, my, Gertrude, but you have a suspicious mind. What if he thinks he has fallen in love with our Nilda and wants to court her?"

Nilda burst out laughing. "Jeffrey? All he wants to do is play tennis and go to whatever social function his mother says he must. His father says he has to finish college and work in the family firm, so he will do that."

Mrs. Schoenleber turned serious. "Don't underestimate Jeffrey. He has a good mind, always has, and he might have learned to use it. He can be crafty and decidedly uncharming when he wants something."

"I'll go freshen up anyway." Nilda left her desk the way it was and climbed the stairs.

Gilda met her at the top of the stairs. "I have another dress ready for you if you want to change."

"Do you think I should?"

"This blue of the dimity matches your eyes. I'll do your hair a bit fancier, add a spritz of lavender toilet water, and you would catch any man's eye, not just Mr. Jeffrey's."

Nilda was just descending the stairs when Charles brought Jeffrey in the front door.

He gazed up at her, and a smile burst across his face. "Miss Carlson, I do believe you grow lovelier every time I see you."

"Why, thank you, Mr. Schmitz. Welcome to Blackduck. Charles can show you to your room, and we will have refreshments out on the verandah when you join us. You have met Miss Walstead, I believe. Oh, and there is no rush." She stepped off the last stair. "See you in a while."

"Yes, you will." He paused but went on past her and followed Charles up the stairs.

She heard him ask Charles if he would have a valet. When Charles responded, "Only if you brought one," Nilda headed out to the verandah, grateful Jeffrey could not see her grin. *Good for you, Charles.*

She went to her office for her notebook and took one of the chairs at the outside table. Butterflies were dancing and sipping in the flower beds, and the purple martins sang at their house and the feeders. Two badminton courts were marked off, and the croquet wickets were all measured for the game. *Peaceful* was the best description she could think of. What a shame to spoil it with social niceties. Why couldn't they make Jeffrey fit into their lifestyle rather than the other way around?

For some reason that thought made her breathe easier.

Chapter 19

Bjorn didn't mind getting up early, especially in the summer when the sun was already up. But this morning he and Ivar got up even earlier than usual to help with the milking and to eat breakfast before they mounted Rosie so they could go to Blackduck.

"Drop this off at the store, will you, please?" Gunlaug handed them two envelopes. "Then this envelope is for Mrs. Schoenleber. Thank you."

Bjorn really enjoyed the ride into town. There were no mountains—in fact, this land was pretty flat—but that meant you didn't have to climb anything and slide back onto the horse's rump, and there were no steep downhills to make you slide forward onto the horse's bony withers. Birds were singing, a rooster crowed, and a line of cows at a barn bellowed their impatience. A barking dog ran down a lane but didn't bother to come clear out to the road. It was the best part of the Norway he remembered without the discomfort of ups and downs.

Ivar asked, "Have you ever played that other game the invitation mentioned, badminton?"

"Nope, never. But Nilda will make sure we learn how before the rest of the people come."

Rosie picked up her pace when she saw Benson's Corner up

ahead. They stopped, and Bjorn slid off the horse to deliver the envelopes. He took them inside Mrs. Benson's store. "Mormor sent this."

"Oh, good." Mrs. Benson smiled at him. "Off to the big town, eh?"

He nodded. "We'll be back for church tomorrow, so this trip is fast. See you then."

"Glad you made it so early," Fritz Larsson greeted them when they arrived at his house a few minutes later. "I was afraid you might not come, Bjorn."

Fritz set his satchel in the back of the buggy, so they did the same. They turned Rosie out into the pasture, and then they were on their way at a fast trot. Buggies were nicer than riding bareback.

"I hear Leif had a grand time in Blackduck," Fritz said. "My aunt was really pleased that he loves to read so much. So much so that we are looking to start a library here in Benson's Corner. Mostly for the school, but everyone will be able to check books out. I'm making a list of books I think we should have, so if you have any ideas, I'll put them on the list."

Books. Bjorn was not much interested in books. But he could probably write the book on logging. "Do you think there are books on making furniture?" he asked.

"Probably not in Norwegian," Fritz said. "You have an extra difficulty, since you learned to read in Norwegian, so now you have to learn to read all over again, but it's a simpler alphabet, if that helps. Knute and Leif have worked really hard at it."

Bjorn knew that. "Far gets a newspaper in Norwegian when he can."

Fritz nodded. "The St. Paul paper, probably. Have you thought about joining one of the logging camps?"

"Not as long as we have trees at home to fell. Is Petter coming to the social?"

"As far as I know."

"I thought he might be one of the drivers delivering the lumber for our hog barn, but he didn't come." Bjorn liked Petter. Petter was getting good at English, and he was always a happy soul, laughing and teasing.

When they arrived in Blackduck, they stopped at the lumberyard to turn in the order Far had sent with them.

"Making more skis?" Mr. Hechstrom asked after reading over it.

"We have several orders to fill. Do you have this here now?" Ivar asked.

"No. I have some, just not that much, but we'll bring it out when it comes. If your father is making skis at this rate, I'd better start keeping a lot more in stock. How's that hog barn coming along?"

"On hold 'til we clear a couple acres of stumps."

"Always more work than the days are long, isn't there? Even as long as our days are for these summer months. Let me know if you need anything else."

They climbed back into the buggy, then trotted across town. George greeted them when they arrived at the Schoenleber house. "You go on in, and I'll take care of your horse and buggy." He paused. "Hope you enjoy the social."

Fritz looked at George. "Anything I should know?"

"Jeffrey Schmitz arrived yesterday."

"Oh, really? Why, I haven't seen him for years. Probably since he and his brother came that summer. What is bringing him up here now?"

George half shrugged and licked his lips, hesitating. "Charles and I are thinking it's not *what* but *who*."

Fritz stared at him. "You think it's Miss Carlson?"

"As I said, I'll take care of the horse and buggy." George took the reins and clucked at the horse as he led it away.

The three young men stared after him. Then the two younger turned to look at Fritz.

"My sister?" Ivar asked.

Fritz nodded, obviously thinking rather seriously. "Come on, let's take our bags to our rooms."

Charles showed Ivar and Bjorn to the same rooms they'd used before. "Dinner will be in an hour, so if any of you would like a bath, you have time. Will you need any help?"

"Thank you, Charles, we can manage." Ivar smiled at him. "Dinner in an hour, you say?"

"Yes, Master Ivar." Charles nodded and went back down the stairs.

Turning to Bjorn, Ivar nodded to the room that connected their chambers. "I'll start the water in the bath. You want to go first or second?"

"You go first." Bjorn crossed his room to look out the window. "Ivar, come quick."

"What?"

"Look." He pointed out the window to where Nilda was walking with another man. "That must be Jeffrey Schmitz. Look at the clothes he's wearing."

Ivar wagged his head. "Silly, I'd say. I saw a picture one time of tennis players. That's what they were wearing."

"All white. How would anyone keep that clean? Especially if you do any kind of real work at all."

"I guess it doesn't matter when you're rich. You hire other people to do your laundry and all your work."

Bjorn shook his head. "I sure hope Nilda doesn't marry someone like that. Why, she'd go live in Minneapolis, and we'd never see her."

"I can't picture her married to anyone like that. She's too smart." Ivar heaved a sigh. "I'll go start the water."

Nilda performed the introductions when everyone gathered for dinner. Why was Bjorn shooting glances at Jeffrey? She heaved a sigh. This did not portend a grand afternoon.

As soon as they finished dinner—fried chicken and mashed potatoes, since those were Jeffrey's favorites as a boy—Jeffrey sat back. "She remembered." He stared at his aunt. "All those years ago, and your cook remembered."

"You might thank her personally after dinner."

"I most certainly will. I seem to remember crispy gingerbread cookies, and there was something else." He wrinkled his brow, trying to dredge it up.

"Chocolate pudding with whipped cream on it," Charles filled in.

Jeffrey stared down at the clear-footed bowl now sitting in front of him. "Well, I never." He closed his eyes in bliss at the first spoonful. "I also remember my father trying to entice your cook to come to Minneapolis to our house. But she would have none of it." He ate half the bowl. "I wonder why I never came back again?"

Mrs. Schoenleber gave a sly smile. "Your father sent both of you to boarding school that fall. Perhaps he was afraid you liked it too much here."

Nilda stared at her employer, then rolled her lips to keep from laughing out loud. This was mighty close to hanging family laundry out to dry in public. She looked across the table to see Fritz hiding his smile in his napkin.

When they rose from the dinner table, Jeffrey headed for the kitchen, and Nilda smiled at Ivar and Bjorn. "How about we go outside and give you some lessons in badminton? Unless you've played that before."

"We played croquet last time we were here." Bjorn spoke for the first time since the introductions.

Good, he is more comfortable now. That was one of the most uncomfortable meals I've had in this house. "Come on, we'll play with partners. You with me and Ivar with Fritz." She showed them how to hold the racket, and the four of them moved to their sides of the net. "The goal is to return the shuttlecock across the net within the lines and try to place it where your opponent can't return it." She tapped the bird over the net to Fritz, and he returned it. They batted it back and forth a couple of times until he missed and she received a point.

"It looks easy, but it isn't. We'll just practice for a time with Fritz and me coaching you."

The first time the bird crossed the net four times before Ivar missed it, earning clapping and cheering.

"See? You're getting it."

Bjorn wiped sweat from his brow. "Ivar makes me run all over the court."

"That's the point." Nilda grinned at him. "You know, this is a game you could play out at the farm. You don't need a lawn."

"As if we ever have time to play like this," Bjorn muttered, tapping his racket on his other hand. "Come on, *Uncle*, let's go again."

"Now, Bjorn, watch your temper." Ivar wiggled his eyebrows.

Nilda glanced at the sidelines, where Jeffrey was pacing. "Fritz, why don't you and Ivar go play a game of croquet and let me work with Bjorn."

Fritz looked at Ivar, and they both shrugged. "Come on, Jeffrey, how about a game of croquet?"

Nilda noticed immediately that Jeffrey's nod was forced. That wasn't what he wanted, but he chose to be polite.

"Come on, Aunt Gertrude, you play too." Fritz waved at

Mrs. Schoenleber, and Jeffrey almost covered up his look of shock when she accepted.

Nilda returned to coaching Bjorn. "I did this to help me get better at it." She held her racket flat and bounced the shuttlecock on it. Handing him a shuttlecock, they both bounced theirs, getting them higher and higher.

She kept one eye on the croquet game. She looked over just in time to see Jeffrey put his foot on the ball with the red stripe and knock the blue one into a flower bed. Jeffrey chortled, Fritz nodded, and Mrs. Schoenleber tapped her yellow ball through the wickets to just miss the final stick. On the next turn, her ball tapped the post.

"Wait a minute, how did you get so far?" Jeffrey stared at her.

"I just let you two play against each other, and I drove for the goal post." She slid her mallet back in the stand. "I think it is time for something cold to drink."

Nilda bit her bottom lip and looked at Bjorn, who coughed to hide his laugh. "Would you like something to drink?" she asked.

He nodded, not daring to talk yet.

When the others arrived for the social, Nilda performed the introductions and saw Lucinda's eyes light up when she met Jeffrey. "I've seen you at a few functions in Minneapolis, but I've not met you before."

"Then I am doubly glad to meet you now, Miss Wall. Where do you live in the Twin Cities?"

"Southeast of St. Paul. At least, that is where our house is, but after my stay here, Mother and I are going to France for a month or perhaps more. We stay at her family's château in Provence. That is where she grew up."

"You do this every year?" And then Jeffrey said something in French.

Smiling, Lucinda replied in rapid French.

Why did this irritate Nilda? She realized it was because it was not polite to use a language not everyone in the room knew. It was, well, hoity-toity, like putting "Esquire" after your name.

When Petter arrived, Nilda introduced him around. She realized with relief that there was no sign of that Mr. Galt. Maybe he had gathered all his interviews and was leaving town. Maybe.

After Petter visited with Ivar and Bjorn for a few minutes, she called for everyone's attention. "Let's see hands. Who would rather play badminton? We have two courts, so eight people can play. Then we also have two courts for croquet, one in the front yard. So, badminton?"

Olivia raised her hand, and Nilda nudged Petter to raise his as well.

"Sure. We can play the next game of croquet." Petter turned to Mrs. Schoenleber. "Do you and Miss Jane want to play with us?"

"I will," Miss Walstead said. "Come on, Gertrude, you can play croquet later."

Mrs. Schoenleber smiled at Petter. "You both promise to take pity on two old ladies?"

Nilda choked. "Be careful what you agree to, Petter. Some people have more skill than is apparent, and they are dangerous."

With everyone laughing, the games began, with the agreement that the winners of both croquet games would meet in another match after. As soon as Jeffrey chose which court he was playing on, Nilda chose the other, making sure Lucinda played against Jeffrey.

After the first round, everyone gathered around the tables for lemonade and iced tea that Cook had at the ready, in addition to crackers and cheese, as well as cookies for those who would rather. Petter and Olivia kept looking at the two older women and shaking their heads.

"I warned you," Nilda said, laughing.

"But we're not playing again," Miss Walstead said, wiping her brow. "We'll cheer for the croquet match."

The next game was for the three on each side with the lesser scores. Then everyone gathered around for the final round with the two teams of three leading scorers from the first game. Jeffrey, Ivar, and Lucinda were on one side, and Fritz, Nilda, and Bjorn were on the other.

"Now, remember," Mrs. Schoenleber cautioned, "this is just a game."

While everyone nodded, Nilda wasn't too sure about that.

From the first whack of the mallets, the audience cheered and groaned. The players laughed and teased each other, but it was every player for himself. When Lucinda knocked Jeffrey's ball off the court, she clapped and cheered with all the rest. But while she pretended to pout when it happened to her, she obviously gave it all she had.

The players to watch, though, were Fritz and Jeffrey. Nilda realized immediately why Mrs. Schoenleber had warned them that it was only a game. Jeffrey reached the halfway post a turn ahead of Fritz. Fritz tried to avoid Jeffrey's ball as he drove for the stake. His ball went through one hoop but not the second. Then Jeffrey abandoned staying on course to go after Fritz. They actually played two turns behind the halfway stake, trying to avoid each other and hit each other.

Fritz's ball hit Jeffrey's. Fritz mashed his foot onto his ball and drove Jeffrey off the course and into a bush. Jeffrey smiled a totally false smile and two plays later sent Fritz's ball up against the foundation of the house.

But while the two of them were focusing on defeating each other, Lucinda, Ivar, Bjorn, and Nilda completed the game. Lucinda's red ball was the first to tap the goal post, and Ivar was second. Fritz and Jeffrey were so intensely and ridiculously engaged in destroying each other that Nilda was laughing too hard and missed the goal post by a foot. She still came in fourth, and Fritz sent Jeffrey's ball halfway to Duluth and finished fifth.

The girls all gathered around Lucinda, clapping and congratulating her. "My father taught me that you keep your eye on the ball and the goal post and let the others worry about knocking each other around."

Fritz came over and shook her hand. "That was some game. I'd play on your team any time."

Jeffrey rounded up the balls and dropped them into the wooden stand. "Fine game, Lucinda. Did you learn that in France?"

"Actually, I did. My father always joined us for a month, and that was the only time he ever took to play. We had some killer games through the years, but the first year I defeated him, I felt like I had won the Olympics."

Nilda clapped her hands. "Supper will be served here on the verandah, so we need to clear off so the food can be brought out. Fritz, how about a sing-along while they do that?"

"I'd be glad to."

Everyone trooped inside and gathered around the piano. Later, after everyone had filled their plates outside, they found places to sit, and the conversations continued. Dusk was beginning to creep in as the guests thanked their hostess and Nilda saw them out the door. For just a moment, she wished Jeffrey had some other place to go too, but when she returned to the parlor, Fritz was playing, her brother and Bjorn were chatting with Miss Walstead, but Jeffrey and Mrs. Schoenleber were nowhere to be seen.

"They're in the library," Miss Walstead said.

"Oh." Nilda wondered what was going on but shrugged instead and went to watch Fritz play.

Sunday morning she rose early enough to have breakfast with the three men, who were packed and ready to leave.

"I wish you could stay longer." She walked them out to their horse and buggy.

"We sure had a good time yesterday." Bjorn smiled and swung his carpetbag into the buggy. "Thank you. When will you be coming home again?"

"I don't know," Nilda replied. "Later in August."

"That's a long time."

"I know. I have a lot to do right now." She had told them about the housing project and providing books for school libraries.

She waved as they trotted out the driveway. If only Jeffrey were leaving today too. Wouldn't it be nice if he could spend the day with Lucinda? She was certainly interested in him.

Nilda definitely was not.

Chapter 20

"I didn't even get a piano lesson." Nilda felt like stamping her foot, but good sense prevailed. At least Jeffrey wasn't beside her right now. Yesterday she'd felt like he was smothering her. All the time, hovering around her, as if he were a lap dog begging for attention. Right now she was grateful for the telephone on her desk. Good thing she'd been in her office just now when the telephone jangled. She rejoiced that it was Fritz.

"You're right. I'm sorry we didn't get a lesson. In fact, I'm sorry we weren't together more yesterday," Fritz told her. "Tell you what. How about I return next week on Thursday and stay until Saturday?" He paused. "Jeffrey is leaving this week, right?"

"Yes." Thank goodness. Whatever had possessed him to act like he was part of the family, or at least had visited frequently? He'd even alluded to the one and only symphony they had been to as if that were a common event.

That morning he had attended church with them as if it were a usual part of his Sundays. Something he'd said another time, though, made her sure church attendance was not part of his family's routine. Besides, how could one stay out at a ball or another social event until the wee hours and then get up to attend church?

They'd played enough badminton and croquet to last quite some time, and now that supper was finished, he'd said he had some things he had to do and retired to his room. His inquiry regarding tennis courts in Blackduck had been met with a solid *no*.

Nilda was just putting her desk in order when a tap at the library door caused her to look up. "Yes?"

"It's me. May I come in?"

She forced some enthusiasm into her voice. "Of course."

Jeffrey jiggled the handle. "It's locked."

She rose and went to unlock the door. "Sorry, I never lock it. I wonder how that happened."

"I like to go for a walk when dusk is falling. Perhaps you'd like to come along."

Not really, but why not. "I'll tell Mrs. Schoenleber that we'll be gone for a while."

"I already told her."

Nilda stared at him. "Sure of yourself, aren't you?"

He shrugged. "I just thought a walk might appeal to you."

He headed for the front door, but she stopped him. "No, the path runs behind the house. It's much more pleasant than the streets."

They went out the back door and crossed the lawn where the extra croquet wickets and badminton net had already been taken down.

"I'd forgotten how big this yard is, and this path was just a trail to the river. Things have changed a lot in Blackduck since I was a boy." Jeffrey waved an arm. "Aunt's house was almost out in the country then. Now houses surround hers, and there are a lot more businesses and people in town."

"Blackduck is a growing town, at least as long as there are huge pine trees still to cut."

"What will you do when the trees are gone?"

"That depends on Mrs. Schoenleber. If she no longer needs me, I will return to the farm that now belongs to my brother." *Not that any of this is really your business.*

"My father has tried to persuade his sister to move closer to the head offices so he can help her if she needs any."

"Really." As if Mrs. Schoenleber needed help. "He would take her away from all her close friends and social contacts?"

"Oh, she would make other friends and social contacts, I'm sure."

The breezy way he brushed off Jane Walstead and Thor Haglund and all of Mrs. Schoenleber's other lovely and influential friends irritated Nilda. Obviously, none of that was important to him.

He frowned. "Isn't this the path where you were attacked?"

His question caught her by surprise. "Yes, why?"

"I just thought that might make you hesitant to walk out here."

"That was months ago, and the land isn't at fault." She paused where the path intersected with one that ran along the riverbank. They stopped and looked out across the river. "Lovely, isn't it?"

"It's hard to believe the number of logs that are shipped down this river every year." He swatted a mosquito on his arm. "Better keep moving."

Nilda tried to think of something to say to start a casual conversation and could think of nothing. And then she realized she didn't really care about conversing with him anyway. They returned to the house in uneasy silence.

By the time they got back, the streetlights had been lit, and the june bugs were attacking the lights and the screen doors of houses. A whippoorwill called its tune, and bats darted about the streetlights, feeding on insects.

As they climbed the stoop, Jeffrey said, "Thank you for the pleasant walk. Would we find drinks available inside?"

"If you want, the bar is always stocked for company."

He opened the door and held it for her. "Will you join me?"

"I'll have Charles bring in tea. I don't much care for liquor."

"Not even brandy?"

"Not really. Would you care for something to eat with your drink?"

"That sounds good." He looked in the parlor to find his aunt and Miss Walstead playing a game of dominos at the low table. "Who's winning?"

"One each."

"Would you join me for a drink?"

"I'll order tea and some of whatever Cook has." Nilda left the room to go to the kitchen. She knew she could have pulled the cord, but right now she needed a drink of water first.

When she pushed open the kitchen door, Cook looked up from fixing a tray. "Is something wrong?"

"Not at all." Nilda headed for the sink. "I just want a drink of water."

"There's cold water in a pitcher in the icebox. You sit down and let me get it for you."

"Thanks, but you finish what you are doing." She took a glass from the drainer on the counter and opened the icebox to stand for a moment in the cool draft escaping. After pouring a glass of water, she shut the door and turned back to see Cook shaking her head. "What?"

"You were that desperate?"

Nilda held the glass to her cheek. "It's muggy outside even though it was a lovely walk."

"Would you like water on the tray also?"

"No, I'll stay with this." She glanced at the tray. "Are the gingerbread men all gone?"

"I'm sorry, I sent those home with your brother. I know how

young Leif loved those cookies. These round ones with the crinkly edges are the same recipe."

"Leif was thrilled. Mrs. Solvang, you are so thoughtful and caring. I can never thank you enough."

"Now, Miss Nilda, you carry on so. I just do my job." She picked up the tray.

"Let me carry that."

"No, that simply would not do."

When Cook spoke that firmly, Nilda knew there was no more cajoling. She held the door open and stepped back into the kitchen to set down her water glass. Exhaustion rolled over her like a wave on the shore. She followed Cook into the parlor, where Jeffrey sat with a half-full glass in his hand and a smile welcoming her.

"Please pardon me," Nilda said, "but all of a sudden I just need to go to bed. Good night, and I'll see you in the morning."

Mrs. Schoenleber frowned. "You're not ill, are you?"

"I don't think so."

"You've had two very full days. Sleep well, my dear." Miss Walstead smiled her beatific smile, which made Nilda feel comforted all over.

"I'm sorry." She nodded to Jeffrey. "Good night." Climbing the stairs took every ounce of strength she could muster.

Gilda met her at the door. "Your bed is turned down, and if you just stand still, I'll help you."

"Thank you." For a change she appreciated the assistance and did what she was told. *Raise your arms. Slip into your nightgown. Now crawl in bed.* Gilda folded the blanket back and pulled up the sheet.

"There now. If you need anything, you call me." She smiled down at Nilda. "Sleep sweet, Miss Nilda. You've earned your rest."

And Nilda did just that.

The next morning she woke to a sparrow trilling its song and a cool breeze lifting the lace curtains at the window. After stretching her toes toward the foot of the bed and her arms over her head, she lay still, listening for anyone awake in the house. Not that she'd hear anything from the kitchen, but she wasn't about to call for Gilda. Dressing swiftly in a simple dimity dress, she washed her face and bundled her hair into a snood. Today was a day to rejoice and be thankful, not that all days weren't for that. But right this minute she felt she could conquer the world, or at least the bookwork she planned to get done. If Jeffrey wanted to help with her projects, she'd give him plenty to do.

Not surprisingly, Mrs. Schoenleber was already at the table, reading her morning paper.

"Do you never sleep?" Nilda asked.

"Someone once told me that as we get older, we need less sleep, but then, I've never needed a lot of sleep. Except after Arvid and the children died. Then it seemed I slept for months. When I was sleeping, I wasn't crying, at least. Although I guess that's not really true either. I so often woke with a wet pillow." She nodded. "But those days are gone, and now we have a lot of work to do, don't we?" She studied Nilda's face. "You look back to yourself."

"I am, so thank you for letting me go to bed. I fear Jeffrey was disappointed."

"Be that as it may, you did what you needed to do." Just as Mrs. Schoenleber was about to ring the bell by her plate, Charles backed into the room, carrying a tray.

"Good morning, Miss Nilda. You look back to health this morning. We were all a bit concerned about you."

"At least exhaustion can be cured by extra sleep, and I didn't even hear Gilda leave the room."

"You didn't stir when I peeked in on you," Mrs. Schoenleber said.

"The next thing I heard after Gilda's good-night was a bird singing his heart out. The world was aglow, and he was announcing it."

Charles set a cup of coffee in front of her and a plate with two eggs, two strips of bacon, and a fresh cinnamon bun. "Can I get you anything else?"

"Are there any strawberries left?"

"I'll ask."

Nilda bowed her head to thank God for the food and bit into the warm roll.

"Good, aren't they?"

Nilda nodded. "Miss Walstead will be delighted."

"What will I be delighted about?" Miss Walstead asked, walking into the room. She sniffed. "Oh, don't tell me. Cook is doing her very best to spoil me beyond measure."

Charles whisked into the room with a plate of rolls and a cup of coffee. He set them in front of her. "I'll bring the rest in a minute."

"What a way to start the day." She sipped her coffee and bit into a bun. "Please don't tell me Cook makes these only when I am here."

"Oh, no." Nilda dipped her bacon in the yolk of her eggs, her eyes darting to the newspaper folded beside her plate. "Look, there's an article here about Mr. Haglund donating the land for building the houses." She read through it. Perhaps that would help generate more support.

She had already been hard at work in her office for over an hour when Jeffrey knocked on her door. He had a cup of coffee in one hand and a roll in the other.

"Can I bring you anything?" he asked as he sat down in a chair near her desk.

"Thank you, but no." She went back to typing another letter. She pulled the sheet of paper out and laid it on the pile to be signed. "Do you know how to type?"

"Heavens, no." He looked at her like she'd accused him of secretly stealing horses. "That's what we have secretaries for at the office."

"Interesting. I've heard that many colleges are now requiring students to type their papers, so I assumed you knew."

"I write mine out and have my secretary type them for me. He also edits, which in my case is a good thing. Did you have breakfast?"

She straightened the stack of papers on the desk. "Of course, some time ago." She looked up at the grandfather clock. "The morning is half gone. How do you manage to get to morning classes? And you start work at the company next week."

"I know. I'm treating each day before that as my vacation. But here I am now, willing to do whatever you need me to do."

"I don't *need* you to do anything, but surely I can figure out some way you can help me. I know, I have several letters that include lists of books for the school libraries. I need them compiled into one sheet." She handed him the letters. "Would you like a table to work on?"

He heaved a sigh. "I was hoping you would like to go for another walk, like we did yesterday."

"Mr. Schmitz . . ."

"When are you going to call me Jeffrey?"

She shrugged. "I'm not. That's not proper."

"But I heard you call Fritz by his first name."

"Well, we have become friends over these several months, and using given names is appropriate." She wasn't sure if it was appropriate, but it was comfortable. "You get those lists compiled, and after dinner, you can go with me to see how they are doing clearing the land for the houses." She ignored his eye-rolling. "Thanks for helping me, as you said you would like to." A sweet smile punctuated her comment.

He set down his empty coffee cup and opened the first envelope. "Do you have a special way you want this done?"

"No. I can alphabetize it later when I type it. Unless you want to break it down according to type, i.e., novels, history, geography, science, etc. According to age levels might be good, but the teachers can do that."

"Let me get them compiled, and then I'll see."

She glanced up a while later to see several sheets of paper with lines crossed out. He flipped back through some pages, looking for something. She went back to typing.

"Why don't you hire someone else to do your typing?" he asked.

She looked up. "Why? That's part of my job."

"But you are writing the same letter over and over. You could hire someone else to do that so you can go on to something more important."

She stared at him. That had never entered her mind. But that would involve another typewriter and desk and finding someone who wanted the work. She nodded. "That's worth thinking about."

He laid the list of books in front of her just before Charles announced that dinner was ready. "There you go."

"Thank you." She made sure her desk was neat with weights on the stacks of paper so breezes from the open windows wouldn't blow them away. They went to the dining room.

Nilda could think of nothing much to say at dinner, but Jeffrey found enough to talk about, almost always about himself, that the air was filled with words.

"We're going out to look at Mr. Haglund's land," Nilda announced. "You two want to come?"

Mrs. Schoenleber smiled. "Thank you, but not this time. I have a meeting at two. You go on and bring back a report. Don't forget that Thor will be here later, and Mathew is coming too. They'll be staying for supper."

Jeffrey said, or rather whined, "I take it there is no quitting time here, as in leave the job and go home? I know that's hard to do when you are working in your home, but surely . . ." He slowed to a stop when he realized three pairs of eyes were drilling him into his chair. "Ah, could you pass the bread, please?"

The soup and rye bread were delicious, but nonetheless, Nilda was glad when dinner was over. Eventually she could fold her napkin and rise. She led the way out to where George was waiting with the small runabout.

George dropped them off at the construction site. "I'll be back as soon as I take Mrs. Schoenleber to her meeting."

"I could have driven us here." Jeffrey pouted. "I do know how to drive a team."

"We have several vehicles but only one team, so how could that have worked?"

"I see. My father is planning on purchasing a motorcar in the next year. Pretty soon horses will be a thing of the past. Keeping up with the times is important, you know."

"Hello, Miss Carlson." Mr. Haglund waved from the second lot. "Be right there."

Jeffrey scowled at the woodlot and shook his head. "For pity's sake. This is what you are so excited about?"

Nilda stared at him, trying to be polite. She could feel the mask settle into place on her face. *Be careful what you say.* "Yes. These will be homes for immigrants who are willing to work hard to live in America. In Norway they would have no land of their own unless they inherited it. They want a better life for their children, just like your father did and does for his."

She almost snorted at the comparison. Her required reading had lately been on the French Revolution. The words that stayed in her head were spoken by Queen Marie Antoinette when someone informed her that the people were rebelling because they had no bread to eat. Her response of "Let them eat cake" made anger seethe somewhere below the polite surface of Nilda's mind.

Here came Mr. Haglund, smiling ebulliently. "Ah, Miss Carlson. Welcome to our attempt at the future."

She smiled. "Mr. Haglund, I'd like you to meet Jeffrey Schmitz." She turned to Jeffrey. "Mr. Haglund has generously donated these ten acres for the town of Blackduck to have housing to offer immigrants who arrive with their families."

Jeffrey stuck out his hand. "Pleased to meet a friend of my aunt's."

"Ah, yes, her nephew from Minneapolis. You are the one about to finish college?"

"I am, yes. I will graduate next May."

"Well, we're glad to have you here. As you can see from all the survey flags, the land has been surveyed and the possible future owners are clearing each plot to build a house. Each house will have nearly half an acre of land that the new owners will clear. The women can plant gardens and have chickens to help feed their families and possibly bring in more income. The men will be at the logging camps, working all winter."

"I see." Jeffrey did not seem to see at all. In fact, did he even know a survey stake when he saw one?

Mr. Haglund said, "We are not giving a handout but a hand up." He added pointedly, "Like your father has done for you in paying for your college education."

And a whole lot else. Nilda made sure her thoughts did not make it to her face.

"So who has been clearing the roads?" she asked.

"Volunteers." Mr. Haglund motioned to the working men. "They cleared enough for the wagons to bring in supplies. I am hoping the city will take over from there. If not, we have plenty of volunteers." He emphasized the last word. "I'll bring the final plans later this afternoon, Miss Carlson."

"Mr. Amundson will be joining us also. Say, five o'clock, after the bank closes." She added the last bit for Jeffrey's sake.

Mr. Haglund nodded. "Good, good. Come, I want you to meet our men. The trail is wide enough that your dress should be safe."

She grinned but made the mistake of glancing at Jeffrey. Stoic, long-suffering, bored? Which best described his face? She watched him glance down at his white shoes. "If you'd rather wait here . . ." she ventured.

"Oh no, I'm sorry. Of course I'm coming." He offered her his arm, but she stepped out ahead of him.

She greeted each of the men in Norwegian, until one answered her in Swedish. She apologized in Swedish and welcomed him again. "My Swedish is, ah . . ." She laughed. "I don't know the word. In English it is *limited*."

The men nodded and laughed along with her.

"This is the assistant to our foreman, Mr. Sandborn." Mr. Haglund waved toward a stocky little man in a jaunty cap who grinned broadly. His moustache was thick enough to hide a small rabbit.

With a thick accent, he said, "I am much pleased to meet you. Unlike all these Scandinavians, I am of Moravia."

Nilda smiled and shook hands. "Welcome to Blackduck, Mr. Sandborn."

Mr. Haglund announced, "Miss Carlson here is the person who first conceived the idea of housing for loggers."

Nilda rather wished he hadn't said that. Now she felt self-conscious.

"Tusen takk," one of the men said, and the others nodded.

"George is here." Jeffrey spoke firmly, sounding relieved.

"We'll see you later, then?" Nilda asked Mr. Haglund.

"Yes. Pleasure to meet you, Mr. Schmitz. Perhaps you will appreciate studying the plans this evening."

Nilda rolled her lips together. Mr. Haglund understood what was going on, but then, one needed to be deaf and blind not to pick up on how Jeffrey, a square peg, was not fitting into any round hole.

When Jeffrey was seated in the buggy, he leaned over and dusted off both his pant legs and shoes.

"Charles will see to cleaning those, if you so desire." She heard the ice in her tone.

"My man will take care of it when I return to Minneapolis." He was frowning. "Or perhaps I will just buy new ones."

Once they reached home again, Nilda had planned to hide out in her office to work some more, but something prompted her to say, "After tea, can I entice you to a game of either croquet or badminton?" She fought hard to make her voice sound relaxed and friendly.

"Are you sure you have time?"

Ah, and she had struggled hard not to be sarcastic. Was verbal volleying part of being polite? Were she to act sweet, would he realize she was acting? "I'd say badminton. I'm sorry I have not learned to play tennis."

"I will gladly teach you when you come to Minneapolis. Badminton, it is."

She blinked. Was he totally oblivious?

"They're out on the verandah," Charles said as he greeted them. "Can I get you anything?" He looked to Jeffrey.

"Can you put a little life into the lemonade?"

"Yes, sir, if you wish."

"I'll be out in a minute." Nilda headed for the powder room, wishing she could go up to her own room and bang something against the wall. Or perhaps out in the stable. Surely she could work off this frustration cleaning stalls, as if George would ever let her do that.

After washing her hands and resettling some pins in her hair, she glared at the face in the mirror. "Miss Walstead would say you are lacking in your hostess skills. What she does not understand is that I have managed not to kill the pompous man."

She walked out to the verandah with a perfect smile in place. If she needed to act gracious until the next morning, she would do that. And make Miss Walstead proud of her.

"Ah, there you are." Jeffrey raised his half-empty glass in salute. He swallowed more of his drink and held it out to Charles. "That could be a bit stronger."

Mrs. Schoenleber caught Nilda's eye with a slight cautioning shake of her head. "You reminded Thor of our meeting?"

"He reminded me before I could." She picked up a glass of lemonade from the table and sat down in the shade. "I met the men clearing the land for the houses. They seem an enthusiastic bunch. Mr. Haglund is delighted with the progress. I hope Mr. Amundson goes out there before he comes here."

Jeffrey cleared his throat and looked over at the badminton court. He had already drained half his second glass.

"Would you mind terribly if I sit here for just a couple of minutes?" Nilda's voice dripped sweetness.

"Oh, sorry. That was rude of me. I've just been looking forward to this."

She smiled and caught the glance that went between her two

mentors. "Would you like to join us on the badminton court?" she asked them.

"No, I think not today, but thank you for the invitation." Miss Walstead's smile was as fake as Nilda's. She stood. "I have some things I need to do, so I will see you at our get-together."

Mrs. Schoenleber nodded in agreement. "You two have a good time. Nilda, is everything ready for tonight?"

"Pretty much." Nilda realized she was being offered an out. "Thank you." She helped herself to another lemon cookie. "Aren't these delicious? We have the best cook anywhere."

Jeffrey was sorting through the badminton rackets. "Next time I come, I'll bring my own racket. I had it balanced especially for my hand."

Next time? If she had her way, there would be no next time.

Nilda held her own on the badminton court until common sense caught up with her again. She quit fighting to win and let Jeffrey have the last set. The scowl on his face was replaced with a condescending smile when she congratulated him.

"I'm going up to dress for tonight, so I will see you a bit before five." She paused on the back patio. "Unless you would rather not be involved in our discussions?"

"No, no. I'll be there. I think I'll sit out here a bit longer. The breeze is picking up and it feels good."

Nilda smiled and went upstairs.

Supper went fairly well, but Nilda thought perhaps it was because Jeffrey would be gone and out of her hair tomorrow morning.

"I will talk to my father about this," Jeffrey said when they were discussing the materials needed for building the houses. "He might agree to help, as he is a very generous man."

Nilda caught the look exchanged between the two older women. But it was true, they had not approached Heinrik on a donation basis, only as an investment opportunity. Maybe he *would* help.

Jeffrey nodded to Mrs. Schoenleber. "Perhaps if you approached him too."

"Oh, I was planning on it, but we are just getting to the stage of needing additional finances."

And then he switched the topic of conversation back to himself.

The next morning, after Jeffrey said his thank-yous and goodbyes, Nilda rode to the train station with him.

He cooed, "I'm looking forward to talking with you now that you have a telephone in your office to make it easier. I'll check the schedules and see what will be produced at the theater this fall. I know you will enjoy that. And any concerts. Have you ever thought of attending a tennis tournament?" He smiled at her, so she forced herself to smile back. "I know you will enjoy getting to know my mother. She'll help you with any concerns you might have about society events in the Twin Cities. It probably seems a bit overwhelming to a country girl like yourself."

"We shall see" was all she could say in response without actually lying. Overwhelming? Hardly. Although the thought of the next business meeting did make her nervous, it was not because of social graces. It was because she was parrying with four stubborn, money-minded businessmen.

Jeffrey took her hand at the station and gave her his most charming smile. "This has been such a pleasure. We have so much to look forward to."

He waved as he stepped into his private car. She waved back.

He hadn't learned a thing.

Chapter 21

I think we need a blessing on the site and the builders before they begin," Nilda said.

Mrs. Schoenleber nodded. "I will telephone Reverend Holtschmidt and tell him we need the blessing on Sunday afternoon. We will provide refreshments."

"That's pretty short notice." Nilda glanced at her calendar. "This is Thursday."

"True, but we have enough time to prepare." Mrs. Schoenleber smiled. "But you are right. I better ask Cook first."

"Good thing she loves a challenge, since we keep throwing so many at her."

Reverend Holtschmidt agreed and set the time for two in the afternoon. "That way people can get home, have dinner, and make it back to the site. Great idea. I wonder why I didn't think of that?"

"It's not like you've been sitting around all summer. I distinctly remember someone telling me they saw you with a mattocks over at the construction site."

Reverend Holtschmidt just smiled. "We'll provide cake and lemonade, that might entice a few townsfolk. I'll mention it to the newspaper too. It will be short and sweet." He chuckled. "Blessing a house before it is even built."

Nilda and her employer took turns on the telephone, letting those involved know about the ceremony. Mrs. Schoenleber used the phone with great reluctance, but she did it.

"Your cook is baking the cakes?" Mr. Haglund asked. "Then I will surely be there. We planned on setting the foundation on Saturday, so this is perfect timing. The foundation will show exactly where the house will sit."

Sunday blazed in with nary a breeze. The folks in church had all brought fans, but even so, women were fanning and patting their faces when they came out. By the time they gathered at the building site at two o'clock, even the dogs were digging holes in the shade. Mr. Haglund and a couple of the men had erected a canvas roof to shade the cake and the servers.

Reverend Holtschmidt signaled to the man with a concertina, who played chords as loudly as possible. Those gathered quieted but for the rustling of fans.

"We are gathered here to pray for God's blessing, even though I think this is one of the most prayed-for projects I've ever seen. I know most of you know these people, but Mrs. Schoenleber and her assistant, Nilda Carlson, are the ones who dreamed this place into being. Thor Haglund donated this land, and these hearty fellows have been clearing the plots." He nodded to the three people who had joined him, and motioned to the gang of men with shovels. He handed Nilda a shovel, Mr. Haglund a mattocks, and Mrs. Schoenleber a whistle. "Now we're going to pray, and then these two will take the first whack at it, and when Mrs. Schoenleber blows the whistle, we'll let the boys loose. Oh, and afterward, cake and lemonade will be served. On the table is also a box to collect donations."

Raising his hands, he began. "Lord God, creator of all things, giver of all good, including ideas. We thank you for your great wisdom and even greater love for your people. Your Word says we are to share what we have with those who haven't, that we are to care for the poor and needy, and also that every man needs to work to provide for his family and for their daily bread. You have been guiding this undertaking from the start, and we pray that you will continue to do so. So, Lord, guide us, give us courage and strong backs, remind those who have sufficient that they are to share what you gave them with others. Give us great ideas through your Holy Spirit that we may all be following you in the path you have set before us. And now, in the name of our Lord Jesus Christ, we commend this property and all who will build it and dwell here to your care. May Jesus Christ be praised."

Everyone said a resounding, "Amen!"

The reverend motioned to Mr. Haglund and Nilda. Nilda knew what to do with a shovel, but the old man seemed at a bit of a loss with the mattocks. Still, he slammed it enthusiastically into the ground a couple of times. Mrs. Schoenleber blew her whistle with surprising exuberance. The crew gave a shout and rammed their shovels into the dirt in the middle of the first house.

Applause broke out, the concertina swung into a peppy polka, and the crowd lined up for their cake. Some even dropped money into the box with a sign that said *Building Fund.*

And with that, the ambitious project was launched.

The next morning when Nilda came down to breakfast, Mrs. Schoenleber, as always, was seated at the table reading the paper.

Nilda sat down near her. "I think I'll go over to the site this morning. For who knows what reason, I'd like to see them beginning."

"You'll have breakfast first?" Mrs. Schoenleber laid down her paper. "I'm sure they've already started."

"I know, I won't stay long. And yes, I remember the meeting here at ten thirty." She smiled at Charles as he set her coffee in front of her. "Thank you. May I have a poached egg on toast?"

"Cook has sliced ham ready also. And strawberries."

Nilda chuckled, shaking her head. "Yes to both."

"Good." He left.

Mrs. Schoenleber snickered. "You might as well give up."

"I am well aware of that. You know that usually I just say whatever Cook is making or has made. I thought of asking for a bun and coffee to take with me, but . . ."

She sighed at her first sip of coffee. "Thank you, Lord, for inventing coffee."

"The Norwegian national food." Mrs. Schoenleber sniffed and went back to her paper.

The day was quite warm out, muggy, and even a little hazy. No matter. Nilda rejoiced in the season, which was actually a little longer than was summer back in Norway. She climbed into the buggy, and away they went.

A while later, George stopped the buggy on the street fronting the property on the west. "You be careful and stay out of their way, miss."

"George, you sound like a mother hen."

"Just doing my job, miss." He assisted her down the step.

Mr. Haglund waved at her, then walked over, steering clear of the busy men. Some were sawing, some moving and stacking a wagonload of lumber, and some were already nailing the subflooring to the floor joists.

Nilda was surprised at the progress they had already made. "What time did you start?"

"They ate breakfast at dawn and were waiting for me when

I arrived at five thirty. They've set the challenge for this house to be move-in ready before the end of the month. And the good news is Mueller announced that the lumberyard is donating the lumber for this first house. Besides, he's given us a good deal on supplies already."

Nilda waved back as several of the men greeted her, all in careful English.

"Did you realize the newspaper was here yesterday?" he continued. "They've decided to chronicle this whole operation. I'm surprised they haven't interviewed you yet."

"The *Bemidji Pioneer* talked with us recently. Perhaps I need to pay more attention to the newspapers. Thank you for the reminder."

Someone called for Mr. Haglund, so she excused herself and returned to the buggy. "See, I was careful."

"Yes, miss." George headed for home. "I do hope you are pleased with what is going on. After all, it was your idea."

"I am, but I do believe this is God's idea, and He is letting me work with it."

"True, but you listened and did. Too many good ideas die before they are born."

Nilda pondered that as they trotted the streets to home.

Mr. Mueller joined the meeting that morning. "I can see this idea is picking up momentum now that the first house is going up. I was a bit dubious at first, but thanks to Thor twisting my arm, I will do what I can."

"Now, Henry, how can you say such a thing?" Mrs. Schoenleber chided.

"I just did, and I never speak idly, as you well know."

"Welcome aboard," Mr. Amundson said. "I have the financial report ready, as you requested." He nodded to Nilda. He read off the list of those who had donated toward the project.

"As you see, other than Thor donating the land, and now the lumberyard the lumber for this first house, we have no other sizeable contributions—yet."

"Most of the other donations are in kind, like the churches feeding the crew. I believe that now that we have newspaper support in both the *American* and the *Pioneer*, our efforts will be more spread out. We have sent letters to all of my contacts, and now we wait to see what response we get." Mrs. Schoenleber looked at each of the men around her table. "This is a way for people of influence to build a reputation of caring for others."

Mr. Haglund nodded. "And if they want to remain anonymous, that is fine too."

That afternoon, when Nilda was hard at work in her office, Charles came to the door. "There is a gentleman from the newspaper here to interview you and Mrs. Schoenleber. A photographer is with him."

Nilda nearly choked on her gasp. "I—ah—right now?" She looked down at her dress.

"You look fine, Miss Nilda. How long before you come, shall I say?"

"I need to stop in the powder room first, and I'll be right there."

"He asked if they could take a picture of you in here."

"Why?"

Charles shrugged.

"Tell him that's fine." Taking a photograph for the newspaper was bad enough, but here in her office was anything but fine. She opened a drawer in her desk and cleared off a good part of the mess.

She managed to put on a smile when the photographer walked through the door. "Good afternoon." She stood to greet him.

"I'm sorry to just drop in like this, but our editor said this article needs to be in this week's paper. And what he says, I do."

Nilda nodded. "I understand. Tell me what you want me to do."

"You just go ahead with what you were doing and ignore me. I need to get these developed right away. Our reporter is interviewing Mrs. Schoenleber right now, so if you would, please join them when I am done."

"Of course." She rolled a piece of paper into the carriage and began to type another letter.

"May I have one of you on the telephone?"

She complied and sank back in her chair when he left the room. *What I will do for the cause.* That thought made her chuckle, so she was smiling when she joined the others out on the verandah.

She nodded when Mrs. Schoenleber introduced her to the reporter. "How can I help you?"

"Mrs. Schoenleber said this all began as your idea. Can you tell me how that came about?"

Please, Lord. She inhaled and nodded. "I am a fairly recent immigrant from Norway, one of the fortunate ones. An uncle sent tickets for me and my younger brother to come join our older brother and his family on their farm near Benson's Corner. We had work, a place to live, and food to eat. Not all immigrants have that when they arrive." She watched his face as he wrote on his pad of paper.

"Good. Good. Please continue."

"Then Mrs. Schoenleber offered me this position and gave me an intensive education, especially in speaking, reading, and writing in English."

"How long ago was this? You speak English extremely well."

"Thank you. I've been working here for almost a year now."

"That's all?"

"Yes." She glanced at Mrs. Schoenleber, who smiled and nodded.

"You must have had some contact with the language before you came here."

Mrs. Schoenleber inserted, "She had some, but she has worked extremely hard here. We enforced an English-only policy from the day she began."

"And would you recommend that to other immigrants?"

"Of course, but few people are given this kind of opportunity. We are going to be offering English classes for those who move into the houses this fall."

"I see." He jotted some other notes and tucked his pad back in his briefcase. "I think I have enough for this first story."

"Pardon me, but what language were you writing in?" Nilda asked.

He took his notepad back out and showed her. "This is called Gregg shorthand. There is a textbook. I have one, if you would like to borrow it to get an idea."

Nilda nodded. "I've learned to type, but I think this would be a good addition to my skills."

"Stop by the newspaper office later, and I'll loan it to you. You can order one too." He stood. "Thank you both for your time. I'm glad the paper will be covering your story and the work ahead."

Charles showed him to the door and returned with the mail. He handed part of the stack to Mrs. Schoenleber and the rest to Nilda. "Looks like you have more work cut out for you."

Nilda flipped through the letters. A square envelope in Jeffrey's handwriting. She held it up for Mrs. Schoenleber to see.

"You have to give him credit for being persistent."

Nilda frowned. "Two telephone calls and now this since he left. He obviously did not get the hint."

"I think there is more behind this than meets the eye." Mrs. Schoenleber pulled the bell rope and smiled at Nilda. "Let's go for a walk around the garden. This has been quite a day already."

Stella appeared, and Mrs. Schoenleber instructed, "We will have refreshments out on the verandah."

"Yes, ma'am." Stella returned to the kitchen.

Nilda expected her employer to stand up, but Mrs. Schoenleber remained seated. "Nilda, I've a favor to ask of you."

"Of course."

"You referred to me several times as Mrs. Schoenleber when the reporter was here, and that is altogether appropriate. But when it is just the two of us and we are working or in private conversation, I would be pleased if you called me simply Gertrude. It is my name, you know."

"Oh dear. That will be difficult for me. You are my employer, not a . . . an equal." Nilda thought about it for a moment. "But since you ask, yes, I shall do so. Thank you, Gertrude." How hard it was!

"Telephone for you, ma'am," Charles announced from the arched doorway.

"For me?" Instead of heading outside, Gertrude went, scowling at the thought, to answer the telephone in the butler's pantry.

Nilda walked outside to wait on the verandah and breathe some fresh air. Just watching the butterflies sipping from the blossoms and the birds spraying water at the birdbath made her shoulders relax and her smile return. Perhaps she could bring her typewriter out here. At least she could take care of handwritten things. What a good idea.

Gertrude joined her. "That call was from Fritz. He asked if he could be any help if he came."

Interesting. Were it Jeffrey, Nilda would have run screaming. But Fritz, now that was a different matter. "I hope you told him yes."

"He'll be here for supper."

"Good." Nilda grinned. "I'll just hand him that stack of mail to start with."

In spite of the heat, their walk was refreshing, the lemonade and cookies even more so, and Nilda returned to her office with a lighter step.

But instead of sitting down at her desk, she turned around and went to the kitchen. "Where's Charles?"

"I'm coming," he answered. "What do you need?"

"Could you please go to the newspaper office and pick up that book on stenography for me? Or should I ask George?"

"I'll do it, but that really is more his job."

"Sorry. I will go ask him." She headed out the kitchen door and found George polishing a harness in the carriage house. She made her request to him, and he smiled at her.

"I'd much prefer that to this. I'll just ride the bicycle over there."

"I think I would like to learn to ride a bicycle."

"We'll have to order a woman's one for you, then."

"What a good idea. Thank you." Why hadn't she thought of that before? But then, when had she had time?

Back at her desk, she stared out the window. Fritz was coming. And before Thursday. Before supper today.

The stack of letters to be signed was growing on her desk when George knocked and stuck his head in. "Here's your book from that reporter, miss."

"Thank you for getting that for me. I wonder how difficult it is going to be to learn it."

"The way you pick up things, it won't take you long." He put the emphasis on *you*. He placed the book on her desk and closed the door gently.

Do not pick that up now, she ordered herself and returned to her typing. When she had finished that group of letters, she signed them and got the envelopes ready for George to take to the post office.

Why was Fritz coming so early? Of course he had to return home on Saturday, unless he put it off until very early Sunday. *You are mooning, Nilda! Wasting time!*

She rose and went to find Gertrude, who was working at her desk. "Do you have an extra accounts ledger to keep track of donations?"

"No, but you can order one at the same time you order your book on shorthand. Or maybe two ledgers. If we have an address for the donor, we can send a thank-you note."

"Do you need more embossed note cards?"

"I already ordered some, but it's not enough. The newspaper office is carrying more supplies like that. Just telephone an order for more. You better order plenty."

Nilda rang the operator and asked to be connected to the newspaper office.

After that it was time to study. At least she could read her French history book out in the shade. She set aside an hour during each day to read so that she would be ready for the discussion with Miss Walstead. Therefore, she kept notes as she read. The French people had revolted, and she could certainly see why.

A glass of strawberry juice magically appeared on the small table beside her chair. "Thank you."

When she finished reading—longer than she had planned—she went inside. Her next duty in her education regimen was practicing the piano. Maybe Fritz would play tonight. She warmed up with a series of scales as he and Mrs. Potts had taught her. Between the typing and the keyboard, her fingers had grown more and more limber. Turning to her lesson book, she played the songs from the last several lessons, the earlier ones memorized now, she had played them so often. Not so with the most recent two. And the current lesson, although she'd played it every day since he assigned it, still befuddled her. Never had she dreamed she would learn to play the piano. More of those dreams God fulfilled almost before she dreamed them.

"You are sounding more proficient all the time." Gertrude sat in a wingback chair and put her feet up on the hassock, something she rarely did.

"Are you feeling all right?"

"Yes, why?" She glanced at her feet. "I know, but I love relaxing like this and listening to you play, especially the songs you have memorized. I telephoned Jane, and she will be coming for supper too. Perhaps we can play a game of cards tonight. This housing project seems to be taking over our lives."

"Jeffrey compiled the book order lists for me. Reluctantly, I might add. He would rather we had taken another walk. I thought I'd have Fritz read through it and see if he has more suggestions. I want the books here in time for school to start." As Nilda spoke, she kept on playing.

"Jeffrey actually did something useful?" Gertrude groaned. "I'm sorry, that was not necessary."

"Well, I for one am extremely happy to have something to do that needs daily work."

"So you have an excuse not to go to Minneapolis?"

"Very astute. That man just will not take no for an answer." And she plunked a particularly loud chord.

Chapter 22

So, not to be rude, but what brought you back early?" Nilda poured a bit more gravy onto her pork chops and mashed potatoes.

Fritz shrugged. "I just kept thinking that perhaps I could help here. How did the blessing go?"

"It raised some interest from the newspaper. A reporter and a photographer were here this morning. They said the editor wanted to run an article about us in the paper this week."

"That's good news." He cut another bite of his pork chop. "Maybe I came sooner because after being here, I am never content with my own cooking." He smiled at Nilda. "And then I thought perhaps you might like to do something, the two of us. I'm game to help with any work you have to do."

Nilda heard willingness in his voice. No, even better, excitement. She thought of Jeffrey doing a simple chore grumpily. What a contrast. "The paperwork for today is under control, but I should go out to the site and get the hours each man has worked and the records of work performed."

Fritz grinned. "I told George not to put my buggy away yet. May I take you out?"

"That would be lovely." Her heart sang.

"But first, these pork chops." Fritz grinned wickedly as he speared another one onto his plate.

After dinner, the sky was starting to cloud over as they rode in the buggy out to the construction site. Darkness crept into the white fluffy clouds. Fritz looked up. "Think it will rain?"

"Quite possibly. Thunderstorms appear out of nowhere in the summer." What did the builders do when it rained? She had not thought of that. Perhaps she would find out.

Thor Haglund had seen them coming. Grinning, he came bouncing over to them before Fritz had even stopped the horse. "Fritz Larsson! Welcome!" He certainly had not greeted Jeffrey this enthusiastically.

Fritz was just as enthusiastic as he pumped the older man's hand. "What are you doing here, Thor? Showing them how it's done?"

"I'm running this show."

Nilda smiled. *Listen to the pride in his voice!*

"You're a bit old to be working construction." Fritz waved an arm toward the half-finished house. "But look at what you all are doing!"

Mr. Haglund cackled. "Just me and a bunch of young whippersnappers." He sobered slightly. "My daughter still plays the piano well, Fritz. You taught her to love it, not just play it."

"I'm so glad, Thor."

Nilda stepped back and followed a short distance behind as Mr. Haglund toured Fritz around the site. Fritz was wearing sturdy shoes, not the flimsy white ones that got all dusty on Mr. Esquire's feet. She realized that Fritz was probably wearing work boots on purpose. He had said he was coming to help out.

Nearly all the workmen greeted her as she passed, and she

returned their greetings. Where would their work records be? A canopy had been raised on poles at the lot where house number three would someday stand, a sort of makeshift tent. She would try over there.

Fritz and Mr. Haglund were nodding and talking excitedly, gesturing at various stages of the project. Fritz touched so many lives, not to mention his English classes and organ playing. He was a wonderful credit to any community. She felt very proud to know him, to know his loving aunt, to be a part of his life—of their lives.

What else did she appreciate about him? No need to think about that very long. His enthusiasm. He taught English quietly and enthusiastically. He played the organ with heart and soul. And look at him and Mr. Haglund now as they scrambled over unfinished walls and squeezed between studs. She was confident that if he lived to a ripe old age as Mr. Haglund was fast doing, he would have the same enthusiasm.

Thunder boomed and rolled, making her jump. She hadn't been paying attention to the sky. The world flashed bright as lightning struck close by. Another crack of thunder, and the clouds overhead split open, dumping water by the oceanful.

"To the tent!" Mr. Haglund called as rain fell so hard you could barely hear over the roar. He started running toward the canopy on lot three.

Fritz took after him, peeling out of his jacket as he ran. Nilda was a good runner, but she had trouble keeping up. Fritz dropped his jacket over her head and shoulders, hooked an arm behind her, and boosted her along.

As they ducked under the canopy, Nilda was panting. Some of the workmen joined them, but most simply stayed out in the rain to continue sawing, hammering, and toting lumber.

A table under the canvas held a couple of water buckets and

ladles. A grin split Mr. Haglund's face as he dipped a ladle into a bucket and extended it toward Fritz. "Water?"

Fritz was grinning too. "Thanks, but I just had some." He bent forward and shook his head like a dog. Water droplets flew everywhere.

Nilda laughed. She was so soaked, the wind was chilling her. Biting down to stop her quivering lip, she dragged Fritz's jacket closer around her. Thunder cracked again, but not as loud and close this time.

Fritz pulled her against his side, pressing her against him. He was just as wet, but for some reason she felt warmer. Together they watched the shower spend itself.

"I hope this doesn't buckle the new flooring." Mr. Haglund bounced away even before the rain ended, heading for the first house.

Nilda looked all around, but apparently the log books were not here. She would come back when Mr. Haglund was not so worried about his flooring.

Fritz stepped out from under the canvas, and Nilda followed. He pointed. "Now the road graders will know exactly where all the low spots are." True. Rivulets were coursing down the street, and huge puddles covered parts of it. "Well, shall we return to Aunt Gertrude's and find some dry clothes?"

She watched the ruined road for a moment. "Will the buggy make it through this fresh mud?"

"If it doesn't, I'll quickly blame my horse."

He gave her a hand up to the seat and climbed in beside her. He clucked to his mare, and she started forward. Keeping her to a walk, he guided the mare to one side, then the other. Clearly, he knew where his wheels were and where the safest route lay.

"You drive on this half-road as if it were a highway."

"This horse and I have gone a lot of miles together. A lot of miles."

He was pressed against her, or was she pressed against him? It didn't matter. They were pressed together. She was absolutely soaked, but that didn't matter. And Fritz didn't seem to mind at all either.

When they reached the main street, the surface flattened out, but it was still slippery and muddy. He held the mare to a walk all the way home.

George must have been watching for them. He greeted them in the drive and held the mare as Fritz hopped to the ground and gave Nilda a hand down. "I figured you'd gotten stuck in the shower," George said.

"What was your first clue?" Fritz patted his wet shirt, a slapping sound. "Please don't wash the buggy. I know you want to. But have it ready for me after breakfast, please."

"I shall." George looked at the wheels, the undercarriage. "Are you certain I shouldn't wash it, Mr. Larsson?"

"Positive. If you do, it will only look like this again five minutes down the road."

"Very well." George led the wet horse away.

Fritz escorted Nilda up onto the porch and paused. They stood facing each other, still close together. Nilda didn't mind a bit. He broke into a broad smile. "You know, silly as it sounds, that was a lot of fun. Getting soaked and all. I loved it."

"So did I." Her smile matched his.

His grin faded. He slowly drew closer, as if he wanted to kiss her. Her breath caught.

Suddenly he stepped back. "Well. We should go dry off before we catch pneumonia." He opened the door and ushered her inside.

A moment ago she had felt happy. Why did she suddenly feel cheated?

The next morning after breakfast, Fritz folded his napkin. "Do you mind if I go over to the building project and see if I can be of help there?"

Gertrude nodded. "Not at all. I'm sure Thor will be glad to put you to work."

With a quick good-bye, Fritz left.

"Now we find out how good our Fritz is at heavy lifting." Gertrude smiled as she ordered tea and walked outside to the verandah with a book in hand.

Nilda returned to her office. She was way behind in the chores she had to get done. This building project was taking far more time than she had anticipated.

Fritz dragged himself back to the house just in time to get ready for supper. "I'll be down as soon as I get cleaned up." Sometimes he took the stairs two at a time. This time he slogged up the steps one by one.

"Your face is sunburned. You need a hat with a wider brim," Gertrude called after him.

He paused on the landing. "At least I don't have blisters, thanks to the leather work gloves Rune made for me. He sure knows how to do many things."

"He used some of the deer hide they tanned." Nilda sat down to get some practice time in before supper. It didn't look like Fritz would feel like giving her a lesson tonight.

The next day he dragged in for supper a little earlier. He washed up and joined Gertrude and Nilda at the table. "Thor allowed me to nail on siding today." He took several pieces of fried chicken. "Teaching school never prepared me for ten hours of hauling, sawing, and nailing siding. That man is a slave driver. In fact, they all are. Totally devoted to the work. And speedy. Much speedier than I am."

"You don't have to do this, you know," Gertrude reminded him. "We have plenty for you to do here."

"I told him I'd be back tomorrow because I want to contribute something."

Nilda peeled the skin off her chicken thigh. The way Cook prepared it was so tasty. "Helping here would be helping behind the scenes. Can you use a typewriter?"

"A bit."

"There's not a lot of difference between that keyboard and the piano. Once your fingers know the patterns." Nilda smiled at him. He did indeed look like he'd been worked to the hilt.

"If I don't show up for breakfast, send someone to check on me. I might have gone to sleep in the bathtub."

"That bad, huh?" Gertrude smirked.

On Thursday morning he went out to the site. That night he burst through the door. "Have you seen the paper?"

"In here, and yes, we have it in front of us." Nilda called from the sun-room. The sound of his excited voice made her smile. She glanced up to see Miss Walstead and Gertrude both wearing a knowing look. "What?"

They glanced at each other. "Nothing, nothing at all." They turned back to their newspapers.

Something was afoot, but what?

Fritz charged into the sun-room. "On the front page, no less." For emphasis he slapped the paper he carried, freeing a cloud of dust to drift to the rug. "Oh, oh. Sorry." He laid the paper down. "That reporter quoted you both, and Thor, and even quotes from others. It'll be great if other papers pick this up."

"Did you see the box on page three?" Nilda flipped the pages.

"And we didn't even ask for this." A two-column, five-inch box encouraged people to volunteer, to donate, and to make their town proud.

"I can't believe this." Fritz read it again. "I have a feeling that if you thought we were busy before, we'll all be dancing at high speed tomorrow. Did you give him permission to include your telephone number?"

"I never dreamed they would do such a grand thing as this." Gertrude was still shaking her head when the telephone jangled. "We need to send them a thank-you letter or gift immediately."

The phone call was someone already promising a donation. Nilda had not had time to set up the ledgers but went ahead and did so while Fritz took over answering the telephone.

The next day, she let Fritz field all the calls in her office so she could man the donation ledger and start writing thank-you notes.

"I'm sorry you feel that way," Fritz answered one caller. "I'm sorry no one offered to help you, but you must be doing well now if you have access to a telephone. Thank you for calling."

Nilda felt her eyes widen. "Someone resents others receiving help? I sure hope I don't know who they are. What a pity."

"I guess some people feel that if they made it on their own, others should be able to do the same."

Nilda stared at the sheet of paper she was holding. How sad. But the more she thought about it, the less sad and more angry she felt. She looked up to find Fritz watching her. "I hope we don't have many people feeling that way. I also hope I never learn who it is, because I would want to go . . ."

Fritz smiled. "Yell at them? Send someone to beat them up?" He got up and wrote the latest donation into the ledger himself.

"Sorry. I got carried away." She reached for the telephone

when it jangled again, sucking in a deep breath before saying hello.

"Nilda, this is Jeffrey. I've not been able to get a call through for hours." He sounded out of sorts, maybe even angry.

"I'm sorry, but I have to keep this line clear. We are having a major response to the article about our housing plan in the paper, and we don't want to miss those calls. I'm sorry, Jeffrey, but I can't talk right now. Good-bye."

He was saying good-bye in an angry, pouty way as she hung up.

Fritz sat down beside the phone. "I get the idea he is being . . . hmm, how should I put it?"

"Persistent. Stubborn. Has no real idea of what we are doing. Cannot think of anyone but himself. Any of those fit?"

Fritz shrugged. "Probably all of them. But you have to understand, Nilda, that is the way he was raised. He has never gone without anything he needed, although he probably did not get everything he wanted."

She shook her head. "We have a meeting here Saturday morning. When do you plan to leave?"

"I'll go after the meeting, and I'll be back late Sunday afternoon."

She found herself grinning. "Thank you. We so appreciate your help."

Why was she grinning so broadly? Because Fritz was . . . Fritz was . . . here.

When the committee convened in the Schoenleber dining room on Saturday morning, Fritz chose to go out to the site to paint. He seemed to be enjoying this new life of a tradesman. Nilda and Mr. Haglund gave their reports of the accomplishments so far.

"All you need to do is visit the site, and you'll see my report." Mr. Haglund nodded at the others around the table. "The men have been sleeping in the first house with breakfast served there by the church. We have our crew of ten, but there have been plenty of volunteers, so all of the sites are cleared to begin raising the houses. We could proceed further, but we agreed to work on a cash basis. There is almost enough cash in the account to pay for the lumber for the second house, so we went ahead with it."

Nilda reported, "I have pages documenting the donations for those in the houses. We're storing the donated furniture in the carriage house here. The women of the Catholic church and the Brethren congregation are sewing pallets that they will stuff with corn leaves and husks or hay, so hopefully everyone will have a bed to sleep on. The list goes on and on, and I am most grateful. But there is a problem: We do not have anyone stepping up to sponsor the building of another house."

Mr. Haglund raised a hand. "I've been pondering this, and I think the fault lies in our including supporting the family through the winter as part of the package. What if we divided the need into three sections? The lumber, the rest of the materials for building, and providing food as needed."

Mr. Amundson nodded. "I think you're right, Thor. We were hoping for a package deal, but it doesn't seem to be working. Can we publicize the change?"

"I will take care of that," Reverend Holtschmidt volunteered.

"I'll help you," Homer Blanding, owner of the grocery store, said.

"Everyone agree?" Nilda asked, grateful when they all nodded.

By the meeting the following week, Nilda was pleased to report that three established immigrant families in Bemidji had banded together to pay for both the lumber and the supplies for one house.

"I hope this stands as an example and a challenge," Nilda added. "How wonderful."

The next evening Fritz arrived in time for supper, served outside where it was cooler. A bit of breeze discouraged the mosquitos, so the verandah was doubly pleasant. His enthusiasm about helping bubbled over, although he seemed embarrassed by the paint that would not wash off his hands.

"Strawberry shortcake for dessert," Charles announced and glared over his shoulder at the offending telephone. "Not again."

Nilda went to answer it. She'd thought of paying the telephone operators not to put some calls through. Like this one. "Hello, Jeffrey. I'm at the wall telephone, so could you please call again in, say, an hour, when I am back in my office?"

"I probably won't be able to get through then."

"All right. Then how are you?"

"Great. I just won the all-city tennis tournament in singles. My partner and I took runner-up in the doubles."

"Congratulations." She could tell he'd been drinking. "Celebrating, are you?"

He didn't catch her sarcasm. "Yes, we have been. We earned it. I wish you had been here."

"Sorry, but we've been busy keeping track of all the assistance people of this area are giving to our enterprise. We're receiving a very generous response."

"That's nice."

Nice? A major outpouring of generosity and caring, and he says it's nice?

"Mother has decided to have a ball this fall," he said, "and the two of you will receive an invitation soon. Father said to set the date the weekend after the fall meeting so you and Aunt will come. So the date is Saturday, October sixth, and it will be an autumn theme."

"I see." Nilda knew she had been shanghaied to attend with no way out. That meant a ball gown and everything that went with it.

"Isn't that exciting? Your first ball, I'm sure."

"Yes." *And my last, if I have my way. Ask him if you can bring Fritz.* She nearly laughed at the thought. "I will go write this on my calendar, and thank you for letting us know well in advance. Congratulations on your grand win, and I must go now, so good-bye."

She heard him sputtering as she clicked the earpiece back on the prong. Uff da.

Fritz was practically glowing when she returned to the verandah. "There's inside construction to be finished yet, but Thor and I are nearly done painting the exterior."

Gertrude's mouth dropped open. "Thor? Painting?"

Fritz laughed. "Almost as stunning as me painting. We'll paint inside too. We decided it would be cheaper and quicker than hanging wallpaper. We should be done Wednesday or Thursday, ready for the first family to move in. The Norwegian logging crew under Mr. Nicholson is pressing to finish it."

Nilda nodded. "Petter has mentioned Mr. Nicholson more than once. His overseer out at the lumber camp. A fine man."

"He is indeed. Mr. Nicholson's crew organized a big party for this Saturday."

Nilda frowned. "But that's tomorrow! I thought you said it would be Wednesday or Thursday."

"Yes, but there are more people in town on Saturday. It's when the farmers out in the country come in. Everyone is invited. Aunt Gertrude, I thought perhaps you would like to provide some of the food for the party."

"Good idea. I'll talk it over with Cook and see what she'd like to do." Gertrude jotted herself a note. "Will this be an afternoon or evening party?"

"I have a feeling it will start early in the afternoon and keep on as long as the crew wants to continue. Do you know who will be the first family to move in?"

Nilda replied, "I do. You know that older man on the building crew, Yousef Sandborn? He's bringing his wife and four children up from Brainerd."

"He's not that much older." Fritz thought a moment. "How did you choose?"

Gertrude answered. "He was the first to sign up and seems the most responsible. His three boys will be in school, and the younger girl will go the next year."

Nilda added, "One of the ladies from the Lutheran church has made curtains for all the windows, and my mor has donated a rug. Their pallets will be stuffed just before they move in."

She watched Fritz as he eagerly tackled his strawberry shortcake, and compared him with Jeffrey. No comparison.

As opposed to a stuffy formal ball, the party on Saturday was a breath of fresh air. Nilda went out to the site after the regular meeting to watch the eager crews putting the finishing touches on the first house. She saw that two more houses had been started. These crews were working mighty fast.

Nilda saw Mr. Nicholson, so she walked over to him. "Are they doing what it looks like they're doing?" She watched the builders carefully hoist a pretty little pine tree up to the roof of the first house.

Beside her, Mr. Nicholson chuckled. "If it looks like we're topping out the house, you're right."

Nilda smiled in delight. "We did that in Norway, but I didn't know it is a custom here in America."

"It's not really a custom all over America, I hear. But look at the men. Last winter, almost all of my crew out in the woods were Norwegians. These builders are nearly all Norwegian, and that's a blessing. They're hard workers and get along well together."

"They're calling to each other in Norwegian." Nilda watched them nail a base to hold the tree upright on the peak of the roof.

"I encourage them to speak English. 'Look,' I say, 'You have a good life here. You're Americans now. You should try and learn English.' I give all my orders in English and translate when I have to. They try, they really do, and they're getting pretty good at common English. But when they get mad, they still swear in Norwegian."

Nilda giggled. That sounded like her nephew Bjorn too.

Mr. Nicholson walked off to talk to a crew of sawyers cutting siding for the second house.

Nilda turned, and her heart went *thump*. There was that investigator, the Pinkerton man, Crawford Galt! What was he doing here? He watched as the crew put the tree up on the ridgepole. He didn't seem to know she was there as he walked over to Mr. Nicholson. They talked a moment and shook hands, so they were introducing themselves. Mr. Nicholson was not pointing out Nilda, and Mr. Galt had not noticed her yet. Good.

Quietly, she moved around until she was directly behind them, then stepped forward so that she could overhear what they were saying.

Mr. Nicholson waved an arm, explaining. "It's called 'topping out.' When the outside framing is completed and the building is the size it is supposed to be, you hoist a tree up onto the roof. They waited on this one until the house was nearly finished, it went up so fast."

"This is a symbol of some sort?" Mr. Galt asked.

"It is. It signifies several things to various people. Mostly, it's a signal that the party is about to begin."

"A party?"

"When Norwegians work, they work hard. And when they party, Mr. Galt, they party hard!"

"I see."

Nilda smiled to herself. Obviously, Mr. Galt did not see, at least not completely; he probably had never seen a good old full-scale party.

A general cheer went up from the work crew and drowned out the conversation for a moment. Nilda could not make out what Mr. Galt and Mr. Nicholson were saying. Someone hauled a table in front of the house, and two men carried a large keg out to set on the table. Two other men came toting yet another table. Women were bringing out food, glasses, plates, and steins. This was really going to be a party!

Mr. Galt asked, "I understand Dreng Nygaard worked in the woods for a while on your crew. Petter Thorvaldson told me he disappeared partway through his contract. Can you tell me more about that?" He had Nilda's full attention instantly.

"Nygaard, that rapscallion! Yes, he was on my crew. You know he froze to death, don't you? And good riddance."

"Oh? Explain, please."

"In the first place, he was no good at any job we tried him on. He couldn't even limb logs right. And he had absolutely no will to work or to pull his own weight. He ate three squares a day and didn't earn any of it. He slacked off constantly, hiding while everyone else was working."

"I can see why you weren't happy with him. But rapscallion?"

Mr. Nicholson lowered his voice slightly, but Nilda could still hear. "He went down to the wanigan—that is, the cookhouse—early one morning. The cook's helper, quite a nice young girl, was preparing potatoes for breakfast. He tried to, well, take full advantage of her. She screamed, and he choked her to quiet her, but two of the men heard her and came running. He tossed her aside—I mean literally, and broke two of her ribs—and ran off."

"Surely his attack was provoked by—"

"No! Mr. Galt, when I tell you she was a nice young girl, she was. Never flirtatious, and the whole crew cared about her in a fatherly way, you know what I'm saying? They were protective of her as if she were a daughter. He knew better than to show his face around there again, so I sent one of the crew into town with a letter to the sheriff, telling him to arrest Nygaard for attempted rape if he found him."

"The picture I got of Nygaard was that he was a decent young man. A gentleman."

"I suppose he could put on an act, maybe, if he wanted to impress someone. But it was just an act. I found out later that before that incident, he also attacked the cook, who is only a little younger than I am, but it made her angry, not frightened, and she beat him off with a frying pan. Later, some of the men told me about his boasting about women he had seduced. He was anything but a gentleman, Mr. Galt. A slacker and a predator, a womanizer and a sneak. *Rapscallion* is a more polite term than what he really was."

Another roar of cheering went up, so apparently someone at the new house had just made a speech. Nilda walked away before Mr. Galt could realize she had been listening. Would he believe Mr. Nicholson? He did not believe her mother or her.

A fiddler and a man with a drum started playing. Some of the men danced with the women, but there were not nearly enough women in attendance, so several men danced with other men simply to be able to dance, and some of them danced alone, with fancy steps and turns. Soon a man with a trumpet joined in, then another fellow with a fiddle. There was so much laughter and boisterous good cheer that Nilda found herself not just smiling, but laughing as well.

From near the new house, a booming bass voice called, *"Skol!"*

"Skol to the Northland! Skol!" Dozens of voices. The men were lifting glasses and steins high, toasting the new house.

"Skol!" It was Gertrude! She sat in her victoria, which was stopped right behind Nilda. Up in the driver's box, George beamed. And Gertrude looked so happy. "Isn't this glorious, Nilda? The whole town is becoming enthusiastic about this charitable enterprise."

Apparently a wrestling match had either been set up or someone had challenged someone else. Over by the house, two men stripped to the waist circled each other, parrying. They slammed together like cymbals, but the crowd was now so thick around them that Nilda soon could not see the wrestlers at all. Suddenly a pair of feet in logging boots poked straight up above the crowd and came down again, accompanied by wild cheering.

Half a dozen boys were lining up along the street, which was blocked by merrymaking. A gun shot—into the air, Nilda hoped—and the boys broke forward running. They ran the length of the street as spectators and well-wishers cheered them on. Most of the boys ran on their toes, the fashionable and accepted way to run fast. Nilda noted that the winner, however, had won by running flat-footed, heel landing first, then toe pushing off. Another race was quickly organized. In this one, only one boy ran on his toes. Norwegians learned fast!

Nilda wished mightily that Fritz were here. He had worked as hard as anyone else, and not because he was a natural-born carpenter. He was a natural-born musician who was giving of himself, helping. But he was in Benson's Corner, giving several music lessons today.

Gertrude asked, "Will you be staying for all of this?"

"No, ma'am. The party is going to roar along for hours yet. I'm ready to return home so I can rest and perhaps write a few more letters."

"Then hop in."

Nilda did so and settled into the victoria beside her employer. George clucked, and they moved off. Nilda wagged her head. "With so many complications, I was afraid the project would fail."

"It was a bit dicey there for a while. But it is a worthy project, and I am so very proud of the way you persevered."

Nilda didn't think her contribution was all that much; after all, it was Gertrude's money and Thor Haglund's organizing skill that had really floated it. "Thank you."

They rode along in silence a few moments. Then Gertrude called, "George, take the long way home past the new Methodist church."

"Yes, ma'am."

Nilda smiled. "From that, I think you want time to talk about something."

"Very astute! I do. Tell me what you think of young Jeffrey."

Oh dear! What should she say about her employer's nephew?

Gertrude was studying her. "The truth."

Nilda licked her lips. "I have been trying desperately to come up with something that would be nice without actually coming out and saying I rather dislike him."

Gertrude chuckled. "Truth well phrased. Please explain."

"I'm not sure I can, either in Norwegian or in English. He irritates me. He is everything you are not. He considers himself above the rest of us, a person of wealth and therefore of power, and we are simply ordinary people. You have never taken that attitude. He cannot hide the fact that he does not care for people. You care deeply. You have shown me what ample money can do to make the world a better place. I suspect the whole concept of spending money for the good of others has never occurred to him. I think my attitude toward him took shape when he signed his letter 'Jeffrey Schmitz, Esq.' Esquire indeed."

Gertrude did not seem at all offended by her opinion. Nilda felt a little better about having it, but still, she was speaking ill of the lady's nephew. Then Gertrude asked, "And what about my nephew Fritz?"

Now that was something Nilda could say without fear of offending. "He is a remarkably giving person who gives freely of his time and talents. He cares very much; for instance, the way he just dove right in to help us with this project. And his desire to help educate the children in this area. And his skill—his gift—as a musician and teacher delights me."

"Mm."

And that was all Gertrude said. Should Nilda push the topic further? She was curious about why she had been asked those questions, but as she thought about it, it was really not her business. It was something Gertrude wanted to know, and surely eventually she would explain why she had asked.

Speaking of Jeffrey had reminded Nilda of the upcoming ball. Humph. Jeffrey seemed to think that little farm girl Nilda should be giddy with delight at being able to do a high-society thing.

Hardly.

Chapter 23

Nilda stared out the window of the library. "Can I say something that . . . something that I am struggling with?" *Oh, please do not be offended.* She bit her lip.

"Nilda, haven't I repeatedly asked you to be frank with me in regard to anything and everything? I am trusting you with everything. I know I hired you to be my assistant, but I believe I look upon you more as my daughter. So, please, whatever it is—tell me." Gertrude wiped her eyes with the handkerchief she always carried. "I'm sorry, the tears surprised me."

Nilda reached in her desk drawer where she kept several squares of soft cotton and blew her nose. "Thank you. I . . ." She puffed out a breath. "Here goes. I have an idea, and I was feeling, ah . . ." She shook her head. "I thought of . . . might it be possible to announce that we will match other donations? I know this sounds outrageous, but perhaps that would encourage others to offer more." She shook her head. "No, that doesn't sound as good when spoken aloud. Sorry."

"No, no, wait. Let's think about this."

"It sounds like we . . ." Nilda stumbled over that word. *We*, such a small word with a world of meaning.

"Continue. We . . . ?"

"Are blowing our own horn. 'See, we can afford to do this.'" She rushed through the last words and threw herself back in her chair.

Gertrude rolled her lips together, tried to stop a bubbling laugh, and then gave up. "You constantly amaze me. To think we've been together barely a year. Our God is so very good."

Nilda stared at her. Laughter was not what she had expected when she started this conversation.

"All right . . . back to the beginning. Your idea." Gertrude gazed at her, a smile still playing about her lips. "Your idea is good, sound. Although anyone with a financial background would laugh us out the door. I can just see the look on Heinrik's face, let alone Mathew's." She nodded. "So, how can we rephrase this?"

She leaned over and picked up the receiver from the telephone on Nilda's desk. "Good morning, Milly. Ring Miss Jane Walstead." After a pause to allow the connection to click into place, she said, "Jane, can you come over, please? I will send George immediately."

Nilda could just hear Miss Walstead's tinny voice coming through the receiver. "Is something wrong?"

Gertrude chuckled. "Not at all. Nilda just came up with the most astounding idea, and we need your assistance."

"I'll be waiting on the front step by the time he gets here. It sounds exciting."

Gertrude sent Charles off to arrange for George and the victoria and to call Cook in. "We need tea and sustenance for three in about twenty minutes."

"Will this be in place of dinner, ma'am?" Mrs. Solvang asked.

"No, but please postpone dinner for about an hour. Thank you. And yes, Jane will most likely eat here." She clapped her hands on the arms of her wingback chair. "I hope you can tell that I am excited."

Nilda nodded, eyes wide. "I got that idea."

Charles knocked on the open door. "The mail is here."

"Wonderful. Bring it in. Surely there is good news in there."

"Is a letter for Miss Nilda from her mother good news?"

Nilda reached for it. "That is always good news. Thank you." She slit open the letter while Gertrude sorted the remainder. Drawing two separate folded pages out, Nilda read her mother's letter first.

Dear Nilda,

First of all, thank you again for my trip to Blackduck. I treasure every memory. Now, here is the letter from Ingeborg that I forgot in all the excitement of our visit. It was still in my bag when I came home.

We are in full canning and preserving here, as you know. So far we have good crops, the peas are done with jars in the cellar. Our strawberries became jam and some have been canned for future drinks. The raspberries are on now. We are canning, drying, and will be shelling beans. The corn, both sweet and field, is ready to be tassled. Leif said that is his job, but Knute is helping him.

Kirstin is learning new words nearly every day. Oh, and I have written back to Ingeborg. To think that we can at last talk again.

Love from
Your Mor

Nilda handed the letter to Gertrude. "You'll enjoy this." She unfolded the other piece of paper.

Dear Gunlaug,

It was wonderful to receive your letter! I praise God that Onkel's edict of having nothing to do with us did not permanently destroy any contact between us. Thank you for telling me about Einar. What a sad end. Please know that when I knew him he was not the bitter, dishonest man you described. I wonder what made him change.

We are doing well here in our town of Blessing, all the praise and thanks goes to our Heavenly Father. It sounds as though you are doing well. I remember Rune as the little boy who worked hard all summer in the seters. To think that he has children approaching adulthood! And Nilda, an adult now. In my heart she is still a tiny girl in braids.

If God allows, I will come to visit you, or you can come to visit me. Either way, the person visiting must bring photographs! Notice I put an exclamation point on that for emphasis.

May blessings abound for you and all yours, dear Gunlaug.

Love always
from your cousin,
Ingeborg Bjorklund

"Oh, my. This is beyond belief." Nilda shook her head. "Me in braids."

Gertrude smiled. "Do you mind if I read that?"

"Of course not. Here." Nilda handed the letter across her desk. "I wonder if they have telephones in North Dakota yet."

Miss Walstead arrived at the same time that Stella brought the tray from the kitchen.

"I'd say that is record time." Gertrude greeted her. "Thank

you for coming." She smiled at Stella. "And tell Cook the same, please."

"Oh, I will. Welcome, Miss Jane." Stella set the tray down, smiled at Nilda too, and shut the door behind her on her way out.

Gertrude raised her glass and nodded for the other two to do the same. "Cheers, and thank God for great ideas."

"Does *skol* work here?" Nilda grinned as she tapped the other two glasses. "I do hope it is a good idea. Thank you for coming, Miss Walstead. This has been an amazing morning already."

"All right, tell her." Gertrude nodded to Nilda.

So Nilda did, with Miss Walstead nodding all the while.

"Interesting. So what do you need from me, since obviously I think it is a good idea also?" Miss Walstead reached for a cookie.

Gertrude explained, "I think we need a way to phrase this so it is not offensive to anyone."

"Other than Mathew? Or Heinrik?"

"You know me so well. In a word, yes." She passed the plate of tiny sandwiches around.

"Simple. Just say an anonymous donor has offered to match the donations of money to the fund."

Nilda and Gertrude looked at each other, heads wagging. "Of course."

"The answer was too simple, that's all." Nilda sighed and shrugged at the same time.

"If the information goes public from Mathew, then no one will ever be sure, even if they think they know." Miss Walstead reached for another cookie. "Leave it to Cook, these are delicious. She whipped them up in such short order? Amazing. And I will not eat another, since I am sure this is not to replace dinner."

When Mathew Amundson arrived at three o'clock, the three women greeted him with wide smiles. "I have a suspicion that I am not going to like what you are hatching up now," he said.

Gertrude grinned. "Now, Mathew, how could you think such a thing? We've devised a solid plan, and we just need you to put the first step into motion."

"I'm listening." He turned as Charles handed him a glass of lemonade.

"Unless you would rather have coffee," Charles said.

"No, thank you, this is fine." He took a swallow, nodded, and stared at Gertrude. "Let me have it."

"We have received notification that an anonymous donor has offered to match all other donations of money."

"I see." But he was shaking his head. "An anonymous donor. And you do know the veracity of this rather dubious offer?"

"Yes."

"And I may assume that this oh-so-generous donor is none other than you."

"Assume what you will. All I ask is that you give this information to the newspaper for this week's edition. Our dream is that this will cause an increase in donations."

"Of course that is what you desire. And the donations will be coming to the bank?"

"Of course."

"And you expect us to take care of all the bookwork?"

"Isn't that what banks do?"

He chugged his lemonade.

Gertrude pressed, "And you'll take care of this?"

"I hope I have to hire on extra help, is what I hope."

All three women sucked in breath and released it at the same time. "Thank you," they chorused.

"Well, it's not like I have much choice." He looked from face to face. "And to whom do I give my congratulations on a good idea?"

The other two women looked at Nilda, who shrugged. "I just hope it helps. Donations have been a bit slower than I hoped."

"Hope springs eternal in the human breast?" he said.

"Man never is, but always to be blest," Miss Walstead finished.

"Yes. Thank you. I had best be off to get to the newspaper. By the way, that was some party out at the site." He nodded to each of them. "I just hope this helps."

"Probably better to pray than just hope." Miss Walstead smiled sweetly, causing him to roll his eyes.

When the newspaper came out on Thursday, there was a box in the lower left-hand side of the front page with the word *Announcement* at the top, and below that, "Exciting News!"

Nilda read the short article aloud. "It covers all the information. Now we wait."

By the end of the next week, there was enough money donated to pay for the lumber of another house. When Gertrude matched it, that covered supplies, including the cooking range. Mr. Renborggen at the mercantile put in an order for four more—just in case, he said.

When Fritz returned on Sunday evening, he congratulated them on all the efforts. "The people of Benson's Corner are gathering donations also. I have a list here of things, other than money, that will be coming in. Rune Carlson has offered three butchered hogs to be divided among the residents and will bring them in after butchering, which depends on the weather. He plans to cut them up and freeze the meat."

"I have a feeling Leif had something to do with this, as the pigs are his responsibility." Nilda jotted herself a note to send him and the family a thank-you letter, just as she was doing for all the other donors.

Another letter from her mother said that she'd heard back from Ingeborg. Nilda sniffed. Tears of joy felt better than tears of sorrow—or frustration. The letter said, *They have a dona-*

tion box at the Bensons' store, and Reverend Skarstead has preached on giving and caring for the less fortunate. I'm proud of my people.

The next morning Nilda walked with Fritz over to the building site. "It's beginning to look real."

Mr. Haglund greeted them. "You don't look dressed for work, young man." He shook Fritz's hand.

"Sorry, but we stole him from you." Nilda grinned at the older man. "This looks so beyond belief."

"We have two houses completed. The first family will be moving in before school begins, the second one not long after that. The next two houses are ready for the finish work—mainly painting, moving the stove in, that kind of thing. We've ordered the lumber for the next two. And we're waiting for enough funds to proceed from there. That man giving orders over there, Yousef, is now the owner of the first house. He is one hard worker. I hate to see him go out to the lumber camps when we can sure use him here."

"Is there a paying job here for him?" Fritz asked.

"I have no answer to that. Of course, all his crews will be gone."

Fritz nodded. "I'm sure there is a way to work this out. We need to bring it before the committee."

"What are you thinking?" Nilda asked as they walked home.

"I'm thinking that if they weathered in a couple more houses, he could spend the winter finishing the insides."

"The committee meets Saturday morning. Would you please introduce this idea?"

"Gladly. But I have to tell you, I won't be back like this again. I need to get ready to teach, as school starts soon and I will be back on my fall schedule."

She heaved a sigh. "I know. But I can't tell you how much

I—we have appreciated your help." *But I like having you here. I love my piano lessons, playing badminton and croquet, listening to you make that piano sing in the evenings.*

She found the invitation to the Schmitz ball in the mail later that morning. She handed it to Gertrude without saying, *I would rather tear it up.*

Chapter 24

"I have something I must tell you before we leave."

Nilda looked up from packing her briefcase. The look on Gertrude's face did not bode well. She pointed to the chairs in front of the crackling fireplace. The weather had turned autumnal with October first.

"Should I call for coffee?" Nilda asked. Tea would obviously not be sufficient.

"I already have."

The knock on the door backed up that statement. Charles entered and set the tray between them.

"Thank you, Charles, and tell Cook the cinnamon buns are a perfect antidote for a gray day." As Charles left the room, they both picked up their coffee cups and settled a cinnamon bun on the napkin in their laps, as if they'd choreographed the scene.

Gertrude set her coffee back down. "Before he left, Jeffrey asked for permission to court you."

Nilda could feel astonishment followed by frustration. She blew out a breath. Drinking coffee through gritted teeth was impossible, so she set her cup down very carefully, so as to not shatter it. She nodded. "Now the way he is acting makes at least a little bit of sense. Except that if he wanted to court me, he would have to behave a whole lot differently." She thought a moment and, eyes widening, stared at Gertrude. "And you answered him?"

"I said that was your decision to make, not mine."

Nilda snorted. "I wouldn't marry him if he were the last man on earth." She shook her head. "No, calm down, Nilda." She took a big bite out of her cinnamon roll and stared into the crackling fire while she thought. "This does not make sense to me. I'm not the kind of woman he needs to marry." She raised a troubled look to her employer. "He knows what I think of the society life. Well, maybe he doesn't. I don't think he is especially perceptive." She poured herself another cup of coffee and then filled Gertrude's cup as well. "I think I am developing a more suspicious mind. There has to be something behind this."

Gertrude nodded. "I have a feeling I know the answer to that, but I have a big favor to ask. Can you just be yourself with Jeffrey as we get through this meeting, and try to enjoy the ball?"

"I will feel like a princess wearing that gown, and now that I know how to waltz and do some other dances, I will have a good time. And you?"

"Oh, I will be there, and each of my brothers will fulfill their duty and dance with me, and otherwise I shall enjoy watching you. After all, I will be your chaperone to make sure there are no unwanted advances. I have a feeling you will be the belle of the ball."

"Mrs. Jones, as usual, amazed me. She finished my ball gown so quickly."

"She is a treasure," Gertrude agreed. "So we are ready to leave tomorrow morning?"

Nilda nodded and pointed to a stack of envelopes. "All the correspondence is caught up. Fritz wrote a letter of thanks for the books and had all his students sign it. Knute just signed his name, but Leif wrote, 'Thank you for more books to read. I already started on them.' We have made at least one boy extremely happy."

"What happened with bookshelves?"

"Rune and the boys built the shelves for their school and said that if no one here would do so, they'd build more for this school."

"But someone here took care of that?"

Nilda nodded. "I would not be surprised if Mr. Haglund doesn't form a new construction company, putting a couple of those lumberjacks to work year-round. He mentioned his barn again and what a good place it was to work in."

Gertrude wore her thinking face. "I believe if he does that, I will look into—that is, we will look into building a house out on the lake like Arvid dreamed. After they finish these houses, of course."

Nilda mused, "I thought of building an apartment house as an investment but keeping the rent low for people of lesser means."

She took plenty of work with her on the train so she wouldn't be able to dwell on Jeffrey. This time, they had a trunk along to bring the ball gowns. By now she knew the routine, so she wasn't intimidated by the train station and all the bustle and noise. When they arrived at the hotel, she talked with Mr. Burns at the desk and greeted the maids in their suite.

"Would you please press the ball gowns and have someone here to do our hair on Saturday?"

"Of course, miss. We are glad to see you back. Will you be doing any shopping this trip?"

Nilda looked to Gertrude, who shrugged. "Possibly we will have some free time on Friday afternoon." Nilda thought a moment. "I know I would like to go to the bookstore on Fifth Street." She wanted to meet the man who had overseen the shipment of all the books they'd ordered.

The morning of the board meeting she woke with butterflies flitting around in her middle. She'd prayed for wisdom and grace to ignore the shenanigans of Jeffrey Schmitz, Esquire, and do her very best to make Gertrude proud of her, and confirm that she had made the right choice in bringing Nilda into her life and business.

When they entered the boardroom, she nodded and responded to those greeting her, then took her place next to Gertrude at the head of the long table. Heinrik did not smile at her as did some of the others. So that was the way it was to be. She smiled anyway and placed her shorthand tablet on the table, along with several sharpened pencils.

Heinrik opened the meeting with the briefest of prayers, obviously doing so because of his father's tradition that Gertrude had resurrected. He then welcomed everyone and turned the meeting over to Gertrude, which probably taxed his graciousness.

Now, Nilda, behave, she told herself. The interesting thing was that Jeffrey was not in attendance. He—or they—had not deemed his leaving school for this meeting of importance. So be it. At least he realized his schooling was of great value, or his father had told him not to bother. *My, what a suspicious mind you have, Miss Carlson.*

"Like the rest of you, we have studied all the proposals and made lists of the strengths and weaknesses of each." Gertrude paused to look around. "You have all done so, correct? And you have your reports with you?"

Nilda looked around. No negatives, although Jonathon didn't look up. Hmm.

"Then let's begin the discussion. Which do you see as the most possible? And the best for the company?"

Nilda did her best to keep up with her notes in shorthand, but after a while, her hand cramped. She laid the pencil down and stretched her fingers in her lap. Good thing she dared to ask Mr. Jurgenson for his notes now.

Finally, Gertrude nodded and said, "Then we agree to our long-range proposal and the processes can begin." She looked around the room. "Since we are all aware that we are running out of timber in Minnesota, anyone want to offer an estimate as to how much time we have?"

"I'd say five years max," Jacob offered. "We already have options on timberland in western Washington, mostly to lease instead of purchase, unless we are forced to. Alaska is, of course, the last great frontier, but that mountainous land will create difficulties beyond anything we've dreamed of."

When they adjourned for dinner, Nilda made her way to the necessary down the hall, grateful she would not have to type all of her notes. She flexed her fingers under the hot water tap.

Gertrude joined her at the next sink. "This meeting is just the tip of the iceberg. It's almost farcical. This afternoon when we go over financial reports . . ." She shook her head. "I have so many questions, but this is not the place to bring them up."

When they joined the others in the dining room, Gertrude asked, "Heinrik, you've met Andrew Carnegie, have you not?"

He nodded. "Yes, of course. A great philanthropist and a good businessman."

She added, "But he has a bad reputation for the way he deals with his workers. You can't read the newspapers without reading about brutality to the miners and the steelworkers."

"He gets the job done." Heinrik appeared finished with the conversation.

Gertrude turned to answer a question from someone else and continued eating. Nilda could tell she was pondering something.

Before they returned to the boardroom, Heinrik stopped his sister. "I would like a meeting with you alone after we are finished here today."

"All right. I'll send Nilda back to the hotel after we close."

"No need, we won't be long."

When they convened again, Gertrude rose. "Now, if we can all stay awake after such a fine dinner . . ." The others chuckled. "I would like to discuss something that has been on my mind more lately." She looked at each person around the table. "I know that my position in this company as chairman is little more than that of a figurehead, but I also see myself as the conscience of this corporation. To refresh your memories, I will read the pertinent clause from our father's will." She picked up a piece of paper and read the clause that specified a percentage of profits to go toward charitable donations and foundations. "Now, my question is, how are we living up to that?"

Pandemonium ensued, the chief argument being that the will had been written years ago, before the company expanded into such great size. Surely she did not expect them to give away so much money in today's world.

She waited for them to settle down. "You know, I am not stupid, and neither was our father. I believe any effort is better than no effort, so in order to stay within the tenets of our father's will, we must return to thinking of benevolence as part of our company policy."

"Our companies provide jobs for who knows how many thousands of people. Surely that can be considered a form of benevolence," Heinrik said.

"True. But we receive a return. It is not charity."

Nilda felt like ducking at the glares sent their way.

"I suppose you have a plan to offer?" Jacob had always been deft at sarcasm.

"Not really. But awareness is the first step to change. And as head of this company, I see it as important that we all become aware. Benevolence starts within."

"Who made you judge?" Jacob snarled.

"There is a difference between judging and recommending. I am not judging when I read you the clause. I am simply pointing out that we have not been honoring it."

Nilda saw heads shaking and heard sighs and grumbling. Gertrude was digging herself a deep hole.

"I challenge that by the next board meeting, we will all be able to report on our efforts and the results thereof. Are there any questions?" At the silence that screamed disgust, she rapped her gavel. "Then we are dismissed for today. I hope we can all think on this overnight and tomorrow morning discuss some possibilities."

"What a joke," Nilda heard someone say. "She is out of her mind," said another. "What a waste of time." She gathered her things and put everything in her briefcase.

"Gertrude, we'll meet in my office," Heinrik ordered.

Gertrude rolled her eyes at Nilda and followed her brother out of the room. Nilda didn't have long to wait before Gertrude rejoined her. Nilda's questioning look earned a shrug.

"We'll talk back in our suite. Here's our driver."

After ordering a light supper to be served in an hour, Gertrude chose to lie down until supper arrived, leaving Nilda wondering.

She shrugged and picked up the telephone to call Jeffrey in answer to a message he had left for her. "May I speak with Jeffrey, please?"

"I'm sorry but he's gone for the evening. May I tell him who called?"

"This is Miss Carlson answering his message."

"And he has your number?"

"Yes, thank you." Nilda hung up and stared at the telephone. "Obviously he has my number or how could he have left a message?" She shook her head and decided to emulate Gertrude. Closing her door, she picked up a throw and pulled it over her legs as she lay down on the bed. And fell asleep.

She woke to a tapping on her shoulder.

It was the maid. "Miss, let me help you get ready for bed. Gertrude said she will see you in the morning."

"Oh, thank you."

A few minutes later, Nilda was properly tucked into bed and drifted right back to sleep. To wake at a tapping at the door. "Yes?"

"I am here to help you dress." The maid again.

Nilda stared at the clock. Morning. She should be up and dressed by now and eating breakfast with Gertrude. How could she have slept so long?

"Yes, please help me. I have to hurry." She threw back the covers and was halfway to the bathroom when the maid came in. "The blue serge business suit."

Thanks to the maid, she was ready in less than half an hour, and after blowing out a breath, she joined Gertrude at the white-clothed table. "Good thing I'm not hungry." Just then her stomach growled, making her out a liar.

"Never fear. You have fifteen minutes before we have to leave. Help yourself."

"Thank you. I—I'm sorry."

"Just eat and relax. You were so sleepy last night, I did not have the heart to wake you up for supper. Besides, we will be there in plenty of time. And if we are late, they will have another cup of coffee, swap some more gossip, and begin when we get there."

Nilda forced herself to concentrate during both the morning and afternoon meetings. She thought that with all the sleep she'd had, she should be at her best, but it didn't seem that way. Anytime there was a lull in the discussion, she wondered what in the world had been so important that Heinrik had requested a private meeting with his sister. Perhaps it wasn't for her to know.

Back at their hotel, they ordered tea and relaxed in comfortable chairs. "Good tea," Gertrude said. "I believe you are dying to know about the conversation."

"Well, yes." Nilda picked up a thin cracker and nibbled on it.

"Heinrik extolled Jeffrey's good traits and declared how life will be so much better for you when the two of you are married."

Nilda stared at her. "That's it? And what did you say?"

"I told him that this would be your decision, and I had nothing to do with your response."

Nilda sensed there was more. "And?"

"And we are looking forward to the ball." She paused. "But then I slipped in that you and Jeffrey did not seem suited, in my opinion."

"I see. So that is why he seemed a bit cool today. To you, that is. He mentioned to me that he is looking forward to the ball and watching Jeffrey and me dancing together. I just nodded."

"Good for you. You need to keep your wits about you tomorrow night."

"I would like to go to the bookstore tomorrow morning if possible."

"Of course. And then we'll come back here and relax and maybe even read some of our new books."

"And perhaps decide not to go at all?" Nilda said, hoping.

"Don't I wish."

Chapter 25

Nilda stared at the piles of books they had purchased. "I believe we are in need of a box, if not more than one."

"See if I let you loose in a real bookstore again." Gertrude studied Nilda, her smile widening. "Watching you was so delightful."

"You seem to have purchased a few yourself." Nilda looked outside the carriage to see people bustling along and electric trolley cars having the right of way. "One of these times when we come here, I would like to go on a tour of these cities where so much is going on. I'd like to see the Carnegie library and the mills and where people live."

"We will make arrangements for that to happen, although a spring tour sounds more inviting to me than a fall or winter one." Gertrude thought a moment. "Regarding the books, the hotel will pack them for us to go along with our other luggage."

They had left the store in time to have a light dinner back in their suite and enjoy a nap and time to read. Two maids came in to assist them in dressing for the ball, making sure Nilda's hair was studded with sparkling hairpins and shining in the lamplight.

"You look beautiful, miss." The maid stepped forward and adjusted the neckline on the royal blue ball gown.

Nilda stared into the mirror, shaking her head. "Is that really me?"

"It is. I hope the shoes are comfortable for dancing, because your dance card will fill up faster than you can believe." Gertrude stood behind her, both of them smiling into the floor-length mirror. Her plum dress, of a more simple design, set off the blue, which set off Nilda's eyes. "And our coach is ready, Your Highness."

Nilda rolled her eyes. "We shall see."

Gertrude was right. When they entered the ballroom at the hotel where the event was being held, Jeffrey stopped, stunned at the shimmery young woman before him.

"Nilda, you are so beautiful." He held out his arm. "Shall we dance?" He twirled her around on the dance floor and took her in his arms for her first waltz. "I was afraid you wouldn't come. I kept trying to get ahold of you but . . ."

She tipped her head to the side. "I've been very busy, and I did return your first message." They swung in a circle and continued around the huge ballroom.

"I should have presented you to my mother. Silly of me."

She just smiled. And felt like she was floating on the music in the strength of his arms. He did indeed dance well. And lead well, so she could enjoy the music and not worry about tripping. When the dance ended, they strolled over to greet his parents.

"Good evening, Miss Carlson," Mr. Schmitz wore the widest smile she had ever seen on his face.

Beside him, Mrs. Schmitz took Nilda's hand in both of hers. "Welcome to our harvest ball. I have been hearing so much about you lately."

"Thank you."

"Excuse us, please. I don't want to miss out on a single dance tonight." Jeffrey had kept ahold of Nilda's other hand.

"You go right ahead. There will be time to talk later when supper is served." Mrs. Schmitz smiled and nodded.

They had danced halfway around the floor when a young man tapped Jeffrey's shoulder. "Move over, brother. You cannot monopolize this lovely young woman all evening."

Jeffrey glared at him but relinquished Nilda with a grumbled introduction. "My brother, Jeremy."

"Really? Well, I'm delighted to meet you."

Jeremy grinned. "I believe you are the best kept secret in our family."

She shrugged. "I have no idea. Besides, Jeffrey has not mentioned *you*."

Jeremy pulled her into his arms and swept her over the floor. "You live up in the Northwoods with my aunt Gertrude?"

"Yes." *And I only come down here for company meetings,* she didn't add.

"No wonder Jeffrey wanted to go visit. I have not been there since we were boys, but I do have good memories."

"Where do you live now?"

"I travel for the company. I just returned from an extended stay in New York."

"And your wife?"

"Oh, I'm not married. But now that I've met you, that could be remedied."

Nilda laughed. "You're as bad as Jeffrey."

"Really? And how is that?" He swung her around, making her skirts swirl. As the music came to a close, he turned his head as another young man tapped his shoulder and cut in. "I will return, Miss Carlson, you can count on that." He bowed and winked at her.

"I'm sorry but we have not met before," she said to her new dance partner. The young man said his name, but it got lost in the music, so Nilda just smiled and kept on dancing. Her new partner was not as smooth as the other two, so they danced without the dips and whirls. Which was fine with her.

By the fifth dance, Jeffrey was waiting and took her hand possessively. "I was beginning to think you were ignoring me."

"How could I do that? I just keep on dancing, but I am counting on you to escort me off the floor before this song is finished and to the ladies' room."

He started to grumble, but then his face cleared. "Of course. Perhaps we should ask Mother to accompany you, beat off other . . ."

She didn't hear the rest, but when halfway through the number he led her off the floor and toward the ladies' room, she was extremely grateful. "Thank you." Once inside, she sank down on the curved-back, tufted sofa, unfolded her fan, and breathed in the cooler air.

"Are you all right, miss?" the attendant asked.

"Yes, I just needed to catch my breath."

"Can I bring you something to drink?"

"Cold water would be wonderful."

She sipped the water, used the facilities, and checked in the mirror to make sure her gown was proper again.

"You look lovely, miss." The attendant straightened the back of the dress. "There now, all is well."

"Thank you." She left the ladies' room and found Jeffrey waiting for her. He led her back to the dance floor.

"I was about to send someone in to make sure you were all right." He stopped. "Just in case I can't get another dance with you, I want you to myself for supper."

"Oh, really?" There he was, back to his not-so-pleasant imperious habits.

"Let me rephrase that. Will you please join me for supper?"

She nodded. "Yes, I will. Thank you." She knew her words were a bit clipped but doubted he would pick up on that.

He was the best dance partner of the evening, though Jeremy managed to claim her for another dance before supper. "Will you please do me the honor of having supper with me?" He half bowed.

"I'm sorry, Jeffrey has already asked me."

"Well, beat out again by my little brother." He smiled. "Perhaps I will join you." He danced her over to where his father and mother were standing. "Here you go, Father, as you requested."

Nilda almost stopped in surprise. "Good evening, again."

Heinrik took her in his arms, and they fell in with the other dancers. "Seems you are indeed the belle of the ball here. Have you noticed the daggers many young women are throwing at you?"

"No, sir, I did not."

"You dance well for someone of the working class."

She looked at him out of the side of her eye. "Excuse me?"

"Pardon me, that didn't come out right. With your background."

No, it certainly hadn't. And on top of that, he did not dance as well as either of his sons. *Smile, Nilda, smile. Do not give him any idea that what he is saying is belittling you. He probably doesn't even realize it.*

Just to break the silence, she commented, "This is a lovely ball. Everyone seems to be having a delightful time."

"Thank you. My wife is very good at organizing events like this. She accomplishes a great deal in the way of raising money for charities." He paused. "We are both looking forward to becoming better acquainted, since Jeffrey speaks so highly of you."

Keep your mouth closed, do not say what you are thinking.

"That's nice." *I told you to keep your mouth closed. Sorry, that slipped out. Will this song never end?*

"In fact, everyone who has worked with you has been singing your praises. Especially my sister." He paused and turned her in a circle. "Even your banker up there in your little town, and the haberdasher."

Nilda stumbled. "Sorry." So he had been what, investigating her? Apparently. This was beyond irritating. It was insulting.

The musicians played the final chords of the song, and a terrible thought struck her. What if his investigation revealed that Crawford Galt was also investigating her? In relation to a death! Apparently if it had, it didn't matter. They were all so unctuous, another word Gertrude had taught her.

"Thank you for the pleasure of this dance, Miss Carlson. I see my older son is coming this way. I hope you enjoy the rest of your stay here."

Why was Jeremy's smile more welcoming than his brother's? Or was she just being critical of Jeffrey?

"Did Father do his welcome-to-the-family spiel?" he asked.

"Well, no. Whatever do you mean?" She felt like walking off the floor. Were all the men of the Schmitz family having trouble with their mouths this evening? She'd noticed them all at the bar or carrying a glass more than once.

"Oops, sorry. I know he can seem rather, ah, *forthright* is a good word, I believe. Will you be remaining in town tomorrow?"

"No, we are leaving in the morning. I know the mail is piling up on my desk, and I promised Mr. Amundson, head of our bank, that I would meet with him Monday morning. We have an ongoing housing project you might have heard of."

"No, I haven't. What is it you are doing?"

She stared at him. He was the first of the Schmitz men to show any interest in what she did. Her smile blossomed.

"Oh, my word, you are stunning when you smile like that."

"Mr. Schmitz! You are a rogue." She tapped his shoulder with her closed fan.

"Ah, I've not been called that for some time. You are not only beautiful, but you can carry on a meaningful conversation." They swirled again. "Now, what is it you are doing?"

"We and the town of Blackduck are building houses on some donated land to help immigrants. In our case, the families of loggers who work in the woods all winter."

"This is all being done with donations? How many houses are you building?"

"We have completed three. One is now occupied, and the second will be shortly. Two more are in the finishing stages, and the next four are waiting for more donations. We have all agreed we will not start construction on a house until the money is in the bank for building materials and supplies."

"And that comes to . . . ?"

The music drew to a close. Another young man tapped on Jeremy's shoulder.

"Sorry, but she is taken for this one." He led her back to the center of the floor. "I know that was rude, but I'm not sure I'll get a chance to talk with you again."

"You are welcome to visit us and see what we are doing."

"Perhaps one of these days. Right now I have to leave again on Tuesday. I get sent various places to solve difficulties." The music began again. "Now, what are the numbers?"

She told him, all the while wondering where this was going.

"Are you sure that is enough?"

"We do things very economically in our town. Most of the work being done is on a volunteer basis."

"I see. I will speak to my accountant, and a check will be in the mail for two houses."

Her mouth dropped open and she stared at him. "Are you serious?"

He shrugged. "Do you need more?"

"Mr. Jeremy Schmitz, you are restoring my faith in your family. I cannot begin to thank you enough."

"You can take me on a tour of Blackduck when I am able to come visit." He grinned at her. "And I hear you are a rather accomplished badminton player. You almost beat my brother, correct?"

"Personally, I think it was an accident." She chuckled. "Beginner's luck."

"I have my doubts that I should believe that, but here he comes, just in time to claim you for supper."

During the supper, she got Jeffrey talking about school and tennis so she only had to nod and smile once in a while. When the dancing began again, she danced once more with Jeffrey and then sought out Gertrude. Her employer was seated at a small side table in the corner with a glass of wine, talking to a matronly lady. It was not polite to intrude, so Nilda positioned herself beyond the lady.

It worked. Gertrude noticed her instantly. "Nilda! Do come join us."

The matronly lady stood up as Nilda approached. "My dear, I have been hearing such good things about you. God bless you as you work to help those in need. Now, if you'll excuse me, I'm going to get myself some more refreshments. Please take my seat." With a smile, she left.

Nilda sat on the chair the lady had just vacated.

Gertrude seemed relaxed, in charge. She fit into a formal occasion like this so comfortably. Nilda envied that a little. "That was the wife of the rector of the Episcopal cathedral. She dislikes these occasions almost as much as I do."

"How long will it be before we can leave gracefully?" Nilda asked.

"Anytime you wish. I saw you dance after supper, so we will not be eating and running. Would you like to leave now? I'm certainly ready."

"So am I." Nilda hesitated. "You're not just saying this to please me, are you?"

"Not at all. I weary quickly of these pretentious balls."

"I will go find Jeffrey and take our leave. Have you seen him?"

"He is over at the bar."

Nilda glanced toward that corner. Glass in hand, Jeffrey was laughing with four or five other young men. "Is it all right to interrupt?"

"Don't bother." Gertrude stood up. "He didn't bring you, I did. Heinrik and his wife are over by the door, and it is Jeffrey's mother who hosted. We can take our leave there." She led the way to the door.

"Wait. You left your wine." Nilda pointed to the half-filled glass on the table.

Gertrude laughed. "That is the drink they poured for me when we arrived. Keep that trick in mind. So long as you have a glass in front of you, they don't urge you to drink."

Nilda chuckled as Gertrude walked over to Heinrik and took his wife's hands in hers.

"Maisie, this was a beautiful event. Just beautiful. You have a great talent. However, Miss Carlson and I are quite weary, and we beg our leave. Thank you for the gracious evening."

"Wait! You can't leave yet," Heinrik exclaimed as Jeffrey's mother waved frantically at someone.

Here came Jeffrey, groping around in his pocket as he approached. He found whatever he was looking for and dropped to one knee in front of Nilda. He held out a little red velvet box and thumbed the lid open. Nilda had never seen a diamond or even a fake diamond as large as this one.

"Nilda Carlson," he cooed, "will you marry me?"

Nilda stammered. What could she do? "I—I think—I mean . . ." As weary as she was, in the next fifteen seconds she would determine the course of the rest of her life. "I want—I don't want . . ." Gertrude could be no help here. She had said it was Nilda's decision.

What do I want?

Nilda drew in a deep breath. "No. I'm sorry, Jeffrey. I'm so sorry to disappoint you, but no. Marriage would be a disaster for both of us." She reached down and closed the lid on the jewelry box.

His face melted into disbelief. "You're not joking, are you?" He stood up. "You mean it."

"Yes. My decision is made."

"You're supposed to be the girl who makes such wise decisions. But this is a stupid decision!" He should have been sad to be refused. Instead he looked angry. Or rather just peeved, not furious. "Nilda, don't you realize that when you marry me, you need never work another day in your life? Never. You'll have servants to take care of everything. You'll be able to go to a ball like this every night if you want. I am offering you every girl's dream: status and wealth. Surely you're not going to turn that down." He flipped open the little box.

She poked it closed again with a finger. "You don't understand, Jeffrey." Her mor's words came back to her. The reason Gunlaug was not happy in the Schoenleber home was because she could not work. Others did the work. "I *want* to work. I want—"

"Go back to the farm you came from and work from dawn to dark every day? When you don't have to? That's foolish!"

Foolish? She and her mor were foolish? Nilda was getting angry. "I enjoyed work on the farm. It's a joy you'll never know. You work hard, and when you're done, you have a lovely garden, happy animals, a warm safe home, and plenty of wholesome food for the table."

"I see. You're playing hard to get. You're an immigrant. What do you want, a dowry? I'll give you a dowry." Now Jeffrey sounded angry, and that would not do. She could not think clearly if they were arguing angrily.

She took a deep breath and lowered her voice. "There are two reasons I'm saying no. One is that I want to work. With Mrs. Schoenleber, I am making a very important and positive difference in people's lives. In whole families' lives. And two, you do not love me, and I do not love you. We could not—"

"Love?" Jeffrey snorted. "Love is for poor people who have no other reason to marry. Why do you think Mother is hosting this ball? It's to celebrate our engagement. I will not take no for an answer."

"Never have you said you love me. You don't even respect me, or you wouldn't call me stupid and foolish. And I know my feelings. No." She stepped back.

Beside her, Heinrik snarled, "Gertrude, talk some sense into her. She's had too much drink. She's spouting nonsense."

For the first time, Nilda looked to Gertrude. Her employer wore a pleasant, peaceful, happy, proud look on her face.

"I told you many times, Heinrik, that it would be Nilda's decision," Gertrude replied. "I will take my leave now. Thank you for the lovely evening."

"Allow me to join you." Nilda nodded to Jeffrey and his parents. "Thank you for the lovely evening."

And she followed Gertrude out the door.

Chapter 26

Nilda noticed that there was no night in St. Paul. With all the electric streetlights, you were never in complete darkness. Their hansom rattled its way from the ball toward their hotel.

"I believe . . ." Gertrude stared out the carriage window. "No, I am certain. I have known Heinrik and Jeffrey all their lives. Jeffrey is a ladies' man, a playboy, a bee who flits from blossom to blossom."

"And plays tennis," Nilda added with a smile.

Gertrude chuckled. "And plays tennis. Marriage has never entered his head. It is Heinrik."

"What do you mean?"

"Don't you see, Nilda? Heinrik understands that I have been grooming you to take over bigger things. I am certain he fears you will take my place in the company rather than him or one of his sons."

"But wouldn't making me his daughter-in-law put me even deeper into the company?"

"No, it would neutralize you. You would be home, keeping house and raising the babies, leaving Heinrik to control the company."

Nilda's head spun. What if Gertrude was right? That Jeffrey . . . that she . . .

"I may be wrong," her employer concluded. "But obviously I believe I'm right."

Nilda thought awhile. "I think you are right too. It would explain his attempts to intrude, his making a show of liking Blackduck, his . . . his disdain. Is that the right word?"

"Perfect word."

"But whether you are right or wrong does not matter. I have no intention of marrying Jeffrey, regardless of the motivation."

"Good. Let us talk of more pleasant things."

Nilda almost giggled. Her heart felt much lighter suddenly. She leaned over and wiggled her toes. "I cannot get these shoes off fast enough."

"Your feet hurt?" Gertrude leaned back against the seat. "I had forgotten how exhausting a ball can be. No wonder they will all sleep much of tomorrow."

"And we will be on the train home. What a trip this has been."

"Will you look at this." Nilda picked up the letter almost reverently. "A letter from Tante Ingeborg to me." She reread the envelope. *Miss Nilda Carlson, Blackduck, Minnesota.* So simple, yet all part of a miracle.

She slit it open, started to pull out the paper, but instead rose and went to find Gertrude. She was sorting mail as well.

"You have to listen to this." She read the return address.

"Well, I'll be. Hurry, what does she say?"

"'Dear Nilda,

"'I know this is surprising since Gunlaug and I have so recently and after so many years made contact again. Her nice long letter has brought me up to date on all of her family, and I am especially intrigued with where you are and what you are doing. That is quite a change from farming and felling those giant trees. Here in the Red River Valley of North Dakota, the only trees are along the riverbanks unless we plant them. And you can believe we have planted trees, at least around the buildings.

"'I know Gunlaug will share her letters with you, so I will get right to the point. God has blessed us far more than we could have ever believed, so I would like to plant some Blessing seeds in Minnesota as well. What a grand thing it is to be helping the immigrants coming to work there. Where would any of us be if others did not help us? We can't be there to volunteer, although we have some great carpenters in our family. As you know, farmers learn to do anything that is needed. But we would like to be able to give an assist, so if you could tell me how much money you need for a house, I will send you a check by return mail.'"

Nilda felt her chin drop to her chest. "Can you believe this?"

"Yes, I can, having met your mother. Our God is not restricted by miles, as we are learning."

Nilda nodded. "With the donation from Jeremy, we can do three more houses than we had hoped." She had told Gertrude on the train of her conversation with the eldest Schmitz son and her delight in him. "I can't wait to tell Fritz. He said he is coming Friday after school is out. He should be here for supper, if Cook will serve a bit later than usual."

"And she agreed with a smile?"

"Oh, yes." Nilda returned to the letter.

"'I will send the check to you, unless you would rather it went right to the bank. I am looking forward to hearing from you. You have cousins here who would be so thrilled to meet part of their family from Norway. I know this is a plea, but could you possibly bring Gunlaug here to visit? We would both be so thrilled, and you would have our undying gratitude. Blessings from Blessing, your tante Ingeborg.'"

Gertrude glanced at the clock. "Isn't Mathew supposed to be here at ten thirty?"

Nilda nodded. "Yes, I'll go get the papers we need for the meeting. And after that, you can be sure I am going to answer Ingeborg's letter." She left the room only to stick her head back in the door. "I'll notify Cook too."

Nilda was just coming out of the kitchen as Charles ushered Mr. Amundson into the house.

"So, how was your trip to the big city? Or cities?" Mathew asked.

They filled him in on their trip as Charles brought in a tray and poured coffee.

"So basically, the Schmitz company is not underwriting any of our activities here?"

"True, but . . ." Nilda told him about her conversation with Jeremy. "I guess I'll believe it when I see it, but that made me feel good."

"I understand." He handed them each a list of the donations that had arrived since they left. "Those articles in the paper, that donation from the people in Bemidji, seeing the houses going up—all of that is, as we had hoped, generating more generosity. With the first family moved in and two more preparing, I am encouraged. And now with what you say, perhaps there will be funds to get several more shells built so the work on the interiors can be finished over the winter. I have to tell you, Thor talked with Henry and told him to go ahead and deliver the lumber for the next four houses, and he would stand behind it. Now we will have the funds to prove him right."

"That is wonderful." Gertrude set her cup and saucer on the table beside her. "Have you gone through all the mail yet?" she asked Nilda. "There might be other donations."

"I got so excited at the letter from Ingeborg, I've not gotten any further."

Mathew handed them each a financial report. "The amazing thing is that all the volunteer work amounts to far more than those totals, if there were any way to compile that. Now, will we have our regular meeting on Saturday morning?"

"Of course. I am looking forward to what Thor has to say." Gertrude shook her head. "I am so proud of our town for the way the people here have joined in the efforts to assist the immigrants like this."

Mr. Amundson nodded. "Now, if it can continue all the way to the end."

"Ever the doubter, but perhaps that goes with being a money person."

"Possibly. I have seen folks too often not live up to their word."

Charles appeared in the doorway, looking grim. "Sheriff Daniel Gruber to see you and Miss Carlson, madam."

Nilda clapped her hand over her mouth.

"Show him in." Gertrude sounded just as grim as Nilda felt.

Mr. Amundson cleared his throat. "I must get back to my duties. Gertrude, blessings. Miss Carlson." He nodded to them and left. Nilda heard him and the sheriff exchange greetings.

The sheriff appeared in the doorway. Nilda stood, but Gertrude remained seated. "Welcome, Dan. Have a chair."

"Thank you." He sat down, so Nilda sat as well. Her breastbone vibrated. Was he going to arrest her?

Charles asked, "May I bring you something?"

The sheriff shook his head, and Charles left. Sheriff Gruber looked at Nilda. "I'm sure you know a Pinkerton man has been poking around."

"Yes. Mr. Crawford Galt."

"He wasn't going to give me a copy of his final report, so I quoted a nonexistent law about deliberately withholding information, and he caved. It has gone into the file about that attempted rape."

"So you know his conclusions," Gertrude pressed.

The sheriff smiled slightly. "When he came, he was certain Nilda was a seductress and that I was incompetent. Talking to Walt Nicholson, he got a different picture. So he tracked down the cook who worked out at Walt's camp. You gotta hand it to him, he was thorough."

Gertrude's eyebrows arched. "Isn't it disconcerting when facts deny your cherished beliefs?"

"Exactly. Well put." The sheriff settled deeper into his chair. "He finally had to admit that maybe, just maybe, Nygaard was a serial lecher and maybe, just maybe, my investigation wasn't so far off after all. In short, Miss Carlson, you are exonerated."

Relief washed over her like a tidal wave. She asked, "Did he say who hired him?"

"I asked him. He said he couldn't reveal that, citing confidentiality. So as he was leaving, I said, 'Wish Dreng's mother my best,' and he just smirked."

Gertrude nodded. "As we've suspected. Thank you for coming, Dan. His investigation was a cloud over our heads, all of us. I'm glad it is finished."

Charles appeared in the doorway. "Miss Carlson, a telegram for you." He handed it to her and turned to Sheriff Gruber.

"Cook seems to think you need a cup of fresh coffee and a sweet roll."

A grin burst forth on the sheriff's face. "You know, Charles, I think she's right." He stood up.

Gertrude smiled. "Better hurry to the kitchen before the rolls cool. I'll join you there shortly, Dan." He left with Charles, and Gertrude looked at Nilda, nodding toward the envelope in her hand.

A telegram? Nilda opened it. "It's from Jeffrey. 'I cannot tell you how disappointed I am and I insist that you reconsider for your own good Stop You are only an immigrant farm girl Stop Do not make yourself out to be more Stop Only marriage to me can give you what you yearn for Stop I expect your swift response Stop Jeffrey.'"

"My, my, my. The saddest part is that he so obviously reveals his disdain for you. *Disdain* is too kind a word. He considers you trash. Will he receive your swift response?"

"Yes, but by mail, not telegram. I understand that the base fee for a telegram allows ten words. He must have spent a fortune sending this. My greatest concern is the effect on you. I am alienating your family. As you said, his father is the one encouraging this." She shook her head. "How will I attend the board meetings and do my job for you if Heinrik Schmitz hates me? I know he does not like to be crossed. I have seen that in action. So will he take out his resentment on you?"

"Nilda, dear, you let me worry about my relationship with my brother. And if you are forced to skip one or two board meetings to let him cool off, then that is the way it is. I told him this was your decision and that I would not coerce or advise you in any way. I believe that I have been faithful in that. And on top of that, he cannot fire me. Our arrangement is written into the will. Violate the will, and he loses his inheritance."

"You seem confident, so I feel better about it."

Gertrude headed for the door. "Let's join Dan in the kitchen. I'm certain Cook made more than one roll."

To her surprise, Nilda realized that Sheriff Daniel Gruber was an ordinary fellow who doted on his daughters. He was actually pleasant to talk to when he was not being official.

After dinner Gertrude called up the buggy for a meeting at her lawyer's office. Sometimes Nilda was included in these meetings, but this time she was not. That was good, because she had so much work to do.

But she couldn't do it. She was too churned up inside, and not just by the situation with Mr. Galt, but . . . but . . . but what?

She took a glass of apple cider out on the verandah. Already the air was so much cooler that she wouldn't be able to enjoy it out here much longer. The thought of winter drawing near so swiftly made her sigh. This weather was so perfect. The mosquitos were gone, and though many of the birds had already left, the cardinal's song still pleased her ear. She couldn't see him, but he would stay around through the winter. The chickadees were here too.

I need to go to the farm. But I have so much to do. Soon, I will go soon.

Donations for the housing project had slowed, but with the big ones promised, all would be well. The family in the first house had been coming to church since they moved in, but she could tell they were struggling with the language barrier.

That's what we need to do next. We discussed starting an English class, so it is time. I will talk with Fritz about how to get started. He'll be here for supper tomorrow night. She went back into the house.

Still she could not concentrate. She went to the piano and opened the cover for the keys. "It Is Well with My Soul." What a fine hymn. Despite feeling churned up, yes, it was well with her soul. Sitting on the bench, she let the song float into her fingers. One by one, she touched the keys to match them with the song in her mind. Key by key, she heard the song come alive. At least she had the tune. She played it again and yet again, using the proper fingering now, not just one finger. But what to do with her left hand, besides keep it in her lap? Perhaps there was a church hymnal in the library. Not that she could locate it.

She sat down at her desk again to think. And her "swift response" to Jeffrey shaped itself in her mind without her actually working on it.

Dear Jeffrey,

Please know that I truly enjoyed the ball, but I am not cut out to become a society wife. I don't believe God designed and prepared me for that. I pray there is a woman out there who is just right for you, but it is not I.

So please do not try to make contact anymore. I will not respond.

Sincerely,
Miss Nilda Carlson

She read through it again, started to fold the paper, and instead laid it on the desk. She would give it a little time before sending it.

By the time Gertrude returned from her appointment, Nilda was settled enough that she could work efficiently again. "It Is Well with My Soul" still played itself over and over in her head, not an unpleasant thing.

At supper Gertrude announced, "We are going to have a meeting here on Saturday afternoon. You and I and Fritz and the attorney. I wonder if I should ask Mathew to come also. I'll think on that." She smiled at Nilda. "I know this seems rather muddled, but it will become clear at the meeting."

"Do I need to do anything to prepare?"

"No, but I will invite Jane too."

Fritz got in late on Friday, wearing his work shoes. After supper Gertrude informed him of the meeting. "I think it is time," was all she would say.

Nilda shrugged when Fritz looked at her.

The lady of the house stood. "Come, let's go sit in front of the fire, catch up on the news, and then, Fritz, if you would play for us, I would be so grateful."

"Of course, my privilege." He paused. "You are all right, aren't you? I mean, this isn't a health thing, is it?"

"No, no, not at all. Just some business that needed taking care of. Charles will bring coffee and dessert to us in a while."

When they were seated and enjoying the warmth of the crackling fire, she asked, "So how is school going?"

"Very well, and you cannot imagine the delight of some of our students with the books. That they can check them out was amazing to them. Some families have donated books too, although not a lot. Our families aren't illiterate, but buying books is not as important as keeping food on the table." He looked at Nilda. "That Leif, he keeps me on my toes with his questions."

"He is in your classroom again?"

"Yes, I teach fifth grade through eighth. I know Knute is under duress, but he is improving, especially in arithmetic. Now that he has realized the principles underlying it, he is ready for algebra. When he was able to figure out how many boards of lumber can be cut from one tree, I think that opened his eyes to the value of education. I so wish Bjorn would come to school, but he feels he is too old for that now." Fritz rolled his eyes. "Little does he know."

"He enjoys coming here."

"That he does. He and Ivar have become really good friends and work well together. You should hear our discussions on the way to your socials." He paused and chuckled. "One day he brought me some fish he had caught. I was so surprised and enjoyed every bite." He ate the last of the apple cake that Cook had baked. "I should have brought you some apples. Mrs. Benson's apple trees are loaded this year."

He moved over to the piano bench and started playing from memory. When Gertrude yawned and kept yawning, she finally interrupted. "I'm about to fall asleep, so I will bid you both good night and see you at breakfast in the morning." She yawned again on her way out the door. "Don't stay up too late. We have a big day tomorrow."

Nilda caught Fritz's questioning look and shook her head. "I have no idea what she is referring to, other than that the committee meets here at ten as usual."

"And she said we have another meeting tomorrow afternoon. Strange."

"I know."

"Why don't you come sit by me, and I'll keep playing. I think this is as relaxing for me as it is to her."

"And me." Nilda could feel the warmth of his body when she joined him on the piano bench. After all, it wasn't designed for more than two. Just watching his hands flow across the keys made her sigh.

"What?" he asked.

"You think my hands will ever move like that?"

He nodded. "Of course, but remember, I've been playing the piano since I was a boy, and Aunt Gertrude insisted that I have piano lessons here at her house since we did not have a piano at home. She also insisted that I continue school and earn a college degree. My father thought I should go into business, but all I wanted to do was play the piano and teach children the excitement of learning new things."

"Not just children, remember?"

"Oh yes, teaching English to immigrants."

"I want to start a class here in Blackduck, especially for the people who are moving into our houses." The urge to lay her head on his shoulder jerked her upright. But it was definitely there.

"So . . . do you hear from Jeffrey anymore?"

"I hope not. I sent him a strongly worded letter."

"You did?" He grinned at her. "I am sure that if he has read it, he is hot under the collar." He picked up a tune that sounded like galloping.

Nilda recognized it. Wagner—which Fritz pronounced *Vahgner*—the "Ride of the Valkyries." "I would love to hear that sometime with a full orchestra."

"And I would love to take you. It's magnificent, what I call a take-no-prisoners piece." He settled into a gentler tune, then segued into a hymn.

"Would you play 'It Is Well with My Soul'? I picked out the tune earlier."

"Did you really? I'll find the music for it so you can learn the whole song. There should be a hymnal in the library."

"I couldn't find it."

"Hmm. We'll make sure there is one here."

She trapped a yawn.

"You too? Then it's time to call it a night, although I would rather be here with you."

"Really?"

"Really." He turned on the bench and took one of her hands

in his. "You have the hands of a piano player, you know. Long fingers, soft." He kissed her hand and let his forehead touch hers. "This is a small bit of heaven right here."

Her breath caught in her throat. Her hand felt warm, a warmth that traveled right up her arm.

He sighed. "Good night. We will enjoy all of tomorrow and sometime, probably in the evening, you will get a long-overdue piano lesson." He shut the cover on the keys. "You are really not interested in Jeffrey?"

Shaking her head, she replied, "Not now and never was."

"Good."

They walked up the stairs together, and at her bedroom door, he stroked her cheek with his hand. "Good night."

She hadn't known what floating really was until she shut the door behind her and crossed to close the window that Gilda had left open so her room would be fresh. Surely it was the chilly room that sent goose bumps up her arms.

The committee meeting in the morning held no surprises, for everyone agreed that the project was going well. Mr. Haglund announced that he had hired Yousef Sandborn to continue to work for him at the building sites, and when the others headed for the lumber camps, he would remain behind and finish the insides of the remaining houses.

Mathew announced the pending donations and started the discussion on how the winter would go. "As Nilda reminded me, those families without the husband here will still need help." The discussion ran from jobs for the wives to education to bringing in firewood. Those men who now had houses were out in the woods, cutting firewood and cleaning up debris while the other crews kept on building.

After the others left, Fritz said to Nilda, "I need some fresh air. Care to go for a walk?"

"Be back by noon for dinner," Gertrude instructed, "and our meeting begins at two."

"We'll hurry."

They were both puffing when they returned, cheeks bright from the brisk wind and fast walking.

At two o'clock, Gertrude convened the meeting in the dining room. She introduced her attorney, then stood at the head of the table. "I have been giving this matter a great deal of thought, and after our last visit to Minneapolis, I realized I needed to do this sooner rather than later. I wrote a will years ago after Arvid died, but it is past time for it to be revised and updated. James, will you read the relevant portions for us, please?"

"Of course. As always, working with you gives me great pleasure." The attorney proceeded to tell them that Fritz Larsson was to be the heir of Gertrude's estate and listed what his responsibilities would be.

Fritz shook his head. "Aunt Gertrude, this is far beyond—"

She interrupted him. "Just listen, please, and know that I am not planning on dying soon."

The lawyer summarized, "The will stipulates that Mr. Larsson will receive the training needed to manage the estate, and she expects him to learn anything else required." The lawyer looked right at Fritz. "He will receive a prescribed amount monthly from the estate in recompense for fulfilling his duties. Do you have any questions?"

Fritz looked stunned. "Many, but according to this, I will learn what I need."

"Correct."

Fritz looked at Gertrude. "I am a schoolteacher in Benson's Corner, and I would like to remain there."

"Is there any reason why you couldn't?" she asked.

"No, but . . . but this wasn't in my plans."

"I know, but plans can be changed as new and better ones open up, agreed?"

The attorney looked at Nilda. "And you, Miss Carlson, will inherit this house and the means to maintain it, along with a monthly amount for your own use as well. And you will inherit her seat on the board of Schmitz Enterprises if you will consider it. The monies from that portion of the inheritance are still under negotiation."

Nilda stared. "But . . ."

Gertrude raised her hand. "Remember, I plan to live a good long time yet, so in reality, our lives will all continue as they are." She motioned for the attorney to continue.

"You, Miss Carlson, will also be in charge of distributing the percentage of the estate that is designated as benevolence."

He continued, but Nilda's mind hit a wall. *If Fritz will be trained, so will you.*

Finally the attorney turned to Miss Walstead. "You have an exceptional gift for training young women. There will be a certain amount set in your name to work with other young women as you have Miss Carlson."

Jane shook her head. "Gertrude. . . ."

She got the same raised hand. "We will discuss this all later, unless you have questions that I cannot answer."

"There are other beneficiaries, such as certain projects that Mrs. Schoenleber is interested in," the lawyer continued, "but this is all that is applicable here. Oh, and I have been designated as the attorney for the probate and applications of this will. I look forward to working with each of you as I am needed. Questions?"

They all shook their heads.

"This is beyond belief," Fritz muttered. "I, for one, would appreciate something to drink."

Gertrude rang the kitchen and put in the order. "Thank you, James. I appreciate your time and wisdom. Fritz, will you please see him out?"

When Fritz returned, he shook his head. "All I have to say is that you better live a good long time yet."

"At least I will have the care I need, if I should need it. Nilda, this leaves you responsible for those who serve us here. While each of them has a designation in the will, I hope you want to live here, and if someday you should marry, that your family will enjoy this as their home."

"How will I ever manage the benevolence fund?"

"Well, you have two good advisors here, and Mathew knows all the financial matters too." She sighed. "There now, that is accomplished."

"Did you talk this over with Heinrik?" Nilda asked.

"No, but he will be meeting with my attorney also. I did not want him to be in on this meeting, because he will become obnoxious, and while I have legally tried to cover all the possibilities . . ." She shrugged. "As far as I'm concerned, affairs will proceed as usual as we all keep on living our lives, and he and the company really have nothing to fear. All they have to do is continue to remit my percentage of the family enterprise."

That night after Gertrude had won two hands at whist, enjoyed Fritz's music, and along with Miss Walstead decided to retire for the night, Nilda and Fritz remained on the piano bench.

"Nilda, do you know that I care for you, a great deal, actually?"

She now knew what was meant by the phrase *her heart leaped.* "You do?"

"I thought you were going to, well, marry Jeffrey, and I didn't want to mess up your life."

"Mess it up!"

"He could give you the world. Every material comfort. A simple schoolteacher cannot give you every material comfort. In fact, not many at all. And I didn't want to destroy your opportunity to enjoy his wealth. Have you any warm feelings for him at all?"

"No, not at all." She shuddered.

"I see that now. I do care, like I've never cared for anyone before, but I couldn't offer you anything but life on a teacher's salary, which isn't much."

"What are you saying?" She was sure he could hear her heart thundering in her chest. Her mouth went dry, but when she looked into his eyes, all she saw was love. Her smile started and grew.

He took her hands, his thumbs rubbing over her knuckles. "I—we have a lot of thinking and talking to do, since this is so new to both of us, but—but I love you."

Those three words dropped into the well of her hopes and dreams and sent out concentric circles. She raised a hand to stroke his face. "I did not understand how I felt, but now that I know you feel the same, I am free of the fear that we would only be friends. But I was grateful for that, because friends do try to spend time together and . . ."

"And, Nilda Carlson, if you marry me, we will have the rest of our lives to explore how friendship that has grown into love can keep on growing."

"I will absolutely marry you."

His kiss was everything she had ever dreamed of—and more. He was right. So many things to talk about and learn about, but they would find ways to do that together.

Lord, I guess you answered my question regarding your plan for my life. This is truly far beyond anything I could have imagined or dreamed of.

She leaned her head on his shoulder as he played Debussy, softly and tenderly. However could she contain the songs of joy bubbling in her heart? No, not contain, but let them spill over to everyone she ever came in contact with. Perhaps she and Fritz could write their own song of joy.

Epilogue

June 1912

Sitting at the table out on the verandah, Nilda flipped back through her journal. Partly she was checking to see if she had failed to finish any notes or lists, but mostly she wanted to relive and rejoice in the months since Fritz had slid an engagement ring on her finger. What a Christmas surprise! She held out her splayed hand to help the ring catch the last rays of sunshine. Never had she dreamed of having a ring like this, one that stored light in its depths and sparkled back at her.

Nearly every Friday night, weather permitting, Fritz rode into town for training in how to manage his aunt's estate. Saturday mornings, Nilda and Fritz would walk to the river or other spots, sharing their news and dreams. Cook would have breakfast ready when they returned, and after that, Fritz would meet with any others that Gertrude felt necessary.

Nilda's big worry kept creeping out through the pages of her journal. How could she remain Gertrude's assistant after Fritz returned to teaching in Benson's Corner in September? She'd prayed so often, and her only idea so far had them living in his house most of the week, spending Saturdays in Blackduck, and then returning to Benson's Corner to play the organ for church. That way Nilda might have enough time in Blackduck to keep up with her duties for Gertrude.

There were certainly no easy answers.

So many pages were taken up with the pros and cons and her frustrations. Nilda stopped to read something her mor had said. "A woman's place is with her husband. 'Whither thou goest, I will go; and where thou lodgest, I will lodge.' In His time, God will make it clear to you. Thank Him in advance for His answers."

And make my heart ready for His plan. For as far as she could see, either way would cause pain. How could she thank God for His answers when she had no idea what they were?

She swatted a mosquito. Time to go inside.

Mr. Haglund and Miss Walstead had come for an evening of whist, so Nilda had no time to finish her reading. Tonight Fritz would arrive. One more week, and school would be out and he could spend more time in town. Even her heart seemed to be grinning.

In the middle of their first game, they heard the telephone ring and Charles answer it. He appeared in the doorway. "Miss Nilda, Fritz is on the telephone."

"Thank you." She rose and headed for her office in the library. Just hearing his voice made her heart speed up.

"I hate to call this late," Fritz said, "but something came up, so I have an extra meeting tonight. I'll leave early tomorrow morning."

Her anticipation for the evening took a nose dive.

Back in the parlor, Mr. Haglund leaped to his feet to pull out her chair. "Your face says you got bad news."

"Not terrible, I suppose, but Fritz had an unexpected meeting tonight and won't be here until tomorrow morning." Curiosity rapped on the door of her mind and demanded entrance.

"That's not so long." Gertrude dealt the cards.

"I know, but this is not like him." Nilda heaved a sigh and ordered herself to pay attention to what she was doing.

When the telephone jangled again, she groaned.

"Miss Nilda."

"I'll take it in my office." She went down the hall again. But when she heard Rune's voice, her heart skipped a beat. It had to be an emergency for him to ride to Benson's Corner at this time of night. "What happened?"

"Hello to you too. The happening is we now have a telephone here at the farm." He chuckled. "Didn't mean to frighten you."

She sank back in her chair. "How wonderful. Now we can talk whenever we want. Oh, Rune, that is marvelous. I hope you put one in each house and also one in the shop. That way you can respond to orders immediately. Oh, this is great."

"I'm way ahead of you. I am calling from the new house, and now I can call the old house and even, yes, the shop too. Ivar said we should put one in the barn. He's teasing, of course."

"Such good news. Please tell everyone hello from us here. As soon as school is out, perhaps Knute and Leif could come visit for a few days, if they would like."

"I'm sure they will. Good night now."

Nilda could have skipped down the hall. Sad news one minute and good news the next. She no longer had to write a letter to her family and wait for an answer. And Fritz would be here in the morning.

"Good news! They now have telephones at the farm. Three of them! One in the shop too."

"Well, that certainly is a nice surprise. Somehow the farm doesn't seem as far away now." Gertrude nodded. "Did you mention that perhaps the boys could come for a visit? Gunlaug too, but I have a feeling she is spending as much time as possible in the garden."

"It also depends on when the sows start to farrow and if a cow is calving. Leif takes caring for his animals very seriously."

"I thought of putting in a garden this year, but I've been too busy." Mr. Haglund smiled at Nilda. "If George won't allow you to work in the garden here, you could come to my house." He paused. "In your spare time, of course."

"You get someone to work up the soil, and I might just surprise you." Nilda laid her cards on the table. "I won."

That night when she wrote in her journal, she stared out the window to see moonlight casting shadows on the lawn. So beautiful. "But, Lord, I am concerned about Fritz's meeting. What if . . . ?" She set her pen back in the inkwell and closed her journal. Shaking her head, she whispered, "I really am not good at waiting—and trusting. Help me, please."

The sun had not yet peeked over the horizon when she was dressed and heading downstairs to get more items crossed off her list. Correspondence was always at the top. She shut the door to her office to keep from waking the rest of the household.

She'd just finished signing five letters and was addressing the envelopes when Charles tapped at the door and brought in steaming coffee.

"You are up mighty early today." He set the tray on the corner of her desk and filled a cup to hand her. "Cook sent some toast with this. She has the cinnamon rolls almost ready for the oven."

Nilda held the cup with one hand and picked up the toast with the other. "Thank her for me."

"I will. Can I get you anything else?"

She shook her head with a smile. "Now I'll have energy to keep going." She licked the butter and jam off her fingertips before rolling an envelope into the carriage. The door clicked closed behind Charles as he left.

With the rest of her tasks crossed off her list and the coffeepot empty, she pushed her chair back in, made sure everything was put away, and made her way to the music room. Sitting at the piano, she flexed her fingers out of habit even though they had been flexing plenty already. As always, she started with scales, then moved to pieces she had memorized by now, and finally to the newest pages in her lesson book.

"Very good. Bravo." Fritz's applause snatched her back from her concentration.

She leaped from the piano bench and flew into his arms. "I didn't hear you come in." She hugged him again and leaned back to see his face. "You must have ridden out before daylight."

"The sky was no longer black." He kissed her soundly. "There, that's better. The fragrance of cinnamon rolls met me outside the door. Have you eaten?"

"Charles brought me coffee and toast a couple of hours ago." She looped her arm through his. "Let's go eat. How did your meeting go?"

"I'll tell you over breakfast. I'm starved."

Nilda huffed. "All right."

In the dining room, Gertrude looked up from her paper and smiled at them. "I love hearing you practice, Nilda. Thank you." She tipped her head for her kiss on the cheek from Fritz. "You left before dawn."

"Couldn't wait." He seated Nilda and took his chair next to her.

Charles set coffee and a roll in front of him. "Welcome home. Cook said the rest of the meal will be ready in about ten minutes, but she didn't want you to faint from hunger."

Nilda let Fritz eat a couple of bites and drink some coffee before she cleared her throat. "You have news?"

He nodded. "I do." He set his cup down and looked from Nilda to Gertrude and back. "The meeting went well." He took another bite and grinned at Nilda. "Oh, all right. I met with the superintendent of our district, and he accepted, but not happily, my resignation. I told him I had another teacher to recommend, and that eased the waters somewhat." He patted Nilda's hand. "I know you've been fretting about ways for us to live together that would allow you to keep working here. I think this way works for everyone."

"But—but you wanted to keep teaching."

"I will be. It will just be the piano and organ, not grade school." He took another sip of his coffee. "Although if I want, I heard they need another teacher here in Blackduck."

"Well, I'll be. Thank you." Gertrude smiled up at Charles as he set her plate before her, then turned to Nilda. "I told you God had a plan. Let's say grace before this banquet gets cold."

Nilda was still in a state of shock. *You did have a plan.* The thought made her want to run to the river and back. Mor was right. She shook her head. So much energy wasted worrying and stewing. Never had she considered Fritz might change his mind.

A week later, Nilda paused at the door of the dining room. She smiled at Fritz as she stopped at her chair. "Good morning, everyone." She had woken reminding herself that today truly was the day before her wedding. After breakfast, George was driving her to the farm to be with her family for her last night as a single woman.

Charles poured her coffee but did not ask her what she wanted.

He just headed for the kitchen. Nilda sent Gertrude a puzzled look. Her employer shrugged as if she was confused as well, but the twinkle in her eyes belied her innocence.

Nilda picked up her coffee cup and inhaled the rich fragrance.

"Are you all packed?"

She nodded. "All things needed for the wedding in a separate trunk as you suggested. Gilda said there would be no wrinkles, although how she'll do that is beyond me."

Charles entered with a beaming smile and a full tray. He paused, and Mrs. Solvang joined him.

What in the world? Nilda could feel her eyes widening. Something was indeed afoot.

Humming the "Wedding March," the two tried to keep formal faces—and failed. "For you, miss—soon to be 'missus.'" They set several plates on the table in front of her. On them were all of her favorite foods as well as a miniature wedding cake.

Shaking her head, Nilda clapped her hands, giggling. "Thank you, thank you. You are unbelievable." But then her emotions started to get the better of her. "I-I . . ." She blinked back tears. "I will never forget this." Her whisper cracked in the middle. She sucked in a breath. The others were blinking too. She gave up and used her napkin to dab her eyes. "Thank you. You are coming to my wedding, right?"

Charles nodded. "Yes, Miss Nilda, we wouldn't miss it."

"The train will be leaving plenty early in the morning." Gertrude blew her nose. "A few of your other friends from Blackduck are coming as well."

Nilda blew out a breath and nodded when George entered the room. "Twenty minutes?"

"Fine. Your trunks are in the buggy." He looked at Fritz. "Your horse is tethered behind."

"Thank you."

The next time I enter this house, I will be Mrs. Fritz Larsson. The thought sent shivers up her back.

When they reached the farm, Leif came running out to greet them. "We're having a picnic out in the woods. I'll put your horse in the corral, Mr. Larsson. Far said to leave your baggage at the old house."

"Thank you, Leif."

As soon as they set Nilda's trunk on the porch, George turned around and headed down the driveway. At the same moment, Knute drove Rosie and the cart up to the empty house.

"Ma said to hurry, so we are. They're already down at the creek." He flicked the reins as soon as they were seated, and they trotted to the timber line, where they left the horse and cart.

"Mor made fried chicken 'cause she knows how you like fried chicken." Knute grinned at Fritz. "I do too."

"Glad you are here, Mr. Larsson," Bjorn called.

"I think you can call me Fritz now. I'm almost a member of the family."

"Does that make you Uncle Fritz, then?"

"It does."

They all talked nonstop, celebrating the meal and catching up on news. When Fritz said he needed to get home, they adjourned to the house to wave him on his way.

In the old house, Leif pointed to Nilda. "Kirstin, this is Tante Nilda."

Kirstin nodded and stopped in front of Nilda. "Tat Nida." Then she raised her hands to be picked up. Grinning, she repeated, "Tat Nida," and patted Nilda's cheeks.

Nilda kissed her chubby fingers. "Good girl. Tante Nilda." She grinned at Leif. "Good job." She swung the little one around while everyone laughed. Kirstin joined in, her giggles as contagious as ever.

The wedding was set for noon the next day, and it arrived quicker than expected. Nilda wore an ankle-length dress with a fitted jacket, the beading on the heavy silk catching the light from the windows. Signe handed her a lovely bouquet of pink and white tulips with matching ribbons. "You are so beautiful. I know Fritz will be speechless."

Nilda hugged her sister-in-law so tightly that neither of them could breathe and then released her with a teary laugh. With a grin, Signe slipped into the sanctuary to take her seat.

The organ music swelled as Fritz played the song that would accompany Nilda's entrance. She hooked her arm through Rune's and walked to the open doors of the sanctuary.

"Thank you, brother," she whispered. Then she puffed out a breath as the altar shimmered through her tears, along with the man at the organ. The music changed to the "Wedding March," and she and Rune paced to the altar, where Reverend Skarstead and Ivar already waited.

Fritz played the final chords and met her, his smile lighting the whole sanctuary.

"Dearly beloved, we are gathered here to celebrate the marriage of Fritz Larsson and Nilda Carlson. Let us pray."

They both repeated their vows with firm voices, smiling. Finally Reverend Skarstead announced, "I now pronounce you man and wife. Fritz, you may kiss your bride."

Nilda smiled at her new husband and kissed him right back.

"Mr. and Mrs. Fritz Larsson."

The people clapped, Fritz took her arm, and they greeted those near the aisle as they walked to the back of the church. Kirstin waved and shrieked, making others laugh.

We're married. We really are married.

"Please join us for wedding cake and coffee down in the basement," Signe called to the guests.

Nilda and Fritz hugged Gertrude and Miss Walstead and family members in the narthex, then joined the others in the basement. When they had cut the cake and greeted everyone, George whispered in Fritz's ear.

Nilda looked at Fritz in question.

"Another surprise." He took her arm and followed the others, who were all heading outside. The Schoenleber train car waited on the tracks at the station.

"What?" Nilda said.

Gertrude smiled at her. "The private car that will take you on your honeymoon."

"But . . ." She looked at Fritz, who shrugged.

"Leave it to my aunt." They mounted the steps to the car.

Nilda shook her head. "What a way to start our new life. Do you know where we are going?"

"I do but hadn't planned on this. You have to admit, our life ahead will be full of surprises."

"And blessings beyond measure."

As the train whistle blew, they both stood in the doorway and waved good-bye. Nilda leaned her cheek against his arm. "Promise me this has not all been a dream."

"People can't dream the same thing. This is indeed real."

"Songs of joy for the rest of our lives?"

"Indeed. For as long as God gives us. Far beyond what we can dream or imagine. His Word says so. And we believe His Word." He turned and kissed her forehead. "Always."

Lauraine Snelling is the award-winning author of more than seventy books, fiction and nonfiction, for adults and young adults. Her books have sold more than five million copies. Besides writing books and articles, she teaches at writers' conferences across the country. She and her husband make their home in Tehachapi, California. Learn more at www.lauraineshelling.com.

Sign Up for Lauraine's Newsletter!

Keep up to date with Lauraine's news on book releases and events by signing up for her email list at laurainesnelling.com.

More From Lauraine Snelling

Don't miss the final stories about the beloved Blessing community! Return once more to Blessing and find familiar faces in new stories of family, love, and friendship. Set at the dawn of the twentieth century, these heartwarming novels follow three couples as they face setbacks, discover hope, and find love.

Song of Blessing: *To Everything a Season, A Harvest of Hope, Streams of Mercy, From This Day Forward*

More Captivating Fiction from Bethany House

After facing desperate heartache and loss, Mercy agrees to escape a bleak future in London and join a bride ship. Wealthy and titled, Joseph leaves home and takes to the sea as the ship's surgeon to escape the pain of losing his family. He has no intention of settling down, but when Mercy becomes his assistant, they must fight against a forbidden love.

A Reluctant Bride by Jody Hedlund, The Bride Ships #1
jodyhedlund.com

In the midst of the Great War, Margot De Wilde spends her days deciphering intercepted messages. But after a sudden loss, her world is turned upside down. Lieutenant Drake Elton returns wounded from the field, followed by a destructive enemy. Immediately smitten with Margot, how can Drake convince a girl who lives entirely in her mind that sometimes life's answers lie in the heart?

The Number of Love by Roseanna M. White, The Codebreakers #1
roseannamwhite.com

In the wake of WWII, a grieving fisherman submits a poem to a local newspaper asking readers to send rocks in honor of loved ones to create something life-giving—but the building halts when tragedy strikes. Decades later, Annie returns to the coastal Maine town where stone ruins spark her curiosity, and her search for answers faces a battle against time.

Whose Waves These Are by Amanda Dykes
amandadykes.com